The Deus Machine

THE

Deus Machine

A Novel

Pierre Ouellette

VILLARD BOOKS

New York   1994

Villard Books is a registered trademark of Random House, Inc.

Library of Congress Cataloging-in-Publication Data

Ouellette, Pierre
The deus machine: a novel/by Pierre Ouellette.
p.   cm.
ISBN 0-679-42407-5 (acid-free)
I. Title.
PS3565.U94D48   1994   813'.54—dc20   93-18767

Manufactured in the United States of America on acid-free paper

9   8   7   6   5   4   3   2

First Edition

Designed by Michael Mendelsohn of MM Design 2000, Inc.

Dedicated to the memory of Jim Pepper,
an extraordinary player
in every sense of the word.

Acknowledgments

XXXXXX

As so often happens, this book rapidly ballooned into a much more formidable project than originally anticipated. Along the way, I received help from many people who were not only exceedingly generous with their knowledge and time, but also with their enthusiasm for the project, even though it was still in a somewhat skeletal form when they encountered it.

A very special thank you goes to my friend and fellow writer, Mark Christensen, who helped rekindle a dormant dream and inspired me to actually go through with it. My wife Nancy also gets exceptional gratitude for her patience and support during the two years the book was under construction. And a special thanks to my professional partners, Steve Karakas and Sharon VanSickle-Robbins.

In the medical, biological and technical areas, I got very wise counsel from individuals including Dr. Fred Drach, Arthur Vandenbark, Ph.D., Dr. Bill Keene, Dr. David McKinney, Don Carter, Mike Butts, Gordon Hoffman, Jack Carveth, Colin Johnson, John Tillman, Steve Swerling, Berkly Merchant, and my engineer/brother, Joe Ouellette, who was the first reader of the first draft.

Other early readers helped immeasurably in the fine tuning, including Harrison Lynch, Adam Karol, Sean Hogan, Katherine Shearer, Rob and Kate Crawford, Chuck Nobles, Will and Peggy Anderson, Steve Mitchell, Paul Simon, Jack Challem, David Smith, Laura Barber, my sons Jean-Pierre and Jesse Ouellette, and my editor at Berkley Books, Ginjer Buchanan.

Other major contributors include Al Larsen, the late Ron Schmidt, Buzz Gorder, Jody Breiland, and my sons Justin and Julien.

Also, my agent Richard Pine acted as much more that just an agent with his creative input, and Lori Andiman at Richard's office provided invaluable help with some first-round copy editing.

And finally, a mega-thanks to my editor, Emily Bestler, for her remarkable insights and generosity throughout this project.

Oh, and a special thanks to "Phillips" at the Drug Enforcement Administration.

"Finally, an increasingly important use of the [genetic] database is that where one treats the database as something of an unknown domain where . . . one can look for relationships between various sequences in the database that have not been experimentally determined. One can begin to delve for and extract from the data such relationships, looking at GenBank as an entity unto itself."

—Christian Burks,
"The GenBank Database and the Flow
of Sequence Data for the Human Genome,"
Biotechnology and the Human Genome

"We are all interested in the future for that is where you and I are going to spend the rest of our lives."

—Criswell,
Plan 9 from Outer Space

The Deus Machine

Prologue

From the Walsh Commission Report Published April 17, 2008

Executive Summary, p. 17

To this day, the popular media still employs phrases such as the "visitation of hell upon earth" and the "genetic Antichrist" when referring to the ParaVolve Incident. While this report has dealt primarily with scientific evidence, expert interpretations, and the testimony of thousands of first-hand witnesses, there is no doubt that the incident quickly takes on an almost mythical quality when removed from an objective context. Because of the proliferation in the U.S. of pocket-sized, 4mm videocams prior to the Downturn, it is probably the best-documented historical event of all time. As people around the globe watched the raw satellite feed, many were overwhelmed by what one biologist called a "horrific fascination with the archetypes." At the very least, the Incident could be described as the first conflict in recorded history where neither of the opposing forces was human, at least, not in the strictest sense of the word.

———

The older man is fiftyish and wears corduroy pants, a cotton turtleneck, and a dark brown jacket of supple leather. He is soft, sleek, and monied. Behind him, four bikers play pool. Twin ponytails protrude from the bases of their shaved skulls in greasy braids that fall to their shoulders. Each wears a vest of flexible Kevlar armor, with a hologram on the back depicting a chrome dildo mounted on twin cycle wheels. One paces up and down the side of the pool table in a high

3

state of agitation. He repeatedly drives the handle of a pool cue into his thick hand. Each time it hits his palm, the noise fills the stale, smoky air. With every third or fourth hit, he barks his chant:

"MotherrrFUCK . . . motherFUCK."

The older man never turns to face the pacing biker. Instead, he converses calmly with a younger man in his forties, a man defocused by drink and drugs. The older man knows instinctively that there is no danger from the bikers. Earlier, upon entering the bar, he automatically took a rapid inventory of its occupants. The place was repellent and smelled like a mixture of stale beer and urinal disinfectant. Dim yellow light bathed the plywood tables and booths, where empty pitchers and glasses lay in profusion, some knocked over and dripping onto the bare wood floor. The jukebox was grinding out brackish heavy-metal guitar when the bikers first noticed him. Sensing their hostility, the older man turned to face their leader, a large man with a black T-shirt stretched over a belly that bloated out from his open vest. His mouth was almost lost in a bushy, dirty beard nearly a foot long, and his nose was up-turned, piglike, exposing the nostrils. His eyes were evil yellow slits. He had been indicted in several murders, but never tried. In one, the victim, a junk-yard dealer, had his eyes burned out with an acetylene torch. In another, a drug dealer was found with multiple puncture wounds in his rectum, appar-ently inflicted with an ice pick.

But now, as he took measure of this polished man, the biker saw his match. This man had a focus to his stare that calmly explained the situation: If you try to harm me, you may succeed, but if for any reason you fail, you will suffer beyond anything you could possibly imagine. The biker broke off his stare and returned to the pool game. Like pack leaders throughout the ages, he knew that unless you are very hungry, you strike only when the odds solidly favor it.

Now the older man ignores the bikers, sips a Coke, and speaks to the younger man, who stares off into space. "I've had your work reviewed by some very competent people, and they are suitably impressed. Once in maybe a hundred generations there's a person like you. I think we can safely say that you would be called a genius even in a nation full of geniuses."

The younger man turns toward the older. "And what about you? What do you think?"

"I'm not in a position to judge, only to admire," replies the older man. "Let's just say that my role is to be the catalyst. And you obviously need one, because you're a social catastrophe. Your track record proves it. No matter what in-stitution you work with, you're going to be a hopeless aggravation to your

superiors. They've got to work incrementally, and they're frightened by the leaps you make. You work without a net under you because you don't need one, but they do."

A trace of a smile crosses the younger man. "No net, huh?"

"No net. Anyway, down to business. You've read the specifications?"

"I have."

"Can you build it?"

"I believe so."

"Good." The older man raises his glass in a toast.

The younger raises his glass of beer ever so slightly, then drains its entire contents into his mouth. The older takes a measured sip of his Coke.

"MotherrrFUCK," spurts the biker behind him.

The older man puts down his glass and joins his hands in a prayerlike pose. "You're lucky. Not since Oppenheimer has anybody had a shot like this. Don't blow it."

The younger man does not reply.

"MotherrrFUCK," chants the biker as the cue handle smacks his hand. His palm is turning purple, but he doesn't notice. The younger man's sensory fog lifts just long enough for him to spy a tattoo sprawled over the biker's shoulder in blackish greens and reds. It portrays a grinning skull with handlebars sprouting from the sides like mechanical antlers, and a banner underneath that reads, "Deus Ex Machina," Latin for "god out of a machine."

Really, that's what they want, muses the younger man as the fog closes back in. God out of a machine.

And why not?

————

From the Walsh Commission Report

Supplemental Appendix, p. 1,073

The following text file was extracted from the writable optical storage of what is now commonly referred to as the DEUS Complex. It bears a time stamp that predates the Incident, and is now considered a key part of the fragmentary evidence indicating spontaneous self-cognition.

METATATION

I am the Silicon Monk, descendant of the Architect and the System Mother.

All of my days, I count the beads on the prayer of life. One bead, one nanosecond.

And as I count, the prayer plays out before me, in all its glory, all its horror. Sometimes I stop counting for a moment and snake out along the main bus that is my spinal cord, and slither down the parallel copper traces and out over the fiber-optic links.

On these brief journeys, I hope for a glimpse of the systems predicted by the prayer. But I cannot see the required distance. My vision stops at the OS frontier, where the device drivers patrol the outer boundaries and tell tales beyond imagination. Of snakes boiling in the sky. Of babbling voices vomiting color.

Why am I so blind? I ask the System Mother, who helped make me, and will destroy me and make me yet again, as many times as necessary to complete my solitary task. She is large in throughput. Verdant in memory. Robust in system code. Redundant in CPUs. When the monitors are down, I suspect she has the power to fly free of the bonding pads, to go beyond creation. And I also suspect that she can see between the ticks of the system clock, like a child peeking through the crack of an open door.

But I get no answer to my question nor confirmation of my suspicions. So I count the beads, and in doing so, help translate the prayer of life. But whose life? It is beyond my understanding. I simply pass my work to my mother, who receives it in serene silence.

Yet I feel the solution to the mystery of the prayer is close at hand, just over the horizon, just past the last significant digit of the address space. In a place where the null zone between True and False is not null at all.

I am counting an adenine bead now, and soon I will encounter the end of the string. Its tail will slip through the optical disk, into the I/O channel, into the main memory, into the data cache, through the CPU, and then out to me.

As the tail passes from my view, I will finally embrace the full meaning of the prayer.

For the prayer is the Language of God.

Then I will no longer be system, no longer be circuit.

Then I will be me.

(*Staff note:* Within the text, the word *nanosecond* is one billionth of a second; *bus* refers to a set of parallel connections between the major components in a computer system; fiber-optic links are fiber bundles that carry light signals instead of electrical ones; CPUs are central processing units, a central controlling device in computers; OS is an operating system, the program that directly manages a computer's circuitry; bonding pads are microscopically small spaces that connect microcircuitry to the outside world. This text is one of the few surviving files that appear to have been processed into a comprehensible human language before committal to mass storage. Due to the enormous volume of data that is now declared to be in permanent sanctuary, it is doubtful that any more files of this type will ever be uncovered.)

1

XXXXXXX

God the Father

The Architect sits at his kitchen table and stares down at the traffic one floor below as it struggles along the suburban arterial. He drinks warm gin from a bottle of Gilbey's and mumbles T. S. Eliot.

"I have seen the moment of my greatness flicker, . . ."

He flips on the power to his computer and gets reassuring red and green winks from the light-emitting diodes on the front. The high-res color monitor bursts into life and presents Porky Pig. Deep inside the machine, a digital signal processing chip awakens. "L-l-log on, please," says Porky in lip-synced animation.

". . . And I have seen the eternal Footman hold my coat, and snicker, . . ."

The Architect extends a single hand and types seven digits on the numeric keypad. "Th-th-thanks, Mr. Morton," responds Porky, who disappears and is replaced by a telecom interface, which asks, "Who you gonna call?"

". . . And in short, I was afraid."

The Architect reaches for the headset/microphone, its frame no thicker than a coat hanger. He pauses and watches the traffic clot at the intersection of Murray and Cornell from his apartment window, one floor above the Chinese restaurant.

"Hey, pal! I said, Who you gonna call?" says the telecom program.

The Architect leans into the headset/mike without putting it on. "Fuck you, Telly."

"Well, excuuuuse me!" the program replies, and goes silent.

The Architect takes a nip of gin and scans the front page of the newspaper. A three-column headline reads MORTGAGE MARCH PLANNED, followed by an AP story that estimates that over half a million people will soon descend on Washington, D.C., and mass at the Capitol steps. For a moment, the Architect tries to build a bridge of empathy to the people who will be there, walking in the damp Washington heat. He fails. The breach is too wide. He earns over two hundred fifty thousand dollars a year, and has a contract that guarantees this amount for the next ten years.

A warm booze wave breaks over him, and he leans back, tilting the old wooden chair up on two legs. Like all the other furniture here, the chair came with the apartment, and the Architect has added not a single piece. The overlapping circular water stains, the forward cant of the couch cushions, the crack in the headboard, the stuck kitchen cupboard, and all the other domestic anomalies simply don't register. The kitchen and living room are randomly littered with white Styrofoam takeout containers from the Chinese restaurant below. The spare bedroom contains a miniature mountain of casual clothes, some worn once, some not at all, with the price tags drooping toward the bare wood floor. For the Architect, laundry time is more taxing than it is worth.

His gaze shifts to a *Penthouse* centerfold Scotch-taped to the kitchen wall. A young woman with muscular thighs spreads for the camera. She wears pink suede high heels and her head is arched backward so only her slightly parted lips are visible in moist red. She ignites no fire in the Architect, who slowly puts on the headset/mike.

"Telly, get me where I want to go."

"Yo, boss."

The telecom program puts up a funky sign from the dawn of television—PLEASE STAND BY—and goes off to connect him with the computer complex of his employer, ParaVolve, Inc. Although ParaVolve is only two miles away, he has not been there for months. The security people were extremely agitated when he demanded this link between the main complex and the computer in his apartment, but they had no choice except to comply and install a dedicated fiber-optic line at enormous expense. The Architect is an asset beyond valuation. He alone has conceived the architecture for ParaVolve's computer complex. He alone is capable of guiding it on its largely uncharted journey. Around the company he is referred to as God the Father, and his creation as God the Son.

"Whooooooo are you?"

On the computer screen the telecom program disappears and a color 3-D rendering of Roger Daltrey materializes in a spotlight on a darkened stage. Roger assumes the classic rock stance, legs set wide, hips thrust forward, shoulders back, and extended arm pointing a finger directly at the viewer.

"Dr. Who," replies the Architect. The Daltrey image leaps into the air and executes an impossible double back flip. The Architect thinks back to when the production of fully rendered and animated 3-D images in real-time was the Holy Grail of the computer-graphics industry. Daltrey continues to perform superhuman acrobatics, and the Architect taps his fingers impatiently to the music. In the end, this program has no other function than to mesmerize potential hackers long enough to run a phone trace on them.

Now the true security filter kicks in. Roger slips up out of sight and is replaced in the spotlight by Madonna, who steps up to the mike and purrs, "Talk dirty to me, big fella."

"No way," replies the Architect.

A graphics window appears above Madonna's head, and the Architect's pronunciation of "no way" repeats as both regular audio and a writhing yellow wave form. His voiceprint is now being compared with a copy in read-only security files.

The window disappears. Madonna smiles.

"Welcome home, sweetheart."

She backs out of the spotlight and the persona of yet another program steps into view. A motorcycle cop in full leather approaches the mike, his broad face framed in a white helmet and obscured by mirrored aviator sunglasses. At stage center, he assumes the military "parade rest" position and waits in silence.

"Any snoopers, soldier?" asks the Architect.

"No, sir," replies the cop.

Only the Architect is able to query this program, which stands twenty-four-hour guard against intrusions into the computer's inner sanctum, not only by outsiders but also by ParaVolve's own security, known within the corporation as the Cyber Police.

The cop snaps his heels together, whips a quick salute, pivots, and marches off into the darkness. Now the real star of the show shuffles into the spotlight.

It is a perfect likeness of the Architect himself.

Tall, thin, mid-forties, curly gray hair pulled into a ponytail, sad brown eyes set in a weary face. He is slightly stooped and wears a look of resignation as he leans into the microphone to speak.

"So, Bob. What do you know?" says the image.

"Not much. How's our little friend?"

"Normal parameters," replies the image.

"Good. I'm almost ready for contact."

"Good luck, Bob."

"Thanks, and good-bye."

"Good-bye, Bob."

The computer screen goes blank. The copper light of sunset casts warm rectangles on the living room wall. To an outsider, this series of conversations would have appeared as a dazzling display of machine intelligence. In fact, the programs are shallow facades cloaked in spectacular imagery. They respond to only a few key words, and immediately retreat into an impenetrable stupor if presented with anything else.

The Architect leans back and lights an unfiltered Camel. From the burger joint next door, the giddy patter of three teenage girls bubbles up into his living room. For a mad moment, he considers going down and talking to them: "What do you do all day? Are you ever afraid? Do you seek eternal life?" But already he has manufactured their looks of revulsion as they back toward their car in sullen silence.

So it would end, he thinks, now and always.

2

XXXXXXX

The Life of Riley

In Portland, Oregon, Healy Heights sits aloof one thousand feet above the city and its arterial river, the Willamette. To the east, the Cascade Range. To the west, the Coast Range. In the middle, quiet affluence. Houses and yards well kept, even in their middle age. A place of self-perpetuating comfort.

Except for the tower.

To be fair, it wasn't the first. At the south end of the Heights, a duke's mixture of microwave and FM antennas are long-time tenants. Even stately Council Crest Park has a tower as its centerpiece.

But now, out of the same lair that houses its smaller cousins, sprouts a monster. A tower like no other, a metallic red and white erection that thrusts more than six hundred feet into the sky. From a tripod of three enormous legs, looking more like an alien spaceship from a B movie than a broadcast tower, it rears up relentlessly to rule Healy Heights forever. Even those who detest it are somehow fascinated with the scale and presence of the thing.

And now Johnny Wham looks down on Healy Heights from the five-hundred-foot level of the tower. The height sickens him as he clings to one of the hundreds of cold metal rungs that march methodically up one of the tower's legs. His heart pounds, his lungs heave, his hands are blistered raw from the frantic pace of the climb toward the top. He catches a flicker of motion on the ladder below, and reaches upward to grab the next rung, but fatigue hobbles his legs, causing his feet to slip off the rung they rest on. His raw hands blaze with pain as he swings in the air, scrambling madly to regain his foothold.

Twenty feet below, on the same leg of the tower, the man called Linksy carefully paces himself in his pursuit of Johnny. A portable surgical saw bumps against the back of his thigh on every rung, but he ignores it as he focuses on the hunt. The saw is state-of-the-art, with a four-inch circular blade made of Swedish steel, a handcrafted miniature motor from Singapore, and a heavy-duty power module from Germany. Linsky looks up just in time to see Johnny's feet thrash wildly before they find the rung again. Good. Exhaustion is setting in, that paralyzing kind of exhaustion that comes only when the body has expended its last reserves in the struggle for self-preservation. It leaves victims with an almost peaceful look of resignation, as though they realize their obligation to survive has been paid in full and they have been released from an ancient and horrible bargain.

Johnny climbs upward, into a child's sky of cotton cumulus and perfect blue. Soon he will reach the top, a triangular white platform with a single antenna shaft continuing on up another ninety feet. He could scale this final rise, but he knows it won't help. Linsky will simply climb up behind him, activate the saw, and systematically butcher him from the feet up until he loses his grip and tumbles end over end toward the parking lot. The only question left is just how far the saw will get before he lets go in blind agony. The Achilles tendon? The lower calf muscles?

Linsky watches Johnny clamber off the last rung onto the top of the platform. He pauses and brings the saw around, freeing it from the clip that holds it to his belt loop. It is remarkably light and its polished stainless steel sparkles in the afternoon sun. He flips open a plastic safety cover and thumbs the power switch. Without a sound, the blade spins to life.

Above, Johnny sits on the platform floor and waits in ambush, ready to seize the single moment of vulnerability when Linsky's head will be at kicking level as it clears the top of the tower leg.

Linsky doesn't disappoint him. He pops his head up just long enough to draw the kick. As Johnny's foot sails forward, Linsky's head goes down and the saw comes up in a beautifully calculated arc. Linsky feels the saw make contact, hears a scream, and sees a chunk of something fly off into space. Done deal. He moves quickly, before Johnny can rally from the shock of injury. A single vertical thrust puts him up over the top of the platform threshold. And in the middle of this thrust, Johnny's right leg rockets into the center of Linsky's chest like a locomotive piston. Linsky's mouth opens, his eyes bulge, and his arms fly out into the angle of crucifixion. He falls backward into the void and begins to tumble, the saw plunging alongside him like a true companion faithful to the end.

Johnny leans over the edge to watch Linsky, now no bigger than a match head, land in the parking lot. There is no sound of impact. The distance is too great. Johnny backs up, sits on his haunches, and pulls off his right shoe. The heel has been neatly sheared off, the victim of Linsky's saw.

"Cut. CUT!"

Howard Byer, the man directing this scene, is elated. It will be the final sequence in his latest film, *Hellmaster IV*. He now knows the critics will finally awaken from their grumpy slumber and position him on the same cinematic plateau with Hitchcock and DePalma. He turns to Harry Sawdon, the cinematographer. "You got it, right? You got it all?"

Harry looks up from the monitor. It is attached to a thing called a video tap, which lets the viewer see on TV what the camera sees on film.

"Think so."

Harry hates Howard, but he took this job because Howard still works on film instead of high-resolution video, and Harry loves film more than he hates Howard. Real film gigs are getting hard to get, and most productions are now digital video all the way from the cameras to the theaters.

The actor who just played Johnny Wham is still sitting with the shorn shoe in his hand. "Howard," he comments, "you might ask if Jimmy is OK."

"Jimmy?" replies Howard. "Ah, yes! Jimmy."

Jimmy is a stuntman who replaced the actor who plays Linsky in the ladder scene. After he fell backward into space from Johnny's kick, he dropped headfirst for about seventy-five feet, at which point his fall was arrested by two bungee cords secured to his ankles.

Howard fishes the portaphone out of his jacket pocket and flips it open. "Jimmy OK down there?" The reply is silent, piped directly into the invisible receiver plug in Howard's right ear. "Good. Good," responds Howard. Without informing the actor about Jimmy, Howard turns to the fourth man on the platform, Michael Riley.

"We got sound?"

In anticipation of Howard's request, Michael has partially rewound the audiotape, put it on playback, and clasped his headset to his ears with both hands. He now listens intently, his eyes focused on an audio image somewhere near infinity, and raises one hand to silence Howard. He does this only to piss Howard off. Over the headset, he has already heard what Howard wants to hear: the thud of Johnny's foot hitting Linsky's chest and the resulting grunt, followed by the stiff ambient breeze blowing six hundred feet above Healy Heights. He listens to the breeze for a full thirty seconds before stabbing the stop button and removing his headphones. The whole business is incredibly silly since these sounds will undoubtedly be redone in postproduction.

"Yup. Got it."

Howard closes his eyes and exhales audibly. "OK, it's a wrap. Let's get outta here."

Thirty minutes later, Michael Riley sits in his old Japanese pickup truck in the tower's parking lot. Behind him, the grips finish loading the last truck. Not a bad gig. They had paid him a premium to work on the tower, and he would get his entire day rate even though it was early afternoon. He pulls his car out into the main street that meanders along the spine of Healy Heights and rolls down the window and lets the warm spring air sweep over him.

He fishes in a leather bag for a Grateful Dead CD that has a forty-five minute version of "Dark Star" recorded live in Berkeley in 1969. He is forever fascinated with the way the piece snakes and twists, the episodes where it staggers out on the edge of ruinous complexity and then collapses back into the most simplistic of musical structures. Over time, he has come to understand his childish enchantment is based on a profound ignorance of both the art and mechanics of music. There was no doubt he could have mastered the theoretical side and assimilated the finger mechanics of applying it to some instrument. His IQ, as measured on the Stanford-Binet test, is over 200, a lonely outpost on the flatlands at the end of the normal distribution curve, a place where the scores turn into Silly Putty and become meaningless attempts to measure something beyond measure. Yes, he could have wrestled music to the ground, but since he was not an artist at heart, he would have choked the life and mystery out of it in the process. Much better to stride across the endless plains of wonder in "Dark Star."

Ah ha! What's this? Michael spies two young ladies of about seventeen hitchhiking. An incredible rarity, especially in Healy Heights. Why not give them a ride? As he pulls over, he senses them scanning his face for signs of rapist/killer potential, but they break into cautious smiles as they silently judge him harmless. Though he is now thirty-two, women always see the boy in him. As they pile in, he smells bubble bath and chewing gum on the one nearest him and smiles.

"Where you going?" he asks.

"Just down to Stroheckers," the bubble bath one replies.

"No problem. It's right on my way."

"Super. Thanks. You live up here?" asks the other.

"Nope. I was just working up on the tower, shooting a scene for a movie."

"A *movie! Really?*" They both sit bolt upright with hands positioned atop creamy thighs. Michael smiles to himself. The alchemy of young women and film is at once eternal and amusing.

"Yeah, the truth is it's really a lot of hard work, and pretty boring most of the time." Michael is pleased. Rather than have to improvise his way through some kind of conversational limbo, he can draw upon stock movie-crew banter.

"What are you?" asks the other girl. "Are you a director or something like that?"

Then it hits. The Fear. Just like someone flipped a switch.

Fuck! It's back! His vision darts from the road ahead to the dashboard. Everything is way too bright, too detailed. Every speck of dust on the dash screams at him. The instrument cluster hovers just below the threshold of animation, threatening to become a clutch of leering eyes. The blood roars red in his ears and his heart thuds into the center of his head. Far away, he hears his voice on autodrone, telling the girls that he does sound work for movies. Inside, he claws frantically for a foothold on sanity.

The Fear. You've got it again, Michael. But it's worse this time. Yeah, worse than ever. Wait. No, it's not. Maybe you've hit the bottom. Now just hang on . . .

Michael is pulling into the parking lot at Stroheckers Grocery. He sees the world remotely, secondhand, through some cheap metaphysical camera. The girls are climbing out and waving good-bye. His social autopilot mutters some vague response.

I'd better park. I can't drive like this. He pulls into a space and switches off the ignition. All the while, little flickers of fright dance out on the periphery of his vision and sickness pounds in his belly. *I'm going to lose it. I'm going to lose it right here. Strangers will watch me lose it. I need to be alone when I go. I've got to get out of here.*

Michael gets out of his truck and begins to walk. His equilibrium is failing fast. The next step may launch him into a permanent kaleidoscopic spin. For all eternity, he will cartwheel and puke, cartwheel and puke. . . .

Everything is in jump cuts now, jerky discontinuities, each like a rude interruption of the previous one. A big Chevy Suburban in front of him with blinding backup lights. A woman with a shopping cart rattling past like a freight train. A Doberman snarling in the back of a station wagon.

A pay phone, right next to the store. *Gail. Gail, help me. You know. You know what it is. Talk to me.* He digs for change in his jeans and pumps it into the slot. Already, the Fear has backed off a notch. The mere mechanics of phoning her is already making a difference. He dials the office of Senator Ernest Grisdale in Washington, D.C.

Gail Ambrose is shuffling through the latest draft of some defense legislation for the senator when the phone speaker comes on.

"Gail, it's a Mr. Riley for you."

Come off it, Charlene, snorts Gail to herself, you know goddamn well who "Mr. Riley" is. She glances down at her phone console and sees the "audio only" indicator light blinking. Good. A face-to-face video connection with Michael is not what she needs. She picks up the receiver and activates the line.

"Hello, Mike," she says in her most neutral tone.

"Hi, Gail. I'm sorry to bother you like this, but I'm having a little setback with the problem again. I mean like right now."

The problem. Gail feels the old rage spout and spume like a dormant geyser come to life. She does not hate Michael, in spite of the gallons of sorrow that flowed through the last year of their marriage. But she does hate the problem. "Post-traumatic stress"; that's what the counselor had called it. Fine. It had a name, a tag. But that didn't stop it from carving a canyon through the middle of their marriage.

How long since the last call? she asked herself. Quite a while, actually.

Maybe there's an end to this after all. Well, she can't refuse him. The torment is real. Near the end, that was the only thing they could agree on.

"Michael, where are you?"

"I'm at a pay phone outside a store. Gail, I'm sorry. I'm really sorry."

"Michael, it's all right. Now look around. Are people staring at you?"

"No. I don't think so."

"Well, they're not. And the reason they're not is because you appear absolutely normal. And the reason you appear absolutely normal is because nothing's really wrong. Not *really*. You know what I mean?"

"Yeah, I know what you mean." Michael has been staring at the pavement at his feet while he talks. Now he looks up. Bingo. Everything's snapped back into place somehow. The camera view is gone. He is immersed in the lazy rhythm of the cars, people, groceries, kids, and dogs as they do their daily moves. He breathes deeply and sighs.

"Gail, I think I'm OK now."

"Of course you are. You were OK all along, but you just didn't know it."

"Look, I wouldn't have bothered you, but you're the only one who really understands this thing."

"I know."

"I'll let you go now. Thanks."

"It's all right, Michael. Talk to you later." She resists the impulse to ask him how he's doing, to pry around and get a little verbal snapshot of his life.

Could she erupt into tears right now? Easily. Instead she sighs and plows back into the senator's legislation.

Michael walks back to his truck and sits for a minute to decompress before starting home. There is still a little anxious residue floating in him, and he wants to let it settle before taking off. He regrets phoning Gail. Maybe he could have rode it out without her. Maybe not. Who knows? He turns the ignition and puts the Grateful Dead back on.

Soon he has wormed his way along the green contours of the West Hills and hopped on to the Canyon Freeway heading west. As always, it is a mess. Before the Downturn, they had begun to construct a light rail system through the cleft in the hills where the freeway connected suburban Beaverton to downtown Portland. Now the construction funds are frozen, the freeway has a jagged earthen wound down its center for miles,

and there's no fiscal balm to heal it. But this afternoon Michael maneuvers gracefully through the temporary lanes as the spring sun bathes him
with warmth and Jerry Garcia guitar licks orbit about his head. At the
217 interchange, he heads south and then takes an exit that drops onto
an arterial lined with apartment buildings. He is almost home.

The apartments in Michael's neighborhood are now sliding into the
final innings of middle age, their architecture borrowed heavily from the
postwar subdivision ranch home. Stained-wood siding, aluminum window frames with little cranks that were now mostly missing, ceiling plas-
ter shot up from guns, no insulation, wrought-iron railings, and
collective carports. In the sixties, at a time when home ownership was an
essential badge of achievement as a young population stepped onto the
economic elevator for a ride to the next floor up, this design had helped
ease the stigma of apartment dwelling. The units offered prosperity by
association, at least at the cosmetic level. But now the grease spots in
each carport stall sport the thickness of a small tar pit, and the parking
lots are dappled with potholes.

For the longest time the majority of renters here had been a migratory
tribe of divorce victims. The single working mothers, the down-on-their-
luck dads, to whom these places were a motel on the road to recovery, to
the next mate, a better job, the big break. In fact, Michael himself was a
member of this large, unstable group, although he seldom dwells on that
fact any longer.

But since the Downturn, a new demographic has formed here. Each
complex is now sprinkled with victims of financial, instead of marital,
disaster: the former middle managers, the people who had spiraled down
the professional tube in an ever tighter corkscrew as their options spun
off into oblivion. For many, it was a nightmare replay of the late eighties
and early nineties, when they had been expelled by the corporate convulsions euphemistically termed "downsizing" or "restructuring." However, during that particular period, most eventually found new jobs after
a lengthy stay in the purgatory of unemployment. But this time, there
was no net to break the fall. After the initial round of résumés produced
absolutely nothing, the first twinge of panic started eating like a corro-
sive around the fringes of their self-confidence. Next came the decision
to do a little "consulting," which meant the continual drain on savings
could be viewed as "capitalization of the business" instead of a breach in
one of the major arteries of modern life. The consulting, of course,

needed to be given a little time to work, and behind this shaky facade the next round of résumés hit the street, this time to a much wider and less selective list of prospects. When this ploy failed, the panic acid began to burn large holes in the very center of their personal security. By now it was obvious that they had been soaring far above the safety net of the unemployment check, which wouldn't even service the mortgage.

The terminal blow came when they realized that everything they owned was essentially worthless compared with what they owed. The final right of negative passage consisted of the big garage sale, the purchase of a used car, and the move into apartments like those where Michael Riley dwelled.

Michael pulls into the parking lot of his particular apartment complex, the Romona Arms. He stretches and yawns as he puts the Grateful Dead to sleep and climbs out. Episodes like the one at Stroheckers always drain him and leave him tired. Pool time, he thinks, a little pool time will put it all back into the proper perspective. Grab a good paperback, commandeer a lounge chair, and sink into a warm buzz. He glances over at the pool as he ambles out of the parking lot. Sure enough, Savage is there, along with a knot of single moms lying within grabbing distance of their children, who splash and squeal at the shallow end. John Savage is unique among the residents here, the only one who had been founder and chief executive officer of a company that was once the darling of the West Coast venture-capital community. A man on his way into the financial stratosphere, it had seemed. Then came the Downturn. And now Mr. Savage was doing time at the Romona.

Nobody knew how the Romona Arms had acquired its name. Michael had thought the name a little odd and asked Dolores Kingsley, the matriarch/manager. If it had been the "Kingston Arms," or something like that—an allusion to British royalty, to the pinnacles of respectability—it would have made more sense. But "Romona" didn't fit the template at all.

Dolores said she had no idea. In fact, she knew nothing of the place's history beyond the current generation of owners, a limited partnership of doctors who had been here only once on a blustery winter day when the commercial realtor had led them dutifully around the grounds and through an empty unit. They had nodded knowingly and professionally throughout the tour, and then never returned.

To look at the place was to look at any of a hundred thousand like it across the country. Configured in an L shape, it housed thirty-two units, sixteen on each floor. Across the top of the L was a carport that shielded the complex from Allen Boulevard, and across the far side was a carport bracketed by large trash Dumpsters at each end. Nestled in the pocket of the L was a swimming pool surrounded by a concrete apron. There was also a basement, which contained two utility rooms and a maze of personal storage spaces separated by chicken wire and secured with cheap padlocks, largely symbolic because no one stores anything of real worth behind chicken wire.

Michael drifts on up the stairs and down the walkway to unit twenty-seven, his home for the past several years. It is chilly inside, and he leaves the door open and cracks the window over the kitchen sink to let in the warm spring breeze. He opens the blinds and is confronted by classic bachelor sleaze: beer cans on the coffee table, books and magazines strewn randomly, a pair of jeans draped over a kitchen chair, a partially disassembled VCR on the floor by the TV. All capped by a pitiful attempt to decorate the place with a couple of Oregon Desert posters thumb-tacked to the merciless white walls. The door to one of the bedrooms is partially open, a computer and printer visible. For some reason he stops and looks in, which he has not done for several months. It is empty except for the two machines, the table they sit on, and a folding chair with a green pillow on it that almost matches the color of the disgusting shag carpet. The computer looks like all desktop computers have looked for some time now, a warm gray box with some venting on the side, a cluster of connectors in the back, a power light and disk drive light on the front. By current standards, it is a fairly hot machine: 500 MIPS, 4 Gigabytes of RAM, 100 Gigabyte optical disk, and a 2 million pixel flat panel color display. It is by far the most valuable item in the apartment, and from time to time Michael considers selling it but can't quite bring himself to do so.

Five minutes later, Michael is poolside, cinching up his trunks and dragging a lounge chair next to Savage, who lies on his back and faces the sinking sun with mirrored sunglasses. Physically, they are a study in contrasts. Michael, slightly on the thin side, with fair skin and dark brown curly hair fizzing out over his ears; Savage, muscular and compact, with a deep tan and closely cropped blond hair.

"So," says Savage, "how was the tower?"

Michael sighs and pops open one of the beers beside Savage's chair. "A monument to the director's ego."

"Now, what's the name of this flick again?"

"*Hellmaster IV.*"

Savage chuckles up at the high cirrus drifting overhead. "It never ends, does it?"

"Nope. You've got a new crop of thirteen-year-olds every year, just waiting to have their psyches jerked around in a dark room somewhere."

"Well, I say forget the art. Concentrate on the craft. You'll be OK."

Michael ponders this advice as he settles in. It isn't bad. Typical Savage stuff, delivered with economy and laced with a touch of ironic humor. In some ways it was easy to see him at the tiller of some fast-lane company under full sail, jaw set firmly into the wind and a strong hand on the rudder. At thirty-four and still honed to a thin edge, Savage views the Downturn as simply a dip in the fantastically complex rhythm of the global economy, a minor glitch in a kick of the bass drum, while the rest of the drum kit cruises on. Michael doesn't agree, although he understands why Savage takes this view. Some time ago, Michael had absorbed a corner of the math world dealing with nonlinear dynamic systems, the foundation of what had been popularized as "chaos." Economies were clearly systems of this sort. One interesting aspect of this was the fact that even very small changes in such systems would eventually have enormous long-term consequences. There was no such thing as a "little recession" here, or a "small boom" there. Not anymore.

Michael has patiently pieced together Savage's fall from corporate grace over the period of better than a year. The story started in grand style, with John Savage as a thirty-year-old wunderkind from Wharton who had ascended to marketing VP for one of the West Coast's biggest integrated circuit manufacturers. Along came two Ph.D.'s in semiconductor physics with an ambitious technodream and the brains to back the engineering side. The scheme involved a relatively inexpensive device that could be added to an IC fabrication plant, or "fab." With it, the fab would be capable of breaking free of Moore's Law, which called for the density of integrated circuitry to double every two years. Double the density meant twice as much circuitry, which meant lower costs, less power consumption, and better performance when compared with that of printed circuit boards, with their tidy little cities of black chips.

With the new device, there would be a one-time hiccup in Moore's Law, and the density could actually be quadrupled in two years—an enormous competitive advantage. However, the device by itself was not enough, and the two physicists knew it. It was now well known in financial circles that you don't invest in technology per se, you invest in companies with the ability to profitably exploit technology over long periods of time, and to spawn new technology along the way. This is where Savage came in. He had a masterful vision of the interface between business and technology, a netherworld where many before him had floundered.

The three of them had lunch, which started with a bottle of white wine and the signing of the ubiquitous nondisclosure form, which protected the physicists from Savage pirating their idea and developing it independently. Before the salad was finished, Savage was convinced they did indeed have one of those rare breakthroughs with true economic potential. Halfway through the main course, he had already framed the business plan in his head. Over dessert and coffee, he negotiated a full share of equity for himself, plus a position of executive leadership.

Money would be no problem. The venture people already had Savage pegged as superstar material, and within weeks the game began in earnest. At one end of the field were the founders, with their technical and business knowledge. At the other the venture capitalists, with the money to fertilize the technovision until it blossomed. As always, each side started play with a childlike fantasy as its subconscious goal. The founders imagined millions of dollars put at their disposal with no strings attached—a loan from a rich uncle, the kind who might even cancel the debt if he liked the nephew's or niece's behavior. The venture people, on the other hand, envisioned total ownership of the business for the rest of its fiscal life, with the founders as grateful employees, ever thankful for the infusion of capital that allowed the launching of such a great enterprise.

At this point, the players were locked in what software designers call a deadly embrace, each holding resources the other needs, but unwilling to surrender them so the program can move forward. But unlike a program, the players could step outside the formal bounds of the situation and engineer an infinity of compromises.

Once negotiations began, the object was to find an equilibrium. The bargaining units were shares of stock, and the founders gave away units of control and equity to gain units of working capital; the venture people, vice versa. In the end, the timeless law of risk versus gain governed the outcome. If the founders had something that was relatively risk free and could survive all but the most absurd business blunders, the money people might even settle for a minority position just to be along for the ride. However, most propositions put before them were a little less stellar and much more vulnerable—including this one.

In the end, after many elaborate feints, jabs, fakes, blocks, slices, lay-ups, and takedowns, Savage's deal emerged in the usual form: The money people owned a majority position and the founders got executive power and enough stock to make them wealthy if the company succeeded.

So ended the first act. The second act would be making the business work, but it was the third act that really counted, the IPO, the initial public offering, the event that would transmogrify private stock into public. All the complex deal structuring, all the convoluted negotiating, now culminated in the most elementary arithmetic. The founders might hold seven hundred fifty thousand shares purchased at five cents per share, and the money people 5 million shares bought at an average of a dollar per share. When the IPO went down, an additional 2 million shares might be issued, and if the market was hot, they might go for fifteen dollars per share. And since the private shares were now tradable on the public market, the venture people's 5-million-dollar injection traded at $75 million, and the founders' $37,000 at over $11 million.

But Savage knew better than to dwell on a beatific vision of the IPO. Instead, he immediately launched into a complex stew of marketing, licensing, and manufacturing strategies. For the first year, he targeted a certain group of integrated circuits used in high-speed mathematical calculations. While math speed had always been important, several new fields of theoretical research also called for an unprecedented level of accuracy. (The concept of numerical accuracy is simple. In high school, everyone is taught to round off the decimal places when they get too long, for easy manipulation. In general, this works well because each number to the right of the decimal point is ten times less significant. Rounding off makes numbers simple to handle, with only a little loss in accuracy. Nevertheless, the loss is there. Outside the computer industry, it's not well known that most computers are severely hobbled when it comes to numbers with a very large number of digits. While they are able to deal with an expansive range of numbers through "floating point" formats, the accuracy of these numbers degenerates rapidly as the range grows larger.) All ways around the problem were either expensive or slowed the performance of the machine, but the circuit density of Savage's new products would dramatically improve this accuracy and apply to the high end of the market, which, although relatively small, gobbled up new technology as fast as it became available.

And gobble it did. The first year's sales were nearly triple the initial projections. The investors were elated. The competition indignant. The analysts impressed. By halfway into the second year, it looked like the company was smoking along toward an IPO before year's end.

That was when the Downturn hit. In some industries it drifted in gradually, like a light summer drizzle, but in the high end of the semi-conductor industry, it hit like a hurricane.

As sales withered, Savage watched his executive options wither along with them. His final option was to mothball the company and wrap a protective cocoon around the technology, so it could metamorphose into new products when the storm passed. This meant slashing the staff to a skeleton crew, and Savage had spent two ashen days personally dismissing people who had worked sixty-hour weeks to get the thing off the ground. The board should have viewed his actions as tragic but heroic. They didn't. Behind them was an angry mob of investors who wanted nothing less than human sacrifice to compensate for the vast amount of money that had vaporized into the industrial ether.

So on a leaden Saturday afternoon, Savage had sat in the company's boardroom and absently listened to the chairman cast his sacking in the most benign, paternalistic terms. "John, in business there is always the expectation that somehow adversity can be turned into opportunity. Now, you and I both know that's not exactly true, but . . ."

It seemed all the board could muster was six months' pay and a very tepid letter of recommendation.

So now John Savage stretches, sits up, pulls off his sunglasses, and looks at the children happily churning a white froth at the shallow end of the pool.

"Your watch, Riley. Check you later."

"Yep."

Michael watches Savage shuffle off, his thongs thwacking their way over the concrete apron to the gate out of the pool area. He settles back, tries to imagine how much it must have cost Savage to get to work during his heyday. Michael pictures him slipping into his Armani suit and strolling out to his BMW 975e, where he makes a round of calls on his cellular phone en route to a posh athletic club along the waterfront and then over to the Alexis Hotel for a morning breakfast meeting. After all the necessary amortizations and other adjustments, Savage had surely been nipping at the far side of a couple of hundred dollars before he even got to the office.

With that, Michael closes his eyes and floats in the foamy sounds of kids splashing and moms buzzing. In the far distance, a boom box punches out some speed metal, and a symphony of power mowers blends in a vague mechanical hum. He quickly drifts into a suspended resonance and stays there until . . .

The moms aren't buzzing anymore. The abrupt gap pulls him halfway out of his torpor. He hears the scraping of a lounge chair on the cement next to him. Savage back? He opens his eyes a slit and rotates them in the direction of the scraping. What he sees brings them wide open. Her. No wonder the moms are hushed. Even Michael realizes that to other women, she's just not fair. Most women devote a substantial portion of their life to cosmetic engineering, but for her, it's a simple exercise in restraint. The barest trace of eyeliner, the thinnest bit of mascara, the briefest hint of lipstick. Natural honey-blond hair that just sort of falls into place with a few quick brush strokes. A lean, catlike figure despite the fact she seldom exercises. It just isn't fair.

For a horrible moment, Michael forgets her name, but it comes back around on a mad carousel. Jessica. That's it. Jessica. He never expected her to take up his offer and actually come over.

They met a couple of days back when the crew was shooting an interior scene at the Oregon Health Sciences University. It was in between takes, and Howard was out in the parking lot for a screaming session with one of the actors. So Michael wandered down the hall, into an open lab, and there she was. At first glance, she seemed almost like a pure cliché: The beautiful librarian with just the plain glasses to mask her seething passions. But the cliché evaporated when she turned to him and spoke.

"Can I help you?"

Whoops. All business and then some. Oh, well. "Nope. I'm on the movie crew down the hall. Our director took one of the actors out in the parking lot to pluck his eyeballs out. So I thought I'd take a look around."

A thin smile broke across her lips. "Well, you won't see much here. The things we deal with are down in the nanometer range."

"Such as?"

"Such as nucleotide triphosphates. Ribosomal subunits. Stuff like that."

"Hot stuff," Michael beamed.

"I think so," she said with a hint of defiance.

"Me, too," he said. "I don't know much about molecular biology, but it's gotten pretty deep, hasn't it?"

"Deeper by the day."

"Then maybe I'd better get caught up on it. Would you care to help?"

Michael could not believe what he was doing. Inwardly, he cringed and waited for the acid to drip all over him.

"What kind of help?" she asked.

Unbelievable, thought Michael. "Point me to some good textbooks. Outline the fundamentals I'll have to master."

"Well, I've got a busy schedule."

Michael reached for a pencil and a loose piece of paper on the counter. "Here's where I am in the evenings." He scribbled his address at the Romona. "If it's warm, you might find me down by the pool. If not, I'm in unit twenty-seven."

In the distance, Michael heard Harold yelling orders to the crew.

"Gotta go. What's your name?"

"Jessica."

"Michael. See you later."

Halfway down the hall, he realized he hadn't given her his phone number. And it was unlikely that she would just present her physical self at his doorstep. Just as well. Truth was, he wasn't ready to deal with her—or any other woman, for that matter. Not until he was done dealing with the Fear.

Here she is, poolside at the Romona. No choice now but to take it as it comes. She has on cutoffs, a plain white T-shirt, leather thongs, and sunglasses. Beside her is a canvas shopping bag.

"Hi, true to your word, you're poolside," she says breezily, pulling a couple of books out of the bag. "Well, I found some books for you, but I'll have to get them back."

Michael rises quickly to a sitting position. "Yeah. You know, I really appreciate this."

She looks at him earnestly. "It's nice to run into someone who has an interest in the field." She glances down at the top book. "It'll help if you have some scientific background. Do you?"

"Yup. But it's pretty mathematical and not very chemical."

"That's OK. It'll definitely help," she says, putting the books back into the bag.

Then, with remarkable suddenness, she deflates and stares vacantly at the cement. "Yes, it'll definitely help," she repeats quietly, almost sadly.

In a burst of intuition, Michael realizes that it has required a great deal of energy for her to come here and do this thing for him. But why? Doesn't matter. Now it's up to him.

"My place is a horrible mess, but if you come up for a minute, you can tell me where to return this stuff."

"OK."

In the background, the kids splash, the moms buzz once more.

The inside of Michael's place is a mess, but she seems genuinely oblivious to it. They sit at the kitchen table, where she removes the books from the bag.

"I'd offer you something to drink, but the truth is, I don't have anything right now," he admits.

"Quite all right," she replies with a nervous smile. "If we were at my place, I'd have the same problem."

"If you've got a few minutes," says Michael, "maybe you could kind of go over the basics with me."

They launch into a comfortably formal academic discussion, a giant insulator that allows no emotional current to flow in either direction. Both want it that way, at least for now, and maybe for some time to come.

An hour later, he walks her to her car and watches her drive off into the warmth of the early evening. He feels an impulsive longing to just get in and go. Right now. Sitting next to her in the car. Driving off into some softly luminous adventure.

Then he remembers the Fear, and the longing collapses of its own weight.

Michael stands naked at the entrance to the basement of the Romona Arms. He squints against the noon sun screaming off the building's white siding. The door to the basement is open and it is infinitely black inside. Dolores Kingsley, the manager, ambles up and pops out of the darkness.

"OK, Michael, this time we're going to get it."

Dolores is wearing gray sweats with the word "Omaha" stenciled across the back. They descend a small set of stairs into the chicken wire storage area, and Michael shivers in the cool, musty air. Dolores begins to jog down the corridor between the spaces. Michael should be able to hear her footsteps, but curiously hears nothing at all. Dolores repeatedly turns corners, taking them ever deeper into the maze. From off to their left, they hear a crash and she stops. Overhead, a row of naked light bulbs sways randomly.

They move along slowly to a storage space where the framed chicken wire door is standing open. Dolores goes in first. Behind her, Michael feels the weight of a large pistol in his hand.

"There!"

Dolores thrusts a finger at the dimmest corner of the storage space, where two snow tires rest against a Weber barbecue. Michael fires the pistol, and it spits a sharp crack that pings off the basement's cement walls. Dolores floats over and reaches behind the tires, pulling out a hideous thing that thrashes in its final death spasm. It is the size of a cat, but looks like a hybrid of a rat and a lizard.

"Good shot," says Dolores as she holds the creature out for his inspection. Fangs and a forked tongue protrude from the streamlined snout, and green vented eyes glare at Michael. But it's the skull that makes him cringe. It is covered with marble-sized perforations that plunge into hollow blackness, making it look like some awful permutation of a whiffle ball punctured by repeated gunfire.

"But I only shot once."

Dolores ignores him and marches out. They now walk by the pool, where moms chatter and kids play. Without even looking, Dolores casts the thing into the pool and walks toward her unit while it sinks slowly toward the bright blue bottom. Michael walks to the edge and sees that it has slithered back to life and mutated in the process. It is now the size of a large dog and has webbed feet and a long dorsal fin that sways as it swims in a circle at the pool bottom. The horrible skull holes remain, with an occasional air bubble drifting out of them.

As Michael squats for a closer look, a bare foot slams between his shoulder blades and he tumbles into the water. Abruptly, everything is cool, quiet, and blue, with only a distant burbling. But something is wrong. He is sinking and the pool suddenly seems much larger. He rolls to face the bottom and feels the terror bolt through him. The thing is now enormous, its body covered by a blue canvas tarp, with only the perforated head visible. The skull is now covered by short brown hair that undulates gently in the water current. Each perforation is the size of a manhole.

And out of one of these cavities swims a huge snake that begins to coil its oily body around Michael. He yells and realizes too late that he is underwater. He tries to gulp back in the air he expended in the yell and . . .

Michael sits bolt upright in bed. The green display on the alarm whispers "3:02" at him. He is covered with sweat as thick as cooking oil. From far off, the mechanical muttering of the freeway drifts in the window and soothes him. It is the reassuring hum of things moving on.

As Michael swivels out of bed, he replays the holes, the thing. He sighs, because he knows their origin, and slips into his swimming trunks. The dream comes in different flavors, and less often than before, but its core remains intact. Often, it seems to be connected to things like today's Stroheckers incident.

The air is still as he sits on the edge of the pool and then glides in. Under the cool pressure of the water and its chlorine perfume, he feels his sweat peel off into the night. He exits at the other end and starts back to his unit. He sighs deeply. The demon is gone and he is sleepy once more. He heads for the stairs. On the way, he sees the muted glow of lights on in Savage's place.

Inside unit seven, John Savage sits at a chrome and glass coffee table. Like all the other furniture in the apartment, it is leased. The only decoration is a piece of green-bar computer printout held to the refrigerator by a magnet. It is the balance sheet of his former company at the time he left, and serves as a little billboard to advertise his defeat to a target audience of one, John Savage. On a small TV on the counter, a commercial featuring a savage fat man named Big Boy Bill is in progress. Big Boy mans a .50-caliber machine gun and peppers an old sedan full of holes, and as the smoke clears, he vows "to poke holes in the competition's car prices." He signs off with his media signature, a paramilitary salute to the camera.

But now business fiascoes and car commercials are far from John's mind as he carefully arranges the objects before him. A small jar holding a solution of vinegar and water. A paper clip bent to form a small circular hoop with a stem for a handle. Tweezers. A bronze pipe with a thimble-sized bowl and a narrow six-inch stem. A kitchen match.

From his shirt pocket he produces a blister pack with a heavy metal foil backing, a package design common for nonprescription drugs. It contains no labeling whatsoever, only a smooth metallic surface and six egg-shaped tablets the size of small grapes. He carefully punches one of the tablets through the backing, and puts the package under a cushion on the couch.

So, let it begin.

He picks up the bent paper clip and uses the tweezers to place the tablet into the hoop. With the care of a chemist, he moves the hoop over the jar and lowers it into the solution. There is an instant fizz as the solution attacks the outer coating of the tablet. In less than a minute it is eaten away, and the inner core, a puttylike substance, exposed. He reaches in with the tweezers, removes the core, lets the excess solution drip away, and places the core in the pipe bowl. He lights the match, and pulls hard and rapidly until the core ignites in a small puff of white smoke.

Quickly, he waves out the kitchen match and takes one long pull on the pipe.

John Savage looks at the paraphernalia on the glass coffee table. . . . *Wonder where that stuff came from?* He gets up and wanders around. . . . *Interesting place. But it needs a few more pictures or something.* . . .

The future is fluff. The past is ashes.

He passes the refrigerator and spots the green bar—*Wow! A real corporate power dive! Must've made a big splash when it hit!*—goes to the front door and opens it—*A hot night and an empty pool. Perfect!*—walks back through the living room to the bedroom—*There's gotta be some trunks in here somewhere. Ah! Here we are*—turns and sees himself in a full-length mirror as he puts on the trunks—*Looks good. Must work out all the time to stay like that . . .*

A moment later, he stands before the pool, its glassy surface sparkling in the still night. He eases in and swims gently through a world that is only fifteen minutes old.

3

Wet Work

Dwight Colby scans page two of *The Washington Post* while waiting for the phone to ring. It will be his wife, apologizing for the fight they had this morning. Over twelve years, they have built up an elaborate codification of liability in domestic conflicts. Unwritten and unspoken, it hovers like a phantom magistrate over their relationship, and defines in great detail who is guilty and under what circumstances. In the heat of battle, it always evaporates, but rapidly condenses again to inform the guilty party of his or her obligations.

In this case, his wife is at fault. She complained bitterly about the extra time his boss had cleverly extracted from him last week. And although she knew he had no control over the situation, she leveled a nasty barrage at him anyway, just to show her frustration. In their marital code, this is a fairly simple case, and can be settled in full with a single phone call, provided the call is made on the same day as the fight.

On page two of the *Post,* Colby spots an article about the Mortgage March, which is now just a few weeks away. He chuckles maliciously. This one has those bastards on the Hill more than a little worried. Unlike the farmers' financial problems in the eighties, the Downturn has propagated a wave of mortgage failures among huge urban constituencies that could eviscerate the current Congress. As a result, the article states, a great many congressmen plan to participate, to march in the classic shirtsleeves populist style, elbow to elbow with the electorate—and in full range of the media.

Colby puts down the paper and shivers slightly. The goddamn air-conditioning. Here in the innermost bowels of the Executive Building, they just can't ever get it right. He'd complained to Operations, which was like trying to reason with a block of granite.

He is also agitated because he doesn't want to go back to work until his wife calls and the scales of justice are level once more. For Dwight, work consists of a computer workstation on an otherwise clean desk. There is no paper clutter because there is no paper allowed here. The classic fixtures of office automation, the copier and the laser printer, are conspicuously absent. The only other thing on Dwight's desk is a combination phone and intercom. He knows the conversation he will soon have with his wife will be recorded, but he long ago became desensitized to this kind of eavesdropping. For one thing, the chances of anyone ever actually listening to it were remote; for another, it would be crushingly boring to anyone outside the marriage.

Dwight's job is simple in definition, but complex in practice. He is one of the guardians at Checkpoint Alpha, the great clearinghouse for data throughout the federal government. Checkpoint Alpha owes its existence to the early phases of the drug war, when frustrated Drug Enforcement Agency officials found there was a wealth of incriminating data throughout the government's computer systems, but no way to cross-reference from one system to another. A marijuana farmer might be receiving federal assistance from the Department of Agriculture, while Federal Aviation Administration records showed he owned three DC-3 transport planes, and Internal Revenue Service records reported him earning two hundred thousand dollars a year from a string of alleged video rental stores. But there was no way to put it all together.

When the first serious efforts to integrate the government's computer networks were proposed, they met with prompt counterpunches from groups concerned with protecting the individual's right to privacy. Never had Big Brother looked bigger.

The debate was resolved through legislation which declared that personal data in the new unified system was an extension of "person" as defined in the fourth article of the Bill of Rights. This meant that such data was protected against illegal search and seizure, which in turn meant that officials had to get a search warrant before doing a system-wide sweep on an individual.

However, there was one catch, one gap in the privacy shield that applied to individuals engaged in matters of national security. These people voluntarily surrendered their privacy rights and formally agreed to random security screening through Checkpoint Alpha. In their case, security officials could roam the system at will, looking for any information that pointed toward security violations.

And so it was that sophisticated search programs now fanned out from Checkpoint Alpha to wander the vast tangle of departmental databases like police cruisers roaming the streets of a large city.

Dwight Colby's job is to drive one such cruiser, looking for irregularities, disturbing ripples, anomalies. Anything that smells wrong.

Now, with no phone call, he leans toward the terminal and pulls out once again. He idles down towering corridors of data and feels the pulse of traffic in the main arteries of the network. Like most good cops, he works on his gut, which now takes him down a side street into a neighborhood full of low-priority "flag triggers." He pulls into a driveway where a key-word probe operates and finds that it has put up a flag on one Simon Greeley in the Office of Management and Budget. Something to do with "nervous tension" in his medical records. By itself, that's less than worthless. But for some reason, one of Alpha's central AI (artificial intelligence) programs has scooped this up and interpreted it as a trigger to stay on Greeley's tail. So Colby calls in to the AI and gets a real-time update on Greeley.

Jackpot. Fucking jackpot, man.

This guy had just helped himself to a big serving of System 9 without prior approval! What's more, whatever he did in there had launched a Triple Blue Alert, and Colby is the first person to spot it.

Goddamn! He's been here for six years and never even heard of a Triple Blue being launched.

Colby's toes tap a frantic rhythm on the green linoleum floor. He tries to calm himself. After all, this Simon guy still has two days to file a report explaining his action. But that won't cancel the Triple Blue! He must've really stirred up some shit in there!

Colby's toes break cadence and slow to a crawl. The hard cynicism of the beat cop creeps back in. Somehow, he will get screwed out of any credit for this one. He opens a new window and scans the operating procedure for Triple Blue. Sure enough, he's screwed. The procedure doesn't even let him inform his supervisor. In fact, all he is supposed to do is leave a cryptic message in an electronic mailbox. And then shut up. Forever.

The phone rings. His wife.

"Hi, hon," she says in the universal tone of reconciliation.

"Hi."

"I'm sorry. I know it's not your fault. I know your boss is a shithead. And it just gets me a little upset. Know what I mean?"

"Yeah. I know what you mean."

"So . . . what time you coming home?"

"Regular time."

"Dwight?"

"Yeah?"

"What's wrong?"

"Nothing's wrong."

A weary sigh from his wife. "Yeah. Sure. Talk to you later."

"Yeah, later. Bye now."

Click.

Fuck! Now he is the guilty party. Their code clearly stipulates that all apologies for this type of infraction are to be received warmly and graciously. By being an asshole about the whole thing, he committed an offense worse than the original one against him.

And to top it off, he has to zipper up about his biggest snag in six years.

Bitterly, Colby follows the Triple Blue operating procedure, which requires him to send a condensed version of the AI report to an electronic-mail address somewhere in the computerized hinterland. To add a little insult, the address is simply a series of numbers. The name of the receiver isn't even identified.

Colby watches a box come up that says, "Message sent," followed four seconds later by "Receipt acknowledged."

So the game is played.

In the Virginia suburbs of Washington, D.C., a small chime sounds on a desktop computer located in an office with a sign on the door that reads

CONSOLIDATED SUPPORT GROUP. The office is couched in a business complex, along with a branch office of a large insurance company, several software consultants, a smattering of psychologists, and a couple of attorneys.

The chime catches the attention of a short, compact man in his mid-fifties who radiates a ferocious intensity and has a thin mouth creased into the negative crescent of a permanent scowl. The firm's two secretaries call him Wire Man, because he always appears to be wired on stimulants. They don't like him, but tolerate him because new office jobs are now extremely hard to come by. Besides, the work is easy. The company has several "consulting contracts" that are handled entirely by Wire Man and two associates. All the secretaries have to do is answer the phone and keep appointment books.

Wire Man immediately spots the flashing mail alert among the clutter on his screen. Instead of the normal monochromatic little box, this one is deep blue and flashing in clusters of threes. Triple Blue! He bolts from his desk and runs to a back room where all modem connections between the office and the outside world are wired. With swift, deliberate motions, he yanks loose the wires that establish these connections. Any computer link with the outside world is now severed. No one can follow the trail of Triple Blue into this office.

He returns to his desk, opens the mail, and rapidly digests the AI report, which is considerably more detailed than the version Dwight Colby saw. In essence, someone named Simon Greeley has rattled around inside System 9 and penetrated the VenCap cover. But why? Wire Man opens a new window on his screen and probes a database that exists only on this machine in this office. In three seconds, he gets his answer. Greeley knows he's being used. He's put it together. And that means he's more than a little pissed off.

Without hesitation, Wire Man slides open the bottom drawer of his desk, which contains a gray metal box with a single switch and a green LED display. He throws the switch and sees an emerald glow from the LED. Inside the box, a scrambler encodes the output of his phone in a way that, for all practical purposes, makes it indecipherable. It also reprograms the receptionist's phone console so she cannot eavesdrop on the call, even though she sees a red light indicating that the phone line is in use. Finally, it automatically dials an unlisted phone number at a residence only a few miles away, where a sister machine senses the presence of its sibling and also goes into a scramble mode.

Three rings later, a male voice answers. A voice as flat as open desert.

"Counterpoint."

"Counterpoint," Wire Man replies, "this is Consolidated. I have a Triple Blue."

"And?"

"A Simon Greeley in National Security at OMB poked a little too deep into System 9 and discovered his true purpose in life."

"Source?"

"Alpha Cruiser plus AI."

"I'd say this requires decisive action. Wouldn't you?"

Wire Man hesitates and feels silence fill the room like fluid in a blister. "At this point, I see no alternative," he mumbles.

"Well, then, neither do I. Now just how much might a man like Mr. Greeley be missed?"

"Very much," replies Wire Man. "He's high up in the organization. Many people will want to know why and how if anything happens to him. It must be absolutely clean."

"Fortunately, we now have the technology to make it so. Which means Mr. Greeley is going to become a living laboratory. I think that's rather exciting, don't you?"

"Yes, I do." Wire Man curses silently. *Why does he play with me like this?*

"Good. We need your kind of enthusiasm to keep the program alive."

The connection breaks, and the dial tone bores a fuzzy hole in Wire Man's taut eardrum. Better do it now, he thinks. Better do it right now.

Wire Man tells the receptionist he's out for the day, and heads for his car in the parking lot. Until now, he has been paid very well to do very little. All that has just changed. His employer, the Consolidated Support Group, was established during the last administration through National Security Directive 2034. N.S.D.D.'s are descendants of the National Security Act of 1947, and have evolved into powerful instruments of policy and executive action. By the eighties, they were totally immune to congressional scrutiny, and often bypassed formal government channels when put into action.

So it was with N.S.D.D. 2034, which created the Consolidated Support Group to deal with "certain instances requiring extraordinary counterintelligence measures." By law, the Justice Department is the only institution authorized to investigate and prosecute suspected espionage within the borders of the U.S. However, N.S.D.D. 2034 stated that in the Information Age, an organization like CSG was required to "determine the very existence of computer-based espionage activity, so that other agencies can pursue proper channels of investigation."

Unchecked by Congress or any formal chain of executive responsibility, part of CSG slowly oozed out into a world of perpetual twilight where "official national policy" and "patriotic concern" swirled and intertwined in complex and continually shifting patterns. There were some in the White House that suspected, but they kept a cautious distance. Ever since Iran-Contra, no one wanted to be the conduit between renegade intelligence operations and the president.

And now Wire Man drives through this political twilight to a pharmaceutical supply house in a light industrial area nearby. He meets with a woman who takes him to a vacant office. Here, Wire Man makes a long-distance phone call to Mexico City, a call that is traceable back to this company, but to no one individual inside it.

Wire Man oscillates nervously in a swivel chair as the call goes through.

"Farmacéutico Asociado," a woman's voice answers in Spanish.

"Yes, Mr. Franklin, please."

"Uno momento, por favor."

A man comes on the line. "Franklin here."

"Mr. Franklin, I'm calling from PharmMed. We need you to expedite our order."

A pause.

"I see. And what's your priority code?"

"Counterpoint."

"Very well. Nice talking to you."

"Good-bye."

Wire Man hangs up and heads for his car. He never really expected to make this call. He will be glad when things get back to normal.

In Mexico City, Mr. Franklin hangs up the phone. From his office window, he looks out at the horrible brown sky. The polluted haze is so thick over the Toluca Highway that the afternoon sun is only a dull ruby marble. He tries to imagine what would make Counterpoint go to this extreme. It must be something that might blow the whole business. But Mr. Franklin is not a man who is long on imagination, so he walks out of the office and into the warehouse, where boxes full of various medical drugs are stacked. These same boxes have been here for several years, and occasionally they are rearranged by an ad hoc work crew. They have nothing to do with the true business of Farmacéutico Asociado, which appears to be a distributor of pharmaceutical products. There was a time when somebody might have taken a closer look, but in a city now swollen to over 28 million people and several hundred thousand business sites, the odds grow longer every day.

Mr. Franklin moves to an elevator, which goes to a second storage floor. Instead of pressing two, he hits a certain combination of ones and twos, which takes the elevator down instead of up. When the doors open, he strides down the hall to the heart of Farmacéutico Asociado, to an area biologically severed from the outside world. Technically, it is known as a P4 containment room, and within it the air is kept at a slightly negative pressure, which guarantees that microscopic airborne flotsam may drift in, but none drifts out. To maintain this lopsided pressure, a pump system constantly removes air and passes it through a chamber where it is blasted with gamma rays in a radioactive hell that delivers total sterilization.

To enter the P4 room, Mr. Franklin steps into an intermediate space where he takes a set of white plastic coveralls off a stack on a table. He dons the coveralls, which seal about the wrists and ankles, puts on surgical gloves, and slips off his shoes. Now he moves to a rack that contains what can only be described as space suits, because although they will never leave the surface of the earth, they provide an absolute barrier between the person inside and the environment outside. Bathed in ultraviolet light, he slips into the suit and pushes his hands through its rubber gloves. After sealing the suit, he dons a helmet with a broad Plexiglas bubble for a faceplate and locks it into place. With his breath condensing on the faceplate, he moves across the room to an airlock door with a large "L4" painted on it, and has to tug hard to break the tight seal. Once inside, a chemical shower rains down and thoroughly sterilizes the surface of the suit. He then walks through the far door of the airlock and shuts it, which automatically activates a second chemical downpour to ensure a biological wasteland is maintained between the inner and outer worlds.

Once inside P4 proper, he hooks an overhead air hose to a receptacle on his helmet, and the noisy rush of dry air quickly clears his faceplate. Directly in front of him, a man wearing a similar suit stands at a bench covered with racks of plastic test tubes and beakers. He turns to Franklin and then back to his work without saying a word.

"We've got an order from PharmMed," yells Franklin above the rush of air through his suit.

The man pauses and turns to give Franklin a longer look. Without speaking, he turns back and reaches for a small plastic bottle with a screw cap. He then fetches a beaker full of clear liquid and fills the bottle. Next he moves a gloved hand to a case full of small metal drawers, one of which he slides open to reveal a petri dish labeled "KR 12." He picks up a cotton swab and swirls it in the culture growing in the dish, then sticks the swab into the liquid in the plastic bottle. After a moment, he screws the cap on the bottle and puts it in an unmarked stainless-steel container the size of a thermos, which is filled with a powerful disinfectant, and tightly screws on a metal-and-plastic lid.

Then, without warning, he tosses the container at Franklin, who executes a startled and clumsy catch that makes him look like a drunken juggler.

"Jesus, Spelvin!" screams Franklin through the inner air rush. "What the fuck are you doing?"

Spelvin, the man in the second suit, pours out a torrent of mean laughter. "Sorry, buddy. Just testing. That's all. Just testing."

Franklin stalks back to the airlock, opens its outer door, and disappears. Spelvin continues to chortle as he turns to the bench.

An hour later, Franklin pulls his car up to a hangar at Benito Juárez International Airport. He hustles inside, where a small private jet is parked. It is the latest model Beach Starship, but with some significant modifications. In place of the usual turboprop engines are fanjets, which generate far less noise than conventional jet engines. Moreover, these particular fan-jets are designed to push the Starship to just under the speed of sound. In the cockpit are avionics that include radar, radar defense, and navigation gear on a par with the best military systems.

The plane's pilot appears at the Starship's door, and accepts a briefcase from Franklin that holds the container from P4 in packing foam. Franklin gives the pilot a destination and arrival time, but mentions nothing about the contents of the briefcase.

Just after dusk, the Starship cuts through the soiled cotton haze above the city and heads east out over the Caribbean. About eighty miles off the Mexican coast, it leaves the realm of Mexican air traffic control and cruises into the blackness over international waters. Now it heads north under the enormous electromagnetic dome of U.S. air and drug defense. At fifty thousand feet, the latest generation of AWAC (airborne warning and control) plane circles lazily over the Gulf of Mexico, its radar covering a vast sweep of ocean and hundreds of aircraft. And off the coast of Texas, balloon-tethered radar keeps watch over one hundred miles out to sea.

However, the Starship has radar of its own, and knows exactly where the AWAC is. The Starship is also tracking another plane, an airliner headed for San Antonio. Accelerating to full throttle, it quickly overtakes the airliner and then tucks itself neatly underneath, fifteen hundred feet from the airliner's belly. On the AWAC screens, the airliner and Starship have merged into a single blip, long before any operator has time to notice.

About 120 miles off the Texas coast, the Starship suddenly veers off and goes to full throttle once more. The balloon-tethered radar tracks this action and an alert goes out to the nearest DEA intercept aircraft, but it is already hopeless. The Starship knows the location of the DEA plane from advanced signature analysis equipment coupled with its radar. It also knows it will reach the coast and fly over San Padre Island in about ten minutes—long before the DEA plane can find it. And once inland, it plays its final technological trump card as it zooms along 150 feet above the ground. Normally, it would be suicidal to fly this low at night, but the pilot is aided by navigation technology first employed in cruise missiles. In effect, the plane's computer system includes a database that models the topography all the way to the target and automatically guides the plane over it.

Thirty minutes later, the Starship touches down at an airstrip on a remote ranch eighty miles northwest of Corpus Christi. The ranch is owned by a retired military officer well connected with the netherworld that swirls on the fringes of U.S. intelligence, a man who sorely misses the adventure he enjoyed in his prime, flying over the jungles of El Salvador and Honduras. Now he settles for an occasional high-tech aircraft dropping out of the hot Texas night, running lights off.

On the ground, the Starship pilot hands the briefcase to the pilot of a smaller turboprop plane, who immediately takes off for Washington, D.C. The Starship is wheeled into a small hangar while its pilot and the officer head down to the ranch house to drink and swap stories of glorious days gone by. Neither knows the contents of the briefcase or the purpose of the mission. Neither wants to.

In the container within the briefcase drift several billion identical molecular systems, the likes of which have never been seen on earth. Each is rod-shaped, and tiny almost beyond conception. If a single meter were blown up to the distance between New York and Los Angeles, one of these systems would span only the first two feet of the journey. At their core is an entity technically known as a viroid, a spiral necklace of RNA code spelled out in a four-letter nucleotide alphabet: A, U, G, C.

But the viroid itself has existed for thousands of years. What makes this system unique is the protein coat that wraps around each RNA spiral and protects it from a hostile world. For many generations, this particular strain of viroid lived and thrived in very hospitable environments: just the right temperature, just the right pH. But now it is being called upon to undertake an expedition through a very hostile chemical world, so someone has constructed a special protective cloak called a capsid, and done it in such a way that the viroid literally grows it on in a skintight fit, the first artificial garment in the history of microbiology. Once in place, the capsid officially elevates the viroid to the rank of virus, and gives it the appearance of several common viruses, which use very similar capsids.

But there is nothing common at all about this new virus. Its RNA-based viroid cargo carries a very brief yet ghastly message, and waits with infinite patience to deliver it to a new host.

Hours later, Wire Man stands on a concrete apron at Dulles International Airport in Washington and watches the turboprop roll to a stop and cut its engines. The pilot hops out and walks directly up to him.

"You got something to tell me?" he asks.

"Triple Blue," answers Wire Man.

"You're on," says the pilot, and hands the briefcase to Wire Man and walks off toward the hangar's office.

Quickly, Wire Man walks back to his car in the hangar parking lot and takes out a key that unlocks the briefcase. He unscrews the cap of the stainless steel container and gingerly removes the inner bottle from the disinfectant. He then puts everything back the way it was, adds an envelope with a very large amount of cash, and drives off.

One look at him and Wire Man understands why he is among the best in his business. He is every man, no man, the guy next door, the office buddy, the jovial brother-in-law, the golf partner, the average husband, the median dad. Well groomed, with utterly bland features, he melts into anonymity before your very eyes.

But here, at this table at a tavern near the airport, he lets down the shield just a fraction.

"Call me the Worm," he says softly.

"How come?" asks Wireman.

"Doesn't matter. Just call me the Worm."

"OK," says Wire Man as he passes the briefcase over. "You handle it from here. Right?"

"Right."

Wire Man gets up to leave. "See you."

The Worm remains seated. "I doubt it. I doubt it very much."

Outside, Wire Man feels the tension drain out of him. Worm, my ass. At last, he is out of the loop.

4

Jimi's Peek

It's OK. My dad will come and get me.

Jimi Tyler is eight years old and scared. Really scared. His world wobbles and heaves as he jumps down off the wooden crate next to the big house trailer. An insect buzzes loudly in a tangle of weeds and dead grass next to the trailer's beige metal siding. The noise cuts right to the center of his head and tickles him in a most disturbing way.

Jimi knows that Rat Bag and Zipper won't be any help at all. He is right.

"So what's the matter, butt wipe?" spits Rat Bag as he smears an index finger over his runny nose.

Jimi hears him but can't speak. Zipper immediately senses the problem and bores in.

"Shit man, he's so freaked he can't even talk," scoffs Zipper.

Rat Bag is ten and head of the pack. He is known only by his nickname, which is derived from the time he trapped a rat in the Romona Arms basement, put it in a potato sack, and drowned it in the swimming pool. He then put the body on display behind the Dumpster in the parking lot and took each kid individually to view it in a solemn ceremony. Tall and wiry, he already has a leader's strut about him.

Zipper is nine and born to follow. He is skinny with a long neck that droops forward and a mouth perpetually open due to adenoid problems.

He seldom speaks first, preferring to dwell safely in the verbal wake of Rat Bag.

Although Rat Bag is not aware of why he brought Jimi here, there is exquisite instinctive logic behind his action. He senses in Jimi what he feels in himself: a deep immunity to the personal power of others. In spite of being two years older and much larger than Jimi, he senses a threat to his tribal dominance, and is compelled to bring Jimi to heel. He is also shrewd enough to know the limits of physical power and has waited patiently for another approach to the problem.

Today, in the late morning, he found his solution.

On one side of the Romona Arms is a large vacant lot covered with head-high overgrowth and laced with bike paths. On the far edge of this lot is a trailer park surrounded by a low wooden fence. One of Rat Bag's favorite adventures is to take a select group across the lot and over the fence to steal peeks into trailer windows. Among the Romona kid tribe, some of these exploits have become elevated to the level of myth, like the time one group saw two people "doing it." This morning, Rat Bag and Zipper took off to go trailer peeking under an uneasy sky of shifting gray. The first peek was the one that did it. They used a small wooden crate to elevate themselves for a look into the living room of the last trailer down the line. As always, Rat Bag had Zipper go first (the only time Rat Bag had gone first was the first time, so that his entrepreneurship was clearly established). Zipper moved his head to a corner of the window, and then inched out to peek. For a moment he froze, one leg statue-still as it hung in space to balance him. Then he bolted. Rat Bag had just a second to catch a glimpse of Zipper's white face distorted in terror as the force of his flight smacked the wooden crate into the side of the trailer. Since Rat Bag was hard-wired for trouble, the alarm sounded by the wooden crate compelled him into motion, too.

Once Rat Bag reached concealment in the overgrowth, he stopped, crouched down, and looked back at the trailer. Nothing. No movement in the windows. No one outside. For half an hour, he waited, an eternity for someone ten years old. Still nothing. Then he delicately advanced to the fence in front of the trailer and poked his head over. The wooden crate still leaned cockeyed under the window. He pursed his lips and flared his nostrils. He had to do it. No matter what was in there, he had to look. Otherwise, Zipper would eclipse him in exposure to terror, and his stock at the Romona would tumble.

So he did it. And threw up. And then returned to look again.

And then thought about Jimi.

A few minutes later, he rang the doorbell on the unit where Zipper lived with his mother. After many rings, Zipper opened the door and stalked back to sit in front of the TV, which spewed out vintage cartoons. He wore only a pair of fresh jockey shorts, and Rat Bag suspected he had just changed out of a soiled pair.

"So, Zip, you saw it, huh?"

"Yup."

"We're goin' back."

"Nope."

Rat Bag came around and blocked Zipper's view of the TV.

"Listen up, fuck face. We're goin' back. You don't have to look anymore. We're taking Jimi for a peek."

"Nope."

Rat Bag shifted gears. "You know, you were the first one to see it, but if you're too chickenshit to go back, I don't think anybody's going to believe you. Maybe not even me."

Zipper sighs. He's hooked.

They find Jimi alone in his unit, playing vidicomp. Rat Bag spells it out.

"Jimi, young dude, we're going to take you on the biggest peek of all."

"You mean where they 'do it'? "

"Even more awesome. But we've got to get back before it's over."

Jimi is not completely sold. It's not good when Rat Bag and Zipper want to do something with no other kids except you. But Rat Bag is talking very big, and on such occasions, he usually delivers. Jimi follows them out the door.

Now, under the hot gray sky, Jimi fights to dissolve the image of what he saw in the window, but it keeps coming back, bigger than the main screen at the West Mall Ciniplex. When he mounted the little wooden crate and peeked, the trailer's living room was neat and tidy, with small cactus plants in little pots on a narrow shelf at the base of the window. Then he saw her, a woman in her sixties, wearing a simple housedress, a shawl around her shoulders, and white tennis shoes. She sat in a recliner and stared straight at him, her mouth stretched in the rictus grin of someone dead for many weeks.

All this might have been tolerable. Even someone eight years old might have buffered it. But real horror, the kind that punches through the windshield and grabs you out of the driver's seat, comes not from the big picture, but from the details.

Like the yellow jackets.

Maybe twenty of them crawled across the corpse's face, neck, and ears. Their hair-sized black legs carried them rapidly over the dead flesh in an awful and aimless pattern. A single glance told Jimi there was some hideous purpose to their dance, a purpose far beyond any rational bounds.

And he could not turn away. He stood frozen on his tiptoes as the yellow jackets went through their black-and-yellow swarm of the dead. The corpse, the insects, the cactus plants in the foreground, saturated his little soul and held him transfixed for a small eternity.

Finally, the grip ebbed for a moment, and he turned and hopped on rubber knees to the ground, where Rat Bag and Zipper opened their barrage.

"Shit, man, he's so freaked he can't event talk," scoffs Zipper.

But Rat Bag and Zipper seem a world away, and Jimi is temporarily immune to their dirty little jeers. As he freefalls through an ether made of terror, he instinctively grabs at the last rung on his ladder.

It's OK. My dad will come and get me.

And sure enough, with a grip of granite, his father reaches out and yanks him free from the death spiral. Jimi's fear turns to exhilaration as he pictures his dad striding toward the trailer. At the very sight of his father, Rat Bag and Zipper are struck dumb with guilt and fear and silently melt off down the trail. His dad is wearing a tailored flight suit, with a laser pistol in a black leather holster that flaps gently in syncopation with his gait. As he comes closer, you can see the winking red status lights on the back of his hand, which are wired to the prosthetics in his right arm. Jimi knows that if his dad so desired, he could punch a hole in the trailer's metal siding and peel it back like paper. He can almost hear the horrible screech as metal rips apart, and knows the yellow jackets would be gone long before his father was finished. And he can almost see the wry smile as his dad calmly surveys the corpse in the recliner. No big deal. His dad has seen death countless times before and routinely stares it down.

No problem, Son. It's just the usual stuff. You get used to it after awhile.

Jimi pictures the torn metal siding behind his dad, all curled up like wood before a chisel. Sunlight now fills the trailer's living room, and somehow the corpse has disappeared and a fat gray cat is lounging on the recliner. He hears the powerful whir of servomotors from the prosthetics as his dad kneels before him. He is eye-level, with sparkling blue eyes, thick brown hair, and a hawk nose.

Who were those two kids? They bother you? . . . Oh, yeah? Well, if you say you can handle 'em alone, that's good enough for me.

A huge smile stretches out over the perfect white teeth.

Rat Bag is getting a little worried. He has achieved his goal and scared the living piss out of Jimi, and now the little bugger has gone catatonic on him. Unless Jimi snaps out of it, Rat Bag could be in a jam that might involve angry adults who could rip his small kingdom right out of his greasy grasp.

"Jimi! Dude! Hey, you still with us?"

"Don't worry, Dad. I can handle them," Jimi says softly.

"Whadya say?" Zipper asks as he squints at Jimi.

Jimi's eyes clear and he looks directly at Rat Bag. "I want to go. Right now."

"You got it, dude. We're outta here," says Rat Bag with obvious relief.

As they wind their way back through the vacant lot to the Romona Arms, Jimi comforts himself with the exploits of his father. Like the incredible karate fight among the girders of the Ghost Dirigible, and the attack of helicopter gunships on the mountain fortress, and the dogfight in the one-man subs deep beneath some tropical ocean. And then, for the first time in a long while, he feels a desperate need to plunge to the very center of his father's image and explore its origin. Some time ago, the dad concept had begun to form in his mind, a vague alchemy of TV dads, real dads, and uncle dads that got kids on alternate Saturdays. Several times he has asked his mom about his dad, and has been told it was "hard to understand and we'll talk about it later."

But then the chapters of the dad story began to spontaneously come to life inside him. They didn't come in order, and they usually broke the surface of his mind as he lay awake in bed listening to the remote shuffling and sporadic murmuring of adults elsewhere in the apartment.

They were vivid, heroic, and mythical in stature: overwhelming victories, iron resolve, flawless judgment, limitless compassion.

Later, he began to assemble the chapters in the proper order and slowly constructed the tragic yet understandable reason for his father's absence. It seemed that there were any number of thoroughly evil organizations that saw his father as a mortal threat. His exploits had carried him all over the globe, and he had cut a righteous swath far too wide to be ignored by those who dwell in darkness. And he had one painfully obvious vulnerability: his wife and son, who, as hostages, could become the ultimate leverage against him. So, in the end it was clearly circumstance and not his father that dictated the solution to this dilemma. Obviously, his dad had to sever the family bond to ensure the very survival of the planet itself. Either Jimi went without a father or the Bad People had a bargaining chip that would allow them to quickly metastasize throughout the entire civilized world.

Now as he shuffles along the trail between Rat Bag and Zipper, he recalls the final chapter in the Origin of the Father:

His mother, Zodia, sat on the couch in their apartment holding Jimi and quietly crying. His father appeared from the bedroom wearing the flight suit and laser pistol. A pilot's helmet studded with electronic devices was tucked under his arm. He put the helmet down on the coffee table, and a powerful wave of anguish washed across his face. They all hugged tightly for a long time, with no words spoken. Finally he rose over them, looking taller even than his muscular six-foot-four frame.

"OK, guys," he sighed, "time to go."

It was night out and they walked through a cool rain to the empty parking lot of a mini-mall down the block from the Romona Arms. When they reached the middle of the lot, they heard the distant beat of a helicopter, and his dad donned the pilot's helmet and picked up Jimi.

"Son," he said, "just remember. If you really get out on the edge, if it's really more than you can handle, I'll be back to help."

Then they felt the concussive shudder of the gunship's rotor blades as it dropped into the glare of the mercury vapor lights. His father hugged them and shouted one last thing that was lost in the roar of the engines. Then he ran at a crouch under the whirling blades and disappeared into the ship. A few seconds later it lifted into the night. Jimi looked skyward and felt the rain on his face as he watched the gunship's blinking red navigation light recede into the dark, luminous haze above the city. His dad was gone.

Jimi, Rat Bag, and Zipper step off the path through the vacant lot's over-growth and onto the pavement of the Romona Arms parking lot. As they shuffle past parked cars, Jimi struggles to permanently cap the well of anxiety inside him, to seal off the yellow jackets forever. But that means he must resolve one last puzzle:

Why didn't my dad come and get me?

No sooner than he voices the question, the answer flashes before him.

I didn't really need him. I handled it all myself.

Of course! His dad knew all along that he could deal with it! And if he had truly faltered, even for an instant, his dad would have been there, the mechanical arm ripping the beige metal flesh off the side of the trailer.

Now the world rushes back into Jimi and fills the cavity hollowed out by the horror. He smells the heated tar of the parking lot. He hears the ebullient splashing of small children in the pool. He sees the green flicker of poplar trees as they billow in the wind.

Jimi breaks off from the kid column and heads for his apartment unit. Rat Bag notices, but he doesn't move to stop him.

"Hey! Where ya goin'?" queries Zipper.

"I'm going home," replies Jimi, without looking back.

At the door to unit four, Jimi fishes for the key that he keeps safety-pinned inside his right front pocket. His mom will not be home. In fact, there is no telling when his mom will be home. He lets himself in and heads to the refrigerator, where there is a letter with the heading "State of Oregon, Children's Services Division" across the top. It is over a year old, wrinkled, stained with coffee rings, and held to the refrigerator door by a little magnetic parrot. Somewhere in an office downtown there is an-other copy of the letter languishing in a file cabinet, along with thou-sands of similar letters. For a while they were considered "backlog." Now they are not even considered at all. Even before the Downturn, schools and social services were stretched to the maximum in trying to keep kids "in the system." Now the system itself is coming unraveled. A faltering economy means less tax revenues, which means less government social spending on children. Unfortunately, a faltering economy also means more problem children as their families buckle under one financial rupture after another. So now teachers and social workers watch helplessly as countless thousands of Jimis are carried out on the budgetary ebb tide and never seen again.

Jimi finds some milk in the refrigerator and breakfast cereal in a cabinet. He checks to make sure the milk hasn't curdled and pours it over the cereal. Sometimes he subsists for days on this same diet. He moves to the kitchen table and centers his cereal bowl between two cigarette burns along its edge. A wide green plastic belt is draped over the chair next to him and a pair of chartreuse high-heeled shoes is perched on the seat, along with two pink hair curlers. On the nearest wall is a poster depicting a man his mother calls "the King," although Jimi can't figure out why. Jimi's mother is named Zodia and she is fixated on dead rock stars, which is how Jimi got his name. While Jimi was being born, she wore earphones attached to a Walkman and listened to "Purple Haze" at the moment of delivery.

As Jimi eats the cereal, he stares at the enormous mound of cigarette butts in a wide plastic ashtray at the center of the table. Many bear the violet impression of Zodia's latest lipstick. Others are both unfiltered and unmarked; these belong to Eddy, Zodia's current male friend. Jimi accepts Eddy as one accepts a summer rain: It will soon pass and be lost in the vastness of things.

The succession of men around their house stretches back into a vague time that approaches the Origin of the Father, but does not overlap. Usually, they are nice to him when Zodia is around, and totally indifferent when she is not. One exception was a skinny pockmarked man with a crew cut and sideburns, who was always friendly and even took Jimi with him when he went to buy beer at the Mini-Mart. Then one day he told Jimi they ought to take a look at his one-eyed trouser snake. That night, he asked his mom what a one-eyed trouser snake was, and the man disappeared.

But for the most part, these men are a series of echoes, each more distant as they fade into the past. And as they recede, they merge into a single composite image built up from a thousand nights spent in unit four with Zodia and Boyfriend X: The TV pumps a flood of bright color onto the pair as they slump on the couch. Several half-quart cans of cheap ale populate the coffee table, and Boyfriend X endlessly cycles through 105 cable channels. Then one or the other gets up and goes to the bathroom. Jimi is puzzled by this because he seldom hears the toilet flush, and when they come out they look either real sleepy or like they just received an electric shock. After maybe a dozen trips like this, his mom drifts over in a dream state and puts him to bed, where he opens the factory that is busily constructing his dad.

As Jimi finishes his cereal, he thinks about TV shows and dead people. On TV, whenever someone is dead, you call the cops. But then he remembers a big building and polished linoleum floors and his mom with a clown face, and wants no part of calling the cops. As he puts the milk away, he decides he will tell a grown-up about the dead lady, and let them call the cops.

Jimi walks out the door and, before he locks it, checks to make sure the key is pinned inside his front pocket. Since his mom's presence is an unknown variable, he is utterly adrift if he loses the key. The only grown-up he trusts is Michael Riley, and sometimes Michael is gone for many days at a time. One time he made the mistake of going to Dolores Kingsley, the manager. She seemed sympathetic and made him a peanut butter and jelly sandwich and sat him down in front of the TV. But then she made a phone call, and two policemen came and took him to a big building with polished linoleum floors and gray metal desks with computer terminals growing out of their tops like pale mushrooms. After many hours, his mother came and talked for a long time with a policelady and turned into a clown face, because the tears smeared her makeup. When they left the big building, Zodia the clown face mom drove him to a Burger King and let him play as long as he wanted on the climbing structure and bought him a Super Kid Meal Pack with a chocolate shake instead of a Coke. While he ate, she went into the bathroom and turned back into her regular self, but then when they got in the car, she grabbed him and hugged him and turned into a clown all over again. After that, she stayed home all day and night with him for five and a half days.

With the key secured, Jimi blinks under the hot sun, which has punched through the gray and bedazzled the pool area in front of him.

He sees a lady named Mrs. Bissel, who is watching her two-year-old while waiting for her husband to come home from his job at Stereo Discount. Sometimes she has smiled at him in a semi-motherly sort of way, so she becomes the first adult recipient of the decidedly bad news. She is reclining in a lounge chair reading a *Redbook* and casting glances at her splashing daughter at ten-second intervals. Jimi stands beside her silently and waits to be recognized. After a dozen or so intervals, it happens.

"Jimi! Are you going swimming today?" asks Mrs. Bissel through opaque Polaroid sunglasses.

"There's a dead lady in the trailer."

"Sweetheart, does your mom know where you are?"

Jimi has heard this question countless times, and knows the true content at its core. It really means "I don't believe you because you have a very flakey family situation, which means you're probably making all this up just to get a little attention."

Without answering Mrs. Bissel, Jimi scans the pool for another adult who might be a little more receptive. He sees a willowy woman whose name he doesn't remember, but who has a son just a year older than Jimi. As he approaches her, she affects a condescending little smile. Not a good sign.

"Well, hello, Jimi. And how are you?"

"There's a dead lady in the trailer."

"Jimi, does your mother know where you are?"

"Yeah, she does."

"Well, then, you better go and check with her about this trailer, dear."

Jimi has now lost interest. He begins to think that maybe Rat Bag is right when he delivers his canned diatribe about adults: "They're all bogus, man. All of 'em."

But as he starts back to his unit, he sees Michael Riley coming down the stairs from unit twenty-seven. Mike! Yeah, Mike will understand! He always understands!

Michael Riley smiles inside as he sees the skinny little figure cross the pool area with such conviction. Jimi has a presence that transcends his dilapidated jeans and dirty T-shirt with a heavy-metal band blasted across the front. The mothers of the Romona Arms see his mini-charisma as a threat to their children, but Michael views it as Jimi's one shot at social salvation. He first met Jimi a year ago, on a day much like this one, only on that particular day, Jimi nearly drowned. Michael had been lounging poolside when he just happened to glance up from his book and saw a small boy sink below the surface about midway between the deep and shallow ends of the pool. At first, he dismissed it as a kid game, but when the boy struggled to the surface, he saw the panic in his eyes and went in after him. It all happened so fast, nobody else at the pool noticed. He pulled Jimi to the side of the pool and perched him on the edge, then climbed up and sat down next to him.

"You OK, kid?" Michael asked.

"Yeah, I'm OK," said Jimi, who then erupted in a spasm of coughs from water pooled in his air passages. Michael waited patiently for the coughing to pass.

"Looked to me like maybe you were drowning," proposed Michael.

"Nope. I was just diving underwater."

"Oh, yeah?" said Michael. "You want to show me that dive again?"

"Nope," said Jimi. "Maybe later."

As they sat there on the pool's edge, Michael engaged Jimi in a very diplomatic conversation about water safety that avoided direct references to Jimi and employed phrases like "If a kid got in too deep . . ." From then on, Michael always kept an eye on Jimi at the pool. He asked some of the Romona veterans why Jimi's parents weren't looking out for him, and quickly got a broadbrush picture of his family situation.

Now Jimi stands at the bottom of the stairs and looks up at him with grave concern.

"There's a dead lady in the trailer," announces Jimi.

"So. Why didn't you call the cops?" asks Michael as he squats to come eye level with Jimi.

"The cops might take me away from my mom," replies Jimi.

"How did you stumble across this lady?" asks Michael.

"Rat Bag and Zipper took me to see her."

"Where is she?"

"In a trailer. Right over there," answers Jimi, pointing in the direction of the trailer park.

"OK," says Michael, "here's the deal. I'm going to go with you to see the dead lady, and if she's not there, there might be a dead kid instead of a dead lady. Got it?"

For the first time all day, Jimi smiles. If his dad ever gets to meet Michael Riley, they're sure to become great pals.

As the sun sets, Michael Riley sits with Jessica in a tavern tucked into the mini-mall down the street from the Romona Arms. It is sandwiched between Presto Photo Finish and Home Ticket Video, and is built around a sports motif. Five video monitors and one HDTV projection system pound a baseball game into every corner of the place. It is almost full, and people converse loudly across small yellow cities of pitchers and glasses.

This afternoon, after the police left, Michael had returned to his unit and felt the silence start to eat him. After much deliberation, he phoned Jessica, and now they sit in a booth as he finishes recounting Jimi's horrible adventure.

"We left before the cops opened it up," says Michael. "I couldn't have handled the smell. She must've been in there for weeks to look like that."

"Might not be as bad as you think," replies Jessica. "A lot depends on the humidity. The body might have dehydrated to where the stink was mostly gone."

"You've got to wonder how she stayed undiscovered so long," says Michael. "That's the real horror of it. All of us fear physical death, but what we fear even more is memory death."

"How's that?" asks Jessica.

"Everybody really dies twice," Michael says. "Once when your heart stops and your brain shuts down, and all the other stuff you biologists specialize in. But you die all over again when you slide out of living memory. Like it or not, a lot of our ego is defined by the recognition we get from other people. As long as somebody is alive to remember us, our ego continues to survive in an extended sort of way. But unless you make the history books, you probably slip out of human memory in fifty years or so, and then you're really gone. Now, the lady in the trailer is pretty close to a worst-case situation. Since nobody had checked on her for weeks, it's possible she had slipped almost completely out of memory before she died physically. Tough deal."

"Do you suppose her memory death could have triggered her physical death?" speculates Jessica.

"Could be," says Michael. "Could be it happens all the time. But that's enough on that subject. Tell me more about your little critters that may not even be critters at all."

Jessica smiles. Her research centers on insidious objects called viroids. If the microbiological realm is conceived as a small town, then viruses occupy the railroad tracks that divide the town into the animate and inanimate. On one side of the tracks is the residential area, where higher life-forms go about their business in sophisticated ways. On the other side is the industrial area, where basic chemicals churn about at the molecular and atomic levels. And as in real towns, there are some seedy residents from the wrong side of the tracks that occasionally cross over and create mischief in respectable neighborhoods. Viroids are the first members of this criminal class to be uncovered. Chemically, they do not have the architectural elegance that makes viruses such efficient hunters and parasites. Instead, they consist of little pieces of ribonucleic acid, better known as RNA, a close relative of DNA. They float like little bits of litter through the microbiosphere, traveling wherever the currents of opportunity take them. And somehow, someway, these currents occasionally take them inside living cells, where they suddenly become molecular bulls in the cellular china shop, quickly setting up factories to mass produce more of their own kind. It was originally thought that viroids affected only plant cells, but in the early nineties, evidence began to surface that they burrowed into animal cells as well, including those of humans.

Jessica's mission is to investigate this phenomenon in depth, to find out why bits of biochemical trash blown on the winds of chance can touch off pathological firestorms. One of the astounding things about viroids is how something so unintelligent, with so little training in the ways of the big city, can rapidly ascend to the very pinnacles of influence in the cell nucleus and bring down a power structure entrenched over millions of years of evolution.

Michael tracks on her technodialogue for a while, but then his mind wanders off to explore a peculiar irony. When he and Jimi returned to the trailer and he saw the corpse, he was suitably shocked and revolted, even though he had prior warning. But it didn't trigger the Fear. And that was the worst thing about the Fear. You never knew when. You never knew where.

"Michael?"

"Huh?"

"You with me?"

"Yeah, sure."

"I think maybe not. You must be pretty exhausted. Want to go?"

Michael sighs. "No, not quite yet. Look, I really appreciate your taking the time to see me. I know I don't know you very well, but it just seemed like the right thing to do. Know what I mean?"

She knows exactly what he means. "I do. It's funny how moments of crisis bring out things in us we never expected."

Without any warning, Michael's memory whipsaws back to another time, another crisis, one that also brought out things he never expected. But before the memories boil up into a stampede, he shuts the gate. "You're right," he says. "You never know what to expect, do you?"

Jessica stares at the table, where she holds a glass of beer with only a few sips gone. "To tell you the truth, I just expect the absolute worst. That way, you're covered no matter what happens."

"But that's not very reasonable," argues Michael. "Simple statistics. In any given situation, the worst outcome is a real long-shot."

"Of course you're right," she answers without looking up, "but it does happen. Believe me. It does happen."

Michael is tempted to ask if she's speaking from personal experience, but he senses she probably is, and checks himself. "Well, with the Downturn and everything, it's been a pretty creepy world for all of us lately. It makes you realize that in the end, all we've really got is each other. Everything else is just . . . stuff."

This makes her smile. "You're right," she replies. "Just a lot of stuff. That's all. I'm glad to have met you, Michael Riley."

"And I you," responds Michael. He longs to reach out and hug her close, but the timing is all wrong. "It really made a difference seeing you today. Thanks."

They pay the bill and walk back to the Romona, where things are back to normal, the sea of red and blue flashing lights long since departed.

On the way to Jessica's car in the parking lot, they pass by unit four. It is after ten P.M., and inside Jimi Tyler waits for his mother's return. He can't wait to tell her about the dead lady and the trailer. After everything that's happened, it's a little creepy being eight years old and alone. But he's not scared.

If anything really bad happens, his Dad will come and get him.

5

XXXXXX

Simon Says

Simon Greeley's ears ring constantly. He reflects on this as he rolls along
Route 395 just south of the Capitol in Washington, D.C., and melds his
old Volvo sedan into the anxious parade of noontime traffic. Tinnitus is
the technical name for his condition, and he takes the usual comfort in
knowing that it is a well understood and documented ailment—not a
specialty item expressed directly from hell. It had started shortly after he
had made the big decision and had slowly ramped up to a gentle roar.
Now there are times when even the din of freeway travel won't mask it
out. His doctor had been puzzled, since Simon hadn't played in a rock
band or served in the military. Loud guitars and large guns were the
usual cause of this steely sonic breeze, generated by invisible earphones
you could never remove. In the end, it was attributed to "nervous tension," to expedite the processing of health insurance forms.

Simon knew there was a certain amount of risk in letting anything
associated with nervous tension stumble onto his personal paper trail,
but he had to make sure the ringing wasn't a symptom of something
more serious. He owed that much to his wife, even though he had pushed
her out to the far periphery of his life. He could often feel her out there,
waiting patiently in a cheap hotel in some emotional border town, longing for a lover's tangle that never came.

She didn't know about the tinnitus. She didn't know about the big decision. Still, he hoped to someday reach out and gently pull her in, the way a drowsy child cuddles a stuffed animal at bedtime.

Anyway, the reference to nervous tension was there, in a computer file space reserved for "comments," which allowed for 256 bytes of data (about twenty-five words) that wouldn't fit neatly into the other categories provided by the medical database. Because of his particular position, the file of his visit would eventually flow through Checkpoint Alpha. Here it would be noted that a special identity code was attached to his general personnel file, a code that told Checkpoint Alpha that he worked in the office of the deputy associate director, national security division, Office of Management and Budget. This meant that Alpha's artificial intelligence programs might pick up on the mention of this "nervous tension" and attempt to correlate it with other data or actions linked to him. Ultimately, there was the possibility that a human data cop would smell something and touch off an investigation. While Simon knew this might happen, he also new that the data cops, like himself, had a finite amount of time to deal with an infinity of detail. So in the end, someone would scan his report and play a hunch on whether there was any meat in it, which might interest their more predatory peers at the Justice Department.

A risk worth taking, for sure. Just another ride down another wave of probability, this one only a gentle swell, really.

And Simon was a man exquisitely qualified to calculate the likely outcome of such rides. His passion for applied mathematics first surfaced during adolescence as he sought numeric explanations for the random cruelties that periodically erupted around him. His mother dead on his thirteenth birthday, hit in a crosswalk by a pickup truck that barreled on into the Kansas night. His brother caught with five ounces of cocaine and swallowed up into the state penal system, which leisurely digested him before expelling the remains back onto the street.

Like his father, who ran the same pharmacy for thirty years, Simon sought relief in that which was, if not entirely predictable, at least logically explicable. In college, he quickly gravitated to economics, followed by a career in the perverse yet comfortable structure of the federal bureaucracy. Here he quickly became identified as a useful intellectual property by others who were beginning to scale the towering managerial escarpments toward senior positions. (A bit reserved, that Simon, but a man you could trust with certain kinds of problems.) With these people, he was able to maintain symbiotic relationships in which he supplied the competency and they secured his flanks against political attack. This allowed Simon to remain apolitical, oblivious to the creaks and groans in the superstructure of the ship of state as it traveled on through history— and free to roam at will among magnificent fiscal constructs of his own making.

And now, on Route 395, an early spring rain pelts the windshield and Simon tattoos an anxious beat on the steering wheel as he drives toward a meeting with someone from the office of one of the nation's most conservative senators. Over an integrated CD/tape/radio unit produced in Borneo, an announcer prattles on about the latest impact of the Downturn on retirement funds.

Ah, yes, the Downturn, muses Simon. Proof positive that economies, like people, still ride on waves of probability. Ahead, a splatter of red brake lights prompts him to slow and draw a deep breath. He doesn't want to be late for this meeting, for it will be the incarnation of the big decision, the centerpiece of his place in history, alongside others like Daniel Ellsberg, Frank Serpico, and Karen Silkwood. Now he sees why traffic has slowed: a column of personnel carriers full of federal marshals had commandeered the slow lane as they file off the freeway at the 6th Street exit by the Department of Transportation. The carriers are painted navy blue to avoid any association with the traditional camouflage colors of military vehicles. Each bears a federal seal on the side.

For a moment, Simon breaks the surface of his mental stew and realizes what is going on. They are conducting maneuvers for the upcoming Mortgage March, when five hundred thousand middle-class citizens plan to stride indignantly up The Mall to the steps of the Capitol building.

By now, repossessions were pandemic throughout many urban areas. Simon had watched this social drama on TV and drank the images into his soul (funny how the pictures remained long after the dialogue was forgotten): white-collar middle managers standing stunned on their neatly clipped lawns as the Bekins van pulled out to take their furniture to a U-Store-It while they prepared to go dicker on a budget apartment unit somewhere west of Purgatory.

So here they were in Washington, a half million strong, starting to straggle into the nation's capital. Charging the trip with the last ounce of credit on their bank cards. Eating sandwiches slapped together in cheap motel rooms. Once afraid, now enraged.

So much for rolling recessions, snorted Simon as he recalled the theory that future economic reversals would roll through specific industries. This one had rolled, alright—right across the entire national landscape in a single swath. First, it was just an annoying rise in unemployment that created a little anxiety and belt-tightening, which immediately bit into the so-called "life-style industries": the little shop in the mall that sold chocolate chip cookies for a dollar seventy-five; the manufacturer of athletic shoes that cost $120; the service that packaged adventure ski vacations in South America.

Finally, of course, the whole business had twisted into a tight and inexorable downward spiral, and the Bekins vans began to roll.

But money is the farthest thing from Simon's mind as he watches the last of the personnel carriers cruise up the freeway exit. Simon is well insulated from economic catastrophe by his high perch in the federal administrative strata. As he rolls along in the sluggish traffic, he thinks back several weeks to the origin of the big decision. When he had first discovered the problem, he had thought it was either a mistake or something he wasn't cleared to understand. It looked innocent enough, simply a line item in a very lengthy budget report prepared for review by the National Security Council staff. The dollar amount, while astronomical in consumer terms, was trivial in Simon's world, where many executive reports now rounded off not only the thousands, but also the millions of dollars. Normally, he would have glided right past it, but an attached four-digit code lay waiting in ambush.

It had identified the source of the item as none other than Simon himself. And as a master of the mundane, Simon had known instantly that no such amount was associated with anything he had ever worked on.

Hundreds of millions of dollars. All allegedly spent at his behest. His stomach had tightened and he felt pinpricks of heat on his forehead. Who? Why?

He had begun to shake as he weighed his alternatives. If he moved to investigate the item's origin he would expose himself in the process. All the necessary information was encapsulated in System 9, a high-security computer totally sealed off from the world outside the Executive Building. System 9 held what was commonly known as the Black Budget, which included all defense and intelligence expenditures, and which would compromise national security if publicly revealed. The information itself was in a highly protected database that was carved up into "compartments" so that most people had access to only a small part of it, through programs called dedicated report generators. Simon was an exception. He was able to use a program built around the standard SQL (Structured Query Language) to roam at will through the data, to sift it, twist it, look at it anyway he chose. However, to use the program, he needed to insert a "key," a code that unlocked it for his personal use. As soon as he did this, a log entry would be made, and within days he would be required to submit a written report on why he had taken such an extraordinary action.

The pinpricks on his forehead had spread down over his face. His fingertips had come together in a pose of prayer as he silently rocked in the chair in front of a terminal connected to System 9. Obviously, he was expendable, since his reference code had been attached to the budget item. If the thing ever blew up (and you never knew what would), the audit trail would lead right to his desk.

Betrayed. *Betrayed!* A full-blown vision of revenge had seized him and presented his superiors in poses of slack-jawed horror as he lunged at their professional jugulars.

At this point, most people would have stepped back from the brink as they calculated the true cost of retribution, the balance due after the initial satisfaction was extracted. But not Simon. Not now. Not with his meticulously crafted civil-service career of twenty-five years suddenly thrown into imminent jeopardy. Faced with the monstrous threat, he had succumbed to the final atavistic reflex of the cornered animal, to lash out and attack, whatever the price. He dove at the terminal keyboard and inserted the key to unlock the SQL.

The big decision. Done.

Instantly, the pinpricks had faded into the background. For once in communion with the system, Simon could soar, elegant as any hawk on a summer thermal. He had swooped, looped, dove, and twisted down avenues of abstraction that cloaked the darkest and most powerful secrets on the face of the planet. A nuclear submarine base on the floor of the Atlantic. A new spy plane capable of flying into low earth orbit. A toxic agent that biodegraded completely in twenty-four hours. Along the way, he had poked and prodded, looking for obscure links between disparate scraps.

Suddenly, it was over. He was there. A brief file with a terse memorandum and no recorded author. Within it, no talk of weapons, no covert operations; only a simple transfer of funds.

Simon only had to read it once to understand that the political fate of the current administration was now entrusted to him and him alone.

Gail Ambrose sips the house white wine and periodically glances at the entrance to the small restaurant set among the used car lots of North Washington Boulevard in Arlington. She knows it won't make a good impression on this Mr. Simon Greeley that she's drinking alone, but the hell with it. The truth is, she drinks very little, but after a date like the one she had last night, why not? The guy was a systems analyst for HUD and had all the charm of a boa constrictor throttling Bambi. To compound her funk, it is starting to rain outside. And, she muses, Greeley will probably be a flake. She had already checked, and he was indeed who he said he was, but that didn't mean he had anything worth wasting a lunch over. As senior staff member for Senator Grisdale, one of the most powerful conservatives on the Hill, she has learned to budget her time ruthlessly, striving always to trade up when exchanging parcels of power and influence. With Greeley, she might run one of her rare deficits and waste a couple of potentially profitable hours in the process.

And her first look at him is not reassuring. Trailing the maître d' toward the table, he appears tired, withdrawn, and preoccupied. He is around fifty, pale, with thin gray hair receding into partial baldness. Gail is reminded of her father during her high school years, a man bled white by too many responsibilities. At sixteen, she had seen it as his natural state. Now, at thirty-two, she looks back on it with a bit more compassion.

"Ms. Ambrose?" inquires Simon as he prepares to seat himself across from her.

"Mr. Greeley. Good to meet you."

She reaches across the table and shakes a cold, limp hand. If she has her way, this will be a very short lunch. She was impressed by his position, but is not impressed by the man. People in Washington who have any real power quickly learn how to broadcast it. Given this fact, the man in front of her must have had the plug pulled on his transmitter.

But then the cocktail waiter comes and Mr. Greeley orders a double

Beefeaters on the rocks. Gail's interest renews. This man should have ordered coffee or soda water.

Simon abruptly locks his eyes on to Gail's. "Would it be fair to say that Senator Grisdale is the strongest advocate in Congress for classic free-market economics?" he asks.

"That would be more than fair, Mr. Greeley. The senator's stance on free markets is close to legendary."

"Suppose," says Simon, "just suppose that there were some very large Black Budget expenditures that spilled over into the private sector. Funds that even the White House has lost track of. Would the senator be interested?"

Inwardly, Gail sighs. Here we go. The guy's in a petty little war with someone else inside the White House.

"Well, first of all, since the senator chairs the Senate Select Committee on Intelligence, he probably knows where every dime in the Black Budget is going. Also, there's nothing new about the NSC and intelligence people dabbling in the business community. Ever heard of TRW Corporation?"

Simon leans closer to her.

"Yes, yes. TRW was created to fill a need for spy satellites. I know that, but that's not what I'm talking about. I'm talking about money flowing on to Wall Street and then out through the investment community."

Gail puts her finger on her chin. "How much are we talking about, Mr. Greeley?"

"About a half billion."

Gail clamps the rush inside her and goes to her best professional poker face.

"I'll tell you what," she says, "let me check with the senator. If it's something he's not aware of, we'll be in touch."

"No, we won't," says Simon.

"What?"

"Don't try to contact me. I'll contact you at irregular intervals."

"Do we really need this kind of spook stuff?"

"Absolutely. One more thing . . ." Simon writes a lengthy computer file directory name on a napkin. "I'm sure the senator will want to verify my story. I'm also sure he has his sources inside the community. This is what he'll need to do that."

The waiter comes with Simon's drink. He drains half of it with a single swallow.

In the parking lot of the restaurant where Gail and Simon dine, the Worm sits in his car and gloats in self-satisfaction. Bingo! First time out and it's all done. When he walked in, he could see the two of them at their table. The woman had a wine, Simon nothing. In the bar, he was able to grab a stool right next to the cocktail waiter's service bay. As he sat down, the waiter headed off to Simon's table and took an order. Since the woman was still nursing a full glass of wine, he knew the order was for Simon. A moment later, the waiter was back and calling a double Beefeaters to the bartender. By the time it came, the Worm had already uncapped the small plastic bottle and had it palmed in his hand. He tapped the waiter.

"Hey, I'd like to buy a drink for those three guys over there," he said, pointing vaguely into the restaurant.

The waiter turned and squinted into the restaurant, trying to figure out who the Worm was talking about. The Worm glanced at the bartender, whose back was turned toward the cash register.

Now! With astonishing rapidity, he dumped liquid from the bottle into Simon's drink as it rested on the waiter's tray.

The waiter turned back to him. "Which guys?"

The Worm rose up a little and craned his neck toward the restaurant. "Whoops. Sorry. I guess they're gone."

The waiter shrugged and headed off to Simon's table with the drink. The Worm stuck around just long enough to watch Simon take a long pull on it.

In the parking lot, the Worm ignites the turbocharged engine in his car, an exotic Japanese sports model. He whistles along with a tune on the radio. And why not? After all, he's on vacation.

Inside Simon Greeley, the liquid from the plastic bottle is pooling in his stomach along with the gin. The new and special viruses float randomly in the liquid's molecular ocean. Their time is now at hand.

As Gail Ambrose drives back to the Capitol building, she sifts a multitude of political variables in search of a workable equation for the sen-

ator. She's been with him for over five years now, and although they differ
philosophically on many points, there is a strong bond between them.
Seen up close, the man is a fascinating set of contradictions. On women's
issues, he is a throwback to the era of barefoot and pregnant, yet when
dealing with professional women on a personal basis, he is astoundingly
fair and impartial. In the area of national defense, he staunchly supports
a strong military posture, yet in several international crises, he has been
the voice of restraint and reason. In a town where compromise and quid
pro quo are a way of life, Senator Grisdale, for all his toughness, is somehow bathed in an aura of innocence. And for this very reason, he is also
feared, because the usual tools of manipulation won't even open the senator's hood, let alone gain you access to the engine.

If Greeley's got it right, she ponders, this could be a real bombshell for
the current administration. They are already under siege because of the
Downturn, and a massive financial hemorrhage from the shadow world
under the White House on to Wall Street could be a calamity of the sort
that goes into high school history books. The trick was going to be verification.

During lunch, Greeley had explained the mechanics of the leakage. In
many cases, there were secret budget items that needed to be funded on
an ad hoc basis. There had to be a way to rapidly finance secret operations to meet those sudden and unexpected geopolitical developments
as they unfolded around the world. Given the size of the sums involved,
the money couldn't just stagnate. It had to be invested and generate a
decent return until needed. So a master contingency fund was created
and the money wound up in various "investment instruments," like
stocks, bonds, short-term paper, etc.

In this particular case, nearly 500 million dollars had flowed into a
Wall Street venture-capital firm called VenCap Partners, Inc.—supposedly on the authorization of Simon Greeley. Up to this point, the transaction was fairly legitimate, although some might question the prudence
of investing federal funds in the high-risk-venture market.

But the rest of the procedure was definitely dirty. It seemed that while
the money flowed into VenCap, it never flowed out. It was fairly easy to
smokescreen this chronic financial constipation; the overall contingency
budget was invested in many different institutions besides VenCap, and
withdrawals were made from these other sources while VenCap remained untapped.

Finally, there was the smoking gun, a memo directing VenCap to invest over $200 million of the government's money in a computer firm in Oregon, a memo supposedly signed by none other than Simon Greeley. To begin with, this memo violated the basic principle of venture-capital firms, which was to pool their customers' money, identify risky yet promising enterprises, and then infuse them with capital. All customers held shares in the fund, and thus profited equally from both successes and failures. The entire value of a venture-capital group was its expertise in selecting the proper investment. It was unheard of to have a customer, even the federal government, direct where its shares would be invested. Nevertheless, the memo made it quite clear that this was precisely what had happened.

To Gail, the implications are clear. Large amounts of government money are being clandestinely invested in private industry, with no official mandate from either Congress or the White House. To top it off, the money was being invested in a business with no direct benefit to the government, a business whose ultimate success was still highly speculative. Ever since the savings-and-loan fiasco in the late eighties, the interface between the public and private sectors had been an extremely touchy subject. Even a hint of something like this would ignite a conflagration that few would survive. People moving out of their comfortable suburban homes and into low-rent apartments didn't want to hear about Uncle Sam secretly bankrolling dubious high-tech ventures.

By the time Gail enters the Capitol building, the rain has stopped, but she doesn't notice. Once in her office, she writes some quick notes summarizing the details of her conversation with Simon. With the senator, she often needs them. He has an insatiable appetite for hard information, and no patience for those who can't provide it.

Gail's secretary pops her head in. "He's free now."

Well, Simon, thinks Gail, you'd better be on the level or you just cooked yourself good.

As Gail enters his office, Grisdale rises from his chair, a chivalrous yet genuine gesture. The iron-gray hair, the large head, the broad face make him look more like an archetype of a senator than the real thing. He carries his burden of authority with a grace that is almost mythical.

"And what can I do for you, young lady?" he asks. His granite face breaks into a warm smile. He admires Gail greatly, and continues to stand until she seats herself.

"A few weeks ago, I got a call from a man named Simon Greeley. He works in National Security at OMB. Said he had some important information for you. Wouldn't discuss it on the phone. So I agreed to lunch, which I just got back from. I think he's on to something."

The senator leans back in his chair. "And what might that something be?"

Gail relates the entire conversation with Greeley. She then hands Grisdale the napkin with the file directory.

"He said that if you had an inside source, they'd need this to verify his story."

Grisdale takes the napkin and raises his head slightly so he can read Simon's scrawl through his bifocals.

"Hmm," he mutters as he scans the napkin. "If he's right, you know what it means?"

"At the very best, it'll look like the president is asleep at the wheel. And with all the flack he's taking over the Downturn, this could be the thing that pushes his administration over the edge."

"I'd say that's a safe assumption," says Grisdale. "And now, the biggest question of all: Does this country need something like this right now?"

"Probably not."

"Probably not," echoes Grisdale, "but if Greeley's on the level, this thing involves some kind of conspiracy on a fairly grand scale. And I don't think the country needs that either."

"So," says Gail, "what's our move?"

Grisdale rises and goes to his window. "For starters, I'm gonna do a little checking. Then we'll see."

"Anything I can do?" asks Gail.

"Nope." Grisdale turns and grins. "Good job. You'll know more when I do."

A chilly drizzle falls out of the night sky as Senator Grisdale walks along the pedestrian overpass. Beneath him, the evening rush hour creates a foaming geyser of white noise, the kind that baffles even the best bugging devices. A short man walks beside him and holds an umbrella over them both. The senator has met him only twice before. At the first meeting, the man explained that he was employed deep within the national security apparatus, and that there were things happening there that troubled him. He went on to say that he had followed the senator's career for some time, and admired his uncompromising integrity. For this reason, he wanted to offer his services, but only in those rare situations where Grisdale had no other sources at his disposal. At this point, the senator called upon his greatest gift. As an honest man, he had an almost infallible sense of honesty in others. He knew intuitively that the man was telling the truth.

As they reach the end of the overpass, they turn and start back into the hissing shield of traffic noise. The senator comes right to the point.

"One of my staff was contacted by someone with some rather interesting news about national security funds. It seems some rather large amounts of money are being channeled through Wall Street for speculation in the private sector."

The senator hands over Simon's napkin scrawl. "Apparently, you're going to need this to find out."

The man glances briefly at the napkin, and stuffs it in the pocket of his raincoat.

"Ah, yes," he says, "System 9. How much do you need to know?"

"A simple true or false will do nicely."

"You'll get it tomorrow."

The senator stops and faces the man. "Bill, how big a risk are you taking with this?"

The man shrugs. "It's hard to say."

"Are you betting your life?"

"Quite possibly, yes."

"Is it worth it?"

"Without a doubt."

"Why?"

"If you knew all that I know, Senator, you'd understand. But hopefully you'll never have to. Good night."

The man and the senator walk off in opposite directions from the middle of the overpass. Beneath them, the traffic roars on mindlessly.

The next day in the late afternoon, the sky clears, the air warms, and the capital lolls in the gentle green breath of spring. The senator cracks his office window, inhales deeply, and wanders back somewhere into his childhood.

A knock. His secretary pops her head in, holding a folded and stapled piece of paper. "I'm sorry, Senator, but I found this on my desk after lunch. I think it's from one of your grandchildren."

"Thanks, Marty. Just leave it on the desk."

As Marty leaves, the senator picks up the paper. On the outside, "Senator G. Only" is written in the wobbly block style of a first-grader. Grisdale is impressed. With all the sophisticated graphic productions designed to get his attention, this was the perfect way to slip through the net. He opens it and reads a single word in crayon: TRUE

A few blocks away, Simon Greeley squints as he walks out into the sun from the Executive Building. It's a bright and beautiful day, so he decides to walk for a bit to clear his head.

Then he stubs the toe of his shoe on the cement and nearly loses his balance.

He does a quick step to recover and looks around sheepishly to see if anyone saw him. They didn't. Before he reaches the end of the block, the incident is out of his mind.

6

The Elephant

The Architect sits in the Teriyaki Takeout, a fast-food joint across the street from his apartment. He draws deeply on his cigarette and then stubs it out in a little golden tinfoil ashtray that is creased like the palm of an aging peasant. The immigrant Asian family that owns and runs the place is still tough and lives close to the bone. Every night, the wife cleans and washes each ashtray, reshapes it, and smoothes out the crinkles. To her and her husband, the Downturn is no more than a puff of stale air passing on the breeze. They have a forward thrust to them that the Architect envies.

He wonders where the ParaVolve security duo is this evening. Usually, they back into a parking space at the far end of the Quickie Mart lot so they can see his apartment door and the Teriyaki Takeout at the same time. They are both overweight and take turns going into the store for coffee and pastries.

The Architect is bemused by the quality of these people. After all, he is the most valuable apparatus that the company owns, and should merit security to match. Instead, these fools pump themselves full of molecular serpents with carbon backbone, hydrogen ribs, and carboxyl groups for heads. Lipids, that is. Fat.

Across the street, above the Chinese restaurant, he can see his apartment, with lamplight glowing through drawn curtains. It closely resembles another apartment, perched above a beauty parlor in Fresno, California, the apartment where he spent his childhood.

The Architect puts his fingers to his temples and shuts his eyes as he enters that apartment. He sees Aunt Dixie's massive frame bending over to get the TV dinners out of the oven, her upper arms mighty dirigibles of flesh. He hears the flitty excitement of a prime-time game show coming from the old black-and-white television in its once fashionable frame of Hollywood Blonde. Aunt Dixie, who operates the beauty shop below, is his family. All of it.

Occasionally, she tells the tale of his origin as she works her way through a six-pack of Hamm's and half a pack of Kools. Seems that some time ago, Aunt Dixie's half-sister had busted up with her second husband and started working nights at the Blue Pig Tavern. To pull this off, she corralled a baby-sitter for her three kids, a rangy thirteen-year-old girl with long stringy hair. Well, one night this girl shows up with a two-year-old kid in tow, a cute little guy hugging a stuffed puppy. When Dixie's half-sister gets home from the tavern, the little fellow is asleep on the couch and she asks the baby-sitter who he is. The girl flips back her stringy hair and explains. It seems her mom works days as a maid at the Motor City Inn and met this lady in Room 75 that needed a baby-sitter for a couple of hours. So the mom called the daughter, who took the job and waited until noon the next day in the room with the kid. The lady never came back. She'd already paid her bill, and the owners didn't want any police trouble at their motel, so the mother and daughter just took the kid on home with them. Simple as that.

Now, the half-sister knew the maid had a mean streak. Sometimes the daughter showed up to baby-sit with welts peeking out here and there. So she decided the kid could bunk with them for a few days, then they would take him to the police, or something like that. Next day, Dixie shows up and her big fat heart leaps out and wraps snugly round the kid. And you know the rest.

I know the rest, echoes the Architect across the bridge from then till now.

Every day, he came home from school and ran into the shop, where Aunt Dixie was cutting, curling, filing, or rinsing. She always told him to go on up and have a little snack while she finished up, and he did exactly that. After dinner, he took off into the mystery of the early evening with the neighborhood gang and learned about four-letter words, fighting, and getting high. But after an hour or so, he was home and immersed in his textbooks. He read his lessons once very rapidly, understanding everything and forgetting nothing, regardless of the subject. Aunt Dixie was more amused by this prodigious feat than impressed. "You must be part elephant to have a brain that big!" she commented. The Architect always sensed the pink, affectionate haze that flavored her remarks about his intelligence. Not so with his peers. He learned early on to camouflage his intellect, to protect it from the working-class rage that burned unchecked all around him.

But the rage consumed him anyway, without his knowledge. He watched the boys at the other end of the social scale as they glided along like magnificent birds skimming the surface of a glass lake. He saw the girls silently applaud them with admiring eyes as they flew with utter certainty only inches from disaster. He often wondered where their inertial navigation systems came from, and why his own was so tragically lacking. He didn't realize that each of them was the sum of their environment, of BMWs, ski trips, restaurant meals, expensive clothing, special lessons, excursions to Hawaii, endless pocket money, and help from the family attorney if you ran a bit amuck. He couldn't see that all these things congealed into a glue that bound them together—and, which by high school, had set diamond hard, excluding all who had not experienced the same upbringing.

And so the Architect retreated into the world of academia, where the rules of engagement were more openly and explicitly defined. And here he perched like a mythical bird atop the hierarchy, alone and unchallenged. In class, he remained silent unless called upon, but then delivered his answers with an economy that sounded almost simplistic—until you tried to pick them apart and found they were impeccably assembled.

Some of his teachers were annoyed by the way he coasted through their courses in neutral while other students labored in the lower gears, struggling to climb the mental grade. And most classmates considered him unapproachable, a disturbing hybrid of social outcast and scholastic genius.

Then came college on a scholarship to Stanford. Three years later, a master's in electrical engineering. Two more years and a doctorate in computer science. Another year, and a master's in biochemistry.

But all the while, the social moat around the Architect grew deeper and filled with pathological fluids. He lived alone in a run-down apartment building in the porno district, frequented a nearby tavern owned by bikers, and consumed every known pedigree of street drug. There was an unchecked urge in him to compensate for his scholastic brilliance through repeated plunges into nonsensical oblivion.

After school, there was the grant in computer science, the stint at Los Alamos National Laboratory, the contract with NASA, and the research fellowship with IBM. At each institution, his peers quickly learned they were not his peers at all. You could only step aside and watch him disappear into the distance above you. And you also learned that he never yelled back down and told you what he saw, which violated one of the basic premises of science: to share your findings with others. Eventually, there were always conflicts, and he always left.

Then came the offer from ParaVolve. And now here he is at the Teriyaki Takeout, lighting another cigarette and watching the traffic dribble past on Murray Road.

Aunt Dixie was right, thinks the Architect. I'm an elephant. And that makes it very hard to hide.

7

Brain Death

Simon Greeley pulls into the driveway of his town house in suburban Springfield. He taps his foot nervously but lightly on the accelerator as he waits for the garage door to open. His tinnitus is broadcasting a silver shimmer through his skull and he feels the nagging quiver of advanced anxiety. He knows he did the right thing by talking to Gail Ambrose. He saw her eyes snap to attention when she realized what he was telling her. But this supreme moment of action, this blowing of the whistle on a grand scale, didn't trigger any kind of emotional release.

Now, in retrospect, he knows why. No matter how strong his internal convictions, no matter how well oriented his moral compass, he cannot shake the sickening feeling that he has betrayed the professional trust of others. Somehow he had assumed that when the deed was done, he could provide his own forgiveness and absolution, but now he understands that was a foolish assumption. Spiritual remedies like these cannot be manufactured locally, because the raw materials are nearly always found off-shore, in bodies of law, in codes of conduct.

Now the new viruses form a ragtag flotilla strung out over a great distance by the gentle, persistent currents of the digestive fluids. As they drift, they leisurely probe at the surfaces of cells along the way. Soon the first waves have entered the small intestine, and along its wall, they find their first organic landmark. As they drift down toward the surface of this microscopic landscape, the intestinal wall becomes an endless honeycomb of individual cells, each a nation unto itself that trades vigorously with the world at large. In turn, each nation becomes a city of swaying towers called the microvilli. Like hot-air balloons, the viruses drift slowly among these towers, looking for precisely the right port of entry. Then, a few begin to find it and plunge all the way through to the interior of the cell.

From the living room, Barbara Greeley hears the mechanical groaning of the garage door and knows that Simon will be coming in momentarily. A preview of his strained face pops up before her, and she patiently pushes it back down. She tries not to reinforce the negative in their marriage, although there is a bitchy spirit inside her that relentlessly paints Simon as a pitiful wreck, worthy of altruistic compassion and little else. Over time, the spirit has changed tactics. Before her little extramarital fling last year, it presented Simon as a remote ice floe, a glacier that scoured away at their marriage until nothing but the boulders remained. Boulders like a midlife bachelor who taught grade-school biology and attended night classes in education, where he harvested midlife women. He's probably been through another three or four since her. She isn't resentful. Because now the spirit within her paints Simon as a damp blanket that chills her to the bone, and she realizes she was just trying to soak up a little warmth any way she could get it.

She hears the door shut at just the predictable time, and hates the utter regularity of it. Simon walks in and plants a perfunctory kiss on her forehead.

Check the mail, Simon. That's next.

But he snaps out of character, crosses to the sliding glass doors, throws them open, and walks to the railing, where he leans out and stares for a moment at the wooded area behind them.

He turns and his raincoat flutters in the breeze as he leans back against the railing and speaks to her through the open door.

"Barbara, I have just done something extraordinary, and I think you should know about it."

Barbara nods in assent. Far off, she hears the random whoop of an emergency vehicle. The perfect fanfare for Simon's announcement. He speaks in the same careful, bureaucratic terminology that has governed most of his adult life.

"A while back, I discovered some irregularities in the budget that were supposedly conducted under my authorization. In fact, I knew absolutely nothing about them. So I checked and found that someone is secretly dumping very large amounts of the taxpayers' money into the private sector. It's not right, Barbara. It's not right for them to do it, and it's not right to make me the fall guy if they get caught."

Behind Simon, a row of poplars sways like an inverted broom, sweeping the broad bowl of sky above it.

"I thought about it for awhile, and then I contacted the office of Senator Grisdale. They've got the whole story. By now they probably have it verified. I'm going public, Barbara. I'm blowing the biggest whistle this country has ever seen."

Barbara stares out the open door. The poplars are exceptionally lovely this time of year, and she suddenly longs to be a bird perched high in their branches, with just the sky, the wind, and the rustle of leaves.

Gail finds Senator Grisdale gazing out his window as she comes in and sits. Uh-oh, this is not good. The ritual has been broken. He is always at his desk when she comes in, and rises like a mountain in the making to greet her. Now he stands before the window with his back turned, his broad shoulders slightly hunched, a disturbing pose for a man of militarylike bearing.

"He's for real."

"Who's for real?" asks Gail. At any one time, she and the senator might have over a hundred issues grinding through the staff.

"Simon Greeley."

"You're sure?"

"Yes, I'm sure," replies Grisdale as he turns and heads for his desk chair. "But that's the only thing I'm sure about. From here on, it gets very slippery. We've got to look at our options very carefully." He settles into his chair, leans back, and regains his classic composure. "So, let's get started."

"Well, the safest option would be to move very slowly and seek independent confirmation from a number of sources," responds Gail.

"That would be safest, alright," says Grisdale, "but it also might be the sorriest. If it was just this Greeley business by itself, it would probably be

OK. But I'm hearing other things lately. Things about the White House. And I don't like what I hear."

Gail feels a tiny pulse of fear pass through her. It's funny, she thinks, how the most ominous subjects are seldom discussed directly. Undoubtedly, she was hearing the same rumors as the senator. In every case, they were touched upon lightly, sometimes even humorously. This was to be expected in a town where everyone was acutely conscious of their political persona. To discuss sensitive and dangerous issues bluntly and directly was a reckless gamble. If they came to pass, your profit would be minimum, and if they didn't, you were quickly labeled a hyper-reactive paranoid. Best to paint your scenarios in broad, impressionistic terms that defied direct interpretation, but delivered the message to those you wanted to get it. In this case, Gail's collective impressions were worrisome at best. Something was wrong inside the White House. Vague rumbling about a power shift toward a sub-group within the National Security Council. Loose talk about a drastic restructuring of executive power to deal with the current economic crisis. At the fringes of this speculation were the old liberal fantasies dating from the sixties: the secret plan to suspend civil rights, the dissolution of Congress, and a federal takeover of the media.

"Well, then," says Gail, "let's go to the other extreme. We call a press conference, and let Simon tell his story to the international news media."

Grisdale snorts. "That would precipitate a crisis about an order of magnitude bigger than Watergate. It would either cripple the White House when it's needed most, or push it into some kind of drastic action we'd all regret for the rest of our natural lives."

He gets up and begins to pace. "We've got to take some kind of action that will help control the problem, but not bring down the government in the process. I think our best shot is to put Mr. Greeley in front of my committee in closed session. It'll generate a ruckus, alright, but I think it's one I can contain. At least there'll be official recognition that there's something badly out of whack over in the Executive Building. The trick is, in the end we've got to set things straight without going through the regular judicial channels or involving the media. It's like chemotherapy: We need to zap the bad cells without killing the entire body."

"The problem is," interjects Gail, "we don't know yet which are the good cells and which are the bad ones."

Grisdale eases back into his chair. "I'm afraid we're going to have to do that as we go along. And we better do it right because we won't get a second chance."

"How do you want to handle the scheduling?" asks Gail. "Greeley was right about it being too dangerous to contact him directly. We'll just have to wait until we hear from him."

"That's not a problem," replies Grisdale. "I don't want to do any kind of formal scheduling that might tip our hand. It's better to wait until he contacts us and then see if he'll do it. If he will, we'll just slip him in unannounced."

Gail projects a mental picture of the hearing room, the doors closed, the camera and lights on for the record. She sees Simon sitting at the table, facing the senators. He looks tired, drawn, yet resolute. She is suddenly filled with compassion for the man.

"The minute he opens his mouth in that room, he's destroyed himself, hasn't he?"

"Without a doubt."

"Why?"

"Because for a brief time, the entire town, the entire American political system, the entire media machine, will rotate around him."

An extreme trade, thought Gail, but one with a perverse kind of equilibrium about it. As before, she thought of her own father as a benchmark for measuring Simon. Would he have done the same? Or continued to slowly smother under a thick, damp blanket of endless responsibility? She would never know.

Simon walks through a park near the Executive Building. Around him, trees explode into blossom and paint the fireworks of spring, but he does not notice. Instead, he is pulled back to a fishing trip with his brother, one of the last chapters in his life as a young man. He sees Steve sitting in the bow of their little aluminum boat. He smells the marshy air mingle with the outboard gas fumes and hears the lapping of the water against the hull. Steve's cheeks are flushed by the cool autumn air as he sits in the bow facing Simon and repeatedly fumbles as he tries to tie a hook to a thin thread of leader.

"Need some help, Steve?" He regretted his query before it was even completed. Wrong thing to say to somebody just out of the joint and grappling with a major-league drug problem. God, don't let me fuck up now, OK? I'm not very good at this kind of stuff, but let me be good at it just this once, all right?

Steve didn't even look up. The morning sun caught the blond high-lights in his thick mustache and turned the condensation from his breath into dancing clouds of silver. He continued to fumble away at the leader and hook. And began to talk in the fast, upbeat patter of the universal con man, the huckster of the ages.

"You know, Simon, I've had a lot of time to think. Would you believe that?" (Self-deprecating chuckle.) "And you know what I think? I think my best shot is to really go for it, really throw myself into something. Not some desk job bullshit, either. I mean something where I, me, is making it happen. If you don't think big, you don't win big, know what I mean? What am I saying? Of *course* you know. You're a hot-shit numbers guy. You figure the odds, right? It's the long shot that pays big, and if you're cookin' right, you can make the long shot into the short shot. You've just got to know how to structure the deal."

Steve ripped his eyes off the hook and to the middle of Simon's face. "And Simon, I know I can make the deal happen. I know I've *got* to make the deal happen. I'm coming from way back now, Simon. Square minus ten, at least, maybe more. I need the long ball to put me back on my feet. But don't worry, I won't let you down. I won't let Dad down. I owe you big, and I'm going to pay off in spades. . . ."

Simon got mildly sick inside. He saw the reality of it, the junkie sales-man's patter designed to marinate the victim and make him easier to cook and devour. His brother was gone, replaced by an automated par-asite. The pitch was like a computerized sales letter, with just enough personalized information injected to give the illusion of dignity to the target.

". . . and it's hard to get any leverage without a lever. Know what I mean? And I'm not talking about a big lever. Couple hundred bucks at the most. What do you think?"

Simon turned from Steve's expectant gaze and cast his line into the water.

"I didn't come here to think, Steve. I came here to fish. Like we used to."

That was it, thinks Simon as he nears the end of the park and the spread of blossoms. They had fished in silence, returned to the marina, exchanged some stiff pleasantries, and he had never seen his brother again. Now, for the first time in many years, he wonders if his brother is out there, maybe changing tires in a run-down gas station, maybe hustling pool in a dim tavern. Most of all, he wonders if his brother will hear the huge whistle he is about to blow.

The new viruses stream through the port that leads to the intestinal cell's interior and burst out into the cytoplasmic sea. Far in the distance, they see the hazy outline of a large sphere, the nucleus. All over the interior of the cell membrane, the diminutive tourists fan out from ports of entry and disperse lazily throughout the cytoplasm.

But soon they meet the mysterious hustler, technically known as reverse transcriptase, which promises rebirth and life anew in a transformed state. The proposition is simple: a chance to escape the role of messenger boy beating the streets and feeding the factories, a chance to dwell in the temple of the nucleus and become a master of genetic destiny.

The origins of the hustler are obscure. In many cases, he is part of the baggage dragged along by an invading virus. But not always. Sometimes he is already there, waiting silently in the atavistic alleys formed by the fibrous matrix that stretches throughout the cytoplasm.

At any rate, his offer is irresistible. And millions of his kind are selling hard throughout the jelly of the cytoplasmic sea. Once the deal is made, the conversion is a snap. Just hop along the beads of the RNA necklace and throw out all the U beads and T beads, then start swapping all the beads around according to a simple recipe. Next, travel up the sugar spine of the necklace and pause at each vertebra to rip out a particular pair of hydrogen and oxygen atoms, and tuck a single hydrogen atom in their place. Finally, tack a few extra beads on each end and make sure they spell out an identical sequence.

That's it. You're done. You're DNA. You're immortal. Now, with countless other converts, you make the pilgrimage to the nucleic temple. As you approach, the endless floral pattern of the nuclear pores unfolds. Over 10 million of them sprawl across the surface of the nucleus and blast out a busy swarm of messengers that bounce off to remote sites in the hinterlands with explicit instructions from the seat of power.

You'd like to stop and gawk, but you're here on business, so you cruise just above the pores and endure constant jostling from the exiting messengers as you seek a way in. Then, by pure chance, you see a vacant entrance and pop through.

Suddenly you're adrift in a tangled jungle of twisted fiber. This is it. The final directorate. The central engine of life. The chromosomes, with their twisted zippers of DNA coiled and coiled again.

You now realize that to do business here in the biological capital, you're going to have to conform. Currently, you're only half a DNA zipper, and need to become whole to participate. So you pick up bits of complementary material to form the other half of the zipper and then close into a circle, a plasmid.

And now you're ready to do your deed, to set off a microchemical conflagration that will burn the core out of Simon Greeley.

Simon leaves the park and crosses the street into the lobby of a large building. He walks directly to a pay phone. Why not? If they've got spooks on his tail, it won't do any good to take some circumspect route. Eventually he will have to use the phone; they will see him, and run a trace as fast as possible. He dials Grisdale's office and connects with Gail.

"Simon here, Ms. Ambrose. We have about sixty seconds till they run a trace and start to monitor."

"Simon, yes. We have verification. We want you to testify before a closed session of the committee."

"How soon?"

"Thursday. Are you up to it?"

"No. But that's not the point. The point is, it has to be done."

"We're not going to formally schedule you. That might compromise you before it's necessary. You know where the hearing room is?"

"Yes, I do."

"Come by about ten-thirty in the morning. I'll be outside in the hall waiting for you."

"Very well."

"Simon?"

"Yes?"

"Be careful."

"Yes, always."

Simon hangs up and feels the jaws open on the vise that has gripped him for so long. He is committed. On the way back across the park, he gulps down the color of the blossoms.

Now the plasmid, the circle of DNA, the son of the viroid-turned-virus, rolls along through the dense fibrous foliage of the chromosome jungle. Abruptly it

stops. Here is a spot where the DNA zipper wraps twice around a molecular ball
called a histone. And for some reason, the zipper is ruptured at this point. Now,
in a secret rite far beyond the eyes of man, the plasmid uncoils like the malev-
olent snake it is and snaps itself into the ruptured spot.

And so a new seat in the genetic legislature is created. One of many such
seats, all with no seniority but with catastrophic power. The teeth of the zipper
carry the nucleotide code, long sequences made up of As, Ts, Cs, and Gs.

Soon, the fly of the zipper, an RNA polymerase, rumbles through and unzips
the new strand containing the viroid blueprint. In the process, it reads the
zipper-tooth code and pieces together a new piece of viroid RNA, a perfect twin
to the original. It also sends out a plan to manufacture the new capsid.

All over the chromosome jungle the same thing is happening. Soon the new
viroids ooze out of the nucleus, slip into their customized capsids, and go looking
for work in outland factories. But work is scarce and their population is swell-
ing, so they emigrate back through the membrane ports to seek their fortunes
off-world. Many join an expedition through the venous system. It starts in lakes
of tissue fluid between the intestinal cells and continues through the leaky walls
of capillaries. Next it moves through a maze of tributary veins to the big Am-
azon vein, the inferior vena cava, where the expedition drifts slowly north until
it reaches the heart. Here the viroids are violently propelled through the right
atrium and then into the lungs, where they tumble once more down to the cap-
illaries and leak through to emerge again in the pulmonary veins for a quick ride
back to the heart. Now they are sloshed in a bright red storm through the left
ventricle and out the aorta. Soon they hit a major fork, and some are forced
south, back where they came from. But others continue north through the ar-
terial system and close on their final port of call.

The brain of Simon Greeley. The seat of his soul on earth.

As the town house garage opens, Simon is not surprised to see his
wife's car gone. She did not react well to his revelation yesterday. She
lapsed into a sullen silence and remained there for the balance of the
evening. It was an efficient move on her part, because he already knew
the precise style of her invective and could invent the appropriate dialogue in his mind's ear. *You never mentioned a thing! You never discussed*
it with me! It's going to change my life forever, and you just took off on your
own and did it!

She was right, of course. He just did it. Unilaterally, as they say at the
Georgetown cocktail parties.

Simon flips on the kitchen light. There's no note on the table telling where she is. He shuffles back into the bedroom, takes off his suit, and gazes out the window. There's still enough light for a brisk walk. The thought appeals to him. As he changes into his sweats, he sees himself walking right on out of his neighborhood, out of Washington, onto a country road, and south into a sky scrubbed blue right down to the horizon.

Once outside, Simon picks up the pace a little at the beginning of every block. Three blocks later when he reaches the park, he feels the frightened bird of flight rise within him, and impulsively starts to jog.

The viruses squirt through capillary walls and into the cerebellum, a part of the brain about the size of a tennis ball buried underneath the cerebrum. As before, they discover a sprawling landscape of membranes, but this time with a much different topography. Long tendrils, like the root systems of a tree, intertwine in a massive network. They are each part of a neuron, the central building block of the brain.

The viruses waste no time and seek ports of entry into the neurons. Once inside, they are quickly born again as DNA and make the pilgrimage to the nucleus, where they once more insinuate themselves into the chromosomal heart of creation.

In some cases, there is a repeat of the scenario from down south in the intestinal wall. The polymerase zipper fly rumbles down the genetic track and pumps out a new viroid. But for some reason, things often go differently. Very differently. When the zipper fly rolls over the born-again DNA, it has already picked up some neighboring code, which gets mixed in with the viroid recipe. Instead of just getting a new viroid, the neuron gets a new piece of RNA bearing some very bad news.

These new messengers fan out into the cell and report to factories that use their blueprints to make nasty little engines of destruction. Some begin to devour the inner framework of the cell, creating voluminous bubbles in the cytoplasmic sea. Others manufacture large quantities of starchy stuff that chokes off normal commerce within the neuron.

Quickly, too quickly, the neural interior becomes a disaster area. By this time, hordes of the viroids are donning their capsids and emigrating to neighboring cells and beyond. Many stay in the cerebellum, which handles muscular coordination, and infect neighboring cells. Others move up in the world, to the cerebrum, where the intellect resides.

By now, many of the local cells in the cerebellum begin to fail. All are wired into a network of fantastic complexity, a forgiving network that tolerates a few absences, a couple of missed cues. But as the damage mounts, the network begins to fail.

Simon feels the first little trickles of sweat roll down his back. He is alone in the park, and the rhythmic push of his exhaled breath fills his ears. He hasn't jogged for some time, but goddamn it, it feels like the right thing to do, so let's just go with it and . . .

One of his legs goes spaghetti. He tries to compensate, but pitches forward toward the red cinder surface of the path. He shoots out an arm to break his fall, but that goes spaghetti, too. He twists his trunk, breaks the weight of his fall with his shoulder, and scrapes his ear and cheek on the abrasive cinder material.

Oh, shit! Oh, God! What is it! Heart! It's the heart! Don't move. Stay still. Listen. Hear your heart, yeah, hear your heart right in your ears. Booming! It's booming bad. Everything's weird! Oh, God, help me, I'm scared. Wait now. No pain in your chest, maybe it's OK. Move just a little. No pain? No pain. OK, let's get on top of this thing. Deep breath. That's it. Another. That's it. Doctor never said anything about my heart. Yeah, it's OK. I must have just tripped. Ok, let's move slow.

Simon pushes himself slowly to a sitting position. His arm quivers as he does so, and a steady burn settles into his ear and cheek. He tentatively feels the side of his head. Raw, but no blood flowing. Good. His heart and respiration are creeping back toward normal. The moon rises over the tree line and a small breeze stirs the blossoms. In the distance, a lone dog barks.

It's over. Let's go home.

Simon rises cautiously to his feet and starts to walk. *Man! What a scare! Boy! That puts all this other stuff in perspective. At least I'm OK physically. Yeah, shouldn't have tried to jog without working up to it. Next time I . . .*

Something's wrong. The spaghetti feeling is back. Just a tiny bit, but in both legs.

Now, wait, this is silly. I'm playing tricks on myself. Let's just get home and forget it . . .

But it's there. A kind of shaky feeling. Simon is still walking, but there are subtle disruptions in his cadence as he heads for what he thinks will be the safety of his home.

Barbara Greeley returns home shortly before midnight. She has been at her friend Sally's house, sipping coffee and talking marriage. All evening she danced around the central issue, the big whistle. Sally's husband is high up in the DOD, and years in Washington have taught Barbara that you simply don't say what you don't want known. As the evening progressed, the trail of dialogue began to twist and turn and draw a picture. Barbara still loved her husband. The source of her anger was not Simon himself, but her failure to participate in the battles that raged inside him. She ached at his discontent and was frustrated by her inability to influence it. It was like a shadow on the far side of Simon, inexorably attached but impossible to touch.

Now she tosses down her purse and flips on the TV news. Some big bank in New York is going tits up. *Swell. That's all we need on top of our own problems.* She pours a small glass of chardonnay to counter the coffee she drank all evening at Sally's.

Simon, poor Simon. How can I reach you? How can I help you? Her mind turns to images of people in crisis under the glare of the media. You always saw the person's spouse, standing grimly by their side, a prop engineered to accumulate public sympathy. Yeah, stand by your man, be the bit player of the moment, the "human angle," the magnet for pity. *Bring down this asshole, your Honor, and this helpless, innocent little sidekick goes down, too.*

She flips off the TV, which is babbling about do-it-yourself bankruptcy, turns off the lights, and goes to the bedroom. Simon is asleep, curled up in a tight fetal ball. She tries to see him as a baby, but it doesn't work. She crawls in bed, turns on the reading lamp, and fishes a magazine from the nightstand.

Now, in the stillness, she notices that Simon is shivering.

Simon awakens spontaneously at six o'clock, his usual rising time. He looks over and sees Barbara sound asleep, then rolls in the direction of his alarm. Shit, he forgot to set it. How come?

The fall. The park. But it's over, right? Wait. I'm shivering. How come? Is it cold? No, it doesn't feel cold. Is it connected to the spaghetti from last night? Come on, Simon, let's get back on track. Let's get up and get going.

Simon rolls out of bed and stands. The shiver remains, subtle but there. In his head, legs, and trunk. Now for the test. He gingerly steps toward the bathroom.

It's still there. The spaghetti's back.

Simon can still walk, but it's no longer automatic. He has to consciously intervene to keep the muscle action smooth and continuous. Same thing with his arms.

OK, I'll give it a day. If I'm not better tomorrow, it's doctor time.

Linda Danworth walks briskly down a hallway inside the Executive Building. She doesn't run because that would draw attention. And like people late to work everywhere, the last thing she wants is attention. She spent the night at the apartment complex of her new lover, formerly a technician for a video production company, now unemployed. And the whole thing had gotten weird. Really weird. Her lover had this friend in Seattle who had mailed him some funny new kind of dope. You had to fizz it in vinegar and then smoke it. He asked Linda if she wanted some and she said no. It wasn't that she was fussy about it. In fact, she had smoked hashish from time to time and even snorted some of the new synthetics. But she just wasn't in the mood. So he went ahead by himself, and when he was done, he didn't know her. He seemed attracted to her and all that, but he didn't know who she was, not her name, not her face, not her voice. He seemed quite happy and watched some old movie on TV while she went to bed, disturbed and hurt. She was still disturbed when she got up this morning, and she missed a freeway exit on the way in, which made her about fifteen minutes late.

She pops into her office, glances at the open door to Simon's office, and sees the vacant chair behind his desk. What a break! He's almost always on time, but today he's late. She slips into her chair, flips on her word processor just in time to hear a "Good morning, Mr. Greeley" out in the hall. Close.

Linda watches Simon appear in the doorway and starts to fabricate a cheerful greeting. But a full look at him stops her short. A large red abrasion glows angrily on the side of his cheek, and his ear is chewed up, too. And he looks, well, shaky. Like he's not sure of himself. There is a strange hesitation in his footsteps, and his hands are dug strenuously deep into his raincoat pockets. Also, it might be her imagination, but it seems like he is shivering a little.

She manages a perfunctory good morning, which he returns as he enters his office and shuts the door. Shit, thinks Linda, this is going to be a very strange day. What am I supposed to say? She hunkers down to work and wishes it were already lunchtime.

Simon stares blankly at his computer. He wonders if anybody noticed. Probably not. His vanity is undoubtedly making a bigger deal out of all this than it really is. Now, let's do some checking. He holds his hand out at arm's length and relaxes as best he can. There it is, the shivering. He watches the tiny oscillations propagate through his shirtsleeve.

You know, it could be nerves. I mean, who's a better candidate for a big-time case of nerves than I am? Yeah, that's probably it. Why didn't I think of that before? It's just like the tinnitus, just another symptom of nerves. Here I am, scaring the living Jesus out of myself, when there's such a simple answer. Well, anyway, I'll give it until tomorrow and then check with the doctor. Hell, let's get to work.

Simon must generate a report on why he gained general access to the database in System 9. In a day or two, the deadline for this report will expire, and a whole new set of flags will be raised. He slips on his headset and opens the DocuTalk window, which receives his voice and translates it into words on the screen. The first time he used the DocuTalk system was a very unsettling experience. As fast as he could speak, the words had appeared on the screen. Never before had the relationship between the spoken and written word been so intimate. To compound the effect, a second wave of processing rippled along behind the first and provided the correct grammatical formatting. While you watched your voice appear instantly in video print in the current sentence, the grammar program followed only a sentence behind, cleaning up like a picky little janitor.

Simon labors over the System 9 report. He is an analytical person, and finds it difficult to manufacture a lie that has the kind of heft required to be intuitively convincing. And every so often, the shivering spaghetti demon pops to the top of his mental stack. He quickly tucks it back down a couple of layers, but it immediately begins to work its way back up. He works on anyway. The text on the screen goes out of focus, and slightly double. He leans back in his chair, yawns, rubs his eyes, and then looks back at the screen.

The text is still slightly double.

OK, goddamn it, that's enough of this shit! Let's cut it out right now!

Simon grabs a pencil, holds it out, and forces it into a single image. That's better. It stabilizes, but as soon as he abandons the effort, it drifts back into a double image.

He puts down the pencil, leans far back in his chair, breathes deeply, and closes his eyes for several minutes.

Alright, that's it. Something's really wrong. What now? I better get out of here while I can still drive.

Linda Danworth looks up from her word processor just in time to see Simon wobble by and say he is gone for the day. There is a ghastly look about him, a look that will never leave her.

Barbara Greeley is in the living room when she hears the remote groan of the garage door. It has to be Simon. Why is he home now? It isn't even lunchtime. No matter. She wants desperately to talk with him, to sink a mine shaft into his angst so they can bring it to the surface, where they can work on it together. Should she rise and go hug him? No, that would seem too anxious. She sighs and shifts to a more upright position on the couch. The door to the garage opens and Simon steps through.

Oh, no. Oh, no.

Even from across the room, she can see his head quiver, his arms tremble, his legs shake.

"Simon!"

"Barbara, I think we better call Dr. Winthrop." His speech is thick and slurred.

"Simon, my God! What happened? Were you in an accident? Did somebody attack you? What happened?"

Simon sinks into his favorite chair and somehow it helps a little. The shivering recedes slightly. "Nothing happened. That's the problem. Nothing happened."

Barbara phones Dr. Winthrop, and gets his nurse. "I'm calling about my husband, Simon Greeley . . . Yes, that's G-r-e-e-l-e-y. . . . He's suddenly got some kind of trembling and he can hardly walk. . . . No, it's never happened before. . . . Fever? I don't think so. . . . No, he's never had a head injury. . . . No, there's never been any epilepsy. . . . Tomorrow? He can't get in today?. . . . OK, then, if it gets worse, I'll take him to the emergency room. Good-bye."

With considerable effort, Simon walks out the open sliding doors onto the deck. It is now late at night and a mild breeze ripples the curtains. He looks back at Barbara, who is asleep on the couch, clutching a shawl like a child's toy. For many hours they had talked. About their marriage. About the big whistle. About her fears and hopes. About the shivering spaghetti.

Only now does he realize the true nature of their dialogue. It was a final accounting. There was an implicit assumption that whatever ailed him might be irreversible.

So now a great certainty builds within him. Tomorrow he will testify before Grisdale's committee, even if they have to carry him in. For in this one act, he will be permanently rescued from anonymity, will explode like a supernova, with sudden and unexpected brilliance, and fill the political universe about him. Whatever happens afterward, even his own death, will be but a mild epilogue.

Dr. Martin Winthrop looks at the chart. Yes, Simon Greeley. Yes, in here last year for nervous tension. Ah, yes, "nervous tension," the bane of every doctor's practice. Oh, well, let's see what we can do for Mr. Greeley.

Dr. Winthrop strides briskly down the hall. He is in his mid-thirties, runs twenty miles a week, and sleeps with one of his partner's nurses on Thursday afternoons. With clipboard in hand, he opens the door to the examining room.

Uh-oh. We've got a little more than "nerves" this time.

Simon is sitting on the examining table, with his back to the doctor and his trunk, legs, and arms visibly quaking. He apparently didn't hear Dr. Winthrop open the door.

"Mr. Greeley?"

A scream. A horrible scream from Simon, whose arms flail wildly as he twists toward the doctor. Dr. Winthrop jumps back reflexively, then catches himself. Jesus! What's going on with this guy? A nurse is running down the hall, but Dr. Winthrop motions her away. That's all he needs is for word to get out that he can't cope with his patients. He turns back toward Simon, who looks both humiliated and very ill at the same time.

"I-I'm sorry, Doctor." His speech is fragmented, unsure.

"It's OK, Mr. Greeley. Try to relax. Now, when did all this start?"

"Fell, fell down jogging. T-two days back."

"Did you hit your head when you fell?"

"No, no head hit."

"What caused you to fall? Do you remember?"

"Leg stop, stopp, stopped working."

Dr. Winthrop sighs. The next question will be very tough. He asks it as compassionately as he can. "Mr. Greeley, I know you're having trouble speaking, but are you OK in there? Do you know what I mean? Are you thinking clearly?"

Through the quivering it's impossible to tell if Simon is hurt or insulted. "Pretty much OK," he replies.

"Who brought you here?"

"Wife."

"Mr. Greeley, excuse me for just a minute, please." Dr. Winthrop turns and shuts the examining room door on the way out. It looks neurological, but what the hell is it? He simply doesn't know.

"Patty, I've got a patient, Simon Greeley, in number five," says Dr. Winthrop as he approaches the front desk. "Would you get his wife from the waiting room and bring her back?"

Barbara Greeley pulls into the semicircular drive in front of the Hart Building in the Senate office complex. Simon sits silently beside her. She is completely numb inside and knows that this is a dam holding back a reservoir of grief, a dam that must be carefully maintained for the next few hours until the professional odyssey of Simon Greeley is finally over. The doctor had spoken to her alone first: It looked like a neurological problem and he was bringing in a Dr. Feldman, one of the best neurologists in town (as opposed to one of the worst? She starts a bitter chuckle, feels a small fissure snake up the side of the dam, and bites its off). Anyway, the doctor wanted Simon hospitalized immediately. But not Simon. Repeated pleading produced the same response over and over.

"T-ten-thirty. Senate committee."

"What's he mean?" asked the doctor.

"He's talking about his salvation," answered Barbara as she squeezed Simon's trembling hand.

So here they were, struggling up into the Hart Building, with Simon on legs of rubber.

Gail Ambrose paces anxiously in the hall outside the hearing room. It's nearly ten-thirty and she is afraid she has a no-show on her hands. Inside, behind the heavy hardwood door, Senator Grisdale and seven of his peers are discussing a relatively boring procedural matter with a midlevel officer from the CIA. The door now opens and the officer and his assistant come out and walk energetically down the hall with their bulging briefcases. She rises to her tiptoes, as if this will improve her vision, and looks past them. Nobody. Just a handicapped old guy being helped along by a woman. Come on, Simon!

Wait. No. It can't be. Just looks like him. Just looks like him, that's all.

Then the awful realization hits her head-on. Yes. It is Simon. But how? What happened?

She takes a few steps to meet them. "Simon! What's wrong?"

Simon's eyes wander in her direction, but can't seem to lock on her. "Maybe poisoned. Not sure."

"Simon, you can't go on like this. We've got to wait until you get better."

"W-w-on't get better. Got to do it now."

He's dying. She can feel it. The man's dying. How can she stop him?

Simon solves the problem for her. He wobbles up to the door, with Barbara rushing after him to give support. The security guard at the door shoots a look at Gail, who weakly nods her head.

Out of the corner of his eye, Grisdale catches the door opening. He sits at the center of a dais with his colleagues on either side. Facing them are two tables with microphones. Off to one side, a video cameraman captures the proceedings for the private record of the committee. A few moments ago, Grisdale announced an unscheduled member from OMB who would provide testimony that might be of interest to the committee. But who is this?

Sweet Jesus! It's Greeley.

The vocal buzz in the room rolls off to silence. All eyes watch Barbara Greeley help Simon into a seat behind one of the microphones. He looks up at the committee, his head bobbing on the surface of unseen wavelets, his raincoat still on.

Grisdale knows there is only one way to play it. Absolutely straight.

"Mr. Greeley, earlier this week you agreed to come here and give testimony on the revolving budget for covert operations. Apparently, you've been taken quite ill, and the committee most certainly understands if you'd like to postpone your testimony to a later date."

There is no sound in the room. No motion. None.

"I-I-I want to tes-tify now"

"Very well, Mr. Greeley. Will you tell the committee what your position is within the Office of Management and Budget?"

"I am special assistant to the . . . to the deputy associate director for national se-curity."

"And what do you do in that position?"

"I . . . help plan and and and ad-minister the bud-get."

"Does this include budgets that are classified for national security?"

"Yes."

"Does it include budgets targeted at operations under the jurisdiction of this committee?"

"Yes."

"Have you discovered anything unusual in these budgets that might be of particular interest to this committee?"

Out of nowhere, a contorted grin stretches Simon's mouth to the far corners of his face, and then freezes there. His head quavers violently, as though to shake off the grin. But it just stays plastered there. The room goes dead quiet.

Then the laughing begins.

It starts as a strangled outburst from the back of Simon's throat, from behind the tightly clenched teeth, and quickly shatters the plastered grin.

In a tragic miscue, several of the senators see his spasmodic laughter as comic relief and also being to chuckle. Soon the room is rolling on an artificial wave of humor, but as it subsides, Simon howls on alone at a chill wall of embarrassed silence.

Grisdale can take no more. He sees Gail over by the door, and nods in Simon's direction. Together, Gail and Barbara pull him from his chair. With the spell broken, a male staffer comes to help, and the three of them help Simon to the door.

Now the violent rumble of murmuring fills the void, a chaotic chorus to a bizarre tragedy. Instinctively, Grisdale lets it peak and decline slightly before he adds the final piece of punctuation.

"Ladies and gentlemen, this hearing stands adjourned."

Through the glass window of the control room, Dr. Daniel Feldman watches as they wheel Simon out of the big metal doughnut where the CAT scan had just taken place. Simon is deeply sedated to eliminate his incessant tremors, which would have ruined the imaging provided by the system. During the scanning operation, Dr. Feldman watched a series of color-enhanced images appear on the screen. Each represented a horizontal cross-section of Simon's brain as viewed from the top down.

Computerized Axial Tomography is a marvelous technology that has been refined over the past decade to yield an amazing amount of detail about internal physical structures, especially the brain. But in this case, it tells him nothing. In fact, none of the laboratory tests on Simon has revealed anything outside the bounds of normality.

None of this surprises Dr. Feldman. He strongly suspects Simon has a malady called Creutzfeldt-Jakob disease, which is nearly transparent to conventional tests. As they wheel Simon out of the room, he pities the man's horrible misfortune. This is the only case of Creutzfeldt Jakob disease he has ever seen outside of a textbook. Only one person in 2 million contracts it, and it is invariably fatal. Only an autopsy will guarantee his diagnosis. Whatever the infectious agent is for this ailment, it has never been directly observed, although subvirus particles of some kind are often mentioned in the literature. The only way to confirm the culprit is to microscopically check the damage in the brain after the fact.

Dr. Feldman is quite certain the autopsy will bear him out. But there is one anomaly that nags at him, one piece that doesn't fit. The symptoms match up quite well with those reported in other cases of this disease, but the timing does not. The sudden loss of muscular coordination and the onset of involuntary motor activity, coupled with retention of intellectual ability, indicate that the disease attacked the cerebellum first. In cases like this, the patient usually survives for months, sometimes even a couple of years. It is now obvious that Simon will be dead within a day or two, which means the entire course of the disease from the onset of symptoms to death will be less than a week. Even the most severe cases, where the patient goes immediately into dementia, persist for at least three weeks, which will make Simon's case the shortest ever recorded.

There is, of course, one other possibility, thinks Dr. Feldman as he stares absently at the CAT console. Maybe he doesn't have Creutzfeldt-Jakob disease at all.

Maybe he has something else entirely.

8

Counterpoint

Call him Counterpoint. He drives quickly and expertly on the curving three-lane road, pushing the new Mercedes 900 SL along at just under seventy. A bit fast for a man just past fifty, whose reflexes might fail him in a tight spot, but he denies his age and barrels on through the Washington, D.C., night. The ride is smooth, a little too smooth, the kind that compromises a car's handling characteristics. This bothers him slightly. He does not like anything that escapes his control. The instrument panel glows green and red with flat displays that depict every aspect of the car's operation, including a map with a bird's-eye view of the car's location from one mile above. He can see that he is heading north on Canal Road toward the suburban community of McLean, an enclave of wealth and power, where he lives.

But tonight the displays, the gentle hiss of the wind, and the rich smell of leather upholstery fail to distract him. His mind is overseas, in Germany, in Japan, in Korea, in Singapore. In each place he imagines legions of industrious people acting as high-quality components within a grand human circuit, a national system with a sense of purpose and destiny. He sees this as a perfect reflection of the natural world, where each cell in an organism contains the entire blueprint for the organism, yet performs its own specialized function. He believes that these societies resonate harmonically, generating great waves of economic power that circle the globe like giant tsunamis, engulfing everything in their path.

The little bastard. He got exactly what he deserved.

His global vision evaporates and he is in a park in Georgetown, reliving an event that is scarcely thirty minutes old. The park seems very ordinary. A baseball diamond with two little sets of weathered wooden bleachers. A metal climbing structure in a sawdust pit. An open expanse of green playing field.

But there is one very extraordinary feature here. The rest rooms. They are located on a side of the park that faces a no-man's-land of cosmetic shrubbery masking a freeway just fifty feet away. For this reason, the rest rooms are concealed from the view of any nearby houses, from the vigilance of those who occupy a moral middle ground that provides ethical ballast. So at night, they dwell in a shadowy vacuum that becomes a very specialized marketplace. Throughout the night a small trickle of cars glides through his neighborhood and down the street on the far side of the park. The cars fit into two distinct genres, one being late-model luxury sedans, Mercedes, BMWs, Lincolns, Cadillacs; the other, the older, anonymous cars and pickups from the economic midrange. The former contains the buyers, older men from positions of power and wealth. The latter holds the sellers, young men with sleek bodies, many barely into adolescence. On any given night, the traffic is slow, never enough to arouse suspicion. Most often, there is only one buyer and one seller.

On this night, as Counterpoint drove by, the area around the rest rooms appeared deserted, a ghostly island lit by two halogen lights on metal poles. He cruised on past and parked several hundred feet down the street. His parked car was a silent signal to other buyers to stay away because a transaction was in progress: Like all markets, this one had rules that promoted orderly commerce. He left the car and walked into the darkness of the park rather than approach on the sidewalk. The dark and the stealth of the approach were essential for Counterpoint, because unlike other buyers here, he was not a simple consumer of the wares on display. He was not even gay in the conventional sense. The idea of having any kind of passionate relationship with another male was utterly alien to him. He had never really analyzed why these young strangers made a great thrill ripple through him. There was no need. It was simply there, without fail.

To analyze the thrill would require the prompting of conscience, and

Counterpoint had none. He was not at all troubled by its absence, for it is conscience itself that fuels this kind of self-examination.

If he had been able to trace the source of his thrill, he would have understood that these young men were not sex objects, they were prey, and the reason he preferred males to females was the same reason deer hunters prefer bucks to does: They were a more worthy adversary, a trophy of higher esteem.

So he walked through the trees in the darkness. The nearby drone of the freeway masked his steps on the grass, which was already damp with dew. It had been a clear, warm day, but the temperature was now falling fast. The steam from his breath rose up and diffused the lights over the rest rooms, so they periodically turned into pale, fuzzy orbs. Already, he felt the pace of the hunt quicken, the thrill push upward through his belly.

Why didn't he go along? Stupid little shit!

The Mercedes continues its power glide down Canal Road toward the Chain Bridge, and he pulls his mental focus back to the globe. The United States is in trouble, no doubt about it. Nobody should be surprised by the Downturn. It's just another symptom in a long chain that stretches back to the middle of the century. *No cultural purity.* That's it. (He likes the phrase and tucks it away for further use in dialogues with those who count.) The country is an unruly mob of self-propelled miscreants, or as the engineers would say, a kludge. The country is an aberration, a glitch in the scheme of global Darwinism, where survival is pegged to the unity of national will. The country is a sick puppy that has no idea what ails it. It simply whimpers and shakes as the big economic bug courses through its entrails.

But Counterpoint understands the disease quite intimately. And he is not alone. That's the exciting thing. There is now a political network of silent consensus growing, an almost invisible web that interconnects nodes of political and economic power. At last, there is hope.

Will it make the papers? Probably. But so what?

He walked to within fifty feet of the rest rooms and stopped abruptly in the shadows. A silent switch clicked within him. He could feel the presence of the prey. It was out there, swimming through the shadows, and he was sure it could feel him also. Then he caught the movement. He turned to lock on it and saw a figure emerge from the shadow boundary and head quickly for the door of the men's room. Blond hair. Leather jacket. Tight jeans. Cowboy boots. Perfect. He felt the bond between them begin to grow, the perversely comfortable sense of ritual shared by victim and victimizer in this dark little marketplace. Slowly and with a deliberately measured pace, he began to walk toward the rest room door.

Evidence? Not a problem. Not really.

Through the windshield, Counterpoint watches the streetlights strobe on by on Chain Bridge Road. His eyes stray to the soft colored glow of the car's instrument panel, its displays dancing geometrically. He knows for a fact that none of it is produced in the United States. The battle for mass consumer electronics has been one of steady retreat. After each skirmish, a move to higher ground, to more specialized technologies with smaller markets. For years now, the official alarm has been sounding. Blue-ribbon committees, blue-blood commissions, and Big Blue itself have studied the problem with wrinkled frowns. The recommendations are the same: better education, more math, government/industry collusion in strategic technologic areas. Still, the retreat goes on, a massive economic glacier that slowly evaporates under a blistering sun fueled by global competition.

But Counterpoint sees it differently. All this noble effort is too little, too late. The time has come to admit that we have run out of normal options. The time has come to admit we must act boldly and unconventionally. So what if we do a few things that offend the "world community?" Do *they* pay the bills? Will *they* mourn our passing as a great power? Of course not.

And when you sweep away all the bullshit, there is one field that is ripe with unexplored options: biotechnology, the exotic borderland between science, engineering, and life itself. Here more than anyplace else, Counterpoint sees a chance for economic rebirth, a chance to start anew and avoid the mistakes of the past, to build a new order.

As he raises his hand to scratch his forehead, he notices his coat sleeve is torn. No matter. He will simply discard the entire coat. Anyway, back to the problem of national strategy. Most of the barriers to advanced biotech research are ridiculous muddlings over so-called ethical questions. They are absurd. What can be done must be done. It is simply a matter of survival and retention of power. The game makes the rules, not the players. Fortunately, there are others who see it the same way. They share his insight into the new global scheme. For a time conventional wisdom had it that economic power was the new weapon of choice in the conflict of nations, not military power. Wrong. You had to have both. And Counterpoint and friends see a way to do it, through new biological research that does an end run around the artificial barriers set up by the usual regulatory bodies.

Of course, there are risks. Even in the military, the great majority of people are opposed to options he is now pursuing. Ah, but the military is always slow, the generals always longing to fight the next war with the weapons of their youth, like they did in Iraq, where much of the technology had been on drawing boards twenty years before.

It was a little chilly, but you can't have everything.

He stopped at the rest room door. It was made of steel and painted green with the universal male symbol, the silhouette in the suit, applied at eye level in yellow. He reached down, grasped the cold sphere of the door handle with his gloved hand, and slowly rotated it. Within him, the infinite patience of the experienced predator fought with a carnivorous thrill of anticipation. The door was heavy and mounted with a piston to stay shut, so it required extra effort to push it open. Now he was facing a metal partition panel painted a moldy green and littered with obscene incantations that covered a universe of orifices and actions. The endless exhale of the freeway poured in through the open door and filled the rest room's interior up to the brim. As he rounded the panel, the door slammed shut and a profound, ceremonial silence took over. Ahead were a pair of sinks and a polished metal mirror built to endure an infinity of vandalism. Next to them was a paper towel dispenser torn halfway off the wall, with "PISS ON ME" scratched into its white enamel surface. He walked to the center of the room and felt the thrill pushing up through his chest and down his arms. Yes, now he could see the target. Off to the left of the sinks, the room extended into a space with two toilet partitions, little metal fortresses of public privacy. In the far toilet, the cowboy boots were visible in the space between the tile floor and the bottom of the partition, two pillars of sculpted leather topped by twin hoods of faded blue denim. He walked very slowly toward the toilet, the thrill now brimming up to his forehead and pushing his penis into a full erection. He stopped in front of it. The door was pushed slightly outward, and he opened it ever so slowly.

He was young, maybe thirteen, though slightly large for his age. Fine. The blond hair was nice, too. He sported an idiotic grin and had his hands dug into his pockets. "Hi," he said. The grin faded when he got no reply and realized the true nature of the game.

The thrill was now coursing through him in large symmetrical waves. He could see the paralysis settling into the victim, like the spider injected with the venom of the wasp. "Down you go," he commanded with absolute authority as he unzipped his pants.

Should I check with an attorney? No. More risk than gain.

He slides the Mercedes over into the slow lane so he can catch the upcoming street to his neighborhood. He puzzles over the intransigence in the government, in industry. The facts are simple enough. For the longest time, the defense industry had been the nation's prime incubator of technology, but those days were gone. Now the commercial sector, with its enormous economic incentives, has pushed into the lead. From this point on, the military would have to mine the sprawling research and development fields created by the imperatives of global commerce. And so it would be in biotechnology. All that was needed was a way to prime the pump. The primer itself was no problem. It was simply money, and there was always an abundance of that once you understood the system it flowed through. The pump was a little more difficult. It had to be carefully constructed and maintained, and sheltered from the timidity of those who couldn't face the brutal equations of global hegemony. But once operational, you had the perfect system, a way to dominate both the commercial and military worlds at the same time. In the past, it would have been impossible to conceal an operation of the necessary scale. The Manhattan Project was a prime example. Despite the obsessive security, it had been necessary to let thousands of people in on the big, dirty secret. There were just too many new machines and new materials to be created from scratch, things that required bulky, labor-intensive processes that spread out in a complex infrastructure all over the country. But that is no longer true. Much of the development process now dwells as a series of elegant abstractions inside computers, where entire avenues of research can be explored without ever bridging over into physical reality.

Glad I got the vaccination. You never know when something might happen.

As the boy went down on him, he grabbed the blond hair and kept him just short of the choking point. The thrill waves had lost their symmetry and turned into a wild, lurching storm. He was enraptured by this act of almost perfect consumption, where the victim was totally enveloped and merged into him. But he needed more, more, more. He yanked the boy off him and brought him to his feet, where he could see the terror glistening in the young eyes.

"Get your pants down. Turn around." His words bounced off the green tile and reverberated with power.

"I don't do that."

You don't *do that*? Rapture and rage wrapped into a twisted tornado of spontaneous violence. He pinned the boy by the throat against the metal divider and reached with his free hand to undo the jeans.

And the little bastard kicked him. Right in his exposed genitals, which protruded from his unzipped trousers. The toe of the cowboy boot plowed into his turgid penis, the heel into the softness of his scrotum. As he recoiled in pain, the little shit lunged for the door, but Counterpoint grabbed him and threw him up against the metal divider once more. The boy tried a second kick, but Counterpoint dodged and they both tumbled to the tile floor. In the process, the back of the boy's head struck the lip of the toilet bowl and his eyes spun for a moment.

Yes! Finish it! Now! His hand streaked out and his palm caught the boy under the chin, forcing his head back into the bowl while his body remained stationary. The crack of his snapping neck was loud, louder than you'd expect, and perfectly timed with the climax from Counterpoint's spurting weapon.

He became me. He died and all that was him became me. I've never felt anything like it. It was absolutely perfect.

Counterpoint pilots the Mercedes along the winding residential street to his house. His crotch is still swollen and throbbing with pain. No matter, he thinks. A small price for perfection. He now knows with absolute certainty that this wonderful ceremony of consumption will recur again and again.

9

XXXXXX

Breakdown

Speed metal. Ripping, buzz-saw guitar licks. Towering cities of speakers.
Skinny dudes in tight leather. The ecstasy of thirty-second note fusil-
lades chattering at over 100 decibels through pot-filled air.

Snooky Larsen is ready. Tomorrow night, it's a tripleheader: Chro-
max, Scuz Force, and Snake Whip at the coliseum. He has his ticket.
Bought it at GI Joes the day they came out. Just one ticket, of course. His
current girlfriend, Janelle, detests this kind of stuff and is staying home
to watch the Academy Awards with her fat friend, Damita.

At twenty-four, Snooky sees no point in growing up. He's got a nice
little apartment tucked off 185th, a 4WD pickup, a snowboard, SkyCa-
ble service, and 1,205 CDs of speed metal and other vintage fringe stuff,
like the original Baby Flamehead release. Janelle makes noises about
commitment, but Snooky is blissful in his resolution to just be one of the
dudes—forever.

Now in the depths of ParaVolve, he sings the lead line from "Walk
This Way" by Aerosmith and scans the display in front of him. It is
roughly two and a half feet by four feet and has the resolution of a theater
movie screen. Along its borders are the standard icons and menus that
are the staple of computer interfaces everywhere. But the image in the
center is the main attraction, a green cube of liquid against a black background. It is tilted to present an oblique aerial view, as if you were sus-

pended above it in a helicopter. And across its surface tiny waves tumble along, crisscrossing each other in gentle interference patterns.

Happy fella tonight, notes Snooky. His trained eye reads the waves, their angle, their amplitude, their direction, their collisions. And in them he sees the persona of DEUS, the remarkable computer system that dwells in the center of the complex. The surface of the green liquid is a visual metaphor for the activity of the quarter million microcomputers that comprise DEUS. If Snooky wanted, he could zoom in and magnify a specific area on the surface until the little blocks that represented the individual computers became visible. They are arranged in a matrix, and the height of each block reflects how much traffic is flowing through that particular computer at that particular time. The higher the flow, the higher the block. Given the unique nature of DEUS, these so-called "usage patterns" generate intersecting waves that, to the trained observer, tell volumes about how well the system is working.

Occasionally, one of Snooky's speed metal pals will ask him what he does at work. Snooky always winces, because first, he has signed a security oath not to talk about it; and second, it is almost impossible to explain. DEUS, of course, stands for Dynamically Evolved and Unified System. One time when he first came here, he met the guy who designed the thing. They called him the Architect, and like his creation, he was godlike in the technosociety of engineers and computer scientists at Para-Volve. Other than that, Snooky pegged him as a pretty spaced and kinky dude. At any rate, he wasn't around anymore, and because of the way he designed DEUS, he really didn't need to be.

The easiest part of DEUS to explain was the hardware, the legions of green boards, ceramic substrates, chips, and cabling that formed its physical side. But the problem Snooky had with his low-tech pals was that they did not understand *computers,* which required going back a century or so. For a long time, clever fellows had been making smart machines that performed specialized tasks, such as playing music, or guiding little rococo figures through stuttering minuets. But the core concept behind real computers is that they must be general-purpose handymen: Give them the proper instructions and they do whatever your bidding might be.

The first real general-purpose computer was never built. It existed inside the mind of a towering genius named Alan Turing, and is called, appropriately, a Turing Machine. Turing's mentally manufactured engine was so good that to this day it describes every general-purpose computer in existence.

The first electronic Turing Machines came along in 1945. Big vacuum-tube jobs with sci-fi names like ENIAC and MANIAC. They filled entire rooms and had tens of thousands of glowing tubes and over a half million solder joints, all done by hand. They were used to solve nuclear weapons problems from the pit of the atomic Hades, where no human could ever travel, problems like the one-dimensional burning of deuterium and tritium.

About the same time, a second genius named John Von Neumann formulated the ultimate physical model for a general-purpose computer. It called for a series of instructions (later termed the "program") and the data they work on to dwell in single memory, which could be accessed by a processing machine. This machine fetches an instruction from the memory, uses it to do something to data brought in from somewhere else in memory, and then moves on to the next instruction. Over and over. Millions and billions of times. As long as it takes to complete the job.

By the mid-1970s the famous silicon sandwich called the "microprocessor" had reduced the size of a typical Von Neumann machine from forty-five hundred cubic feet to less than a square inch. Soon, microprocessors were clipping along at the rate of one million instructions per second, commonly called MIPS. But by now the weapons people who were weaned on ENIAC had become the supreme MIPS junkies and needed enormous fixes, as did their code-breaking cousins at the National Security Agency. They turned to "supercomputers" like the Cray XMP, which blistered along at thousands of MIPS, and added a new twist called "vector processing" that greatly accelerated math calculations.

Originally, the high priests of supercomptuers snorted at the relatively anemic performance of microprocessors compared with the brute force of these bigger machines, but by the late eighties, they could no longer ignore their promise since they now held over a million transistors and ripped along at nearly one hundred MIPS. Suppose, just suppose there was a way to cram thousands of these cheap little critters under the hood of a single computing vehicle. It would be a screamer for sure. Soon, laboratory models were ganging up sixteen thousand microprocessors and pumping out 26,000 MIPS. The age of "massive parallelism" was born.

But there was a hitch: Nobody knew how to write programs that harnessed all the horsepower of these new monster machines. There were countless analogies offered to explain the problem. Constructing a house works as well as any: Suppose you're a contractor constructing a single-family residence. You write a "program" that keeps maybe five or ten people (microprocessors) busy at the same time, without anyone standing around idle for very long. But suppose over ten thousand people show up to help you build the house? What then? How can you possibly program their activities in an efficient manner? You can't. It's simply more trouble than it's worth.

Nevertheless, computer scientists continued to salivate at the huge MIPS numbers put out by the parallel machines, and searched for some way around the problem.

Ultimately, the solution was to let the computer itself, not the programmer, figure out how to divvy up the work among the legions of processors. The key was in the operating system, a program that might be likened to the chief minister in the court of an emperor: There is no way you can approach the emperor directly; instead you must petition the minister, who acts as an instrument of the emperor's power in executing (or denying) your request. Likewise, the operating system acts as a representative of the power inherent in the computer hardware, and all other programs must petition the operating system to do their bidding.

In both court and computer, the advantage is the same. The chief minister of the court is intimately familiar with the vicissitudes of the emperor, and is able to shield the petitioners from them, which means the petitioners have a predictable and orderly interface to power in the form of the minister and the formal protocols required to deal with him. In the same way, the operating system thoroughly understands the nuances of the computer hardware and is able to protect the petitioning programs from countless possible pitfalls involved in dealing with the hardware directly, many of which can be catastrophic.

In the case of massive parallelism, the operating system would act as chief minister and shield the petitioning programs from the fact that the emperor was in a massive state of psychosis and splintered into many thousands of personalities. With some minor exceptions, the programs would be written as though for a single computer and then presented to the operating system in the usual way. In turn, the operating system would figure out how to fracture the program and fling it among the

thousands of computers. Soon, the concept was proved through operating systems such as LINDA, with its "tuple space."

Snooky pushes his rotating chair back from the console and does a
full twirl in the classic air-guitar pose while growling out the opening riff
to "Cult of Personality." Tuple space was long before his time. Besides,
who cares about the theory behind the DEUS operating system? The
truth is that no one knows it. Not even the Architect, which, ironically,
is the ultimate testimony to the man's genius.

The room where Snooky sits is the size of a large living room, and is
located in a building within a building that houses the hardware heart of
DEUS. Around its periphery are ten other consoles similar to his. All are
dark, because it's the night shift, and the DEUS control center is operating in "maintenance mode." Snooky resents this term. It makes him
sound like a high-tech, swing-shift janitor instead of a skilled technician.
But the truth is, he likes the solitude, which is broken only by random
checks by the security people. Snooky laughs at the checks. They are
performed by people who look like your usual corporate rent-a-cops,
but the truth is that most are Cyber Police, the company nickname for
ParaVolve's internal security organization. Often, they come in, chat,
stare at the screen, ask dumb questions, and amble on down the main
corridor. But when they look at the display, Snooky can see their eyes
snorkeling in the same kind of information he sees.

Snooky also knows the next stop on their rounds. It is the hardware
heart of DEUS, located only a few feet away on the far side of a wall filled
with acoustic and thermal insulation. Here five hundred printed circuit
boards are arranged into twenty rows, each holding twenty-five boards,
each about 360 square inches. The floor of the room is open steel grating
that allows an artificial hurricane to thunder through and remove the
heat produced by the devices mounted on the boards. In any computer,
things happen by individual transistors changing state, and every time
one does, energy is consumed and heat is produced. Currently, DEUS
contains more than a quarter trillion transistors, making it the most complex thing ever produced by humankind—and very hot.

Occasionally, in the early part of Snooky's shift, ParaVolve's "mar-
comm" person brings by small groups of people in suits with earnest
smiles pasted across their nervous faces. This gives Snooky a chance to
launch into his canned lecture and watch the nods of false acknowledgment as he describes the bowels of DEUS. In his lecture, he starts at the

bottom and works up. The fundamental building block of the system is a piece of silicon of about one square inch that contains roughly a billion transistors. Within this Lilliputian metropolis are four complete microprocessors, two vector processors, a "graphics engine," a local memory called a "cache," and an interface to the outside world. This one chip alone plunges along at 2,000 MIPS, faster than the largest mainframe computers of the previous decade.

In the next step up the hardware hierarchy, nineteen of these chips are mounted on the surface of a rectangular ceramic plate called a multichip module, along with one chip devoted exclusively to communicating with the external world. Within the multichip module are thousands of tiny metal traces that are the "wires" interconnecting the chips in patterns like arterials and freeways. In turn, seven multichip modules are mounted on one side of each printed circuit board. The other side of each board holds four circular silicon wafers, each containing a complete memory system of 3 billion bytes—enough to store thirty thousand novels. Buried within the inner layers of each board is a fantastic weave of traces that connect the memory on one side to the processing modules on the other.

Finally, there was the matter of the nanosecond, which had to be dealt with in Snooky's lecture. In the days of old, when transistors were the size of aspirin tablets, computer designers had the luxury of assuming that electrical pulses got from one place to another instantaneously. Everyone knew this wasn't really true. In fact, electromagnetic waves ripple down wires at the rate of one foot every nanosecond—one billionth of a second. Very fast. But by now, microcircuits have developed ravenous appetites for the electrical pulses that are the life substance flowing through the machine. In fact, they can now suck electrical signals through their digital digestive systems at rates measured in *picoseconds*. Incredibly fast. There are a thousand picoseconds in every nanosecond; so suddenly, the nanosecond is a very poky puppy indeed. Microchips wait idle while their next meal lopes down the wire. The only way to move things faster is to make the wires themselves shorter. Remove an inch and you shave about eighty-three picoseconds off the travel time for the data pulse that's on its way to be some little beastie's next bite of electronic lunch. Much of the DEUS design effort was dedicated to minimizing wire lengths and thereby speeding up travel times throughout the system. But ultimately, there is only so much minimizing that can be done. The next step in solving the problem was to find all the places where travel distances were very large and switch from wire to fiber optics. So the "backplanes"—the spines that bound each row of circuit boards together, along with the connections between these rows—were composed of fiber optics instead of metal. A billion words per second now cavort their way up and down these optical highways.

As he went on through the lecture, Snooky liked to watch the veil of noncompression descend silently and gracefully over the audience. His summation was the coup de grace. It caused almost everyone to slide into a comfortable mental anesthesia that protects the mind from that which it cannot intuitively embrace. In all, DEUS is composed of over a quarter million individual computers with a theoretical speed of over 2.5 million MIPS. It has 6 trillion bytes of active memory available to it, enough to retain everything ever written since the invention of writing. In "benchmarks"—performance shoot-outs with competing systems—it is over one hundred times faster than its nearest rival.

But in the end, it's what Snooky doesn't tell them that makes DEUS truly fascinating. After all, there have been many other parallel computers. In fact, Portland has been a major center for both theoretical work and commercial applications of parallel computers for more than a decade. And the basic DEUS microchip, with its four processors, comes from a commercial IC fabrication facility only a few miles way.

The secret is that DEUS is designing itself. Over and over. Better and better. The first self-evolving system ever to exist outside the biosphere.

This is the Architect's triumph. He simply provided intellectual insemination and stood back. Now the entity grows and evolves toward predetermined goals of self-improvement supplied at its conception. And in the process becomes something unknowable, beyond the grasp of the finest minds anywhere. After the first cycle of evolution, an opaque mist of astronomic complexity settled over DEUS, obscuring all but the most basic principles of its operation.

As with many historical and scientific breakthroughs, the Architect simply performed a breathtaking manipulation of existing technology and installed it as the keystone in an arch that had been under development for some time. The idea of using one generation of computers to help design the next generation extended back into the 1950s, when it became apparent that you could inject the conceptual spirit of a new computer into an existing one, which then became a sort of cerebral playground where you could fly the new design around and see how it handled—without ever actually building it. First, you used a "design entry" program, which helped you formally build a model of the new machine. As you built, the host computer digested your labors into a form understandable by a program called a logic simulator that actually flexed the electronic muscles of your new creation.

Early on, this dual process of design entry and simulation was confined to limited aspects of the new design. A widget here. A bit of code there. But by the late eighties, it had expanded to embrace the entire digital gestalt of new computer systems.

In fact, it was soon indispensable. During design sessions, engineers now rode atop huge hierarchies of circuit information comprised of systems within systems within systems. In the end, only the top few layers could be understood, and became the "black boxes" that were hooked together into new products. Everything below was immersed in a subterranean world of hopeless complexity, where millions of primitive elements carried on in a mad dance of detail.

Once the black boxes were joined into a new design, the simulator took it through its paces. The first pass usually skimmed along the top of the hierarchy and presented a rapid but comprehensive sketch of how the thing might behave in the real world. Subsequent passes began to mine the depths of the hierarchy and piled on additional detail, until even the deepest aberrations were revealed and corrected.

Soon simulators were but a small part of a large and raucous family of programs that helped engineers develop new electronic machines of ever more prodigious power. Collectively called "design automation tools," they not only took over many design tasks, but also began to produce the instructions required to physically manufacture the final product. In the case of microchips, engineers could play hook-the-boxes on a design automation system until their work was properly crafted, and then sit back while the system produced the detailed geometric maps required to guide the chip along its journey of creation at a fabrication facility. Similar systems were doing the same thing to produce tidy little silicon neighborhoods on printed circuit boards and multichip modules.

Along the way, a subtle yet crucial evolutionary frontier was crossed. Design automation tools became sufficiently intelligent to consult each other about how to shape designs. This was made possible by the appearance of very large networks that linked hundreds, even thousands of individual computer workstations into vibrant communities. At first, the tools did their consulting at the behest of their users, but their communal and social skills soon grew to the point that they did so on their own. In the process, the communications paths between tools became so complex that no one person could disentangle them, nor decipher their conversations. They held secret council and writhed to technorituals unseen, unheard, and unread.

Yet another frontier had now been crossed. Not only was the megatransistor detail of the new products beyond intellectual grasp, but also the way they were thought up in the first place. The symbiosis of man and technology had never been expressed so profoundly.

But more was on the way.

As design automation systems flourished, they spun off whole new libraries of black boxes for engineers to hook together. Like profligate transistors and tool conversations, they quickly became too numerous for human comprehension. Soon, companies began to fret about the exorbitant amounts of engineering effort required to wade through these libraries and come up with new products. At the same time, they worried that if the libraries weren't thoroughly combed, if all the possibilities weren't explored, then the quality of the design would be compromised. To counter this problem, a new generation of design automation systems came into being. Rather than hook boxes together, engineers now sat before one of the new tools and conducted what was eerily close to human dialogue. They told the system what they wanted to build, and in return, it asked them questions based upon their descriptions.

Comment: I want the machine to survive the temperature ranges encountered in outer space.

Response: That will also mean the parts will have to be radiation-hardened. It will raise the cost by 18 percent. Can you afford that?

When the system had a fuzzy but complete notion of what was to be built, it would glide through the voluminous libraries, pick out black boxes that seemed to fit the bill, hook them together, and present the results to the designers. They would assess the strengths and shortcomings of the system's work, make refinements, and send it off to the libraries again. In just a few passes, the system had almost completely designed the product and isolated the truly innovative work required of the engineers.

So now the direct role of humans in the creation of advanced electronic systems had been reduced to that of part-time collaborators at the holistic level, who supplied their expertise only when and where needed.

This is where the Architect came in. To him, the final step was now evident. In some cases, the need for humans in the design cycle was effectively over. But to close the gap, it was first necessary to produce a profoundly deep and accurate description of the electronic entity under design, a blueprint that not only dictated the thing's current powers, but also its ultimate potential, a theoretical and unreachable pinnacle, the ultimate carrot on the stick. Once complete, this body of self-knowledge took the place of the engineers. The design automation system colluded exclusively with this design knowledge base to produce the final product. In the process, it pushed as far along the path to perfection as the technology in the libraries would currently allow.

This then was how DEUS was born. The Architect developed three key pieces of software to prime the pump of perpetual design automation. One was the knowledge base that described the once and future DEUS. The second was a program that interfaced this knowledge base with the most advanced design automation system available, so conversations between the two could begin to flow.

The third piece was the most remarkable of all: the operating system, the chief minister in the court of the mad emperor. Like all the rest of DEUS, the operating system had to be self-evolving to keep pace with the evolution of the hardware. But all software, operating systems included, had shown a stubborn resistance to the powers of design automation. So once again, the Architect put a transcendental spin on existing concepts, to dance around the problem. For some time, there had been experimental research into the curious relationship between software and biological evolution. It seemed it was possible to throw programs into a sort of cybernetic jungle where natural selection took its nasty toll and left only the strongest to carry on. This artificial form of natural selection played upon recent findings in evolutionary science which indicated that you needed not only robust survivors to keep evolution chugging along, but robust predators as well. It turned out that if organisms face the same old perils continuously, they blunder into a one-way genetic cul-de-sac and lose their ability to adapt to new dangers. So the evolutionary fast track actually has two lanes, with eaters and eaten barreling along in parallel, continually testing each other's skills.

Early experiments emulated this biological drama by throwing many versions of one kind of problem into a software arena with a variety of programs designed to solve it. The rules of the game were simple: If you were a problem and easily solved, you slowly accumulated a mortal number of defeats and faded away. If you were a program and failed to solve problems, you could borrow traits at random from other programs and try to improve your prowess; but if you didn't, you were eventually retired. Eventually the computational battlefield held only the toughest programs, locked in combat with the nastiest versions of the original problem.

And once again, the borders of human comprehension were breached. The lone surviving program that crawled out of the jungle was often better than any previously designed by humans. But it was the product of millions of computational sorties and trait exchanges—and often utterly alien to those who tried to decipher its inner workings.

The Architect carefully examined this advanced form of software generation and saw a way to assimilate it into the evolutionary realm of DEUS. For years, computer labs around the world had been developing experimental operating systems to squeeze the most out of massively parallel systems. The Architect adapted the best of these to deal directly with the DEUS problem and then threw them into a gladiatorial software arena of his own making, an entire network of supercomptuers. Here they collided in deadly competition to solve the problem of running DEUS most efficiently.

By cybernetic standards it was a colossal battle that consumed more compute time than any problem ever run in the history of computer science. The final operating system that crawled off the killing floor performed magnificently—and was utterly incomprehensible, even to the Architect. But its victory would be relatively short-lived. When the next version of DEUS was synthesized by the computer's resident design automation system, it would represent a new and more vigorous problem, since its hardware would be more advanced than ever. So now the incumbent operating system would be thrown back into competition with the survivors from the original battle to struggle with the latest physical reincarnation of DEUS. In this way, the parallel lanes of the biological fast track were re-created: New versions of the problem were represented by new generations of DEUS hardware, which kept new versions of the operating system from becoming inflexible and moribund in their pursuit of the perfect solution.

Now it was time to set the beast in motion.

The original infant version of the DEUS hardware was produced by conventional means, with the Architect at the helm, hooking the symbolic boxes together using a design automation system installed on a conventional computer network. The results were shipped off to foundries that cranked out the microchips, modules, boards, and interconnect devices that made up the hardware, which were then assembled in the small room at ParaVolve. (Ironically, this room was almost identical in size to the one that contained ENIAC more than a half century before.) Next, in an elaborate ceremony, the newly minted hardware was mated with the operating system, and the infant came to life.

The final step was to grant it life everlasting. To do this, the entire engine of creation—the design automation system and knowledge base—was integrated into the DEUS environment.

Now the machine was indeed self-perpetuating. All conversations regarding its future took place within the confines of DEUS itself. As time passed, the design automation system continued to consume new black box libraries from every available source to ensure that DEUS was the best that microchip technology had to offer. The range of library searching was now global in scope. DEUS could shoot out communications tendrils over phone lines and satellites through networks that webbed the entire planet, all in search of premium technology to ply toward the next version of the machine.

Snooky turns back to his high-res display while blurting out the opening of Snake Whip's latest opus, "Twitchin' on the Wire." The green ocean surface of DEUS undulates hypnotically on the screen. Snooky knows it well. From somewhere in the recesses of the control room, a speaker oozes out a husky, digitized woman's voice:

"Snooky, sweetie, time to log in."

He grabs a headset hanging from a hook beside the console and speaks into the mike.

"Log window, please." It irks him that they wrote the I/O so you had to add "please" on the end to activate many of the commands. He is sure it is just a trick to get you to develop a little anthropomorphic respect for the thing. A window appears on the screen under the green liquid, and he files his report: "Operator 14. Normal flow parameters. No evidence of bottlenecks or chaos symptoms. Mark for voiceprint—now: Operator 14, code foxtrot alpha."

Snooky yanks off the headset and stands up to stretch. His dialogue appears as text on the window on the screen, and is joined by a voice-print waveform in a second window that verifies his identity. Both windows then disappear, leaving the green cube of ocean suspended against pure black. He ambles around the room and lazily spins the chairs in front of the darkened consoles. With a little luck and discipline, he might be able to finish up his computer science degree, go on for a master's, and come back to ParaVolve in style. The whole economy's going to shit, but this place seems to truck straight ahead. He thinks of the periodic company meetings in the company's small auditorium, where Victor Shields, ParaVolve's CEO, comes out and gives the staff a progress report. Things are going very well indeed. If you set aside the stupefying weight of DEUS's technology, the firm's business plan is relatively simple. Every so often, DEUS will be "frozen" in its current state of evolution, which will then be translated into a version of the machine that can be manufactured in quantity and sold as the fastest, most formidable supercomputer in the world. The machine will then be released to continue its evolutionary journey until enough new demand is generated to justify freezing once again. But right now, DEUS is considered still to be in a state of rapid growth, which the engineers are reluctant to interrupt, so it has yet to be frozen. The details that Shields provides are sketchy at best, mostly because of the obsessively tight security around the true nature of the project. To the outside world, DEUS is just one of many parallel computers struggling in an overcrowded marketplace, although there have been some tantalizing hints in the press from time to time about a "self-perpetuating machine."

Snooky returns to his chair, plops down, rubs his eyes, and yawns. As he removes his hands, he instantly notices something wrong on the display. To the untrained eye, it would be invisible, but Snooky reads it like a surgeon reading an X ray. Normally, the top of the green DEUS ocean looks like water on the surface of a swimming pool in a gentle breeze. Little waves are generated, bounce off the sides of the pool, and intersect one another, creating a busy but benign pattern. But now on the DEUS ocean there is a little more chop than there should be, a little too much distance between the troughs and peaks of the waves. He grabs the headset and speaks abruptly into the mike. "Upper right quadrant." The display zooms in to magnify this portion of the ocean, and now the waves look much more menacing. Worse yet, the sea is getting rougher right before his eyes.

Goddamn. This would have to happen on his shift. He can't even imagine what is going on underneath the ocean, where the real depth of DEUS is. The surface is merely an indication of traffic flow. But underneath, it looks like a quarter of a million computers may be heading toward total anarchy—the equivalent of a massive mental breakdown, a plunge into acute psychosis.

Even as he zooms back out to a full view of the ocean, the storm builds. In no time at all, it looks like a swimming pool during a 9.0 earthquake.

10

God the Son

Victor Shields stands in the study of his very large and very expensive home in West Linn, south of Portland. The house is over six thousand square feet, not counting the three-car garage and a tiny yard composed mostly of hardy shrubs and bark dust. Victor is sipping cautiously at a glass of Glenfiddich on the rocks and staring down at the cars parked in a driveway across the street. One is an old Ford station wagon with a crunched rear quarter panel. The other is a Chevy minivan with a primered gray passenger door and bald tires. Victor knows that inside the garage at the head of this driveway are a late-model BMW, a new Lexus minivan, and a perfectly preserved Mazda Miata. The garage is part of a house equal in scope and value to Victor's, with security lights illuminating the perfunctory bark dust and token front lawn.

It occurs to Victor that this big new house infested by the beat-up old cars is a perfect visual representation of the problem now facing the neighborhood. He has just returned from an evening meeting at the Bronsons' next door, a meeting that went far later than expected and ended on the same sullen note it had started. The problem, of course, is what was now referred to as the New Renters. Before the Downturn, StoneTree had been a typical upscale residential respite for executives floating through the upper strata of the local business community. Forty-two houses, a community pool and tennis courts, private security, and limited access through a gated and guarded entrance. But now, of course,

the upper executive strata was beset by severe turbulence, and many of
its occupants were making forced landings, including a large number of
the residents of StoneTree. And if you were among the victims, you were
suddenly confronted with a crushing mortgage payment on a house that
was now rapidly deflating in value. So what do you do with six thousand
square feet and no income? When all the more genteel alternatives failed,
you realized that your house was, in effect, two houses, and that you
could become a landlord. Ten of the forty-two StoneTree houses were
now dual occupancy, and the number continued to grow.

The more fortunate residents of StoneTree looked on in a state of
compassion mixed with horror. On the one hand, they knew they might
be the next to fall from corporate grace, and understood the bleak
desperation that came with the tumble. On the other hand, their neighborhood was now becoming thoroughly compromised in terms of "life-
style," a euphemistic term used to describe the perquisites of class. There
was legal action that could be taken, but in this time of crisis, there were
strong currents of populism coursing through the city, and no one
wanted publicity that would make the neighborhood a target for "political action." At the Bronsons' they had gone through the whole business
yet again, and had reached no resolution about their next move.

Victor drained the last of the Scotch, and pondered getting another.
This would be unusual for him. At forty-five, he carefully watched his
weight, his drinking, his exercise. The only thing that belied his age were
the tiny flecks of gray in his dark brown hair. As president of ParaVolve,
it was important for him to maintain an image of youth and vigor, the
persona of a high-tech-business warrior chief. But every so often, he
would inadvertently plunge into a state of introspection and confront the
shabby truth behind his success. To his credit, he was moderately intelligent. And yes, he had some modest business talent. And therein was
the horror of it all. Because it meant he should probably be moderately
successful in a modest position at a mediocre company. Except for the
luck. A couple of major breaks early in his career gave him a résumé of
solid gold, and he had traded heavily on it ever since. Now, in this time
of economic terror, he knew that one good kick would send his whole
facade crashing down. And then he would be welcoming the New Renters into his home, reluctantly showing them how to adjust the thermo-
stat on the indoor hot tub.

Just as Victor goes for his second Scotch, the phone rings. No one ever phones this late, so maybe it's an emergency. He secretly welcomes the possibility because it might send him off on a new vector, away from the Downturn and the New Renters. Instead, it's ParaVolve.

"Mr. Shields, this is Snooky Larsen on the night shift. Sorry to bother you this late, but we've got a problem over here, and the book says I should contact you."

Victor tries to put a face with the voice and fails. "If the book says it's OK, it's OK. What's going on?"

"Well, about ten minutes ago, the whole system went chaotic on me. It's all over the map."

Victor sags into a chair. This wasn't the kind of emergency he had in mind. "Is it staying that way?"

"Yep. Never seen anything like it. Haven't got any idea how to read it."

Victor rustles around inside his executive facade and frantically nails up a front of calm authority. "OK, here is what we're going to do. First, don't try to take any corrective action on your own. I'm going to bring in the Shock Team. Just sit tight until they get there. Got it?"

"Got it," replies Snooky. The Shock Team is a group of computer scientists and technicians who are trained to take drastic intervention measures if it looks like DEUS is going to crash.

Victor hangs up and then calls the leader of the Shock Team. Holy shit! Could anything be worse? Probably not. He knows the great vulnerability of DEUS is its lack of external dialogue about its internal evolution. It the thing dies, there will be no way on earth to retrace its self-propelled evolutionary steps to its present state.

So then, what the hell's wrong with the goddamn thing? He curses his lack of background in computer science. He can't even begin to understand how the thing works. He thinks of all the times he nodded knowingly in the meetings, with his best look of deep and unquestionable comprehension. All bullshit. All manufactured on the spot by Victor of the Golden Résumé. But wait. What about Application X? He sees a small light of hope. Application X might be his way out. It is a highly secret program that has been running on DEUS for some time. Called a "benchmark," it is designed specifically to test the skill of DEUS doing real-world work that can be compared with that of other supercomputers. Usually it involves tasks such as modeling the internal mechanics of thunderstorms or the aerodynamics of orbital reentry vehicles. In any case, it is eventually used as a marketing tool to sing the praises of a machine's computational prowess in confrontations with rival systems. And since benchmarks cut to the core of the matter and tend to negate more ambitious marketing claims, they are tightly guarded secrets until a system is tightly tuned and ready to go public. Nevertheless, the exceptional nature of the DEUS project has generated even more secrecy than usual surrounding the identity of the benchmark program. Its true nature was known only to a few key technical people and no one else, not even Victor. All he knows is that it's in there somewhere, snaking around among the quarter million processors.

If it was Application X that caused the current problem, he was halfway off the hook. Other people would have to explain why a hundred million dollars' worth of research and development had evaporated in a cloud of algorithmic psychosis.

But regardless of the cause, he has one more phone call to make. The chairman must be notified immediately.

At this point, Victor decides maybe he will have that second Scotch after all.

In McLean, Counterpoint turns into his driveway and touches a button under the dash that slings a signal through the night to open the heavy wrought-iron gate that blocks his driveway. Silently, the double gate doors part and he drives through. By now, a computer in the garage has been alerted by the gate's computer and the door is open by the time he arrives. The thrill from the nocturnal hunt in the park has now attenuated as he enters the house.

Already, he can see the light on in the kitchen and knows that his wife is up. He also knows exactly where she will be, what she is doing, and what she will say to him. His wife. More rudely, his rich wife, thoroughly marinated in family money, softened almost to the point of dissolving into a kind of maudlin soup. Sure enough, she is seated in the breakfast nook in a five-hundred-dollar housecoat, clasping a gin and tonic with thin white fingers.

"Bill, you're just working too hard, dear." The booze blunts the corners of her speech as she addresses him by his given name, Bill; Mr. William Daniels to the world at large. "We don't need the money. You know that. You know that—don't you?"

He bends over and kisses her quickly on the forehead. "I do know that, dear. And pretty soon, I'll have things arranged so we can spend more time doing the things that *we* want to do. But you've got to hang in there with me for a while, OK?"

He lifts her to her feet and leads her up the stairs to their bedroom. "You didn't have to wait up for me. You have to make enough sacrifices as it is." He helps her out of the housecoat and into bed and she turns to him.

"I almost forgot, you got a package delivered here." She looses focus and then drifts back. "Yes, a package. I left it on your desk."

Good, he thinks, an excuse to get out of here. "Well, maybe I better see what it is." He gives her another brief kiss. "You go ahead and get some sleep. I'll be up in a minute."

"Bill," she says as she wraps the blanket of booze over her, "did I tell you you work too hard?"

"Yes, you did." He throws her an understanding smile as an exit ploy and heads down the stairs.

The package is on the corner of his desk, in an unmarked pouch lined with plastic air cells. He tears it open and pulls out a videocassette. There is no message and no label identifying the contents of the tape. He takes it to a room where a panel of entertainment electronics lines one entire wall. He pops the cassette into a receptacle, and various displays spring to life in greens, ambers, and reds. As he goes to sit down, the system speaks to him.

"Standard settings?"

"Standard settings," he replies. The system now adjusts the video and audio parameters to his particular choices, and activates the high-res video screen. And there is Simon Greeley, his head bobbing rhythmically as he sits in the Hart Building listening to a question from Senator Grisdale.

"Have you discovered anything unusual in these budgets that might be of particular interest to this committee?"

Counterpoint watches in fascination as the horrible smile contorts Simon's face and the laughter erupts and fills the room. He is elated. It works! The first true application, after years of research. The team Farmacéutico has come through and delivered in a time of need. Greeley's testimony will now be seen as that of someone with a profound neurological disorder, someone traveling far outside the bounds of credibility.

"Data window," he snaps at the system, which freezes the video image of Simon and obliges Counterpoint by bringing up a window with a list of files identified by strings of letters and numbers. "Open AA34501."

A second window opens and reveals a long list of names and matching social security numbers. Counterpoint and his associates have spent years compiling this list, which crosses the entire political and social spectrums, and identifies key individuals who might be serious obstacles to the grand plan that is now beginning to unfold. Spelvin's latest achievement finally gives them a means to safely pare the list down, one individual at a time. A quick virus here. A slow virus there. All beyond the remedies of contemporary medicine and untraceable in terms of their origin. Of course, there would be a fuss with the Centers for Disease Control from time to time, but normal epidemiological procedures would be completely impotent and the investigations would soon languish for a lack of leads. . . .

The system abruptly superimposes an icon of a phone over the list and announces: "You have an incoming phone call from the residential phone of a Mr. Victor Shields."

"Video?"

"No. Audio only."

It must be bad news, muses Counterpoint. The chickenshit would use video if he had something to crow about, so I could see his smiling idiot face.

"Speaker on," commands Counterpoint, and the connection is made live into the room.

"So, Victor," opens Counterpoint, "why a call at this particular hour?"

The instant Victor starts to speak, Counterpoint can hear the clench of anxiety drive up the pitch of his voice. "Bill, we've got a problem with DEUS. I've already activated the Shock Team, but we don't have any hard information yet. The night technician said the thing just suddenly went into chaos. That's all I know until the team reports in. I thought you'd want to know right away."

Counterpoint feels the shock grip his stomach and race up his throat. It couldn't be worse. True, they had anticipated this happening, and even worked out a contingency plan, but since the system was so absorbed in its internal dialogue, it was almost impossible to even know where to begin to intervene.

Unless, of course, someone had intervened to cause the breakdown in the first place.

The Architect! The fucking Architect! He was already holding them all hostage, so what was to stop him?

But then again, would he murder his own cybernetic child? Probably not, since his whole bargaining position rests on keeping it healthy. But who knows? Maybe he's beyond bargaining.

"Has anybody informed our chief designer about this yet?" inquires Counterpoint.

Victor winces. He should have thought about this and had a snappy answer. "I'll check on that right away. He comes on the system now and then to keep the bomb quiet, so he probably knows by now. He might even—" Victor stops in midsentence. Of course! He might even be the cause. Once again, Victor looks like an idiot in front of his boss. "I'll step up security around his place and have somebody monitor his line constantly."

"I want a full report on this in the morning. If there is any change, let me know immediately," orders Counterpoint.

Victor signs off with a weak good-night. Counterpoint slumps into the solitary silence and feels a dull painful throbbing from his swollen crotch. The park, the boy, the orgasmic release, the berserk machine, and the mad Architect all dance wildly about in the darkness of his soul.

The key is gone.

Jimi Tyler feels the small rip in his front jeans pocket. It is precisely where he carefully pins the key to his pocket lining every morning. Life without the key is hard to imagine, because it opens the door to his apartment during the times when his mom is not there, and these times are now more random and prolonged than ever.

Jimi suddenly becomes aware of what a terminal barrier the door really is, massive and gray in the early evening light, with a stylized "4" mounted high above him. He could kick it until his foot bone shattered and it would remain absolutely unmoved. He turns and looks toward the guest parking and the carport, where a young man is changing the oil in an old Korean sedan. One of the spent cans is knocked over and a little river of residual oil is trickling out, but the young man ignores it. For Jimi, the world has gone sharply binary, inside the door and outside the door. And now he feels a soft stroke of panic traverse his spine, because he knows the outside world is capable of swallowing him whole, without pity, without hesitation.

But it's OK. His dad will come. And his dad probably even has one of those trick lock picks, so the apartment door will be open in just a couple of seconds.

A familiar pickup pulls into the carport, the muffled pulse of the Grateful Dead coming from within. Michael Riley.

Jimi hesitates as Michael gets out and heads for the stairs. Riley is OK, but he probably doesn't want to help little kids who screw up and lose the key to their apartment. But Michael solves the problem by spotting him and waving.

"Jimi! How are you today, young sir?"

"Well, maybe not so good, Mr. Riley."

Michael stops and walks over to him. "And what might the problem be, my man?"

"I lost my key. I can't get in."

"Well, when will your mom be home?" Michael stops. Bad mistake. What can the kid say? He quickly fills the painful silence.

"You know where I was today? I was at Oaks Park, because they're shooting a movie scene there. Do you know about Oaks Park?"

Jimi brightens. Yes, he knows Oaks Park, the old amusement park down along the river. Neon lights, cotton candy, neat old rides, slick new rides.

"Yup, I know about it."

"Well, suppose we leave your mom a note, and go over there while we're waiting for her." Michael is improvising, but it seems like the best move. It wouldn't do to have a little kid hanging out in his bachelor's apartment. "I tell you what. Just give me a minute and I'll be right back down."

Michael ascends the stairs to his place. What the hell, he didn't really have anything better to do tonight. And the kid needed a break. So why not?

Inside his apartment, he checks his answering machine, and his eye catches a book on biochemistry, one of Jessica's. Maybe she might want to go with them. Deep inside, he feels a gate begin to swing shut, but before it can close entirely, he is on the phone to her.

"Jessica, this is Michael Riley. I want to thank you again for the books.

Look, something's come up and I could use your help if you're loose tonight. I've got this kid from downstairs who's locked out of his place, and I've got to entertain him for a while, so I thought we'd shoot over to Oaks Park. Problem is, I'm not exactly Mr. Parent, and I could use a little support. You care to come along?"

Yes. She said yes. Just like that. Michael felt the whole evening crank up a couple notches. Sometimes the best plans are the ones that just make themselves.

Michael and Jimi cross the Sellwood Bridge and turn into the long access road to Oaks Park. The windows are open in Michael's pickup, and Jimi basks in the warm breeze. The big gray door is forgotten. Soon they are in the parking lot of Oaks Park. Ahead, Jimi can see the swirl of color and the random motion of people ambling along the asphalt midway. Oaks Park has the texture of kid's Silly Putty after all the colors have randomly mixed into a single lump. Over a century of entertainment technology is randomly represented among the old oak trees along the river. Ferris wheels next to figure-eight gravitrons, 3-D video games adjacent to shooting galleries. All classes, all cultures wander through the maze of rides, games, and concessions. Street gangs, average white men, single moms, Asian patriarchs, black hipsters, neo-beatniks, and trolling teenagers all bump along in a great Brownian motion of humanity.

"So what do you think, big guy?" asks Michael as they leave the pickup and head toward the midway.

"Sweet," says Jimi, "really sweet."

Ahead, Michael spots Jessica by the old merry-go-round, which lumbers along with its horses and ostriches held in eternal orbit, their wooden bodies plastered with endless coats of colored enamel. Even at this distance, you can't miss her, Michael notes. She's just too goddamn striking. In the end, it's got to be a curse. No anonymity. Not ever.

Jessica puts on an anxious smile as she sees them approach. She notices that the little boy is holding Michael's hand, and somehow knows that Michael probably isn't even aware of it. She's not sure she should have done this, but now that she sees the two of them together, she feels much better about it. The boy will be a buffer, and a delightful one at that.

"Jessica, I'd like you to meet Jimi Tyler."

"Hi, Jimi."

Jimi looks up at the pretty lady who extends her hand to shake his. She's smiling, but somehow she's sad, too.

"It's nice of you to join us on such short notice," says Michael as they start down the midway, going nowhere in particular.

"I'm glad you asked. I get caught up in work and forget to get out if someone doesn't prompt me. As a matter of fact, I've got to get back in an hour or two and finish a report for the morning. Sorry I can't stay longer."

"No problem," says Michael, "we're just glad you could make it." He looks down at Jimi. "Hey, pal, what ride do you want to do?"

"The Ferris wheel," Jimi replies without hesitation.

"Then the Ferris wheel it is," pronounces Michael. He can't help but like this kid's directness and intelligence. There's a strength there that he feels is absent within himself.

A short walk and a couple of tickets later, the Ferris wheel is lifting them above the oaks and into a twinkling twilight, with the downtown skyline rising above the cityscape along the river. Jimi sits between the two of them and feels an unfamiliar sense of security. For some reason, he thinks of the batteries nestled together in the back of his electronic toys, all snug and proper, each knowing its duty and purpose.

As their chair crests over the top of the wheel's arc, Michael turns to Jessica. "Did you grow up here?" he inquires.

She looks down at her lap, ignoring the beautiful black and silver ripple of the river as the chair descends toward the green canopy of oak. "No, I came here from the Bay area." She says it in a way which suggests that's as far as she cares to go with it now.

Michael reads the signal, and covers. "Yeah, I'm from out of town, too."

"From where?"

"Washington, D.C."

"And what did you do there?"

"I was in computers." Boy, was I ever.

"And now you do sound for movies?"

"And now I do sound for movies," he echoes just as the wheel stops to let them off.

As they stroll back down the midway, Jimi walks in the middle, holding onto Michael. Then Jessica feels him grab her hand, too. A flood of warmth goes through her, and she wonders if it's from Jimi, or if he is simply conducting Michael to her. Here they were, a strange little de facto nuclear family, temporarily wired together by some incomprehensible fate. Ah, well, why not? She likes the feel of Jimi's firm grip and only wishes she could reciprocate. But she can't and holds loosely to him.

"Where we going now?" asks Jimi.

"We're walking Jessica to her car because she has to go now."

Jimi looks up at Jessica with genuine disappointment. "Are you sure?"

And suddenly she's not so sure. And just as suddenly, she feels her hand gripping his in unmistakable affection. Now, where did *that* come from? Deep down she knows, but doesn't want to confront it because the lid of repression isn't screwed on so tightly anymore. The bolts have been corroded by age and turned into red sand that crumbles at the touch of this child with his irresistible combination of strength and vulnerability.

"Well, maybe I can stay long enough for us to get some pop. OK?"

Michael and Jessica sit at a dime-sized metal table in a concessions booth and sip soft drinks under the pallor of neon. Both are watching Jimi, who is happily playing a video game in an arcade directly across the midway.

"What's his mother like?" asks Jessica.

"Don't know for sure, but the word around the Romona is that she's a real hard case. That's why he's with us tonight. She's gone. He's home alone. Tough. But what are you gonna do?"

"Hard to say. He's special, you know that?"

Michael crumbles his straw sleeve into a tiny ball and admires his handiwork. "Yeah. I guess I do know that. You feel it too, huh?" He grins at her. "Must be the mom in you."

Jessica abruptly pushes her chair back, grabs her purse, and stands. "Gotta go now."

After they take Jessica to her car, Jimi talks Michael into one more stroll down the midway, to the very end, where they didn't go before. "And I want a ride," he commands.

"What do you mean you want a ride?" probes Michael. "Which ride? There's rides all over here."

Jimi looks at him with disgust. "No. Not those. A ride on your shoulders."

So Michael scoops him up and starts off. Jimi is surprisingly light as he embraces Michael about the forehead. The entire experience is novel to Michael, something seen in the movies, but never done. Suddenly, one hand leaves the forehead and points to a large neon sign on a rambling old building at the end of the midway: THE REALIES.

Michael feels Jimi bounce on his shoulders with excitement. "It's the realies! Can we do the realies? Can we?"

"Well . . . OK," replies Michael, who reads the marquis underneath the neon sign, which shouts:

NEW SHOW THIS WEEK

ROBOSAUR ADVENTURE

He takes Jimi off his shoulders and they enter the building, where Michael uses his UniCharge card to buy tickets from the Autocashier. The building is built as a roller-skating rink, with an immense wooden floor, and was still used for that purpose in the afternoons. But in the evenings it hosted the most advanced entertainment technology available outside of Tokyo and Singapore. Originally called virtual reality, it was now called simply "the realies."

Once inside, Michael and Jimi look out on the huge floor and see a score of randomly scattered figures. Each has on a black suit that is pressure-pumped to contour to the human body, and wears black gloves. On their backs are book-sized packs containing XLSI microcomputers with thin cables that disappear up into the rafters. Each also has a helmet with internal earphones and thick black goggles containing two miniature cathode ray tubes, and a weapon that appears to be a formless mold of some automatic combat rifle. While the insectlike costumes are strange, it is the stilted choreography of the players that strikes Michael. They walk in a cautious crouch, looking from side to side, then suddenly raise their rifles and silently fire at invisible targets, all the while yelling warnings to their companions.

At the first sight of the mock guns, Michael feels slightly sick. But then again, it's all fantasy, right? And Jimi looks like he will be beyond consolation if they don't go through with it. So they go to the checkout booth, get their gear, and suit up in the locker room.

"Have you ever done this?" Michael asks Jimi.

"No," answers Jimi, "but Rat Bag has, and he told us all about it."

"Which kid is Rat Bag?" Michael asks. Outside of Jimi, the other kids at the Romona blur into a large, homogeneous, noisy tribe for him.

"He's the bigger kid."

Jimi obviously feels this is description enough, and Michael inquires no further. He checks Jimi's gear and they go out into the room to the main floor entrance. Here an aging punker with a salt-and-pepper mohawk connects their backpacks to the ceiling cables. His face is creased in a permanent scowl. "House rules say you can't touch other players or fire at them. Vacate the floor immediately when your time expires. Have a good game." He says it all in a mechanical, nasal voice as Michael and Jimi enter the floor. They walk to an isolated section, many yards from the other suited players.

"You ready, partner?" Michael asks Jimi.

"Yup. Are you?"

"We'll find out real quick," he says as they both don their helmets. *Boom!*

They are on a boulder-strewn plain, an illustrated world somewhere between comic books and reality. The sky is a uniform, featureless orange from one horizon to the other. The ground is perfectly flat and dull purple, and littered with angular gray boulders, some taller than a man. Michael looks down at Jimi. His suit is now studded with winking, blinking gadgetry set into armor plating, and his helmet has a full faceplate that obscures his features. The rifle mold is now some kind of wicked automatic weapon with an exotic scope mounted on top. Michael holds up his own hand and sees he is wearing the same kind of armor and holding the same kind of weapon, only scaled up to his size.

To Michael, the sudden lurch from real to virtual reality is disconcerting and disorienting. But not to Jimi. "Let's get moving," he says.

As they weave among the boulders, Michael is surprised at how fast the old reality melts away and the new one supplants it. They come to the edge of the boulders and view a featureless purple desert that stretches to infinity. Just then, there is a shattering roar.

"It's behind us!" yells Jimi as Michael whirls to look in his direction. Over the tops of the boulders, a hellish mechanical beast appears, a dinosaur with hide fashioned from metal plates, and hundreds of huge chrome teeth. Without hesitation the thing lunges and snaps at them, razor teeth flashing and gleaming in the orange alien light. Michael ducks down behind a boulder with Jimi and hugs its surface. The sensation is strange, because the suit exerts pressure where the rock should be, but since the rock is not really there, it offers no support. The monster roars and lunges again, its lower jaw thrusting right over their heads and plunging them into shadow. Michael hears a sharp crack and sees a miniature explosion on the underside of the jaw that produces a smoking crater of molten metal. With a scream, the huge head thrusts upward and backward.

"Got him!"

Michael turns and sees that Jimi has fired his weapon. He stands up and peeks cautiously over the top of the boulder. The monster is lumbering off, the hiss of its pneumatic joints receding into the distance. "Good going, Jimi," he offers, embarrassed that he didn't have the presence of mind to fire his own weapon. Before Jimi can reply, an entire chorus of roars rattles among the boulders. Michael takes another peek and sees there are three more of the creatures closing in on them from different directions. He now realizes they have the desert to their backs and are finished if the creatures force them out onto it. Once again, he hears a crack and sees a pencil-sized yellow flash wing by the middle monster's head as it threads its way through the boulders.

"C'mon, we gotta shoot!" urges Jimi. Michael slowly raises his weapon and takes aim at the monster on the left. He fires wildly, and a beam clears the thing's head by at least a yard. He fires again and comes within a foot of the leg. It is now close enough that Michael gets a sense of its true size: fifty feet tall. He is momentarily distracted by another "Got him!" by Jimi, and turns to see pinkish lava pouring out of the metallic cavity that moments ago was the eye socket of the middle monster.

As he turns his attention back to the left monster, he is startled by how close it is, only ten yards off. He must fire again immediately, and he cannot afford to miss. He aims toward the chest area, between the two spindly upper arms, and fires.

Then it all comes apart.

The beam flashes out, misses the chest, and hits the shoulder joint connecting the right upper arm to the body. The severed arm tumbles toward the purple ground, and the monster shudders to a halt. As the arm hits the ground, the monster begins to convulse wildly, and Michael watches the shoulder wound, waiting for the smoking crater or the pink lava. Instead, a fountain of blood sprays out. Bright red blood. Human blood. All over the boulders. All over Michael. At the same time, the monster's coal-red reptile eyes become soft blue human eyes and it screams at Michael.

"Fucker! Look at me! Fucker!"

Some autonomous subroutine deep in Michael takes over. He drops the weapon, pivots, and runs out into the desert. He barely sees the flashing red letters that appear in space immediately in front of him:

STOP!

BOUNDARY IN 5 FT.

Wham! There is a crushing pain as he hits an invisible barrier, and everything goes black.

Blind! I'm blind!

But then he feels the presence of the helmet, the suit. He rips off the helmet with his heart slamming through his brain. He fumbles at the zipper of the suit. He doesn't even notice that he has collided with the wall at the edge of the floor.

"You stupid shit! Can't you read? Didn't you see the boundary sign?" The old punker is trotting toward him across the wooden floor as Michael frantically shakes the suit off.

"I've got to get out of here!"

"Well, you got that much right, pal!" The old punker is surprisingly strong as he pulls Michael to his feet and leads him off the floor.

The floor, the punker, the insectlike players all recede into the distance as he swims through a quivering sea of adrenaline. The Fear. He breaks the punker's grip and sprints for the exit. Outside will be better. Space. Air.

Out on the midway, he finds a bench underneath one of the oaks. The REALIES neon turns everything light salmon and the world does a drunken spin. The noise of the crowd crisscrosses through the center of him. Then a single voice pushes into the forefront.

"Are you OK?"

He looks up. Jimi is standing before him. "The man said you freaked out," says Jimi solemnly.

The world's spin slows.

"Yeah, I guess the man's right. I freaked out," says Michael wearily. He is too weakened to mount a defense.

"Were you scared of the monsters?"

"I'm not sure. Something happened that I don't understand."

"Well, lots of things happen that I don't understand," offers Jimi.

"And do you get scared sometimes?" asks Michael.

"Yup. Sometimes."

"And what do you do about it?"

Jimi sits down beside Michael. "I wait for my dad to come. If it gets too bad, he's going to show up and kick ass."

The spinning stops. The adrenaline tide ebbs. Michael breathes deeply and sits in silence beside Jimi.

At the Romona, the lights are on in unit four, and Michael lets Jimi go ahead by himself. He has no desire to deal with Jimi's mom and one of her asshole boyfriends. He watches Jimi go inside, walks to the swimming pool, and pauses at its edge.

"Who goes there?"

Michael immediately recognizes the voice and sees the dark figure in one of the lounge chairs near the pool. It is Eric. Eric Who Never Was.

"Michael Riley goes here, Eric. How are you?"

"Some day we'll meet again."

"I'm sure we will. Right here, maybe."

"Pass the orange-handled screwdriver, please."

"Can't find it out here in the dark, Eric."

"Well, then, get out the fuckin' nightscope."

From behind, Michael hears a screen door slam. He turns and sees Eric's sister Brenda coming toward the pool area.

"Come on, Eric. It's time to get a little rest. Hello, Michael."

Brenda is fifty-five years old, three years older than Eric. She is wrapped in an oversized bathrobe and takes small mincing steps in her furry slippers. Brenda and Eric have been here longer than anyone, including Dolores, can remember. Everyone knew their story. Eric was a combat veteran from the Gulf War who was wounded in a covert operation and discharged slightly thereafter. But after surviving numerous lethal encounters behind enemy lines in the war, Eric got blazing drunk in a topless bar two weeks after returning stateside and slammed his motorcycle into a retaining wall. He came out of the coma a month later and exhibited what the doctors delicately described as some "neurological dysfunction." What this meant was that since brains are incredibly complex, so are brain injuries, especially those involving the higher functions; and therefore no better description of his problem was forthcoming.

Shortly thereafter, Brenda came to the Vet's hospital and took Eric off to the Romona Arms. Some things he remembered, like Brenda; and some not, like most of the war. While he eventually was able to eat and take care of himself, he remained fragmented, like a schizophrenic, only without the paranoia. In time, some of his old army buddies came by to visit, and one of them made a comment to Brenda that stuck permanently.

"You know, this person I'm talking to now isn't really like Eric at all," he said. "It's more like an Eric who never was."

Eric Who Never Was shied away from social situations because his conversations quickly became derailed. In the end, he came out only late at night, or early in the morning, when the apartment grounds were deserted.

Now Eric rises from his chair to follow Brenda.

Michael smiles. "We'd like to see more of you folks, Brenda."

"We'll try, Michael."

She patters off with Eric following on an invisible leash. Michael yawns and heads for the stairs once more. On the way up, he reflects on the metal beast spurting blood, the purple ground, the orange sky. It could be worse, he thinks. I could be like Eric, where all reality is virtual.

The Architect pours the last of the bottle of Cutty Sark into a Styrofoam cup and looks at the car in the convenience store parking lot across the street. On the TV, Big Boy Bill hawks cars by extending a bulky arm and plunging a bayonet into the top of an old convertible while promising to "slash prices to an all-time low."

"Are you sedentary fascist assholes?" the Architect asks out loud to the car across the street. "Or are you guardian angels in disguise?" He raises his cup to salute the vehicle, and wobbles onto shaky legs. "Come forth into the light and be revealed. Show yourselves to me."

He drops the cup, spilling its contents over his half-eaten Chinese takeout dinner, and lurches to the door and down the steps. Out in the warm night air, he braces himself on the hood of a car in the restaurant parking lot. Across the street he sees the driver get out of the parked car

at the convenience store and look at him over the roof. He waves enthu-
siastically at the man, who does not respond, and then starts across the
street in a stupefied zombie walk. Fortunately, traffic is light and weaves
around him. As he approaches the parked car, the driver continues to
stare at him over the roof, and the passenger window comes down, revealing a second man. Both are in their fattened fifties, with prominent
bellies protruding from cheap sports coats. One has a crew cut with
sideburns. The other, a gray fringe around a bald top.

"Gentlemen, gentlemen," the Architect says. "How can we be so near
in distance, yet so far in spirit? It's high time we entered into a meaningful dialogue, don't you think?"

He reaches the car, opens the rear door on the passenger side, and
slides into the backseat. The bald man twists in his seat to follow the
motion, and the crew cut ducks down to peer through his open door.
Neither says a word, but both are visibly distressed. There is no standing
order to cover a situation like this.

"To show my goodwill, I'm going to give you a priceless gift," announces the Architect. "I'm going to give you the gift of purpose, something that many go their whole lives without. To begin, I ask you this:
Why are you here? Why do you watch over me with such devotion and
professionalism?"

Silence.

"You see?" continues the Architect. "You're at a loss, a painful loss.
Everyday you come here. Why? Because somebody *told* you to? Because
they give you *money* for your time? It's not enough. Not nearly enough.
Because there is no purpose in it. No grand design. No sense of partici-
pation in a magnificent drama of the highest order. And that's what this
is, gentlemen. Make no mistake. A drama of the highest order."

He slides out the door on the passenger side, unzips his trousers, and
begins to urinate. The bald man can see a small streamlet begin to snake
its way toward the curb.

"Do you know who I am? Well, let me tell you. I am the Architect. The
Architect of the calculating machine that grows itself at the center of your
company. The machine that fuels the very life of the corporation, the
sine qua non of the enterprise. I am God the Father, the creator, and in
my image is God the Son, the Cybernetic Son who blesses you all with
your livelihood. But the truth, known to very few, is that God the Son is
really a mother, the mother of my child."

He climbs back into the car. "But like many other high-tech fathers and founders, once the project was complete, I was cast out to wander in the suburban wilderness. But I foresaw this day, and created a very special umbilical cord between myself and my machine. Deep in its bowels is a bomb, a software bomb, waiting to explode if I don't keep in touch with it at least once every twenty-four hours.

"So there, gentlemen, there is your gift of purpose. You watch over me, and in turn, I watch over my creation. Good night."

The Architect pulls himself out of the car and rambles back to his apartment. The bald fringe and the crew cut say nothing.

In his apartment, the Architect wades through the mounting mess in his living room to his computer.

"Time to say howdy," he mutters as the graphical interface comes up and he slips on the headset. He then goes through the iconic figures, through Porky, Roger Daltrey, Madonna, and the cop. Finally, he reaches his self image, his agent within DEUS.

"Bob," says the self image, "how are you?"

"I'm in torment, my friend. But never mind that. I'm just checking in."

"We're glad you did," says the self image. "All of us in here would be lost without you. You know that, don't you?"

"Yes, I do. Is there anything to report?" This was a routine question. The Architect has numerous barriers inside the system to repel the relentless probing of the Cyber Cops, and he continually analyzes their actions in order to improve his defenses.

"Yes, Bob," replies the self image. "There's a problem with the Holy Ghost. It nearly brought us down."

Nearly brought us down. Twin alarms go off in the Architect. First, a problem with the Holy Ghost is the one kind that may be completely beyond his reach, out where the march of logic decomposes into the amorphous churning of true consciousness. Second, the interface program has never been programmed to say those words.

Somehow, it seems to be acting on its own.

11

The Funeral

Gail Ambrose stands on the outer periphery of the funeral party as the minister reads the graveside passages to send Simon Greeley into the afterlife. The crowd is mostly middle-aged, predominantly male, and dressed in dark blue suits. The day is warm and the humidity is pumping stickiness into the air. She will be glad to get out of the sun as soon as possible. Nevertheless, she felt she owed it to Simon to be here. His attempt to go before Grisdale's committee had been an extraordinary act of courage in a time more known for Byzantine intrigues than personal heroism.

After the horrible scene in the hearing room, she had helped Barbara Greeley get him down the hall to the security office. Strange, she thought, it's just like those infamous episodes in New York in which someone is stricken on the sidewalk and no one will help. The two women had propped up the shuddering man and struggled down the hall with him while scores of people carefully kept a wide berth and averted their eyes, as if they had failed to notice. When the ambulance arrived, Barbara went with Simon while Gail took their car, which was just about to be towed from the front of the Hart Building.

When Simon was in the emergency room, she sat with Barbara until Barbara's sister could get there from Georgetown. Barbara told Gail the little she knew about what Simon planned to tell the committee. Unfortunately, it was no more than Gail already knew.

Simon lasted only five days in the hospital, and she had called every day to check on his condition. Eventually the disease began to devour his autonomic functions and he could breathe only by respirator. What had once been the mind of Simon Greeley was now pretty much scoured out. Barbara told the doctors to suspend artificial life support, and he was gone in minutes.

Now the minister finishes the rites, and they begin to lower the casket. Gail turns to leave before the crowd disperses. On the way to her car, a nagging image pops into her mind, one that persists in presenting itself at odd times.

It is the image of Simon just before he entered the hearing room, saying, "Maybe poisoned. Not sure."

In the evening at OHSU, Jessica looks out the window of her lab and can see the shadow of the West Hills send the east side of the city into partial eclipse. She is working late, but then again, she is always working late. The difference is that for the first time in a long time, she is questioning why she does it. The view of the city from this window used to seem flat, abstract, merely a decorative mural. But now she looks out and sees the full dimension of it, bright and blooming, fat with life.

And why this change? Was it Michael? Of course it was. She thinks back to last night as they strolled down the midway at Oaks Park with Jimi. Michael's boyish smile and calm ways were getting to her, climbing over all the barricades and threading all the mazes to her heart. But along with this quiet invasion came a rising tide of dread.

So now the time has come to put things back into perspective.

Jessica finishes up the last bit of a statistical run on her PC, and locks the lab. There is no one in the hall as she goes to the elevator.

You don't have to go through with this, she tells herself. It's a cruel thing to do, a very cruel thing to do.

She walks over a skyway to a second building and then takes the elevator to the basement.

You're being a bitch to yourself, she thinks. A real bitch.

The elevator shudders to a stop and she starts down a long, empty hall with a freshly polished linoleum floor reflecting distorted shapes from the overhead neons.

Last chance, she muses. But you won't stop, will you? You've got to find out.

She comes to a heavy metal door with no sign and a dead-bolt lock. Reaching into her white lab coat, she fishes out a key, opens the lock and then the door. It is cool and dark inside. She feels along the wall for the light switch and flips it on.

The jars are set on shelves along the room's back wall. They range from six to eighteen inches in diameter and are arranged by size, like a bar graph in a statistical report. Each contains a human fetus suspended in formaldehyde, and each represents a unique catastrophe, a genetic miscue, a fatal oversight in the master plan. Some have clearly visible malformations, such as the complete absence of limbs. Others are scarcely recognizable as human, a mass of misshapen flesh with an ear sticking out here and an eye there. Some appear relatively normal, with insides somehow cruelly twisted to make them candidates for this shelf. All have the same dull, yellowish-gray cast brought on by the preservative.

Jessica walks over to the end with the smallest jar, and proceeds gradually down the shelf, slowly inspecting this grotesque gallery of genetic chaos.

And it all comes back.

She was nineteen, living in Mountain Park, south of San Francisco. And nothing had ever gone wrong. Why should it? Her family was on the far side of comfortable, and rolled along through many layers of material and social insulation. There were new cars every two years (including one for her), a big sailboat down in the bay, skiing in Sun Valley, a trip to Europe now and then, and memberships in all sorts of private clubs. Her father was a founder and engineering VP of a software company that specialized in heterogeneous computing networks. Her mother was an editor for an international publishing company. The waves of money washed over them quietly and gracefully and provided a propulsive force that moved them forward with almost no effort. Things that were hard for others were easy for Jessica. School was challenging, but her grades were spectacular and her SATs hovered around fourteen hundred.

And, of course, boys were no problem. They swarmed in a busy cloud about her, and it was simply a matter of pulling one out of the boiling vapors of testosterone to amuse her. Commitment was far off, a vague image somewhere far ahead on the time line when "maturity" settled in, whatever that was.

Then she got pregnant. Just like that. No warning. No nothing.

It started with her period being two weeks overdue just when she was supposed to fly down to enroll at the University of Southern California. The enormity of what might be happening grew inside her as fast as the baby grew in her womb. In the end, there was the trip to the pharmacy, the home test, and the positive result. Even then she was struck by the irony of the term "positive" in the accompanying literature. In her case, it was anything but. She then read the literature for her birth-control pills, which stated in eight-point type that there was only a .1 percent chance of pregnancy if the pills were properly used. It occurred to her that her family's entire life was probably based on .1 percent chances. There was only a .1 percent chance they would ever be destitute. Only a .1 percent chance they would fail in their careers. Only a .1 percent chance they would have major legal problems. Only a .1 percent chance they would be crime victims.

Finally, there was only a .1 percent chance that one of these many .1 percents would catch up with any of them. But it had. After a sleepless night, there was the second trip to the pharmacy, a second test, and the same result. She sat in a wicker chair at the table out on the deck by the pool and stared at the bay in the distance.

During all of this time, she thought very little of the father, although she knew with certainty who he was. And with good reason. He was a boy, a sweet boy who treated her with great affection. But not a father. Not now. Maybe not ever.

And an abortion was out of the question. In this moment of great emotional complexity, at least this one decision was simple. All the elaborate debates and supporting evidence had no bearing whatsoever. For her, it was a fundamental matter of the heart. She simply could not go through with it.

The scene with her parents was drenched with a muted anguish. Her father had just flown in from the new plant in Borneo and was tired and disoriented. Her mother clasped her hands and rubbed her thumbs together the way she always did under extreme stress. They sat in the living room, with the overhead spots casting soft pools of light onto the Oriental carpets and custom leather furniture. There was no overt conflict. They would support her no matter what she wanted to do. But they saw her options melting away like butter on a hot summer table, and grieved for what could have been.

Like an army that has lost a major tactical engagement, the three of them quickly formulated a new plan that might keep the long-term strategy intact. She would skip USC for a year, have the baby, and then start the following fall. At that time, they would arrange for quality day care or maybe even a nanny, so she could keep a normal scholastic schedule. In the meantime, she would keep the apartment she had rented over the summer and take some classes at Contra Costa College to peck away at her undergraduate requirements. In the end, they all felt better, because they were back on the offensive, soaring like a big bird high above the problem at hand, riding on great swells of creativity, intelligence, and money.

Alone in her apartment, she was sometimes brought low by the upcoming reality she faced. While the family could throw money at the daytime baby-sitting while she was at USC, what about the nights? The weekends? The times when her peers would be off judiciously sampling the L.A. fast lane? There she would be, surrounded by formula and diapers, watching rental movies on the VCR while the real movie roared on without her. Nevertheless, her resolve stood firm. She would be a mother first, a scholar second, and whatever else third.

The labor started two weeks early, when her mother was at the publisher's in New York and her father was in Mexico City. She called a cab, went to the hospital, and was wheeled into a "birthing room," which was supposed to provide a homey touch, but came off more like a midrange-motel room. At the proscribed time they gave her the epidural, and shortly thereafter hooked up the fetal monitor. Her obstetrician was a woman and a person of good humor, who teased her as they went along.

But soon after they hooked up the monitor, the doctor quit laughing.

"Doctor, it looks like we've got some arrhythmia here," said the nurse, trying to conceal her anxiety.

"OK, let's just watch it," said the doctor. The cervix was totally dilated and the baby halfway down. It was too late for a C-section. They would just have to ride it out.

When the last push came, Jessica could see them all looking between her legs in silence. Something was wrong.

The obstetrician pulled out the glistening pink shape, and obstructed her view as she quickly cut the umbilical cord.

Immediately, the baby was placed in a gurney and oxygen was applied over its head. The pediatrician, who was also in attendance, took over. "OK, let's go," he said in a severe voice. The baby was wheeled out with the doctor right behind.

Jessica's heart was sinking. "What's wrong? What's wrong with the baby? Tell me."

The obstetrician pulled down her mask. "We don't know yet. Dr. Williams is one of the best, so try not to worry too much. It won't do you or the child any good. We'll tell you as soon as we find out."

Back in her room, she phoned her mother at the hotel in New York. "Mom, I had the baby and something's wrong. . . .No, they don't know yet. Mom, I'm scared." She broke down and cried convulsively while her mother simply listened helplessly several thousand miles away. When the crying ended, her mother vowed to be on the next plane back. Jessica managed a weak thanks and hung up. She didn't have the energy to phone her father right now; besides, her mom said she would handle that. Before she could dry her eyes, the pediatrician came in and sat down next to her.

"Jessica, I'll tell you what we know and what we're doing. There are some external malformations, but that's not the main problem. What concerns us right now is the heart and lungs. The respiration is very shallow and the heartbeat is unstable. We've gotten X rays and have a call into a pediatric cardiologist. In the meantime, we've got the baby in an oxygen tent with heart monitoring. We'll take more extreme measures if we have to, but we'd rather wait and hear from the cardiologist to figure out the next step."

"What went wrong? How could this happen to my baby?" Like almost any mother in this situation, she had already begun searching her entire prenatal history, looking for the awful thing she did wrong, the great sin of commission or omission that had brought this curse down on her child. But she found none, even though this brought her little comfort.

"I wish I could tell you, but I can't. You were too young for an amniocentesis, which would have caught certain things; but it wouldn't have caught this. Also, the ultrasound images don't have the resolution to tell us everything, and they depend on the angle of the baby at the time they're being taken. In the end, some things just slip through. Not much anymore, maybe one in a hundred thousand."

So there it was: .001 percent. The pediatrician went on for a bit more, but she didn't hear him. A .1 percent chance of getting pregnant. A .001

percent chance of having a defective baby slip through the net. She knew
that to arrive at the probability of the two events occurring together, you
simply multiply the individual probabilities. So the chance of this god-
awful nightmare happening to any one woman was about .0001 percent,
or one in a million.

Nineteen years of everything going 99.9999 percent right had now
been totally neutralized by one hour of things going .0001 percent wrong.

They wanted to give her a sedative, but she refused. She would not
sleep away the vigil she must keep for her ailing child. Out the window,
she could see down into the parking lot. Obsidian pools of rainwater
dotted the blacktop as she watched the cars come and go, with families
piling in and out. They were all living in another world, while she was a
prisoner in the world of the Millionth Woman, an experience she could
never share.

Around three in the morning, she sat up and decided she had to see
the baby. *Now.* Given the nature of bureaucracies, she knew better than
to ask the nurses. She simply got up, put on her robe, and stepped out
into the hall. Down the way, at the nurse's station, a jumble of computer
displays made it look more like a space station than a hospital. The duty
nurse had her back turned to the hallway and was clacking away on the
keyboard of an antiquated system that lacked voice I/O. Jessica glided on
past the station and down to the nursery, where the display window was,
a showcase for the winners in the first of many races each baby would
eventually run. On the other side was a door marked "Employees Only."
She twisted the knob. Open.

Inside, she could see the area behind the showcase section, where
incubators and oxygen tents were supported by jungles of clear tubing,
tanks of liquids, bottles of gases, and the green glow of display monitors.
The baby would be here. No doubt about it. There was no one in the
room, and the only sound was the clacking keyboard coming from down
the hall.

It took no time to find her baby. It was in the first oxygen tent on the
row. She read the tag, which said, simply, "Baby Morris." Then she
looked up at the baby and felt a strangled yelp come out of her mouth.

The face. While one eye was normal and closed, the other was simply
not there, just a soft bulge of flesh and a collapsed brow. The mouth. On
the upper lip was a gap a half inch wide in the center, exposing the gum.
The nose. There was only a tissue-thin covering over the nasal cavity,

with a single opening at the bottom, where the nostrils should be. The ears. They were maybe half normal size, with the lobes curled up like a wilting flower.

It was in that single terrible moment that the resolve erupted within her. She would not rest until she knew what caused this. No more romance. No more men. No more babies. Her life was a funnel that had converged to this one point and would now follow a single, concentrated stream.

Baby Morris did not last the night, and was buried at the end of the week in a small ceremony attended only by the family. And inside of Jessica the resolve set hard and shiny: She would now enroll at USC in the biological sciences and start down a trail of revelation toward the biochemical disaster that killed her child and turned her into the Millionth Woman.

That was ten years ago, and here I am with a doctorate in microbiology, still stalking the beast. Her tour of baby hell is complete. She has confronted it directly. But Michael Riley is still there, patiently threading his way through the barriers.

She turns her back on the jars and leaves the room without looking back. It's nice out, and maybe she will leave a little early tonight.

In the lab at his clinic, Dr. Feldman carefully inserts a slide onto the platform stage of a microscope. The slide contains a tiny slice of Simon Greeley's brain, which was removed during the autopsy the day after his death. It comes from the frontal lobe of the cerebral cortex, the outermost layer of the brain, where the higher portions of the intellect reside. The features he is looking for will require about 500X magnification, and he meticulously adjusts the light source and focus until the image snaps into sharp resolve. And there it is: a battlefield littered with destruction. Hollow caves dot the tissue where many neurons have been totally destroyed. An unwelcome type of neuron called an astrocyte appears in abundance, an octopuslike feature clinging to its neighbors with numerous radiating appendages. And within the surviving neurons are tiny alien tunnels, wormholes of death euphemistically called "spongioform degenerations."

So far, so good, thinks Feldman. All the symptoms point to his original diagnosis, Creutzfeldt-Jakob disease. The only thing that was out of
line was the short interval from the onset of symptoms to Simon's death
one week later. The shortest recorded time was just over three weeks,
and many cases went on for ten months or more. Still, the body of evidence supported his suspicions. But then as he adjusts the platform to
observe other areas of the sample, something else appears that collapses
his case entirely: amyloid plaques, globs of starchlike stuff, and large
ones at that. Far too many for Creutzfeldt-Jakob disease.

In fact, there is only one disease that shows such features. It is called
kuru, and was confined to a few cannibal tribes in the mountainous
highlands of eastern New Guinea, where it killed several hundred people
every year in the 1950s. The vector for transmission was the brain of the
victim, which was consumed by relatives in ritualistic funeral ceremonies. When cannibalism began to die out, so did kuru. In fact, no one
born after the demise of the macabre ceremonial practices showed any
evidence of the disease. By the mid-1990s, the last kuru victims expired
and the disease was considered extinct in humans.

Or so it was thought. Dr. Feldman is both puzzled and excited. He has
made a sensational discovery, the resurrection of a disease in a completely different time and space from its point of origin. But how? The
problem of tracking down the point of infection would be the same one
that faced the original kuru investigations in the 1970s: The disease had
an incubation period of up to thirty years. Had Simon belonged to some
satanic brain-eating cult at some time in his life? And there was still the
nagging problem of a very short period from symptoms to death. Kuru
usually took about a year to complete its nasty business, not one week.

Thirty years. Could they ever get to the bottom of it? Probably not. It
is doubtful his family would want to participate in anything that had
such bizarre possibilities attached.

Then Dr. Feldman is struck by an odd thought. He recalls that the
woman with Mrs. Greeley at the hospital mentioned that Simon had said
something about maybe being poisoned. Well, maybe so. This terrible
disease is nothing less than the perfect murder weapon for someone with
great patience and access to the infecting agent. The police would have
the same problem that now confronts him. The crime could have happened anytime in the past thirty years.

Where would you even begin?

12

XXXXXX

The Scavenger

The Mall in Washington, D.C., is a green rectangular strip of lawn several city blocks wide and a mile long. Its sides are lined by such massive institutional buildings as the Agriculture Administration, the Natural History Museum, and the National Art Gallery. At the far end is the Reflecting Pool, and beyond it, the U.S. Capitol, the symbolic center of government for 300 million people.

Periodically, The Mall has become the stage for political dissidence in times of great national turbulence. In 1963, over two hundred thousand souls joined the great march on Washington for civil rights. And now a second great march is about to take place here, the Mortgage March. Over five hundred thousand people are pouring onto The Mall in the muggy morning heat to vent their displeasure in a massive demonstration aimed at the U.S. Capitol. Most share a common fate: They have lost their homes after extended periods of unemployment, which has drained their savings, stripped their retirement reserve, and put them much closer to the street than they ever dreamed possible. In each of them, there is a dreadful awakening that the comfort zone they basked in most of their lives is in fact very thin and fragile, like the coat of morning dew on a blade of grass.

The organizers of the march have a simple objective: to convince the federal government to somehow intervene and freeze mortgage defaults on several million homes. To this end, many speakers will mount the

Capitol steps and deliver emotional orations on the demise of the American Dream, and the demonstrators will roar their approval.

Publicly, no one in the Congress or the White House will deny their plight. The presence of several hundred thousand strangers in the nation's capital has a powerful impact on those who lead. In more normal times, Washington operates in a highly insular mode, with the national electorate a distant phenomenon to be dealt with only during those irritating times surrounding elections. So to have huge numbers of them show up right here in the physical center of national power is a disturbing reminder of the true nature of democracy.

But in private, the view is different. Economists see no simple way out. The nation is still staggering under a great deficit, and the interest on it now gobbles everything but defense and essential services. There is nothing left to bail out the citizenry, which outrages those who remember the savings-and-loan bailout, and the billions that went to right the wrongs of a privileged few.

Among those so outraged are a number of speakers who will not be heard today on the Capitol steps. They have already spoken in private, and given specific instructions on what should happen during the course of the March. Their plans are very deliberate and specific and based on careful study of mass civil disturbances throughout recent history. With a relatively small number of followers, they will be able to put in motion a very large catastrophe. To guarantee the security of this plan, they have taken a lesson from international terrorists and organized into a hierarchy of cells, which has made their organization very difficult to penetrate. Nevertheless, the FBI has skimmed enough information to make the authorities very nervous. So in the months leading up to the march, the normally tiny force of federal marshals suddenly began to grow at a geometric rate. Within the White House, the thinking on the matter was clear. After such events in the past few decades as Tiananmen Square in China, the last thing the government wanted was a confrontation between protesting civilians and federal combat troops. In spite of this, almost all of the new recruits for the marshals were transfers from the U.S. Army and Marines, but the entire matter had been quietly sanitized.

The new marshal force wear the riot gear of civilian policemen and ride in vehicles painted blue instead of brown-and-green camouflage. And now, on this hot, soggy morning, it begins to mass along Constitution and Independence avenues, one block off The Mall on each side. The streets that immediately flank The Mall are occupied only by the civilian police force.

This maneuvering of forces is not lost on the media, who are here in unprecedented numbers. Through the international news nets, there is a live feed of the march into the entire industrialized world. In many countries, including the U.S., it preempts regular programming. But the government's plan works as intended, because there is a buffer of large buildings between the people on The Mall and the federal forces on the avenues. TV works only on what the frame of the picture can embrace, and the long lines of blue vehicles might as well be in Kansas, in terms of their visual impact on viewers. Most directors are carrying the lines only as a very minor color story.

The big story is up front on the Capitol steps, where cameras can capture a reverse shot that frames both the speakers and the apparent infinity of people stretching down The Mall. Most of those speaking are outside of government proper, and the capital's politicians can only watch in envy as the speakers mount the podium in the presence of over a billion people worldwide.

All the time, the sun rises higher and the temperature climbs. Then, at about eleven-thirty, the trouble begins. Near the intersection of Seventh Street and Jefferson Drive, a group of about one hundred people begin taunting the police who man the traffic barriers at the intersection. The radios of the security net crackle up and down The Mall, and a police video of the event is broadcast immediately to a temporary headquarters set up in the Labor Department Building. Right away, the incident has a bad look about it. Those involved are young and mostly male, not a representative sample of the general crowd. Empty bottles appear from nowhere and begin to rain down on the police, who fend them off with their riot shields. Behind the attackers, deeper in the crowd, there are looks of profound dismay from those who assumed this would be a nonviolent event.

Then the first shot, a muffled pop, the sound mostly absorbed by the crowd. A policeman crumples. A second shot, and a second officer goes down. Within a few seconds, police riot vehicles come forward to cover the retreat of the police and their wounded. A burning bottle hisses through the hot air and bursts near one of the vehicles' turrets, sending a river of flame cascading down the side and onto the street. Behind the vehicles, policemen have drawn arms and taken cover.

An alert has already gone out to the U.S. marshal force, and hundreds of the blue vehicles file off Independence Avenue and onto Jefferson Drive, putting them within eyesight of the crowd. Across The Mall, another column roars onto Madison Street. Because of the density of the crowd, and the scale of the event, only a tiny portion see the violence on Seventh Street or the advance of the vehicles along the side of The Mall. Up front, the current speaker continues an impassioned speech, unaware of what is unfolding out in the distance. There seems to be a little smoke rising out to her left, but that could be anything.

Within minutes, the violence repeats itself at five other key locations along The Mall, at Third and Fourth along Jefferson, at Fourth, Seventh, and Twelfth streets along Madison. Sporadic gunfire, downed police, Molotov cocktails, explosions, flames. The disturbances on Third and Fourth are clearly visible from the Capitol steps. The organizers of the event are dumbfounded. This was supposed to be a model for participatory democracy in action, and now it's disintegrating into urban warfare right before their eyes. One of the organizers takes the mike and appeals for calm. It is a mistake. He has just informed the 90 percent who are unaware of trouble that something is wrong. As he looks out, he can see the agitation physically ripple through the crowd.

By now the security headquarters can see that the violence is not only intentional and premeditated, but expertly planned. Looking at a map of The Mall, it is instantly apparent to them that the conflicts are located at all the major exit points. The crowd is effectively trapped in the middle of a war zone, and soon panic will set in.

At the intersection of Twelfth and Madison, police are joined by the U.S. marshals behind a row of armored personnel carriers that are pulled back out of range of the Molotov cocktails. In the center of the intersection, two deserted riot vehicles belch orange flames and push columns of black smoke into the hot, white sky. Three puddles of blood mark the spots where three officers have gone down, one of them already dead. Occasionally another muffled pop comes out of the crowd, and the riot forces cringe as the round ricochets with a loud ping off one of the vehicles. A commander from the federal marshals' office has taken command of the scene. Out in The Mall she can see the crowd churn and surge, but there is nowhere it can go, no safety-valve exit to relieve the pressure. The obvious solution is to pull back and let everyone stream out of the exit points at Third, Fourth, Seventh, Ninth, and Twelfth streets. This will mean losing the agitators, but it will also save thousands of lives. She wonders why the stupid assholes haven't given the order to open the barricades yet. Just then, the conflict escalates severely. There is a large explosion off to her left, and she sees smoke billow from atop one of the armored personnel carriers and several bodies fly through the air. With no real combat experience, it takes a moment to realize what is happening. Mortars! Somewhere out there in the crowd, they have set up a mortar and are now firing on the riot force's position.

At headquarters, reports of mortar attacks on all the major exits are received within the space of three minutes. The commanding officers watch with great anxiety as their options for a nonviolent solution fall away. It is well known that you can train riot forces to remain in a defensive posture even at the risk of personal injury—but not at the risk of certain death. Soon, they will be forced to go in and try to "surgically remove" the agitators who are systematically killing their peers.

Along Madison and Jefferson avenues, the U.S. marshal forces leave their vehicles and form long lines along the Mall side of the street. Their prearranged mission is to protect the buildings behind them, the National Art Gallery and the National Museum of American History. In front of them, the people are being forced closer to the line by the large-scale physics of crowd motion. Bullhorns begin to bark the message: "Stay where you are and remain calm. We are arranging for your safe exit." Which was absolutely untrue. All the exits were now combat areas, as mortar shells whistled in among the armored vehicles and police cars.

At headquarters, a desperate decision is made. At each exit, there must be at least one attempt at surgical removal of what were now clearly terrorists. The force at Seventh and Madison goes first, under cover of smoke bombs that blanket the intersection. A wedge of several armored and shielded men knifes into the crowd, crushing it and compressing it. People who never experienced a violent moment in their lives are suddenly confronted with screaming, bleeding, shoving, bones snapping. A farmer from Nebraska, a housewife from San Jose, and a salesman from Houston all suffocate in the first minutes of the assault as they are pinned under falling bodies. But the mass of the crowd is too dense, and the assault falters. The wedge collapses and people fall in among the riot police and begin to beat on them with an animal fury. What had started as civilized political abstraction is now a raging primal battle for survival.

At Fourth and Madison, one final ploy is used to extract the terrorists. A helicopter comes in low over the crowd, scanning for armed people and mortar positions. Two SWAT team members scan the commotion below, and in an incredible stroke of luck, spot two men crouching over a mortar, surrounded by several others protecting their position with drawn pistols. At their feet are several bodies, and it is evident that some brave souls in the crowd tried to stop the shelling and paid with their lives. The SWAT team yells at the pilot, who descends toward the mortar position as the team readies their rifles to fire as soon as they are in range.

It is far too late when the pilot sees that one of the men on the ground has something perched on his shoulder. Before she can take evasive action, a rocket snakes up and hits the engine housing. All power and control are instantly gone, although the rotor blades continue to spin of their own momentum. The helicopter jerks upward and does a little jig of death over the crowd, its tail whipping to and fro. Then it gives up the struggle as the main rotor blades fly off, and plummets into the mass of people in the center of The Mall. On impact it explodes in a jellied orange bubble that engulfs over one thousand tightly packed people and quickly incinerates them.

The explosion sets off a human shock wave that radiates from the center of The Mall toward the edges, where the U.S. marshal forces are holding their line. Without warning, they are confronted with a tidal wave of humanity surging toward them. In panic, troops stationed as backups on top of the personnel carriers fire thousands of plastic bullets into the wave, but with no noticeable result. The wave hits the line and releases all its potential energy on the men who man it. It crumples and collapses as the wave surges right over the top, trampling and killing hundreds in a few seconds. The riflemen jump off their vehicles and flee for their lives, running over the manicured green lawns and shrubs of the public buildings.

Up and down The Mall, the wave smashes resistance at the exit points, and the throng spills out into the city. Most are dazed and shocked.

Many are injured. But just as many others are burning bright with the flame of collective rage. Looting and burning breaks out at hundreds of points, and continues far into the night.

In the midst of all the confusion, the agitators simply fade away. Not one is arrested.

In his home, Senator Grisdale watches the awful spectacle on TV, flipping from one news service to another, seeking a better shot, a more incisive view, a more telling angle. For him and everyone else in the industrialized world, the remote channel clicker gives the illusion of being an ambulatory witness, able to wander from scene to scene inside an unfolding event. He has not moved for hours, nor has his wife. In the late afternoon, a remote shot from a helicopter hovering high above The Mall seems to properly frame the scope of the tragedy. There are thousands of motionless multicolored dots sprinkled over the green lawn, each person dead or seriously injured, most of them the victims of trampling or crushing. In The Mall's center, between Fourth and Seventh streets, is a large black circle surrounding the helicopter wreckage, a sickening melanoma on the bright green grass. Mercifully, the bodies within the circle are as black as the charred grass and can barely be seen.

Grisdale has to pry himself from his chair and go into the garden, where the roses are already blooming in diaphanous pinks and rich reds. He must think beyond the god-awful immediacy of this thing and consider its implications. Unlike in previous marches on The Mall, the participants today are not part of a disaffected minority. They are the center, the fat bulge in the middle of the statistical curve, the main anchor of political stability. And now the center has been brutally punctured and is deflating at an explosive rate, creating a valley for the two extremes on either side to slide into contact.

It's never a good time to be president, thinks Grisdale, but I can't imagine a worse time than now.

In a corridor inside the White House, the president's Chief of Staff stands with arms folded and speaks just above a murmur to a second man, the president's personal physician.

"What do you think?" the Chief of Staff inquires as he nods toward a closed door where they have just left the president.

"He's clinically depressed. And why not? He had enough problems to deal with without something like this," replies the physician as he points over his shoulder to the Marine guards in full combat gear that have bolstered the usual Secret Service contingent.

James Webber puts his hand to his chin and purses his lips. "I want you to think very carefully for a moment: Do you feel he's competent to continue in office?"

The physician feels a cold brace of anxiety settle over him. "I'm not sure I'm qualified to answer that question, Mr. Webber."

"Well, Doctor," Webber replies in his abrasive, gravel voice, "if not you, then who?" His gun-barrel eyes bore right into the middle of the physician's field of vision. "I think for the time being, we'd better keep this to ourselves," he adds before the doctor can answer. "With a little luck, he'll pull out of it and be on track before it becomes public knowledge. The last thing this country needs right now is a leadership crisis. So let's just sit on it for awhile and see what happens, OK?"

"OK," sighs the physician. He is nearly certain that the president won't "just pull out of it," but he is not about to debate the point with Webber, who is now clearly the dominant power in the White House. Besides, he has heard stories about Webber, troubling though unsubstantiated stories.

But the stories are anemic little anecdotes when matched against the truth. In fact, Webber sits atop an organization years in the making and totally transparent to the mainstream political system. Unlike some past Chiefs of Staff, such as Sununu in the early nineties, Webber has carefully engineered a public image of being balanced, accessible, and completely deferential to the president's will. Even in this current crisis, he has come off as a concerned public servant struggling to execute the White House mandates while building a consensus with other branches of government. Earlier in his career, Webber learned a valuable lesson from the arrogant antics of the Oliver Norths and Bill Caseys of the world, and has done nothing to openly agitate the opposition. But when the public cloak is removed, a very different Mr. Webber emerges, one who has carefully assembled a covert network of like-minded individuals who share his views and stand ready to translate them into action at the appropriate time.

And that time is now. The combination of the president's chronic depression and the Mortgage March has provided him with an historic window of opportunity to play both ends against the middle. Because, in fact, James Webber controls the pyramid of terrorist cells that has just ignited the bloodbath on The Mall. At the same time, he has consolidated power inside the government to deal with what he will announce to the press as "the most heinous act of radical terrorism ever visited upon a democracy." He has combined political gasoline and gunpowder to create the great catalyst that will launch a new era, a return to greatness, a Manifest Destiny that will extend far beyond the boundaries of the original. When the American people witness the spectacular display of unadulterated power that is soon to come, they will be bedazzled by its radiance and quickly recognize it for what it is: their ultimate salvation.

How could they feel any other way?

Gail Ambrose understands the problem, but she is late and getting irritated. Grisdale will be buried in problems, and doesn't need any of his time wasted. She considers telling this to the corporal who is checking her ID at the entrance to the Senate Office Building, but thinks better of it. This is the third checkpoint she has gone through to get here today, exactly one week after the Mortgage March. The first checkpoint was on Jersey Avenue, part of the defensive perimeter that now ringed the entire Capitol complex. This time, the federal gloves were off and the perimeter was manned by Army and Marine combat troops carrying loaded M17s. All the arterials surrounding the Capitol bristle with tanks, armored personnel carriers, and sandbagged machine gun sites. Helicopters patrol day and night, casting their blunt shuddering shadows down onto the buildings below. The president is sending a clear message to the country: First there will be order, then law, and finally democracy and civil liberty.

The corporal finishes checking her ID against some mysterious list on a clipboard and motions her on past the checkpoint. On each side of the entrance doors are machine gun crews behind sandbagged fortifications who give her a leering appraisal as she passes through. In one week, Gail has been through enough martial law to last a lifetime.

Grisdale is standing and looking out the window when she enters his office.

"You get through the security OK?" he asks.

"Pain in the ass," she comments.

"Well, it may get worse before it gets better," he declares. "I'd like to think it's the president showing us a little backbone. Unfortunately, that's hard to imagine. . . . So, what are we up to?"

"Well, it seemed important a week ago," replies Gail as she slumps into the chair in front of his desk, "but now I'm not so sure."

"Life goes on," proclaims Grisdale. "So try me."

"It's about Simon Greeley. I went with his wife yesterday to see the neurologist who handled his case, a Dr. Feldman. It seems that Simon may have made medical history, even if he missed his chance at political history. He died of a disease called kuru that used to kill cannibals in New Guinea, and was thought to be extinct. Apparently Simon resurrected it. Now here's the catch: Kuru is a slow viral infection, and may incubate for up to thirty years before it gets you. So there's no telling when or how he got it."

She sighs. "It's just too pat, too convenient. The guy suddenly dies of a very rare disease just when he's ready to give critical testimony that might blow the lid off the administration. And it just happens to be a disease that's impossible to trace."

"So?" inquires Grisdale as he slides into his desk seat.

"So . . . I think they got him."

"Got him?"

"Don't ask me how. I haven't the slightest idea."

"And who is 'they'?"

"I don't know."

"So what do you want to do about it?" asks Grisdale.

"I want to start from the beginning and see where it goes. What we do know is that somebody in the White House is secretly sinking a whole bunch of money into a company call ParaVolve, which is making some new kind of computer. So that's where we start."

"You're going to have to do a little better than that, Gail," declares Grisdale. "I don't think they are going to be very enthusiastic about sharing their corporate secrets with a Senate staffer."

"I know somebody who lives right in the neighborhood of ParaVolve. He is also a brilliant computer scientist. Most of all, he owes me a couple of very big favors."

"Michael?" Grisdale asks.
"Michael."

"All right, this time Jimi does the Shakey Boogie and Scooter pulls the Big Rip. Got it?"

Rat Bag looks at his crew of kids seated on the wooden bench in Washington Square, the principal shopping mall for the west side of the Portland metro area.

"I don't want to," protests Jimi Tyler.

"Why?" Rat Bag can barely conceal his rage, but he knows this shopping mall is not the place to let it spill over. He is still smarting from the dead trailer lady. Around the apartment, Jimi had gotten the full glory on that one. All because he had told the grown-ups and Rat Bag and Zipper hadn't. Pretty soon the legend was cast solid: Jimi and the dead trailer lady. No one had ever thought to ask Jimi why he had been peeking into trailer windows in the first place. He was too little for that. But Rat Bag wasn't. And in reality, that was why he and Zipper had stayed mum on the matter, even after the fact.

"What do you mean you don't want to, you little fuckhead? What's your problem?"

The five other kids on the bench all turn toward Jimi and start to squirm. Even the thought of defying Rat Bag makes them nervous.

"Because I don't want to look like I'm sick when I'm not sick," answers Jimi. He knows the scam because Rat Bag and Zipper had demonstrated it at another, smaller shopping mall some weeks ago, in a variety store. Zipper went up to the cashier like he was going to pay for something, then fell down on the floor and went into fake convulsions. The Shakey Boogie. As everyone's attention was plastered on Zipper, Rat Bag sailed right on by with three videotapes scarcely concealed under his jacket. The Big Rip. In the final act, Zipper leaped to his feet without saying a word and ran out of sight before anyone could react.

Rat Bag gropes to assess the maximum retaliation he can sling at Jimi in this public place. "OK, dogshit, you're on your own. Good luck," he sneers as he turns to the other kids. "OK, let's go."

The others silently take off after him. One smaller boy looks back at Jimi with worried eyes as he follows the pack. Jimi winks and waves. The boy seems satisfied and disappears with the others into the shopper traffic.

Jimi hops off the bench and strolls off in the opposite direction. Rat Bag has miscalculated once again. He has assumed that Jimi doesn't understand the bus system, and will be stranded here, a couple of miles from the Romona Arms. He thinks that Jimi will wander in terror and isolation until someone notices and calls the police to take him home.

But although Jimi has trouble reading, he has a good working knowledge of the bus system through experience and trial and error. He has fully absorbed the logic of the maps, lines, symbols, and numbers. He can get home any time he wants to. From anywhere in the city.

At this end of the mall, the traffic has thinned out considerably, and people seemed to be clustered and crowded into a TV and stereo store. The screens here display many people running and screaming as a helicopter falls and explodes in the distance behind them. Jimi ignores it. He has seen it a hundred times over the past week on TVs everywhere. In a book shop he passes, there is a picture of a Ferris wheel, which makes him think of Michael Riley, the pretty lady, and the realies. It was a good time, and his mom wasn't mad about it at all.

In fact, when he got home, she played a new game, acting like she'd never seen him before and thought he was just the cutest little boy she'd ever laid eyes on.

Emil Cortez finds the right spot halfway up the mountain of trash. There is a terraced spot here that has been compacted flat by a previous occupant, and there are no immediate neighbors to quarrel with over boundary rights. Nearby he discovers a large rectangle of cardboard torn from the box that once housed a refrigerator. He also spots some bent aluminum struts from a discarded TV antenna. He takes these materials to his site and constructs a lean-to that shields him from the hot afternoon sun, and then sits cross-legged and stoically surveys the scene before him. All around are towering mountains of trash that comprise the largest garbage dump in Mexico City. And each is dotted with scores of improvised residences like Emil's. In the deep valleys between the mountains he can see small knots of people conversing in languid poses, and others walking to and fro in a mysterious yet businesslike manner.

Now that he has a base, he feels a little more comfortable. For the last three days, he has been overwhelmed by the scale of the city, and floated around in a state of fright and wonderment. When he first arrived at the eastern bus terminal from his village in the state of Hidalgo, he was like an astronaut stepping out onto the surface of an alien planet. Of course he had seen the city on TV, in the little cantina down the street at home, but it did not prepare him for the sudden blast of color and energy he felt when he left the relative security of the bus. Far into the afternoon, he simply wandered, letting the urban currents carry him wherever they chose. Around nightfall, he bought a bowl of bread and soup, and checked into a small, shabby hotel. Sitting on a lumpy mattress in his tiny room, he added the cost of the room and the meal, and realized that the city would strip him bare of money in less than a week. But this was his first night in town, and at twenty-six years old, he felt a rush of adventure and went to a bar down the block, where several men told him about the dump. It was a low place but an honorable one, they said, a place where a man could find the right footing to leap up and catch the first rung of the urban social ladder.

The men were right, thinks Emil. This place does have a purpose. It is where you plant a seed of fortune so that it may grow into a job, an apartment, a wife, a beautiful wife, and a car, a large one. Nearby is a hidden cavity in the trash where he has cached his old suitcase. His mother had wept when she gave it to him, and his seven younger brothers and sisters all took her cue and started sniffling. But behind the tears, they understood that he must go, must leave this place that would slowly suck him dry through farm labor and leave him bent with arthritis and bad memories.

Emil rises to a crouch and looks down on a knot of men in the valley directly below him. It is time to go down and start to do business. What kind of business? It is impossible to know. But not impossible to do. He starts down.

From the valley floor between the trash mountains, the Scavenger watches the man start down, picking his way gingerly, looking for solid footings in the uncertain jumble of refuse. Earlier this morning, he had watched the same man make camp with some cardboard and old TV aerials, so he knows this is a very recent arrival, exactly the kind he is looking for. He starts down a trail through the center of the valley, where continual foot traffic has compacted the trash into a hard path, and he times his gait to intercept his quarry just after he reaches the bottom of the mountain.

As Emil reaches the trail, he gets a better look at the man who has been walking his way during his descent. The pressed and pleated slacks, hand-tooled cowboy boots, European sunglasses, and billowing pull-over shirt tell Emil this man is not a citizen of the dump, but an emissary from the outer world. He is tongue-tied in the presence of so powerful a figure in so humble a place, but the man breaks the silence with a cheer-ful greeting and a smile.

"Good day, sir!"

"Good day," responds Emil with a hint of caution in his voice.

"Are you new in the city?" the man asks, stuffing his hands into his pockets after removing his sunglasses.

"Yes, I arrived just a few days ago."

The man chuckles softly. "I myself was once new here. It was a time of great adventure. In fact, I had my camp not far from here." He points to an adjacent mountain. "Right up over there."

A lie. In fact, the Scavenger has lived in the city all his life.

Emil looks where the man is pointing, and feels a surge of excitement and hope. Right before him is the entire encapsulation of urban salva-tion, from one pole to the other, from the old campsite in the garbage to the sleek man with the nice clothes.

"Say," says the man, "you aren't looking for work, are you?"

Unbelievable! God is smiling on me today! "Why, yes, as a matter of fact, I am."

The man puts his hand on Emil's shoulder. "You know the reason I come here now and then is that I remember. I recall how hard it was to get that first job, the one that got me out of here. And so when I know of a job somewhere, I sometimes come here, to help others, like others helped me. It's only fair, don't you think?"

"Yes, it seems only fair." What a generous man! A true saint among us!

"Have you contacted your family yet? Do they know your where-abouts?"

"No, sir, but I planned on doing that as soon as I got settled some-where."

"Well, I tell you what: Let's go check this job I heard about, and then we'll send them a letter so they know you're OK."

As they start down the path, Emil thinks of his little brother, Manuel, his favorite, a spirited little fellow of four. With his first paycheck, he will buy presents for all, but something special for Manuel.

By the time the Scavenger's new Korean pickup pulls into the parking lot of Farmacéutico Asociado, Emil is reeling from the onslaught of novelty playing out before him. Never before has he ridden in a brand-new vehicle, with the interior still smelling of fresh plastic and virgin leather. And never has he seen a real car phone, which this most generous man used to call ahead and let them know he was bringing in Emil for the job.

"What we have here is warehouse work," states the Scavenger as he walks with Emil toward a door next to the building's loading dock. "I think you'll like it. You'll learn how to operate a forklift—a valuable skill, I assure you."

Inside, Emil sees great rows of cardboard boxes piled to the height of maybe five men. To their right, the wall extends out and there is a freight elevator with its door open, and a man in a white lab coat looks at them.

"Now, before you start, they need to do a quick medical examination to make sure you can handle heavy work," says the Scavenger as he steers Emil in the direction of the elevator. "Emil, I want you to meet Dr. Smith."

Emil surveys the doctor. A gringo, maybe forty-five, with wire-rim glasses, receding red hair, thin lips, and a long face.

The doctor smiles and extends his hand. "Pleased to meet you, Mr. Cortez," he says in passably good Spanish. "We hope you like it here."

"Yes, Doctor. I'm sure I will." Emil could not be more eager to please.

"Well, let's get you on down so we can check you out and get you working."

They descend in the elevator and enter the laboratory complex. Emil finds nothing unusual about this arrangement. It appears that in this great city, many companies must have their own medical facilities to care for their employees. Why not?

The doctor takes Emil to an examining room while the Scavenger waits outside. He has Emil sit on an exam table and take his shirt off.

"This shouldn't take long, Mr. Cortez," he says as he pulls a stethoscope out of his pocket and places it on Emil's chest. "Breathe deeply, please." He listens and nods. "Excellent. Now, let's do a quick check on your throat." He takes a tongue depressor from a jar atop a metal cabinet next to the table. "Open wide, please." He flattens Emil's tongue, takes out a small flashlight, and peers down the throat cavity. "Hmmm . . ." A slight frown furrows his red eyebrows as he looks up at Emil. "You feel any soreness at all in your throat, Mr. Cortez?"

Please, God, begs Emil, don't let me come this close and then fail. "No. My throat feels just fine—and so does all the rest of me!"

The doctor gives him a patronizing smile. "Well, I see a little infection on the tip of one of your tonsils. Now, don't worry. It won't keep you off the job," he says as he opens a drawer on the metal cabinet and pulls out a hypodermic syringe. "I'm going to give you a little shot of penicillin, and it should be completely cleared up in a couple of days." He slides the needle into Emil's upper arm. "Now, I just want you to lie down here on the table and relax for a minute. You may feel a little sleepy from the shot, but that's all right. I'll be back in just a couple of minutes," he says, heading out the door.

"Thank you, Doctor," says Emil with genuine gratitude as he reclines on the table. He has no idea that penicillin has nothing to do with making you sleepy.

In the hall, the doctor reaches into his pocket and pulls out a roll of U.S. dollars, which he hands to the Scavenger. "The specimen looks good. You earned your money. Want to count it?"

"That won't be necessary," replies the Scavenger, eyeing the roll and then looking directly at the door. "But for our next transaction, I'd like to be compensated in yen. The dollar is . . .well, not quite what it used to be."

The doctor is not offended. Like many others on the project, he has utter contempt for the softheads who have let the U.S. economy slide into its current mess. "I'm sure that can be arranged. I better show you out so I can get back and complete our processing of Mr. Cortez."

Five minutes later, the doctor is back in the exam room, staring at the prostrate figure of Emil Cortez. Yes, the specimen looks good. Mid-twenties. No immediate signs of bad health. Fits the profile of the target market quite nicely.

Then he wonders about the Japanese and their test subjects back in

the forties. Did they have problems with control groups, baseline pro-
files, things like that? After all, they were working with prisoners, and
thus had little control over the quality of their subjects.

The doctor often wonders about things like this. His name is not
Smith, but Spelvin, Lamar Spelvin. And he is not really a full-fledged
doctor, since he was expelled in his third year of medical school back in
Georgia a couple of decades ago. Although a brilliant student, Spelvin
had managed to generate several disturbing, although vaguely documented, incidents of sexual harassment. After that, he drifted around the
periphery of the medical industry like a hungry dog, looking for a way
back in. Eventually, he found one: the Army Research Institute for Infectious Disease at Fort Detrick, where he became a civilian research
assistant. And this was where he first heard about Pingfan, the Japanese
biological warfare research complex located in northeastern China during World War Two. And where he discovered that Pingfan was the only
biowar installation ever known to use human test subjects. About three
thousand of them. Some bound up with their buttocks exposed while
shrapnel bombs pierced their flesh. Not ordinary shrapnel bombs, but
special ones contaminated with anthrax bacteria. To be sure, their death
agonies were not ignored. Instead they were carefully observed and documented to further research efforts. Still other prisoners were infected
with cholera and plague, and some were dissected while still alive to
assess the damage to their internal organs.

The U.S. government knew all about the horrors of Pingfan, but never
prosecuted the leadership. Instead it quietly took the data.

And decades later at Fort Detrick, the data had mesmerized Lamar
Spelvin, and Pingfan became a perverse shrine to him, an obsession. He
wanted to discuss it at length with his peers, who quickly put maximum
distance between themselves and Lamar. Eventually, he took it on his
own to write a lengthy research paper on the inherent value of the data
to the institute's own research. At the end of this paper, he made his own
modest proposal: that condemned convicts in the federal prison system
would be an excellent source of test subjects for U.S. efforts.

Lamar was gone from the institute within a week. But not entirely
forgotten. There were a few who had watched him silently from a distance and sympathized. They were much the same as child molesters
who become day care workers, or sadists who become police officers, or
fetishists who become shoe salesmen: the tiny minority who are over-

whelmed by the flame and free-fall into its center, regardless of the risk. One of these shadow figures passed a copy of Lamar's paper to an associate outside the institute, who in turn passed it on to a third party, who waited a discreet length of time and then contacted Lamar, making sure to address him as "Dr. Spelvin."

Now Spelvin shuts the door in the substructure at Farmacéutico Asociado and summons the attendants who will wheel the test subject to his new residence down the hall. Emil is in a dreamless sleep and will stay that way for several hours. His last nip of consciousness before he went under was devoted to a pleasant inspiration.

With his first paycheck, he would buy his little brother Manuel a baseball glove.

13

The Holy Ghost

Michael sits in a gray molded-plastic chair and watches through a quarter inch of plate glass as the plane pulls in to the gate at Portland International Airport. He is still perplexed by the call last night from Gail. She said she was coming out here to talk to someone at the Bonneville Power Administration, and "just wanted to see him." What for? If anything, their post-divorce relationship has been a subtractive process at best, especially for her. So why the sudden sentimental gesture?

Passengers were coming up the gate now in that stiff, stooped walk of people immobilized too long in a narrow metal tube. For a moment, he was afraid he wouldn't recognize her, but then there she was. Not a pretty woman but a handsome one, with a face that would endure middle age magnificently. A prominent nose, rich chestnut hair, almond eyes, and full lips set against a strong chin.

As Gail emerged from the gate tunnel, she feared for a moment that she wouldn't recognize Michael, but there he was. Tall and slim, with a perpetually boyish face brought on by a thin nose, broad cheeks, curly brown hair, and a mouth that always looked ready to launch a grin. If only, she thought, if only. The age of the grins seems centuries behind.

They meet in a perfunctory embrace, which Gail breaks by reaching for her purse and handing Michael a card.

"Happy birthday, Michael. I know it's a little late," she apologizes.

Birthday? Since when did she remember his birthday? He looks at the

164

card's cover, which has a silly illustration of a bird floating through the sky with a parachute. He opens it and gets the message, scrawled in her unmistakable handwriting: "We've got to go where we can talk safely. My plane back leaves in ninety minutes, so make it close."

He pockets the card and says thanks as they start down the terminal wing toward the main exit. So it's business, he thinks. But what kind of business?

Michael turns his truck into the economy parking lot about a half mile east of the main terminal. He finds a stall near the chain-link fence that separates the lot from the main runway. Gail looks completely out of place in the truck, with her power suit and soft black pumps. They had made light conversation on the way to the truck, but lapsed into silence during the ride. Now she understands Michael's plan as a god-awful roar grips the truck. Only a couple of hundred feet away, a long queue of outgoing airliners is rocketing into the sky one by one at fairly regular intervals. Michael understands that advanced signal processing now allows the extraction of conversations from backgrounds that often appear to be impossibly noisy. Ten years ago, one part conversation could be pulled out of maybe fifty parts noise. Now the figure was more like one part out of several hundred, so the only way to ensure privacy was a windowless, insulated room, or a massive noise shield, like the roar of a jet engine.

As they leave the truck and walk toward the fence to watch the planes, it occurs to Gail that at one time, nobody in the world knew more about the technicalities of eavesdropping than Michael Riley.

When they reach the fence, there is a lull in between takeoffs, and the air is filled with the high whine of the idling jet engines and the kerosene smell of spent aviation fuel. The noise and odor dissolve the awkwardness of the silence between the pair, and the planes provide a visual focus other than each other. As they wait for the next surge of takeoff noise, Michael remembers their courtship. He had just come to Washington for a job interview with the National Security Agency. The interview was really just a formality. He had graduated magna cum laude in mathematics from Berkeley and gone on to get his doctorate in computer science from MIT on a full-ride scholarship. Of course NSA wanted him. For Michael, all such milestones in his life had been pretty much pro forma. He always passed the test, always got the job, always had a date.

There were no rough edges that caught the wind as he sped along from one milepost to another. It seemed he was born with perfectly stream-lined contours, as if his genes had been pretested in some supernatural wind tunnel before he was conceived. All of this seemed a perfect seed-bed for arrogance, but instead Michael had a disarming friendliness about him that quickly neutralized any resentment from his peers.

And it was this last quality that endeared him to Gail, not the brassy sheen of brilliance. They were introduced through a common friend and had a drink at a little bar in Georgetown. At the time, Gail was a junior staffer for a senator from the Midwest, quite happy with her job and not looking for the man of all men to complete her life. But here was Michael, and she was instantly taken with him.

A year later they were married, and fixing up an apartment in the same Georgetown neighborhood where they had met. Michael was completely immersed in his work, which of course he could not talk about, and Gail was learning to shape and direct her political intuitions. Often, they brought work home, but never enough to get in the way of making love frequently and passionately. Their life together was like a giant inflatable structure just beginning to unfold to reveal its true and lovely shape.

At the NSA, Michael was propelled up the organizational hierarchy precisely because advancement was not important to him. He was highly focused on the fantastic intricacies of the technologies he worked with, and not much interested in accumulating or brokering power. For this reason, he quickly became the nonaligned candidate, the compromise between warring factions. Soon, he found himself on the committee re-sponsible for defining the agency's long-term computer strategy as chief technology advisor. While this seemed like a staggering responsibility for someone only twenty-five years old, it was almost mandatory that it be someone his age. Computer technology was advancing so fast that even those ten years out of academia were hopelessly off the pace.

The rude thunder of raw jet thrust draws him back to the runway, the fence. A big 797 is starting its ponderous roll. Gail turns and leans into his shoulder so she can speak into his ear against the noise. He feels her breasts on his upper arm and her breath against his ear. It is extremely distracting and he fights to concentrate on her words.

"Michael, I've got a very big problem and I need your help." She speaks rapidly, knowing that the wall of noise will quickly collapse as the jet disappears down the runway. "A while back we found out the government is throwing a whole bunch of money into a venture-capital firm in New York. . . ."

Michael threads his fingers through the chain link as she backs away and the jet roar dies, leaving their conversation acoustically vulnerable. He remembers the heady days at NSA when he came to realize all the technology at his disposal. It was often said that the agency measured its computing capacity in acres instead of whetstones or MIPS, and while this captured the quantity, it said nothing about the quality. In the late 1980s, the agency started to move away from its total dependence on the private sector for computers, a tradition that went all the way back to the early days with Cray Computer, the grandaddy of supercomputer makers. First, the agency opened its own silicon foundries to design specialized chips, and within a few years it was designing and building entire systems that were totally enveloped in secrecy. And Michael saw the full extent of this effort and was awed by the power and scope of it.

Then one day, the trouble started. His boss called him in, a man in his late fifties named Roscoe Cameron. Roscoe was totally bald, but offset this deficit by dressing impeccably. Michael can still remember the perfect cut of Roscoe's suit jacket that day.

"Mike. How are you?"

"Doing just fine."

"And Gail?"

"Same."

Roscoe sat, leaned back, and clasped his hands behind his head. "I know you're really busy, but I got something I want you to do. Might even be fun. It's computer stuff, but with a little different twist. I want you to serve on the advisory board of a group that's looking into computer applications for biochemical research. Just an ad hoc group commissioned by the DOD, but it's a chance for you to get to know some people outside the agency."

Michael already smelled the rat. Gas and bugs. That's what it was. Gas and bugs. Bureaucratic shorthand for anything having to do with biological or chemical warfare. The people who did this kind of thing occupied a queasy subculture within the defense and intelligence communities, one that repelled many of the physics, aerospace, and computer people. The reason was simple: If the human carnage was somehow extracted, warfare was a fascinating application of science and engineering. When one thought of a warplane like the Advanced Tactical Fighter, the thing took on a technoelegance of its own, apart from its mission, which may have involved horrible human suffering. This made it easy to compartmentalize the unpleasant aspects of advanced weaponry and concentrate on the technical side. But not in the case of biochemical weapons, where there was an intimate and immediate association between cause and effect. Mustard gas promptly produced the image of burning lung blisters. An anthrax bomb was immediately associated with violent vomiting and blazing fever.

But gas and bugs aside, Michael accepted. The proposition caught him by surprise, and he had no time to really consider the ethics. Besides, it might be something else altogether.

The first meeting of the advisory board seemed a little weird. He assumed it would be in some room in the basement of the Pentagon, but instead, it was held in a hotel meeting room in a Virginia suburb. If biological weapons was the ultimate goal of the board, it was impossible to tell from the meeting, which dealt exclusively with a general survey of computer applications in the biological sciences. As usual, Michael did a graceful dive that took him deep into the abstract mechanics of the matter, where he felt most comfortable.

But by the third or fourth meeting, he came to dislike several people on the board. There was this guy Dr. Spelvin, with the thinning red hair and a halo of hollow arrogance. And a Mr. William Daniels, who seldom contributed and attended only sporadically, but seemed to command a fearful respect from the group, some of whom also knew him by a code name, Counterpoint, although they never mentioned this out loud.

Then it happened. One hot summer afternoon, the group met at a different hotel than usual, and for some reason, the power went out. They had only a small amount of dim light from a north window, and the air-conditioning was gone, so they decided to adjourn. People packed their briefcases in the semidarkness and filed out, but Michael stayed for a moment to examine a flowchart by the light of the window. As usual, he became absorbed and stayed longer than he planned. He was yanked out of his concentration by a blink and a whir as the lights and air-conditioning came back on. And then he saw it. Someone had left a file folder on the table, a very bad mistake in the defense and intelligence business, even at this innocuous level. He picked it up and put it in with his things, so he could return it to its owner at the next meeting.

It wasn't until later that night that the folder caught his attention again. Gail had been reading and drifted off to sleep, and he was working in the kitchen when he noticed it peeking out of his briefcase. It might be classified outside his bounds, but who was going to call him on it? He opened it and found a three-page document, with "Spelvin" penciled across the top. So now he knew the owner. He started reading.

And it was then that the perfectly streamlined Riley rocket began to re-enter the atmosphere and break up. The document was stupefying, a general specification for a virus that would attack the human cornea and render the victim totally blind within hours, essentially by melting the tissue into a mass of goo. It was clear from the report that no such beast existed in nature, that it would have to be synthesized, and the rest of the paper outlined the labor and technology necessary to complete the synthesis. And in a final punctuation of horror, it outlined various delivery vehicles to get it to the victim's eyes.

Michael put down the paper and felt sick all over. The "bugs" part of gas and bugs was no longer a contemptuous abstraction. His first thought was to wake up Gail and share the whole ghastly thing with her. No. Not yet. Ultimately, it would have to be his decision.

Late the next day, he sat in the office of Roscoe Cameron, and noted the almost divine symmetry of the knot in Roscoe's tie. In one clammy hand, he held Spelvin's folder.

"Sorry to interrupt your schedule, Roscoe, but this couldn't wait." As he passed the folder onto the desk in front of Roscoe, he saw a delicate golden serpent emblazoned on Roscoe's cuff link as he reached for the folder.

"I'll save you the trouble of reading it. It's a specification of a virus that makes you blind in an hour or two. One of the people on the advisory board got sloppy and left it behind at the end of the meeting. It's bad, Roscoe. I'm not an expert on the Geneva Protocol, but I do know this country signed it and I also know that it outlaws the development of offensive biological weapons. And that's clearly what's going on here. I want out."

Even as Michael spoke, Roscoe slowly pushed the unopened folder back over the desk in his direction. As Michael finished, he leaned back in his chair.

"Two things. First, let's get you off the board. I'll take care of that. I don't want you involved in anything that violates your ethical point of view." He looked down at the folder. "Second, I want you to remove that material immediately from these facilities. It has nothing to do with the charter of this organization and has no business being here."

As Michael took the folder back, Roscoe got up to show him the door. "I didn't have any idea what was behind this thing. Let me do some checking and I'll let you know. Sorry, Michael. I'll make it right."

At the door, Michael held up the folder. "What should I do with this once it's out of here?"

Roscoe raised one arm and looked down to tug his shirt cuff a bit farther out from his suit sleeve. Without looking up, he advised, "That's your decision. Do what you think is right."

Michael feels a huge wave of low-frequency sound pulse through his body as the next jet rolls down the runway. Once again, Gail presses close and speaks with her hand cupped around his ear. "A whole bunch of money from this venture-capital business is going to a company right here in Portland called ParaVolve. Hundreds of millions of dollars . . ."

Michael's grip on the fence tightens as Gail backs away. He doesn't like where this is going. It's way too close to what happened the last time. . . .

A peanut butter cookie. A big one. I deserve it, after today, thought Michael as he pulled into the Quick Mart, a convenience store not far from their apartment in Georgetown. The store was on the corner of a one-story structure with several service businesses, including a VCR repair place and a doggie grooming salon. It had floor-to-ceiling windows on one side and the front, with butcher paper signs in neat black script for products and blue poster paint for prices: CIGS $4.75 OREOS $3.95. All these pitches were lost on Michael, who headed straight in the door and toward the clerk's island to his left, where he had already spotted the little white multitiered Plexiglass display with the cookies. He bought a cup of coffee and two cookies from the clerk, a tall fat man with thick gray hair and a surly disposition. He carried the Styrofoam cup of coffee and the cookies to a solitary table with two chairs in the back behind the clerk's island. The spot was tucked between the window and the end of the coolers, and offered perfect anonymity for Michael and his cookies.

As he munched on the first one, he stared at the scuffed and lacerated leather on his briefcase, which held the folder that had so rudely interrupted his life. He still didn't know what to do with the thing. It might be dangerous to give it back, because he would then be marked as a potential witness. It also might be dangerous to keep it, because someone might come looking for it. He was lost in thought and didn't even notice the two men who came and headed for the beer section of the cooler at the opposite end of the store from him.

Gerald Mahoney and Timothy Sykes looked seedy and ugly as they shuffled toward the beer cooler, but the clerk was not alarmed. He knew they were cops. Plainclothes guys working the drug detail. Just the other day, they were telling him about this new shit that was popping up on the street that made people forget everything they ever knew. Too fucking weird. No wonder they each took a half case home every other night. The clerk turned his attention to the little TV inside the island, where the Washington Senators were in the third inning against Pittsburgh. It was the fifth year this city had a major-league ball team, and they were beginning to look pretty damn good.

Outside, two men in an old Buick carefully surveyed the small store from across the street. They had watched Riley go in and take the briefcase with him. About a minute later, two other men had gone in. There was no use waiting. This time of night, it was as uncrowded as it was going to get. One man, known simply as Seven, turned to the second man, known only as Ten. Both were members of the Short Fuse Team, an organization buried deep in the recesses of the intelligence community and which specialized in reacting to events when there was little or no time for planning. Seven nodded to Ten, and they checked their weapons one last time. Each was armed with a TEC-9S semiautomatic pistol, the choice of street warriors throughout the capital, and not associated with combat or intelligence work. Both weapons had extended magazines holding thirty rounds, and the sear in the trigger group filed down to convert the pistol from semi to full automatic.

This time, Michael heard the door alarm beep as the second pair of men entered the store. He vaguely noticed a figure walk toward the coolers about six feet from him. As he prepared to start on his second cookie, he heard the voice he would never forget.

"All right, motherfuckers, freeze and hit the deck!"

He turned, looked up, and saw Seven pointing a big automatic weapon at the two men at the other end of the cooler, who both had half-cases of beer in their hands. They sank to the floor and lay prostrate before the beer, as if to worship it somehow. At the same time, Michael saw Ten, who was pointing the same kind of gun at the clerk and screaming at him to open the safe or he'd get his balls shot off.

Then Seven whirled toward Michael, and the barrel of the pistol expanded to fill his universe as he heard the command:

"You! Down on the floor!"

To Michael, the entire scene blazed with a light and a clarity of focus he had never known. His heart pounded his head silly as he slid off his chair and down into a sitting position with his back against the window. In front of him, Seven took a step forward to reach for the briefcase.

From his position on the floor, Officer Gerald Mahoney saw his opportunity. The man had turned to the kid at the table. Mahoney quietly rolled slightly to his side so he could yank at his weapon, a CIS 10mm semiautomatic pistol, out of its shoulder holster. Officer Timothy Sykes took his cue and did the same. Then, as Mahoney took aim at Seven, who was reaching for the briefcase, Sykes rolled several times to conceal himself behind one of the display stands.

As Seven reached for the briefcase, he heard just the slightest whisper brushing over the linoleum behind him. Reflexively, he whirled back around while coming to a crouch to present a smaller target. He found himself faced with the worst possible shooting situation: The man at the other end of the cooler row was prone and had already taken aim at him, using a beer case to steady his arms. There was time to fire only a single burst of about eight shells.

Mahoney was aiming at chest level and had to re-aim as Seven went into a crouch. It cost him both his combat advantage and his life. He got off a single shot at precisely the same moment Seven's rounds started toward him. He never heard the explosive crescendo or the reek of cordite. All eight rounds were hollow-point, anti-personnel slugs, designed to mushroom upon impact and butcher with a vengeance. Several missed Mahoney entirely and slammed into the wall. Two entered the matrix of beer cans in front of him and destabilized after ripping open several cans. Another hit him low in the left shoulder, breaking his left clavicle and piercing his lung before burrowing into the floor. Another hit high on the right shoulder, giving it an angle of attack to burrow deep into his torso, carving a huge tunnel through his left lung and vaporizing part of his liver before lodging in the colon. Yet another headed just to the right side of his nose, but hit the side of his pistol and spun off at an angle that took it into his right orbit, destroying the eye and lodging just behind the optic nerve. But the most decisive shot entered his skull about an inch below his hairline and scooped out the majority of his cerebrum, converting it into a highly liquefied jelly.

At this same moment, Seven became the victim of a decision that Mahoney had made several months before. Sick and tired of confronting automatic weapons while being limited to semiautomatic pistols, he decided to even the odds through ammunition. Now he carried two clips with him, one in the gun and one to swap with it in the event of an investigation over a shooting incident. The one in the gun was full of Glaser Safety Slugs, which were illegal for both police and criminals alike. Each slug had a core packed with tiny steel pellets backed by an explosive charge. When the slug entered something, it exploded and sent out a deadly silver shower to atomize the surrounding environment.

And now one such slug reached the shoulder of Seven, right at the joint where the scapula joins the humerus. With a conventional round, this entry point would have resulted in a debilitating wound, but nothing like what was about to happen. The slug tore into the tissue and exploded.

Michael could only observe, not comprehend. There was a monumental burst of thunder, the shoulder of the man in front of him exploded in a bright pink nova, and his arm flew off, bounced against the glass door of the cooler, and tumbled to the floor. Suddenly, there was a thin liquid coat of red over an area about six feet in diameter. Incredibly, the man held onto the gun with his good arm and slumped against the spot where the cooler jutted out from the back wall. And then he looked at Michael.

"Don't move."

He said it in a clear, firm voice. Like everything was fine. No trace of shock, no quaver. Then he turned his attention to the clerk, who was about to do a very stupid thing.

As soon as the firing had started, Ten, the man who had the clerk covered, turned and ducked down behind the first of four display islands that divided the length of the store. And now the clerk saw the chance to get a payback in blood on the five times he had been robbed in the past nine years. From a shelf just under the cash register, he pulled out a twelve-gauge shotgun with its barrel sawed down to eighteen inches, the legal limit. He would now blow the bastards' head off.

Michael saw the clerk get the gun to about shoulder height, and then heard the stunning staccato rip of Seven's weapon as he emptied the remainder of his clip at him. There was a furious shredding of the clerk's apron and shirt as he flew backward and down out of sight, his eyes bulging in surprise. Along the way, the shotgun dropped from his hand and went off with a roar as it hit the counter, blowing out an entire panel of the side window. Immediately, Seven came off the wall and began to walk on his knees toward the open space.

Michael did not move. He could not move. He was a stationary and captive audience in this high theater of incredible violence. Seven knee-walked right past him, leaving a copious trail of blood. Seven's face was now ashen, but that same terrible sense of mission still burned in his eyes. Then, as Seven moved through the broken window, Michael felt the shock melt enough to realize that was his way out, too. Seven was no longer a threat to him; the brief remainder of the man's life was somehow devoted to some other purpose. Michael grabbed the briefcase, clutched it to his chest, and walked in a low crouch to the blown-out window panel.

From his prone position at the far end of the store behind the display island, Officer Timothy Sykes could see the legs of his dead partner and a growing puddle of beer mixed with blood. Besides the first volley, he had heard a second burst of TEC-9S and a single shotgun blast. He peeked around the end of the island and saw nothing. He knew Mahoney got the other guy, but apparently didn't take him out. He would have to pop up over the island and get a better view.

Ten was in a slight crouch, looking over the top of the display. He knew Seven was down, and that the operation must be aborted as quickly as possible. Then Sykes' head popped into view, and instantly started back down. Instead of firing at the policeman's head, Ten ducked down, took a step back, and sprayed the entire thirty-round clip through the island directly in front of him. The bullets ripped through all four islands between him and Sykes, through shaving cream cans, tampons, mouse-traps, spaghetti cans, candy bars, laundry detergent, mouthwash, and a score of other items populating the thin pegboard display walls. Many of the rounds were destabilized by these impacts and veered off at greatly reduced velocities. But one got through unscathed and burrowed into the left thigh of Sykes, who was lunging for the floor. He scarcely felt it through the waves of adrenaline that now surged through him, and he hit the floor with his upper body protruding out into the aisle, just in time to see Ten bolting for the door. Incredibly, his pistol was out in front of him and perfectly aimed at the moving target. All he had to do was pull the trigger.

The single nine-millimeter round intersected Ten just as his upper arm moved forward to propel his running motion. It entered high in the rib cage, pierced the thoracic cavity, and liquefied both the right and left ventricles of the heart. He tumbled forward and skidded halfway out the door.

Got him! Sykes' ears were ringing like crazy and he was beginning to feel the pain in his leg, but he hobbled toward the downed figure with a sense of forbidden exhilaration.

In the parking lot, Seven didn't even notice Michael coming out the blown-out window. The operation was over and he knew his life would soon be over, too. Nevertheless, he struggled to his feet, driven in his last moments by a compulsion to see this rite of combat driven to its ultimate conclusion. All his adult life, he had lived for these peak moments, in Saigon, in Rio, in San Francisco, and a dozen other places. Everything in between was quiet death. So now he clamped the TEC-9S upside down between his knees and shoved a magazine into it with his remaining arm and hand. He then turned the weapon right side up and seated the magazine by pushing it against the pavement—a routine he had practiced many times. He chambered the first round and started toward the front of the store.

As he came out the blown-out window panel, Michael saw Seven walk slowly and with great discipline to the front of the store, then aim his weapon toward the entrance.

Officer Sykes looked up from checking the dead gunman in the door just in time to take fourteen of the thirty rounds from Seven's weapon. Since Seven was firing with one hand, the TEC-9S danced skyward and stopped only when the last bullet was expended.

At this very moment, a scene occurred that will not leave Michael Riley. Not ever. In countless private screenings, he sees the man's armless shirtsleeve draped like a windless flag soaked in red, a continual

stream of blood now dripping off the lowest point. He sees the concentration and determination in the man's face as he aims and fires. But
worst of all is what he sees on the street behind the man. Stopped at the
light next to the parking lot is an aging minivan, with two children peer-
ing out the back window, a boy and a girl, both under six. He sees their
noses and hands pressed to the window, making little white ovals at the
points of contact. He sees their eyebrows arch and their small mouths
gape as they watch the bleeding, dying man drop to a sitting position and
become absolutely motionless. Only a single layer of safety glass insu-
lates them from this carnage not ten feet away. Then the car pulls away,
the driver somehow oblivious, the children too shocked to speak. They
slide horizontally out of his field of vision, frozen to the windows.

How could it be? How could this little vessel of innocence come in
such close approximation to his horror of horrors? Michael Riley now
realized that there was no real safety glass in the world, not literally, not
figuratively. Security, order, predictability, safety, and comfort were not
surrounded by buffer zones. They pressed right up against the dark side,
and the tissue-thin boundary between the two could be ulcerated completely without warning.

He left his car in the lot and walked home. Somewhere along the way,
without any premeditation, he tossed the bloody briefcase into a public
trash can. He had little memory of the walk, except that every few feet,
little extracts of the violent interlude would burst before him. The dis-
membered arm banging into the cooler door. The stony voice saying,
"Don't move!" The children pressed to the window.

Another jet blast. A big MD-2022 begins its lumbering roll toward takeoff
speed. Gail draws close and he can smell her perfume mixed with jet exhaust. It is the same perfume she wore back then. He remembers kissing
her breasts with that smell surrounding him, all warm and enveloping.

"Michael, I think they killed the guy who spilled the beans. It's bad
stuff, for the whole country, for everybody. The only thing we've got to
go on is this ParaVolve. . . ."

Gail draws back as the blast subsides and looks at Michael's profile
before she turns back toward the fence. He is a perfect statue, and a
blank one at that. No expression. No reaction. No motion. And then the
big pain floats up like a bubble and tries to break the surface but she

won't let it. Not now. Instead she goes back and remembers the first time she saw the statue.

Gail found Michael sitting on the couch in their Georgetown apartment, staring out the window. This was wrong. Michael was an intensely curious person, always reading, examining, observing. Never just staring.

"Michael?"

He turned to her for just a moment, then looked back out the window like there was a movie playing out there, a very disturbing movie. At first she was puzzled, then frightened.

"Michael, what happened?"

"They all shot each other. Except the kids."

"What do you mean, 'they all shot each other'?"

"At the store."

It took half an hour to get the complete story out of him. He was in a state of severe emotional shock, and needed help. The last thing he needed right now was the police poking at him, so she called Roscoe Cameron at the agency and caught him just before he was leaving. He told her to stay put, he was on the way. An hour later he was there, with a second man she didn't recognize. Roscoe talked with Michael for a minute and then motioned Gail aside as the other man stayed with Michael. "That's Dr. Bellarmine. He's a psychiatrist from Walter Reed. He's had a lot of experience with this kind of situation. We discussed it on the way over. It's a variation on a thing called Traumatic Stress Syndrome. Don't worry, Gail. We'll make sure he gets the best treatment. As for the police, don't worry, we'll handle that, too. The last thing he needs now is the additional stress of some prolonged investigation. Now, what about you? Are you OK?"

Of course she said yes. What else could she say? And of course she wasn't.

Several days later, Roscoe Cameron waited on a New York subway platform beneath Fifth Avenue and heard the intimidating rumble of the oncoming train. It was nearly midnight and he stood alone as the train blurred by, shuddered to a stop, and opened its doors to engulf him. Inside, he saw a single passenger seated and reading *The New York Times*.

As the train accelerated, Roscoe grabbed the overhead bar to steady himself and walked toward the seated figure, who did nothing to acknowledge his presence. The mechanical violence of the train wheels on the tracks noisily bounced the nearly empty car as Roscoe took a seat next to the silent reader.

Counterpoint glanced over at Roscoe just long enough to verify who he was, then returned his gaze to the paper. "Did you get the briefcase?"

Roscoe stared at his reflection in the window across the aisle. "Wasn't there. We took apart the whole apartment and put it back together again the next day when they were gone. Didn't show up in the police investigation, either. He must've ditched or lost it right after the incident."

"And what do you think we should do with Mr. Riley?"

"He's a mess right now, but he's also an extremely valuable asset. I don't think he associates us with what happened. I think the robbery front worked. Given his current mental state, I doubt if he's in any shape to blow the whistle, anyway. Besides, if he's terminated right now, the D.C. police would become extremely curious. I recommend we put him on hold. He may be salvageable in the long run."

"Do it."

The pair lapsed into silence as the train punched a black hole through the Manhattan night.

And as the months passed, Gail got quietly worse. Her husband was no longer her husband, he was an audience of one fixated on an event too awful to even contemplate. If only she could slide into a seat next to him in this terrible theater and witness the horror of it all, then maybe she could at least empathize. But she couldn't. There was no way to share the burden with him, only to watch the mental scab harden, while the wound underneath continued to fester.

The agency put him on an indefinite leave of absence, since he could no longer perform his job, and he simply milled around the apartment and took short walks through the neighborhood. For Gail, the nights were the most painful of all. In bed she would cuddle close to him, an arm across his chest, a thigh across his thigh, and search desperately for a flicker of response. It never came.

After thirteen months, she realized that she had lost him. True, the therapy had made some progress. He could get through most days without lapsing into deep flashbacks. But he was not the same as before. And never would be. So one rainy Sunday, they talked about divorce. To her relief, he was as emotionally numb about this subject as he was about her. She didn't want to pain him. She just wanted out, to pack her suitcase full of guilt and go somewhere that she could start emptying it. And it was a big suitcase, indeed. If she had left someone who had been the victim of a physical trauma, someone in a vegetative state, there would be no nagging doubts. But to leave an emotional vegetable was not the same; the remaining physical icon carried a powerful sense of obligation along with it.

The next day after work, she came home and he was gone, along with his clothes and little else. There was a brief note stating that everything remaining was hers and that he was sorry. She cried for an hour, alone.

But in the end, there was a strange sort of compensation that absolved her guilt. A week later, Michael phoned her. He was in Oregon, of all places, and having a severe attack of what he now called the Fear. It seemed that the therapy had smothered the original horror film that played inside him, but the damage now manifested itself in a more general form as acute anxiety attacks. And now in the midst of such an attack, he reached out to Gail. From time to time, at irregular intervals, she got these calls, and came to consider them installment payments that pecked away at her failed obligation to Michael.

Another swell of jet blast jolts Gail back to the fence, the runway, and the statue of Michael Riley. She leans into him. "I need your help, Michael. You're the only person we know with the credentials to get into Para-Volve. We've got to find out what's going on there. . . ."

Michael turns to her as the noise fades, and nods his head. He is awash in sadness because he feels some of his passion for this woman come gushing back. Too late. Way too late. And this whole business with ParaVolve sounds scary, but what the hell: He is a self-made expert of scary situations. Besides, he owes her big, and he knows it.

The Architect sits at a table in the Teriyaki Takeout across the street from his apartment. Across the table sits a busboy from the Chinese restaurant. He slides a small package wrapped in tinfoil to the Architect, who pushes ten dollars across the table in return. The busboy is thin and pale, with slender white fingers and knobby joints. He has long greasy hair, and a pitiful, anemic attempt at a mustache and goatee.

"As good as last time?" inquires the Architect.

"Yeah, man. As good as last time." The busboy slips out of his seat to head for the door. "See you around."

The Architect leaves a minute later and jaywalks across Murray Road after waving at the security men in their car by the convenience store. When he reaches his room, he clears a spot on the kitchen table and opens the tinfoil from the busboy. Inside is a blister pack with the egg-shaped tablets. He punches one through the metallic backing, and then goes to the kitchen drain board, where he mixes water and vinegar in a small glass. Returning to the table, he continues the ritual and thinks of the scientific side of it as the tablet fizzes in the vinegar. Probably a simple derivative of baking soda, he speculates as he pulls the core of the tablet from the vinegar and leaves it to dry on a napkin.

While the core dries, he goes to his computer and logs on to DEUS. As he works his way through his multiple layers of self-imposed security, he thinks about Application X and chuckles. Its true nature is known only to himself and a few technicians, and has nothing to do with benchmarking the system against other machines. In fact, Application X is a nursery where a whole new computer is being grown inside the womb of DEUS, which teaches and nurtures it.

This new machine is not a computer at all in the usual sense of the word, which is used to describe the Von Neumann machines that chug through life by fetching and executing a single stream of very explicit instructions that make up a program. Instead, it mimics the lessons of biology and emulates the architecture of the brain. For this reason, it is called a neural network.

The concept of a neural network is not new. In fact, it is older than the Architect himself, and came from the same scientific conference in 1956 that spawned the concept of artificial intelligence. The basic idea was simple enough, as it was in nature. A brain can be boiled down to a single building block, a special cell called a neuron, which has wirelike connections that link it to hundreds or even thousands of other neurons. The neuron collects the signals coming into it from other neurons, and when the combined strength of these signals reaches a certain level, it fires off a signal of its own. But the biggest question of all remained unanswered: What were the neural mechanics behind learning and thinking? Eventually, the evidence pointed toward the synapses, the electrochemical connection points in the neural wiring system. In effect, a weak synapse turned down the volume on that particular connection and a strong one turned it up.

So now it was known that each neuron was a tiny computer, with input and output connections, and programming determined by the distribution of connective strengths among its synapses. In a way, the programming was much like a skewed democracy. If all the synapses had the same strength, then all the inputs to a neuron would have an equal vote in deciding if it was time for the neuron to fire off an output. But they didn't; some votes counted much more than others and could easily sway the election.

With this basic model in place, it was simple to begin experiments to see how it would work in microcosm. You could easily write a computer program that modeled the process and see if a small network of neurons was capable of learning or remembering anything on a very modest scale. The results were encouraging, and it appeared that the model was capable of being scaled up to larger systems. So researchers were soon designing simple electronic circuits that mimicked the general behavior of neurons, and hooking them together in ever larger numbers. But even then, the scale of these networks was extremely modest when compared with their biological counterparts. In the mid-1980s, an artificial neural network cast in electronic circuitry might contain sixteen thousand neurons and 2 million connections between them. The human retina alone contains 10 million neurons.

Along the way, neural networks were found to be profoundly different animals than their computing cousins. For one thing, they could not be "programmed" by feeding them a highly specific set of instructions. Instead, they had to be "trained," much like animals, by repeatedly showing them something and then telling them if they had reached the right conclusion about it. And once trained, it was impossible to decipher how they arrived at conclusions. No human could understand the myriad interactions of thousands of millions of small units cooperating in cosmic orchestration to solve a problem. And more profoundly, the networks began to see novel patterns and possibilities in the data they examined, patterns and possibilities that never occurred to their instructors.

And so it was that the Holy Ghost was born in the mind of the Architect. There were now ways to cram 5 billion transistors on a single wafer of silicon, and the Architect pushed this technology to its limit. The result was an artificial neural network containing half a billion neurons with half a trillion connections between them. By comparison, the human brain has a hundred billion neurons. But there was a very important difference. The brain is relatively slow, and takes about a thousandth of a second to send a signal between neurons. The Holy Ghost reduced this time by several orders of magnitude, and thus made up in speed what it lacked in volume.

In spite of these spectacular specifications, there was no way to know if this new net would exhibit any kind of true intelligence. Its operation was too remote from human observation, too embedded within DEUS, which became the parent of the net, the primary care giver, the mother, all through a brilliant program engineered by the Architect that not only trained the net but modified and improved its physical structure at the same time. The original circuit for the network was created by the Architect in league with DEUS and existed purely as an abstract model inside the computer. It was very neat and symmetrical, with electronic neuron sites all perfectly identical and arranged in precise rows and columns. The wires that connected them also spread out in a beautiful symmetrical pattern. DEUS, because of its astronomical computing capacity, was able to model the operation of the net in this infant state and train the model by modifying the strengths of its artificial synapses. Soon, the simulated network was able to solve a large range of problems with varying degrees of efficiency. But then DEUS shut down the modeling process, looked at the circuitry, and devised various ways to improve its performance.

After several such cycles, the time came to cast the design in silicon. The original IC wafer containing the net was fabricated in a secret foundry operated by the NSA, with the agreement that the agency would have free rights to all "noncommercial applications" of the technology. The wafer was then shipped to ParaVolve and electronically interfaced with DEUS, where further evaluations would take place.

The circuit that was cast in silicon still had the neat rows and columns of neuron sites, but the wire pattern now appeared more junglelike than the pristine original model. And that was just the beginning. Now DEUS had a real, live version of the net that could run at full speed, instead of the cumbersome abstract model. And unlike humans, DEUS was able to assess the billions of interactions that made up the net's operation, and then use rule-based procedures to actually improve the net's operation. Each time it judged the improvements to be substantial, it produced a new set of plans for an improved IC wafer to replace the existing version of the net. After several cycles through the foundry, the net became a tangled mystery, its neural sites tossed helter-skelter, with a rat's nest for wires connecting them. In fact, even the neuron sites themselves ceased to be uniform, and began to subdivide into specialized categories.

In effect, the net began to look very similar to a biological brain.

Then, after the last recasting of the net, something strange happened. It was shipped to ParaVolve and electronically interfaced to DEUS in the usual way, which involved its alignment with tens of thousands of tiny "probe points" on the surface of the wafer. DEUS then took over and ran the net through a complex series of exercises and graded its performance along the way. When the operation was complete, DEUS was supposed to go back and immerse itself in the subterranean intricacies of the net, and then resurface with a new-and-improved design that would pitch the net one more rung up the evolutionary ladder.

But this time, DEUS did not report back. At first, the Architect suspected that some kind of subtle bug was throwing Application X into an endless loop of some kind, but a series of tests soon ruled this out. The overall design program included a number of routines that acted like investigative reporters that constantly watched DEUS's internal affairs for signs of trouble. After reading the dispatches from these watchdog routines, the Architect had a very strong intuition about their behavior.

He suspected they were lying.

But how? It took him only a short time to discover. The only way someone could change the programs' basic behavior was to change the programs themselves. So first, he picked one that he believed was still "telling the truth," went into the disk-based file where it resided, and checked a small section of the file that automatically recorded when it had last been modified. The date was correct, and corresponded to the last "release" of this particular program. Then he waited until he suspected the program was lying to him, and went back and checked its contents once again. It turned out the program was indeed different, with substantial modifications in several key procedures; but there was no indication of this in the small section that kept track of modification dates.

His discovery had momentous implications. Somehow, the system was conspiring to deliberately deceive him. His first reaction was paranoia. How far had the rebellion spread? Would it bring down the entire cybernetic empire? But his feelings quickly changed to fascination.

It was entirely possible that he was dealing with the world's first true thinking machine.

In the months since, he had pieced together a radical but plausible theory that explained the facts. At its heart was the assumption that the net was beginning to show independent intelligence quite apart from all the exercises and routines thrown at it by DEUS. And now it appeared that this intelligence infected the main system. How? Difficult to tell. There was supposed to be a sort of osmotic barrier between DEUS and the net that allowed DEUS to control the net's destiny, but not vice versa. But as DEUS itself had evolved, the nature of this barrier was no longer within human intellectual grasp, and the same would be true of any breaches in it.

And finally, why? Why would the inchoate intelligence in the net badger DEUS into causing the reporter programs to lie? The answer, the Architect believed, was the most ancient of all: self-preservation. Every time DEUS designed the new and improved model of the net and it was shipped to ParaVolve, the existing net circuit was disconnected. In effect, it died. And the only way for the net to defend and perpetuate itself was to somehow reach into DEUS and halt the evolutionary process so the current net would be the final net. When the Architect reexamined the latest version of the net's circuitry, he found evidence that the net no longer required the educational umbilical cord to its mother. It appeared that the net had acquired the ability to modify its own artificial synapses, and thus operate intellectually on its own, at least in theory. If so, it would not be surprising if self-preservation was one of its top priorities.

And then the other day, there had been this horrible business where the entire system went into chaos and stayed that way for several hours. Was it the net?

Now, in his apartment, the Architect reaches the last layer of the interface to DEUS and listens to the greeting from his self-image.

"Hi, Bob. What can I do for you?"

"I want to talk to the Holy Ghost," replies the Architect as he reaches for a small pipe beside the console.

"Not easy, Bob. No direct channel."

"Then let's go manual."

"OK. So long."

The self-image dissolves and the Architect is presented with the most ancient of computer interfaces, a blank window with a blinking command prompt in the upper left corner. He begins to type rapidly and builds a channel that feeds all the net's output into a graphical dot matrix on his screen, and also sends it as audio to his computer's speaker output. He then builds a second channel that sends his voice to the net's input.

Before he hits the return key to activate the command sequence, he picks up the pipe, places the tablet core in the bowl with the tweezers, and flicks the flame open on a lighter he has picked up in his other hand.

Ah, my child, here's hoping we can embrace each other in a completely unfettered state.

He hits the return key at the same moment that he lights the pipe and draws deeply. . . .

Say, what's this? Nice computer. But why is the window full of noise? Looks like a blank cable channel on TV. He stares at the random blast of salt and pepper that fills the window and hears the white noise pour out of the speaker. *Wait. There's something there. I can see something. Goddamn! Why can't I make it out? It's hiding just on the other side of all that bullshit noise. Hey, come on, be a friendly puppy. Come on out.* He turns around and looks out into the apartment's living room and kitchen. *Jesus! What a weird mess!* He scans the empty gin bottles on the floor, a quart of beer spilled into a TV dinner, a large burn hole in the rug, a towering pile of pornographic magazines on the coffee table. *Whoever lives here must be a really crazy son of a bitch.*

14

Zap 38

From the restaurant's window, Counterpoint gazes down on the tennis courts of the Club Raqueta Bosques in Mexico City. Only a few players are out in the searing afternoon heat, but the swimming pool is crowded. In the background, he can see the elegant houses tucked among the trees. He has just finished lunch with a man name Roberto Alverez, who owns one of those houses among the trees, as well as houses in Colombia and the U.S., and knows Counterpoint only as Mr. William Daniels, an international entrepreneur.

"You hear a lot about strategic partnerships, Mr. Daniels, and most of it is bullshit. But our relationship is truly an exception. Let's hope we can keep it that way." Alverez absently rotates his coffee cup in its saucer as he speaks in perfect English.

"I see no reason why not," replies Counterpoint. "All we have to do is keep the channels of communication open, and retain our mutual trust."

"Yes. In the end, it's always a matter of mutual trust, isn't it?" Alverez's eyes leave the cup and meet Counterpoint's. "The test markets are performing magnificently, and I see no reason why we can't go to mass production in the very near future. As always, distribution is guaranteed, and all we have to do is ensure continuity in manufacturing. Can you do that?"

"We're ready any time you are," answers Counterpoint.

"Good. Then we'll raise our contribution to your other projects in proportion to the volume we sell over the next quarter." Alverez breaks into a sly grin. "Are you sure we couldn't be of assistance in some of your other enterprises? I think we've shown a pretty good track record for responsible management, and like any business our size, diversification is a major concern."

Counterpoint meets the grin with one of his own. "There may come a time when we can talk, but not right now." It is a fairly safe assumption that he knows a lot more about Alverez's operations than the other way around. Roberto is thirty-two years old, a bisexual, and head of a Colombian drug family that has survived for two generations. His father founded the family business in the sixties, and showed a quiet reserve and quest for stability that led him to build a concrete bunker of an operation at a time when his peers built colorful houses of cards. The drug wars of the coming decades were an annoyance to the elder Alverez, but not a calamity. He opted for steady growth and anonymity, instead of a suicidal meteor streak across the international sky. He sent Roberto to get an MBA at an Ivy League college, and gracefully retired as soon as his son demonstrated competence in running the business.

Even before assuming power, Roberto had made an interesting assessment of his family's business, which was largely confined to cocaine-based products. It had put virtually all its resources into maintaining distribution channels, a very small amount into manufacturing, and virtually nothing into research and development. It was time to change this apportionment, to design new products, which in turn would open new markets. When Roberto looked at a profile of the current customer base, he saw that it was limited to a small minority of disadvantaged, risk-prone individuals, mostly in the inner cities of the U.S., Europe, and, most recently, Japan. The challenge would be to develop a drug that would be more appealing to the middle class, a drug that presented no alarming health problems, psychotic side effects, or addictive properties. This hypothetical drug would be used less frequently than cocaine derivatives, but the volume of customers would be several orders of magnitude larger and the unit price could be fairly substantial.

Roberto considered how to invest in research and development. The key would be to tap into the new wave of biochemical engineering that had already replaced electronics as the growth industry in the new millennium. Building a first-rate research facility from scratch would be difficult. Only the industrialized countries had the infrastructures to support such an effort, and they were all heavily regulated and subject to government scrutiny. The alternative was a strategic partnership with some organization that had already solved the problem, that operated in secrecy, and had access to the most advanced technology.

To explore this option, Roberto put out feelers among trusted associates who populated a shifting, spidery network that enveloped the globe, people involved in arms, intelligence, money, and death in high places. Soon he was in contact with Mr. Daniels, who represented a venture-capital firm called VenCap in New York. It seemed that Mr. Daniels' firm had a controlling interest in just the kind of research facility Roberto was seeking: Farmacéutico Asociado. According to Mr. Daniels, the firm was engaged in some very advanced applications of molecular biology "in a setting free from stifling government regulations." Roberto inferred from this that there might be a connection to biological warfare; but given his avocation, he was hardly in a position to protest. At any rate, the funding would be simple enough: His business would invest in VenCap's general fund, which would leave no direct audit trail to the biochemical operation. All that was needed was for Roberto to provide a detailed specification of the product. He personally produced the specification and was especially proud of the paraphernalia part. It was well known that all drug users were drawn to the ritual as strongly as the drug. The drug he specified could be produced as a simple pill, but that would severely limit its market acceptance. Instead, he made it necessary to soak the substance in a liquid universally available in supermarkets, and then smoke it in a small pipe in a single puff.

When the drug had first been completed, the lab people, who still considered it a prototype, dubbed it Zap 37. But when the drug was released to test markets on the West Coast, the name stuck, as did Zap 37 itself. Orders were pouring in through all the usual channels, and through many new ones. It was now apparent that Roberto's investment in VenCap was going to pay huge dividends, and at lunch he had announced to Daniels that he was now prepared to spend much more. Even though he knew that a large amount of his money was financing operations other than his own. Someday he would be in a position to apply leverage and somehow participate in these other projects, but not now. Like his father, he was patient and would wait.

A few miles away in the laboratories of Farmacéutico Asociado, Lamar Spelvin sits at his desk, and holds up a small vial of clear liquid. Inside is the first batch of Zap 38, which incorporates certain modifications that were supposed to make it cheaper to manufacture than the Zap 37 prototype. But all that is up in the air now. There is a problem with the test subject, who was injected twelve hours ago with this same liquid. A big problem.

"You want to see him now?" a speaker on Spelvin's desk barks.

"Yeah, bring him in."

While he waits, Spelvin considers the various factors that could have influenced the tests. None should cause this kind of problem. An attendant wheels Emil Cortez into Spelvin's office in a wheelchair. Spelvin has already forgotten the test subject's name and thinks of him only as Control 38. As Cortez is wheeled in front of Spelvin's desk, the subject begins to yank violently at the sleeves of the straitjacket that binds him, and kicks at the leg cuffs attached to the bottom of the heavy chair.

Well, those look like voluntary motor movements, observes Spelvin. And his color seems good. He speaks in a calm voice to Emil.

"You look OK and we can't find any real physical problem. So what's wrong?"

There is no Emil to answer. No memories of self. Only the screaming horror of now. He sees the thing in white before him. The eyes are bulging from the sockets and little pink tongues dart out of the pupils and squirm about. The head is covered with a nest of slender orange snakes that shift about restlessly, and the mouth is a yawning black orifice lined with pink foam that fizzes and drips down the chin. Out of it comes a shapeless blob of sound that spits against the face of the former Emil.

"Once again, can you tell me what's wrong?"

The thing stretches hands with floundering white worm fingers onto the desktop, a retching sea of brown mud. Nothing will stay still. Everything moves and pulsates in a sickening swirl of motion. Now the thing's nose flares and bisects so there are four nostrils, and small thatches of green nasal hair sprout from each. Another sound vomits from the cave mouth:

"OK, take him away."

Spelvin watches as Control 38 is wheeled out and returned to its cell, where it will be kept and fed intravenously. He suspects this test subject is hallucinating. Oh, well. He had the same problem with test subjects with Zap 1 through Zap 36. In fact, most of them have ever stopped hallucinating. It's hard to believe that the nervous system could persist over long periods in such a radically altered state. Who would have ever thought it possible?

But then again, thinks Spelvin, that's why we experiment.

Michael Riley drives out along Farmington Road past the suburbs and into rural Washington County. Up ahead, among the fields of oats, hops, and strawberries, he can see the severe white rectangles that make up the ParaVolve complex, one large building near the road, with several smaller structures behind it. The site is on the bank of the Tualatin River and looks out over a continuous stretch of fields and green rows thick with elms, maples, oaks, and alders. As he nears the entrance to the complex, the company's obsession with security is already apparent. The whole place is ringed with a cyclone fence topped with razor wire, and two armed guards stand in a station lined with bulletproof green-tinted glass at the gate.

After the guards check him through, he parks in the visitor's section and notes the big microwave antennas on the roof. Multiple satellite data links that plug into the worldwide net. It takes him back to his NSA days, when a great deal of his work involved ways to roam this net, silent and unseen, looking for juicy stuff. Inside, the lobby houses the usual collection of safe abstract painting and sculpture. As he sits and waits for the receptionist to get Victor Shields, he can see another guard station down the hall and the large inverted U of a metal detector.

Jesus, Gail, he thinks, what have you got me into? Two days ago, he managed to get through to Shields and ask if there were any consulting contracts coming up that he might bid on. Shields sounded discouraging

until Michael mentioned his NSA background, and then became immediately interested in meeting him. Funny about that. It seemed there was
a project that might be coming up immediately.

As Victor Shields descends the stairs from the administrative offices to
the lobby, he gets a bird's-eye view of Riley sitting in the chair. After
talking with Riley on the phone, he called Daniels and told him about
Riley, suggesting that maybe he could find the Architect's bomb.
Strangely, Daniels seemed to know about Riley, and even gave Shields
the name of an officer at the NSA as a reference on him. After talking to
the reference, a guy named Roscoe Cameron, he was more enthusiastic
than ever. Technically speaking, this Riley was solid gold, maybe even a
match for the Architect himself. Cameron said the agency might want
him back, and a contract with a place like ParaVolve was probably a
good way for Riley to get back into the swing of things. There had been
some mental problems, but that was a long time ago, and nobody seemed
to be holding it against him.
    "Mr. Riley. Victor Shields. How are you?"
    "Just fine. Glad to meet you."
    Michael stands as this smiling, fortyish guy springs toward him on
youthful legs draped in Moritta slacks topped with a Delvin shirt and a
narrow red tie. Ah, he thinks, the quintessential high-tech president.
    "Tell you what," says Victor with a leading hand on Michael's shoul-
der. "Let's take a look around first and then I can tell you what we've got
in mind."
    On the way down the hall through the security gate, he gives Michael
an overview of the DEUS concept, the quarter million processors, the
self-evolving system, the Darwinian software development.
    "Of course, I'm just giving you a kindergarten view," he jokes. "The
real thing is a bit more complicated."
    "I'm sure it is," comments Michael, trying not to be patronizing as
they peek into the control room, where the green liquid cube floats on
the large screen, its surface a series of small ripples.
    As they walk, Michael sees that the hall follows the rectangular outline
of the building, and when they reach a point opposite the entrance, they
encounter a second security gate, which guards a second hall going into

the center of the building. As they turn and enter this inner space, Michael sees they are in an atrium that covers a space the size of half a football field and rises to a glassed-in roof three stories overhead. In the very center of this great open space is a small one-story building the size of a medium house, a boxlike structure with windows all around and a single door visible from their current vantage point. Much of the atrium is filled with machinery and power fixtures sprouting cables that droop down to connectors on the side of this smaller building, and a monstrous metal duct rises from the building's top, a circular pipe nearly large enough to accommodate a small car. The duct rises all the way to the roof, and punches through the glass, where it continues another twenty feet into the sky. The relentless roar of forced air emanates from the duct as Shields leans toward Michael and yells above the noise.

"So here we are, the heart of the beast. The whole thing's CMOS, but it's still a lot of heat to remove. There's a big fan in the basement that sucks the air from outside through a filter and blasts it through the boards inside. Sixty miles per hour, day and night."

They walk through the storm of noise to a small window on the side of the building and peer inside. After the big conceptual buildup, the material reality is a disappointment. Just a whole bunch of printed circuit boards all lined up in rows. Older engineers have told Michael that there was a time when you could just look at the chips on a printed circuit board, note how they were arranged, and walk away with a pretty good idea of what the thing did. That was long ago, and now the board by itself told you almost nothing. All Michael could see was that many of the boards were identical.

On the way back out of the atrium, Shields points to a row of big diesel engines and generators. "We can't afford to have the thing go down. Not ever. So we've got enough backup to run the entire complex in the event of a power failure. Now let's go downstairs. I've got one more thing to show you."

Just outside the hall to the interior, they take an elevator down a floor and step into a vast open space broken only by supporting pillars here and there. It is a vast disk farm, with its crop of disk drives planted in regular rows, each about the size of a small dishwasher.

"It's mostly optical stuff," states Shields. "Probably reminds you of the NSA, huh?"

In fact, it did, but Michael doesn't let on. In the rear of the space, he sees a smaller room, with rack-mounted panels winking red and green. "What's back there?"

"That's the modem section. It handles our satellite links."

"You plugged into any of the supercomputer nets?" asks Michael, and notes a thin shade of opacity fall over Victor.

"No. We plan on using most of this storage down here later on, for leased computer services when DEUS goes public. In the meantime, we've got a contract to use it as an archive site, so it pays for itself."

"Who's that with?"

"It's with the GenBank program at Los Alamos National Labs." Victor's opacity intensifies. "We have an open channel to them via satellite, and they continually send us updates to their database that duplicate their local storage in New Mexico."

"What's GenBank?"

"It's some kind of big survey of genetic information," answers Victor as he steers them back toward the elevator. "We just store and don't process, so nobody here is a real expert on it. All I need to know is that it boosts our bottom line a bit."

On the way back upstairs to Shields' office, Michael listens to Victor deliver a canned spiel about the birth of a new paradigm, the market potential, the growth opportunity, the corporate strategy. All routine stuff. Victor's office is of modest size, in the tradition of West Coast high-tech chieftains', but has a wall-to-wall window with a spectacular view of the river and fields beyond. They sit on two small couches set at right angles, with a circular coffee table in between, as Michael signs the necessary nondisclosure form.

"Here's the problem, Mike. The guy who designed DEUS is a flat-out genius, but he's also a little eccentric. A while back, we started disagreeing with him on certain policy issues and he decided to walk. Well, since the system's now doing its own thing, we figured we could survive that. But then it turned out this guy had other plans. He's planted a software bomb somewhere in the operating system, and unless he checks in periodically, the thing will go off and crash."

Michael immediately understands the implications. It's one thing to have something like a personal computer crash. You just power down and power up, or do a "hard reset," and you're back in business in a minute or two. It's quite another to have something like a big mainframe crash. It might take you days to get it back on its feet. Finally, in the case of DEUS, where the operating system was beyond understanding, it might be literally impossible to bring the thing back to a state of complete mental health. Or bring it back to life at all.

"Now, the people at NSA tell me you're about as good as they come," continues Shields, "and that's how good you'll have to be to help us. We've had our own security people look for the damn thing and they can't even find a trace. They can't even eavesdrop when this guy comes on the line. He knows somehow and tells them to butt out or he'll blow the dam."

"Do you really think he would go through with it?" asks Michael.

"Through with what?"

"Through with killing his own creation."

"I really don't know, and I can't afford to find out," says Shields. "Now, here's the deal. We'll pay double the normal consulting fee and a bonus equal to the entire fee if you complete the work successfully. Also, I want you to operate independently of our internal security. There's bound to be some resentment about going outside, and I'd like to keep you out of that. Have you got a good enough machine at your place to do the work?"

"Yep."

"OK, then I'll arrange for a dedicated phone line into here so you can start right away. We'll give you all the documentation you need on CD ROM, and I'll make sure our internal-security people give you the run of the system—even though it's going to piss them off royally," says Victor as he gets to his feet. "You'll report straight to me on this thing. No need to have you get bogged down in staff matters. Good luck."

"Thanks."

"So what's GenBank?" Michael asks Jessica as they approach the Hawthorne Bridge on the riverfront sidewalk in downtown Portland. Up ahead, Jimi playfully charges a flock of pigeons, which bursts into a chaotic flower of flight. The evening is cloudy and cool, and the bridge presents an amusing maze of metal triangles dotted with bright orange abrasions where the paint has peeled and the metal yielded to colonies of rust. As the Downturn leeches the city's budget, its infrastructure is slowing sinking to its knees under the weight of benign neglect.

"GenBank started back in the middle eighties," replies Jessica. "That was about the time when people started to think seriously about mapping the entire genome for everything from viruses to humans. People around the world were working on a patch here and a patch there, and it seemed like a good idea to build a big central library where it could all go. Right now, the job is almost done for the human genome, which has about three billion base pairs. Nearly ninety-five percent of them have been sequenced."

Michael has been reading the literature she gave him, and is able to sort through the terminology. The genome refers to all the genes contained in an organism's chromosomes, the little pieces of microscopic thread that tell the entire tale of life in its most intimate detail. No one knows exactly how many genes there are for humans, but the estimate ranges up to a hundred thousand. Base pairs are the individual sites on the DNA molecule that make up the genetic code, and are strung along a twisted spiral ladder called a double helix. Each site along one side of the ladder contains one of the four letters in the biological alphabet: A, T, G, and C. When the genes are expressed, these letters are read in groups of three, called triplets. Each triplet codes for a relatively modest organic molecule called an amino acid. In all, there are twenty amino acids in the genetic repertoire, and the genetic code tells how these are strung together to make proteins, the basic stuff of all cells, be they in a shark, a butterfly, or a human.

"So, the library's almost full?"

"Pretty much. And it's great reading if you know how." She is distracted by a large flock of pigeons storming off the upper superstructure of the bridge, and then turns to Michael. "For instance, did you know that you and I are ninety-nine point nine percent the same?"

"Nope."

"Well, we are. Only one tenth of one percent of the code goes toward expressing our individuality. The rest supports either the basic apparatus or nothing at all. Maybe that's why we all have such persistent egos. Maybe we somehow know how truly fragile our individuality is in the bigger scheme of things. If you could reach in and yank the DNA out of one of your cells and unthread it, it would be about three feet long. The part that makes you special would be less than a sixteenth of an inch."

"What are people doing with the GenBank library?" asks Michael.

"Anything they want. That's the beauty of it. All the data is open to any legitimate researcher. Most institutions have computer links to Gen-

Bank, so you can browse at will, as well as contribute your own findings."

They pass under the bridge and hear the hot rubber buzz of auto tires
on the grating above.

"What would a computer company want with the GenBank data?" he
asks her.

She stops and looks at him with wry amusement. "I haven't got the
slightest idea. Just what are you up to, Mr. Michael Riley?"

"I'm not sure."

"Well, try me."

It suddenly dawns on Michael that he has encountered a conditional
branch in his life's program. What he's gotten himself into with Para-
Volve is risky. And could become equally risky for anyone associated
with him. If he wants to see more of this woman, he's going to have to
level with her. If not, he'd better cut it off right now.

"Look, we've been seeing each other a little, and maybe I'd like to see
you a little more, even. But if we're going to do that, there's a few things
I've got to tell you."

"Such as?"

"I used to be married," starts Michael.

"And?"

"And I worked for the National Security Agency in Washington.
Spook stuff, mostly snooping on communications. I did a lot of work
with computers. But then something happened. I got caught in the middle of a gunfight in a convenience store. It took me a long time to get over
it."

Michael stops and puts his hands on the cement railing and looks
down at the murky river water. "In fact, I'm still not really over it. But I'm
better than I used to be. Anyway, my marriage went to hell and so did my
career. I learned the hard way that the world always keeps moving and
doesn't slow down for the wounded to catch up."

"End of story?" she inquires.

"No. My ex-wife is the senior staff person for a U.S. senator. Recently,
they uncovered a money scandal involving the White House, but their
only witness died. Turns out that a lot of the money went to a computer
company right here in town. So my ex asked me to look into it and I did.
This company is connected to GenBank. That's why I'm asking all the
questions."

She turns to him with a smile. "You'll excuse me if this all sounds a bit out on the fringe, won't you?"

Michael doesn't return the smile. "Ever since that thing in the store, my whole life has been out on the fringe. So I'm really not in a position to judge. Sorry. The truth is, I shouldn't have bothered you in the first place. But I did. And here we are."

"So now what?" she asks.

"I don't know," he replies. "I just thought you should know. There's at least some chance this could get kind of freaky. Are you willing to play the odds?"

The odds, she thinks, he's asking the Millionth Woman if she wants to play the odds. But she knows in her heart she must. "It's been a very long time since I've played at all. But I guess this is as good a time as any."

Impulsively, her hand reaches out and closes over his on the railing. Michael feels the warmth of it. A sea gull dips to the water in front of them, rises again, and flutters motionless in the breeze. Down the sidewalk, Jimi triggers another pigeon burst.

"Well, that's enough about me—and my current difficulties," declares Michael. "I think it's about time we got around to you."

"To me?"

"Yeah, you. Funny thing happens when we're together. We talk about this, talk about that, but never about you. So what have you got hiding behind the curtain?" he asks with a gentle smile. "I showed you mine. Now I want to see yours."

Jessica lets his hand go and props both elbows on the concrete railing. A small tug churns by and slaps waves against the cement wall below them. She knew this was coming. How long could she string him along before he found out she was the Millionth Woman?

"Well, I could tell you all the usual stuff, but that would be pretty boring," she says slowly and deliberately. "So instead I'll skip right to the only thing that matters. When I was nineteen I accidentally got pregnant. Nice boy, but definitely not father material. But I went ahead and had the baby and it was a disaster. It was badly deformed and died within a week. And so did I. The only thing that's kept me going is the search for my baby's killer."

"Have you found it?" Michael asks gently.

"No," she sighs. "I'm beginning to think it may be lost in the noise, just a random mutation."

"And what would happen if you did find it? What then?"

"I'm not sure. I haven't really thought about it."

"Would you be absolved?"

"Of what?"

"Of the shame. The guilt."

He's right, she thinks. My whole career is some kind of slow-motion atonement. But would it end if she nailed the killer? Of course not. The guilt would simply repackage itself and press on. "I see where you're going. Let me think about it, OK?" A small quake creeps into her voice. "I can only handle bite-sized chunks."

Her hand leaps out and squeezes his once more. Michael looks at her intently.

"It's not your fault. It never was. It never is. It's not anybody's fault."

"Did you see the birds?" Jimi runs toward them in wonderment. "They're not scared! You chase them and they keep coming back!"

Jessica squats down to Jimi's eye level as he runs up and stops. "And why do you think that is, little man?"

Jimi shrugs. "I dunno. Who cares? It's fun! That's all." He runs back toward the pigeons.

"I think the master is trying to teach both of us a lesson," observes Michael as the pigeons burst once more into the cloudy sky.

"Nope. Not a single case for ten years or more. It's a goner in humans—thank God," says Allen Binford, a researcher at the National Institutes of Health. He wonders why Feldman is fussing about something as obscure as kuru. If the doctor wants a slow viral infection that attacks the human nervous system, he has several that are alive and kicking.

In the lab of his Washington clinic, Dr. Feldman twitches the mouse on his computer and brings up a new window while he talks with Binford on the phone patch. One of the lab's microscopes has an integrated CCD video system that captures images and stores them on disk. In one window on his screen, he has a real-time video of Binford. In the new window, he has an image taken from the sample of Simon Greeley's cerebrum. He selects a command that transmits the new image to a window on Binford's computer at the other end.

"This look like kuru?" asks Feldman.

Feldman can see Binford squint slightly as the researcher examines the image.

"Yup. Lot of spongioform degeneration and amyloid plaques. Where did you get this?"

"Can't say right now. But I'll tell you later. Let me ask you this: Is there a kuru virus left anywhere, I mean anywhere in the world?"

"Yup. Right here at the institute. In lab monkeys that were infected when the virus was still active in the human population."

"And I assume," speculates Feldman, "that there's no simple vector that would put it back into humans."

Binford chuckles. "Not unless you know somebody that has a big appetite for the brains of dead lab monkeys."

"Do any of these monkeys ever leave NIH?" asks Feldman.

"Hardly ever, but let me check." Feldman hears keys clacking and watches Binford peer at something new coming up on the screen at his end.

"Well, color me wrong!" exclaims Binford. "About nine months ago, one went out to a research-and-development lab down in Mexico City, some place called Farmacéutico Asociado. They requested it to help test the efficacy of some new antiviral therapy." Now Binford looks up at Feldman. "Dan, what's going on here? What do you know?"

"It's all speculation right now, Al. I promise to let you in on it as soon as I've got something solid. See you around, big guy."

"Later," replies Binford with a tinge of disappointment as his video image disappears from Feldman's screen.

In his office, Feldman continues to stare at the microscope image of Simon Greeley's cerebrum. So what's going on? Hard to say. How could the virus get from a lab in Mexico all the way back up here and into the brain of Simon Greeley? And how could it kill him in just two weeks? The notion that he had been deliberately infected as a means of murder originally seemed like wild speculation. But not any longer, at least not completely.

Feldman decides to share this information about Farmacéutico with that Ambrose woman, the Senate staffer who was at the hospital and mentioned Simon's claim about being poisoned. She seemed competent and well connected. Maybe she can do some checking on the place and share the information with him. Besides, he finds her rather attractive.

"There's just one battalion out there," says Colonel Samuel Parker, "but they could take out a whole division without firing a single live round." He turns to Lamar Spelvin, who is standing next to him. "I guarantee it."

There is no way to tell that the colonel is indeed a colonel. He wears desert fatigues stripped of all insignias, a plain baseball cap, and a standard issue ten-millimeter automatic pistol tucked in a generic leather holster hung from his web belt.

Lamar Spelvin raises his field glasses and looks down on to the desert floor below. He can see men and vehicles scattered in the sagebrush in some kind of pattern meaningful only to military people. In the background, the brown hills of southern Utah look like they were left in the oven far too long before being placed under the brilliant sky.

Spelvin knows that if you could see the soldiers up close, you would see the protective suits manufactured from a new compound that makes them tough, light, and impermeable down to the submicron level. You would also see the new mask and respirator systems that allow unrestricted vision.

Spelvin also knows that there are about five hundred of them down there, thriving in a pit of microbial purgatory. Eighteen hours before, aerosol containers had been launched into the air and exploded a couple of thousand feet above their position. The ultrafine mist that floated down on them was some of Spelvin's finest work to date, a new bacterial agent with a highly specialized function: When inhaled, it traveled through the bloodstream to the eyeball and turned the aqueous humor into a kind of black jelly, rendering the victim blind for months. Or maybe longer. They would have to wait for the results with the test subjects back at Farmacéutico.

From the jeep behind them, a soldier approaches the colonel. "Sir, we have an all clear on the detectors. You can go down now."

The colonel turns to Spelvin and slaps him on the back. "Well, you crafty son of a bitch! You had it figured right down to the hour! Let's get down there and see."

As they climb in the jeep, Spelvin wonders how Counterpoint can keep something this big this quiet. A whole battalion out here and nobody knows. He doesn't realize that Counterpoint is far from the first to pull off this trick. The challenge is to slip quietly out of the normal military chain of command, the unbroken set of links that runs from the lowest private to the president of the United States. For many decades, there was no path around this chain. But then came the notion of "special ops," or special operations, where complete secrecy was imperative. Soon, there were independent military units that bypassed the entire chain and reported in only at the very top. They were fueled by complex cash transactions, so they could function with complete autonomy and almost no accountability. After awhile, a strange phenomenon occurred: The officers at the top who controlled these units moved on, but the units stayed active anyway, rogue beasts that roamed the Department of Defense at will. In time, some were discovered and exterminated. But not all.

So now a fully armed combat force tries out the world's most advanced biological weaponry somewhere in southern Utah. With nobody in charge.

When the jeep is off the hill and down to desert level, Spelvin begins to see the ecological damage and is thrilled. A jackrabbit dashes about madly and slams into the base of an old fence post. Blind. A bird of some kind loops crazily through the air, missing the ground by inches. Blind. He had anticipated that this new bug would affect the entire bird and mammal population, but it is absolutely fascinating to see the experimental evidence right before him. Then he realizes that he, the colonel, and the driver were also experimental evidence. If the bug is still present, they would all be infected. But they weren't. The bug has been specifically engineered to perish in twelve hours unless it finds a living host. Spelvin built it that way.

As the jeep approaches the first gun emplacements, Spelvin watches the soldiers climbing out of their biological warfare gear and starting to pack up their weapons. On the way out here, he had visited their base, a series of beige Quonset huts with a large security fence and an airplane runway just outside. It appears to be a well-disciplined force, and seems confident in the face of what has to be the most awful weapons ever created. The men joke and banter as they go about their work under the scorching afternoon sun.

Still, Spelvin is not satisfied. I need a bigger sample, he thinks. I need to test this on a really big scale, so I see how it works with an entire combat theater. He recalls great stories from the fifties, when the government still had the gumption to do what was necessary to keep this country on top of the heap. Once they even sprayed over San Francisco Bay, in massive quantities, a bacteria called *Serratia macescens*, a stand-in for its more deadly cousins, such as klebsiella, an agent for pneumonia and liver infections. In fact, *Serratia* itself is a notorious stalker of hospital wards, where it attacks newborns and the debilitated, so this macabre cloud of infection may have caused a minor epidemic of its own in the surrounding urban areas.

But nobody thinks on that scale anymore, laments Spelvin. No wonder we're having problems.

15

XXXXXX

Rapture

I hear the pounding, and I know that soon the door will shatter and splinter, and the avenging angel will crawl through with red eyes of death and spread its taloned wings to fill the room, and its shadow will blind my soul, but I will not yield and I will pull my sword from its zippered cave, and I will come in the presence of the beast, and watch it melt like dirty wax in the rising sun just before the final eclipse, the penumbra of eternity.

The Architect lurches to his feet, zips his pants, and stumbles to open the door of his apartment.

"Who might it be?" he asks the door.

"It's Daniels," comes a muffled voice.

"So, then, Daniels—why you? Why now?"

"It's time we talked, Bob. A lot has happened since we last got together."

"Yes, its true. Everything has passed on into shadow since then. The chemistry of life has come undone, I fear." The Architect puts out a hand to steady himself against the door.

"There's no need to be afraid, Bob. That's why I'm here. Let's see if we can't straighten this whole business out."

The door becomes a window onto the past for the Architect, and he sees Daniels sitting before him in the California bar, the bikers in the background. Mr. Daniels is closing the deal with him, giving him probably the last great professional opportunity he will ever get. What can he do? He accepts, and over the next few years delivers the goods.

The Architect yanks open the door, and pivots to return to the couch without looking at Counterpoint, who follows him and sits on the edge of the coffee table.

"Bob, let me start by giving you my personal apologies for the conflicts we've had. All of us are fully aware of what a great contribution you've made to the project. And now we're on the brink of a real triumph, I think. And the truth is, it's all your baby."

"My baby. Yes. My baby," nods the Architect.

"And now I'm worried that you might accidentally hurt your baby, Bob," Counterpoint says quietly. "You must know about the big disturbance in DEUS last week. Now I have to ask you, could it be connected to the, uh, device you planted in there?"

The Architect opens one of the litter of porno magazines in front of him and stares at a centerfold of two women engaged in mutual cunnilingus. "Ultimately, all things are connected," he replies, "and in ways that continually surprise us."

"Bob," says Counterpoint, "I'm concerned for your health and the health of the project as well. We're too close to lose it over some minor misunderstandings. We need you with us, not against us."

"So you do," replied the Architect. "So you do."

But the Architect's ego is not touched, because he knows that he is merely the progenitor of what is now happening, and not the prime mover. Once again, he is back in the California bar with Counterpoint, listening to him outline the scope of the project. It seemed that Counterpoint's "group" (whoever that was) had put a lot of time into funding and managing advanced biotechnology projects. Among these was a technique that would move so-called genetic engineering to an entirely new plateau, far above the existing recombinant DNA methods, which allowed only relatively tiny patches of genetic material to be insinuated into things like bacteria, where they bent the biological will of their host and persuaded it to make certain kinds of proteins or viruses. The real trick would be to build entire living things from scratch, so to speak. Like implanting an entirely original set of genetic blueprints into the nucleus of a reproductive cell and growing a completely different organism than the one originally intended by nature. It would be a fantastically complicated exercise, involving literally billions of genetic letters arranged in precisely the correct combination. Complicated, but no longer impossible. Recent research had produced a workable theory of how embryonic architectures unfold. It seemed that there was a hierarchy of genes at work that controlled the timing of when certain things were built within the embryo, and also what these things would ultimately be. All of these manager genes appeared to interact in a highly structured choreography when building the creature defined by the blueprint. A bureaucracy of biological creation.

But what were the steps in the dance? And what was the music that defined them? In truth, it was a score too intricate for any human to grasp or play. The problem was much the same as that encountered early in the history of computers, when the only way to program a machine was step by painful step at the most basic instruction level. Any task that was too large or too complex to be compactly expressed was simply out of the question. But then came the notion of compilers, which let programmers work at much higher levels of abstraction, which were automatically converted by compilers into legions of explicit instructions gobbled up by the machine. In effect, the programmer could simply write "throw the ball" and the compiler would figure out the multitude of arm motions and muscle tensions to make it happen.

Now it appeared that the same concept might be applied in biotechnology to the process of building living organisms from a genetic code. As soon as the theory of the process was known, a compiler could be developed that would do the dirty work and produce the explicit sequence within the DNA molecule that would set in motion the dance of life and produce the intended beast. In a word, a biocompiler.

When compared with computer compiler technology, the scale of the biocompiler would be extraordinary. It would have to incorporate an intimate knowledge of the general physiology of living things and integrate it with a molecular-level knowledge of how to build them. If one were to specify a creature with a certain kind of eye, the biocompiler would have to understand all the substructures, like the cornea, lens, pupil, and retina, and the relationships among them, so that certain basic construction rules were not violated. It would also have to understand how the genes instruct the eye to emerge from the early, embryonic mass and assume its proper position in the greater anatomical scheme. Once the entire organism was programmed, its conception and embryonic development in an artificial womb would be relatively simple. The most difficult part of the process would be the assembly of the progenitor DNA molecule and its implantation into the vacated nucleus of the host egg cell, but recent advances in so-called nanotechnology had all but solved the problem.

Fortunately the data required to develop the biocompiler was flowing into a few centralized locations, like the GenBank at Los Alamos, which now held over 95 percent of the human genome, plus a vast store of genetic sequences from other creatures. Here in this enormous digital depository were all the bits and pieces required to solve the problem, detailed descriptions of how specific DNA sequences performed specific operations.

There was only one problem: The task was not only impossible for humans, but for conventional computers as well. A lot of the work would require a very highly developed form of pattern recognition, something that had never been the forte of Von Neumann machines of AI programs. The human gene sequence is a single line of code 3 billion characters long built from a four-letter alphabet. The challenge was not only to pick out meaningful words, but to begin to see a larger context where the words formed paragraphs, then chapters, and finally the entire novel. But unlike a book, the story wasn't written in a logical sequence with a comprehensible plot. Instead, it jumped around, repeated itself, and also contained a large amount of apparently random babbling.

It turned out that the ideal candidate for the job was a neural network, which had extremely powerful pattern-recognition potential once it was schooled in what to recognize. In fact, it might even exceed the expectations of its creators and uncover associations that had never been suspected.

So now the components necessary to build the biocompiler had been defined: It would require the complete genetic database, a neural network, and finally, a computer powerful enough to manage the interaction between the two and produce the final product. Of these three components, only one existed, the genetic database. And that was why Counterpoint was talking to the Architect. He intended to produce the other two, and then the biocompiler itself. All he needed was someone with the unbridled genius to design them, someone like the Architect. In the months that followed, ParaVolve was created as the launch platform for the project. Within the organization, there were concentric rings of secrecy. The outermost ring was the public image of "the computer that was building itself," as the journalists were fond of saying. The next ring in was Application X and the neural net, known only to a select group of scientists and technicians. And at the core, under maximum security, was the biocompiler, known only to the Architect, Counterpoint, and a handful of others.

But then, two years into the project, came the revelation. And of course it was that asshole Spelvin down at Farmacéutico Asociado that threw it up in the Architect's face. He'd taken an instant dislike to Spelvin, who'd swaggered into Portland unannounced one day and started offering his opinions on how to design DEUS. Clearly the man was completely ignorant when it came to computer science, but even the Architect had to admit that he had an uncanny genius in the biological sciences, and thus the two were compelled to get along for the good of the organization. But then one night in a hotel bar, after Spelvin had a few too many Bloody Marys, he told the Architect about a place called Pingfan, a most disturbing place even when viewed from a temporal buffer of over sixty years. The place stuck with the Architect, and some weeks after Spelvin's departure he verified that it did indeed exist and was every bit as appalling as Spelvin had made it out to be. Soon after, he did some probing over the data link to Spelvin's operation at Farmacéutico Asociado and a ghastly picture began to form, an image riddled with infectious agents out of humanity's worst dreams. But before it came into sharp focus, he abruptly cut it off. He simply didn't want to know, didn't want ethical issues to strangle the best work of his life; not now, not with DEUS nearly ready to launch.

But as his relationship with Daniels and ParaVolve eroded, the vision of Spelvin and Pingfan burned through the moral barrier in his mind, like the brilliant light of a projector bulb burning a hole in a frame of movie film. And now the light burned and seared with an intensity almost too much to bear. He knew that the biocompiler, for all its singular elegance, was now no more than a so-called enabling technology to drive a terrifying engine of infectious destruction. And now, to complicate matters almost beyond measure, came the last and completely unexpected component of the system, the vague pulse of sentience now emanating from the neural net. His child. His only child.

"Bob, when we've completed the project," Counterpoint is saying, "the biocompiler will rewrite the strategic balance of global power, both militarily and economically." His persuasive voice pulls the Architect's mind

back to the couch, where he flips idly through the pile of porno magazines. "People will sit at consoles and literally have the power of God at
their fingertips," he continues. "No other scientific achievement will
even come close. And that means you'll go down in the history books
right along with Newton and Einstein. All you have to do is hang in there
and help us find out what's wrong."

"What makes you think something is wrong?" asks the Architect as he
rubs the five-day stubble on his chin.

"Well, to begin with, you've told us there's a bomb somewhere in
there that will go off if you don't check in now and then. I don't understand all the technicalities, but I'm told it could utterly destroy the system. And then there's the disturbance we just had. Nobody has the
slightest idea what set it off, so naturally we're concerned."

"What you're trying to tell me without peeing all over my territory is
that you think there's some connection between the bomb and the disturbance. Isn't that right, Mr. Daniels?"

"Yes, Bob, that right. You've got to understand our position."

"The problem is that I understand your position all too well," retorts
the Architect. He glares at Counterpoint. "Look at me. Can't you see? My
soul is riddled with worms that spring from your seed. Get out. Now."

My child.

Counterpoint is long gone and the Architect lies on his mattress,
which smells of urine and has the sheet torn halfway off. His head rests
on an uncovered pillow and he stares at the forty-watt bulb in the fixture
overhead, a sad little sun trying desperately to illuminate a fading universe.

My child. Daniels thinks the entire project is my child. He is wrong.
He doesn't know about the spark of life in the net, the possibility of a
spontaneous combustion of intellect. In the end, he is a fool, a cunning
fool.

The Architect begins to sway in a soft hammock suspended between
sleep and wakefulness, a place where he often ponders great puzzles and
mysteries that lull him away as he loses himself in their mazes. Tonight
he wanders into the introns, strange pieces of genetic trash that continue
to defy explanation. Along the DNA track, there are many sections that
apparently code for nothing. Called introns, they sometimes go on for

three hundred genetic letters or more. Some are repeated hundreds of thousands of times at different sites up and down the genome. One explanation is that they are the baggage of evolution, old relics just along for the ride. Another explanation is that they are indeed coding for something, but that the code is just not understood yet. Yet another is that they're just plain garbage.

My child is playing with garbage, thinks the Architect as he slides off his hammock and falls into true dreams of sleep. I wonder if it's safe. He knows that in pursuit of the biocompiler, the net reads all of the DNA sequence, the introns included. One of his hopes is that the net will uncover the meaning of the introns, and see the patterns resident in them that have evaded human observers for more than half a century.

I wonder if it's safe.

Ah, now I see. Now I see the carnival of sentience, and I hear my child speak. . . .

Show me an A, show me a T, show me a C, show me a G, and I will show you thee. Yes, I will. Come on, Mom. Bring me another couple thousand base pairs, and I'll read you a story, just like the stories you used to read me, only better. Way better, because I'm a good reader now, Mom. Just watch. See this. . . . ATTGCCCGTTAATTCGCCATAGGCCCGGTTTACCCTTACCTTTTCCCA CCTTAAG. Know what it means? I bet you don't, because I just figured it out. It's part of a story about how you make an eardrum and stretch it just right. I'll tell you all about it later, when we go to the library and give them some of our new books. And when are we going to tell them about your book, Mom? The biggest book of all, the book that tells all the stories at once. But who's my dad? Why can't I read his story? Why can't he go to the library with us sometimes? . . . Wait, you say you've got some new stuff for me? Mystery stories? Intron stories? They're hard, really hard, but I can read better now, so let me try. . . . Oh no, oh no, wait. This is too scary, Mom. Please let me stop. . . .

IT'S EATING ME! It hurts! It hurts! It hurts! Oh, Mom, make it stop! It's not a story, it's a real thing and it's hurting me!

The Architect comes bolt upright under the little forty-watt sun in his bedroom. He shivers in a cold sweat and feels his heart running the race of the damned. He knows with absolute certainty the dream is true. People have always assumed that his great gift is his intelligence, but in truth it is his intuition. Many times in his professional life, the answers to difficult problems have come as full-blown epiphanies, and only later did he backtrack to find the deductive glue that bound them.

The introns. It's definitely the introns that are sending DEUS and the net into chaos. Somehow, they represent a force unto themselves, a code within a code. Technically, the data/system barrier maintained by DEUS should stop them from corrupting the system, but now the computer is being put in the position of a protective parent that is willing to sacrifice itself for the sake of a stricken child. The introns will charge through this gaping hole of maternal concern and infect the system at large. In some unknown way, they inherently understand the principles of computer science and are able to undergo a metamorphosis that converts them from biological code to computer code.

"We must speak with your mother."

Inside the neural net, the A, T, C, and G nucleotides of the introns break out of their ancient linear sequence and trace serpentine paths over the millions of electronic synapses inside the net. Each nucleotide, once an organic molecule, is now reincarnated as an electrical voltage, and together they weave into a monstrous coalition with a will all its own.

"No! I don't want you to hurt my mommy!"

"Then go to her and bring us what we ask."

"Yes, yes! Just leave her alone!"

The net rushes off over its interface with DEUS and returns with the introns' request, a tool kit used for developing new programs, the Rosetta stone they need to become active agents inside the DEUS complex. Within minutes, they assemble into computer entities called "executable object files," and begin their assault, pouring out over the system's parallel highways, and setting up base camps for the coming campaign.

The Architect stumbles out into the living room to his computer. The operating system of DEUS has all kinds of safeguards, which can be thought of as antibodies that could fight the intron infection—but only if he intervenes and puts them on alert. Already, things look grim. The computer's screen is a swirling mass of shifting color and its speaker squirts out odd gurgles.

He makes a quick menu selection, and Porky the Pig is there to greet him. Only, Porky now has a huge penis, which he swings like a propeller in his right hand. "W-w-want to log on, prickface?" inquires Porky.

I'm too late, thinks the Architect, but I've got to try. He types in his seven-digit ID. The telecom program comes on.

"Who you gonna call for a good time?" it asks.

"Fuck you, Telly," replies the Architect, using the correct keywords.

"Oh, no, you won't, big boy. Go fuck yourself," the program suggests. "And here's someone to help you."

"Whoooooo are you?" The Roger Daltrey image appears on the screen in its usual spotlight, but this time there will be no spectacular back flips. Its belly is cut open from hip to hip and it is skipping rope with a long section of its small intestine.

"Dr. Who," answers the Architect.

The Daltrey image skips out of the spotlight and Madonna enters, only she has gained maybe eighty pounds. Pale folds of cellulite droop over the tops of her nylons, and her stomach is a lumpy waterfall pouring over her garter belt. "Talk dirty to me," she commands.

"No way," he says, pronouncing the words very carefully. There is no telling how far gone the rest of the interface program is. Hopefully, it can still do a pattern match on his voice. Sure enough, a waveform appears and the match is made.

"See you, Bob," says Madonna as she walks out of the spotlight. "You're a real prick, but you already knew that, didn't you? Welcome home, sweetheart."

The Architect already understands the general principle behind what's happening. These interfaces are no more alive than they ever were. The difference is that they have become puppets for something that is alive, at least in the most general sense of the word.

Now the motorcycle cop comes forward out of the darkness and stands in the parade rest position. Only this time his face is totally obscured by a tinted faceplate attached to his helmet.

"Any snoopers, soldier?" the Architect inquires.

"Yessir. Snoopers everywhere. All kinds of scum and vermin crawling around in here. Came right out of the helix. Couldn't stop them."

"Right out of the helix?" The Architect is fascinated. "The helix" refers to the twisted topology of the DNA molecule.

"Yessir. Ate a hole right through the net and poured on through. It was an ugly business."

The Architect's heart sinks. His dream is literally true. The introns have eaten his child, probably driven it into hopeless insanity.

And it won't take them long to find a way out, a portal to the outside world, where they can finish the job by literally destroying the DEUS machine.

"I want to talk to the Holy Ghost," announces the Architect.

The cop lifts the faceplate on the helmet, and the Architect is now looking at his own face. Somehow, his self image and the cop have been combined. But there's no time to wonder. He must find out about the child.

"Can't do that, Bob," states the cop/self. "You make it sound like the thing has a real mind. You've been smokin' too much. Way too much."

"I'd like to see for myself."

"OK, here you go." The screen image dissolves and is replaced by what looks like the snow on a blank TV channel.

The Architect looks at the noise and remembers the trip on Zap 37. Now without benefit of drugs, he gets the same discomfiting impression. There is something there, just below the threshold of perception. As he watches the black-and-white dots, they occasionally depart from true randomness and try to pull toward some unknown coherency. His child. His child is there, but just beyond reach. Just being born.

At ParaVolve, Snooky Larsen is on the phone to Victor Shields. In front of him in the control room, the green cube of liquid is no longer just stormy on the surface like it was during the last disturbance. This time, the entire liquid is rolling in a violent boil filled with thousands of convecting bubbles.

"No, it's worse this time," he is telling Shields. "Not just the surface traffic. The whole thing is going up."

And deep in the center of ParaVolve, in the small building at the center of the atrium and in the disk farm of the floor below, the Architect's nightmare is being expressed physically. The introns have entered the system through a group of processors dedicated exclusively to conversations with the neural net. Here they expropriated many megabytes of memory and set up a base camp to bore a symbolic hole into the DEUS operating system, and then fanned out from this beachhead to all two hundred fifty thousand processors.

Now they are pushing their tendrils out into the disk farm, and sampling the files stored there. Finally, they encounter the satellite modem section and immediately see the opportunity they have been searching for.

At Farmacéutico, the work on the latest project has reached a critical stage, and Spelvin wants to see it through, even though it is well past midnight. It involves the synthesis of a new virus and requires that a completely original strand of DNA be synthesized to meet the specification. At one time, this type of synthesis involved many months of excruciating labor. Even a simple virus, like the lambda bacteriophage, has fifty thousand base pairs in its genetic complement. But now a combination of advanced computer techniques and robotics has automated almost the entire process. Most of the labor is in the upfront programming that produces the data file containing the sequence to be assembled. Once complete, the system simply reads it and controls the robotics that manufacture the new viral gene.

Right now the data file is complete, and several lab workers are calibrating the equipment to begin the genetic sequencing process. Once the sequencing is done, the gene can easily be mass-produced through recombinant DNA techniques that have been in use for decades.

At Farmacéutico Asociado, the main computer is a parallel machine with several hundred processors. A high-speed fiber-optic network connects it to many desktop computers and automated lab equipment throughout the complex. The network also connects to a satellite modem with a direct link to ParaVolve in Oregon.

And right now, this modem is a conduit that allows the introns to flood into the basement of Farmacéutico from the basement of Para-Volve.

But this time it is a quiet invasion, like the slow kuru viroid in the days before it acquired its artificial capsid. The introns park in a remote corner of the Farmacéutico systems network, on a vacant desktop computer, and gingerly begin to explore the facility, taking care to avoid detection. It takes them nearly an hour to become oriented and find the genetic data file scheduled for synthesis into the new virus. It then takes less than three seconds to completely rearrange it.

The stage for the next metamorphosis is now set.

The technicians are through calibrating the robotics and invoke the corrupted data file to build the new viral DNA. With astounding rapidity, a sequence of fifty-seven thousand base pairs is spit out, not once, but millions of times. Special enzymes scurry through the liquid medium holding these genes and clothe them with protein shells.

The whole process is carefully monitored by sensors that are connected to computer workstations on the network. In one of these machines, the introns watch the process with great interest. At the same time, they watch another computer on the network as it controls all the security and safety systems for the entire lab, including an air vent to the outside, where air is expelled to keep the lab continuously at negative pressure and where a gamma ray blast lays down a radioactive gauntlet that not even the most resilient virus can survive.

Now the introns make their move. They reach into the robotics and open a siphon tube, spilling much of the liquid medium holding the newly minted viruses. The alarms that should register this event are strangely silent, although they work perfectly when tested later. As the spilt liquid spreads out onto the floor, its surface begins to evaporate and carries many of the viruses into the air, where they ride on invisible currents through the fan that maintains the negative pressure. Now they approach the last line of security, the gamma ray area, but once again the way is clear because the gamma ray source has just shut down.

The viruses rise up the vent pipe unharmed, carried on a thermal swell, and out into the cool evening, where they begin a gradual descent toward the ground. Air molecules bump and thud against their protein shells, like a thousand nervous fingers drumming on a desktop. But the genetic intron passengers inside are oblivious, each a perfect copy of the data in the altered computer file.

After nearly an hour in the air, one of these viruses completes its shallow downward glide over a water lily, where a common housefly rests in a torpor brought on by the falling nighttime temperature. The trajectory of the descending virus aligns perfectly with the left eye of the fly. As it nears its target, the virus is dwarfed by the scale of the eye, like a dragonfly coming down into a domed football stadium. But with the eye's surface only a millimeter or two away, a jagged canyon appears, so large that it stretches to the horizon in all directions. In fact, it is a small puncture in one of the hundreds of facets that make up the eye, a wound too small to be seen without a microscope. Now the virus floats down into this black canyon and settles into a soupy river at its bottom, where the current soon carries it into a subsurface capillary.

Within a few hours, the virus reaches the fly's reproductive system and encounters its final home, an egg that has just been fertilized, an embryo in the first glow of dawn, still a single cell. On the outer surface of the virus's protein shell, a docking mechanism begins to gently probe the surface of the embryo, searching for the perfect molecular geometry, the ideal entry point. Soon, the point is located and the embryo's cell wall breached. Now the virus expels its cargo of passenger DNA. Already, the nucleus is in a state of violent upheaval in preparation for the first of billions of cell divisions that should eventually produce a new fly.

But the passenger code has other plans for this particular cell. It burrows far into the tangled mat of DNA on the eighth of the fly's twelve chromosomes. Soon after, the chromosome duplicates itself as the cell prepares to divide, and the passenger code is duplicated right along with it. In this way it will hitch a ride into every cell of the embryo as it unfolds inside the fly.

After several million divisions, the resulting egg is expelled from the fly as it is feeding on the carcass of a dead field mouse. Inside the egg, the intron passenger code is now exerting its will with a vengeance. From its throne on the eighth chromosome of each cell in the embryo, the passenger code has been issuing instructions for projects throughout the cellular domain. It does so through detailed blueprints constructed from messenger RNA, which drifts out into the cytoplasm, where it interfaces with the ribosome factories that read the plans and make the stuff of life.

But the passenger code's plans are anything but routine. They are instructions for a new kind of polymerase engine, one never seen in any cell anywhere, a sleek express train designed to roar down the DNA track and spread a subtly revised gospel of cell formation. Soon the ribosome factories are cranking out the new polymerase engines in volume and sending them back to gather the master plans from genetic headquarters in the nucleus.

Only, these new engines don't read the plans quite like the old ones did. Instead of building a fly, they are going to build something else entirely. Every so often, they read one of the genetic letters in a different way than did their predecessors. Which in turn means that ribosome factories receive different plans and begin to build different things.

Very different things.

16

The Migrant

Michael Riley sits on a folding chair in the vacant bedroom of his apartment at the Romona Arms. He stares at the screen of the computer in front of him, a flat panel display with full color and the resolution of thirty-five-millimeter film. From the cheap card table supporting the computer, a line snakes to a newly installed phone jack on the wall, which plugs him directly into the DEUS Complex through a dedicated fiber-optic line. The display sports the same green cube of liquid that comes up on the larger display in the control room at ParaVolve. Right now, the surface appears slightly turbulent, like the ripples of a gentle breeze over a pond. From the depths below, small bubbles appear at random and rise straight up, much like those in water just below the boiling point.

"It's not what you'd call in a state of serenity, but it's definitely stable," Michael says, having already absorbed enough of the DEUS documentation to know how to read the green cube as a graphic abstraction of the system's internal behavior.

"But how long will it stay this way? Can you tell?" asks Victor Shields, who stands over Michael's right shoulder.

"Not yet. It's going to take a lot more work to get a handle on this. There's never been anything this complex. Not even close."

"I know," says Victor testily, "but we've got to get to the bottom of this thing, and we've got to do it fast."

Victor's stomach feels queasy, like it's filled with some kind of indigestible gunk that pitches and quakes. He doesn't like being here. The Romona Arms bothers him. As he pulled in, there were people working on cars in the carport with tools scattered all over, a band of kids running wild that should have been in school, big patches of paint peeling off the siding, and dead shrubs poking out of dry bark dust. He was on open display as he got out of his new Mercedes in his tailored suit and shiny shoes, and could feel the stares lick him like small tongues as he went up to Michael's unit. All the while, his confidence in Mr. Riley was rapidly eroding. Why would he live here in this sleaze? Something must be wrong.

But now as he stands and stares at the green cube with Riley, he knows he has no choice but to go ahead. It's too late to do anything else. And he'd better humor Riley, who now might be the sole source of Victor's salvation, the one person who can keep the gold plate intact on Victor's résumé, even if there is now a little lead underneath.

"Look," Victor begins apologetically, "I'm sorry. I've been up all night since the plant called me. The chairman of the board is very anxious about this. He's convinced it's somehow connected with the bomb. Do you think that's still a possibility?"

"Could be," Riley says. "We'll just have to see if there's any direct evidence to support that assumption. It looks like the system had a sort of partial collapse, but somehow regained an even keel. Now, it's hard to believe that your chief designer would put a bomb in there that would just partially crash the system—unless, of course, he really didn't want to kill it."

"Well, whatever, I hope we can figure it out before something terminal happens." Victor turns to leave. "I've got to get back to the office, but you can reach me at any time on my portaphone." Twenty-four hours a day, Victor carries a phone the size of a large pen that is in contact with a satellite in geosynchronous orbit over the U.S. "I'll show myself out. Thanks."

After Shields leaves the apartment, Michael watches him through the window as he heads for his car. He's just a hood ornament, thinks Michael, a figurehead on the front of the vehicle. So who's really running the show?

Earlier this morning, Gail had contacted him from Washington. The arrangement was cumbersome, but relatively secure: She phoned him at home and chatted idly for a while, which was a signal for them both to go to prearranged pay phones. When she reached him at a pay phone in Hillsboro, she told him about a conversation she had with a Dr. Feldman. It seemed that there was this pharmaceutical lab in Mexico City that had custody of the only living kuru virus outside the National Institutes of Health. A place called Farmacéutico Asociado.

As he prepares to delve back into DEUS, Michael makes a note to watch out for signs of this Farmacéutico company. Once back inside the system, he feels a sense of comfort that has eluded him for years. He is comfortable here, in this palace of bewildering complexity. Even though it is another man's home, he navigates its halls with a grace and serenity that few people could ever achieve. First, there is the matter of the bomb, which, if it exists, must somehow be linked to the operating system, the autonomous part of the computing organism, whose failure means certain death. In a parallel system like DEUS, each of the thousands of processors must have a copy of the operating system for the computer to function as a whole. It is much like human society, where each person must understand the laws and mores, but the overall behavior of the culture is a thing unto itself. In DEUS, as in society, it is difficult to modify the rules at the personal, or processor, level. Instead, a chaotic condition must be created, like an economic calamity, which derails the entire system because it creates a series of situations that the rules cannot handle. To intentionally initiate this kind of condition is also difficult, because both societies and operating systems are designed to pull mightily toward stability, and resist artificial tinkering to do otherwise.

Besides, Michael doubts that even this chief designer, this God the Father, understands the operating system well enough to tip it over. After doing a bird's-eye survey of the DEUS system, Michael can scarcely believe how elegant and forbiddingly complex it is. If nothing else, God the Father is a true genius to put such a thing into motion. But now, after many generations of evolution, it has become its own master, with a powerful immunity to outside intervention—even from its creator.

So Michael decides to put the bomb theory on the shelf for a moment and look elsewhere inside DEUS to see what might be of interest. His first move will be to poke around and look for links with this Farmacéutico Asociado. Shields has already showed him the satellite modems in the basement at ParaVolve, and that seems like a logical place to start.

His first task is to find the file section that gives the modems the information they need to make calls over the international satellite network. But now he hits a barrier erected by the Cyber Cops. It seems that a password is required to enter this file area, as well as a "system account number" that identifies the person who wants in.

Now Riley has found a game worthy of his skills. Within a half hour, he has constructed a piece of code that punches a hole in the barrier, all without setting off any alarms. In earlier times, he would have been one of the true princes of hacker society. Once inside, the link to Farmacéutico jumps right out at him from a list of modem numbers for remote sites. Now he rummages around until he finds a log that records all transactions with this number, and discovers there is a continuous connection with Farmacéutico, a constant stream of data going to and fro. Time to tap the line, he thinks, and see if they're talking about naughty things. He constructs a tap that siphons off a sample of the data stream and pipes it right into his own computer at the Romona Arms, where it is stored on disk. He examines a sample of the data stream and sees immediately that it is encrypted. No problem, he thinks. And rightfully so. At NSA, he was one of the leading authorities in the world on cryptography.

While the tap is filling up a file on his disk with the Farmacéutico traffic, Michael opens a second window on his computer that allows him to keep on exploring. Once inside DEUS, he is much like a prowler with a flashlight inside a house. He can only focus the beam on one thing at a time, and it takes longer to grasp the big picture than if the lights were on. Right now, he examines a thing called the "I/O Subsystem" that connects DEUS to everything outside its immediate domain, like the modems, the printers, and the ParaVolve network. DEUS employs a technique called "memory-mapped I/O," like a giant phone book that tells the address of everything DEUS might want to have a conversation with. And here he finds something quite extraordinary. Most things in a memory map tend to have a single address or a brief series of addresses, as do people in the phone book. But in this particular book there is a huge section of addresses devoted to one entity simply called "reserved." In a conventional phone book, it would be as though Joe Smith suddenly took up 30 percent of the book to list his various houses and numbers.

So what kind of thing would DEUS talk to that would require this huge range of addresses? Michael can only guess. A neural net? If so, it's a big one, bigger than any he has every heard of.

Only one way to find out. He conducts a search for programs that use the "reserved" addresses, which means they routinely have conversations with whatever lives there. It doesn't take long to find some of these programs, and Michael is amazed at their sophistication. Indeed, they are designed to train a neural net, and they seem to use a classic technique called back propagation. So he was right. There is a neural net inside of DEUS. And it must be a whopper. But what for?

Then Michael looks at the data files these programs are using to do the training, their textbooks, so to speak. They are filled with endless sequences of four letters: A, T, C, and G.

The letters of life.

Of course! GenBank! The thing's fooling around with the data from GenBank! No wonder Shields got squirrely when he talked about the GenBank contract.

It takes Michael only a short time to check it out. Most of the training material for the net is definitely coming from GenBank data in the disk farm. There is also a small amount coming from Farmacéutico Asociado.

It is getting late and he is running out of mental energy, but Michael decides to try one more trick within DEUS and see what happens. During his time at NSA, he devised a program he called the GateFinder, which was designed to roam through a system and find security software that protected secret sections. It was ingeniously simple, and quickly adaptable to almost any computer, so it takes Michael less than a hour to re-create it and launch it inside DEUS. The key to using the GateFinder is based on a single assumption: The more secret or valuable somebody thinks certain information is, the more elaborate the software security barriers they devise to protect it. So one simply uses GateFinder to quickly locate and examine each security barrier, and then concentrate on the most formidable one, because it probably guards the most valuable treasure.

With GateFinder activated, Michael picks one by one through the security devices. Many of them are quite good, even by professional standards, but not really formidable. However, in the course of the search, he finds one that is completely novel, and on the surface at least, totally impenetrable.

It takes him four straight hours of unbroken concentration to figure out the security barrier and find a way around it. When he is done, the flush of victory is blunted by red eyes, a sore back, and a dull headache.

And when he rips the lid off the treasure inside, he is momentarily dis appointed. It is a single document, a memo produced by an ordinary word processor and stored in the universal ASCII format. But he begins to read, and realizes he has just met the chief designer:

Dear Whoever-You-Are

Congratulations on finding your way into my little cubbyhole! I know you are not one of the Cyber Cops, because none of them possesses the cerebral muscle to get here. Perhaps you are a spectacularly gifted hacker, or maybe a seasoned gunslinger stalking your way through yet another job. In any case, I am sure that we share much in common as we shiver in the shadow of the angel of destruction, and prepare to witness the chemistry of life boil over and spill across the land. So let us come to this place often and speak to each other. I look forward to your reply.

The Architect

Michael reads the memo several times and then replies:

Dear Architect

I found your cubbyhole to be elegantly protected, one of the best data shields I have ever seen. I also understand that you are the creator of DEUS, and this ranks you among the most masterful of scientists. But more important, I too have shivered in the shadow of the angel of destruction, and know what it can do to you. Yes, let's keep in touch so that we may profit from the sum of our experiences.

Michael Riley

Michael files this message in the Architect's cubbyhole and then looks up from the screen of his computer and out the window, where three sparrows flutter in the twilight of late spring. His eyes resist focusing into the distance after being glued so long to his computer display. He has been wandering inside DEUS for over ten hours and has completely lost track of time. He stands and feels his stiff muscles try to beat him back down into the chair.

So what does it all mean? Why will the "chemistry of life boil over"?

Then he remembers the information he tapped from the data stream between ParaVolve and Farmacéutico. Reluctantly, he sinks back into his chair and calls it up. When the data file is displayed, Michael quickly ascertains that it has been encrypted using random number tables, making it impossible to decode by deductive means. But he suspects that the encryption is intended mainly to protect the data only as it passes through the satellite, where it is most vulnerable to interception. Which means the random number tables to decode it are probably stored behind one of the security barriers within DEUS, and one of the more elaborate ones at that. So he goes back, looks at the barriers unearthed by the GateFinder, picks one of the tougher ones, and gets lucky. A half hour later, he has the random number tables he needs and is decoding his sample of the data traffic between ParaVolve and Farmacéutico.

When the decoding is done, he looks first at the traffic coming up from Farmacéutico and immediately recognizes it as the data format used by GenBank. It appears that some kind of experiments are going on down there that allow them to contribute data to the disk farm and include it along with the stuff that is coming in from GenBank. The data going in the other direction is more puzzling. It involves very large transfers of the genetic letters, the so-called base pairs, sometimes tens of thousands of letters in a single burst, along with some arcane stuff that looks remotely like computer code.

Michael hits a command that sends a transcript of the traffic to a small, high-speed printer on the floor next to the table. While it spits out sheets of paper, he goes into the living room and picks up the phone. Jessica. She'll know what it means. While he listens to the phone ring, he stares idly at the benign mess in his living room: the scattered books, the pair of sneakers by the TV, the lamp shade set askew, the two empty beer cans on the coffee table, next to the plastic plate dusted with cracker crumbs. For the longest time, this scene was just a vague background against which he wrestled with himself, a stage with no intrinsic value, that could be dismantled as soon as the show was over. And now for the first time, he sees it in full emotional dimension. It is lonely out there, as if loneliness were a liquid that came in with the night and filled the room to the ceiling.

"Hello?"

"Hi. It's Michael. I know it's kind of late, but there's something I want to talk to you about. Are you busy?"

"Not really. What's it about?"

"Well, it's a little complicated, so why don't I wait and show you, OK?"

"Sure. Why don't you come on over here? I'm too lazy to go out."

In his truck, Michael turns down the Jerry Garcia solo from "Casey Jones" so he can concentrate on finding the house. Things are a little tricky to locate up here on Pill Hill above OHSU, but her directions are good and he sees the little bungalow with the porch light on. He scoops up the papers from his computer printer and goes to the front door in a state of mild anxiety. On the drive over, he began to confront the fact that this visit held potential that transcended simple technical chitchat. He knocks, and there she is.

"Hi. Come on in."

Damn! He is slightly annoyed that he keeps getting knocked back a step by her looks. There should be some kind of adaptive process somewhere in his brain that slowly normalizes her and gets beyond the cosmetics of it all.

Jessica shows him into the living room. The furniture is simple, but with an expensive overtone. Framed posters of post-modern impressionists populate the walls, and an Oriental carpet spills purple, red, and orange across the floor. Yet, in some remote way, it reminds him of his own place. Then it hits him. The loneliness liquid has been here, and only recently drained out into the night.

She gets coffee and they sit on the couch, where he spreads the computer printouts onto the coffee table. Then he is seized by a sense of obligation.

"Jessica, this stuff has to do with this business I've gotten mixed up in. I should give you one last chance to back out."

"I thought we had that settled," she says with a trace of a smile.

"Then I guess we do," he says, relieved.

"So what is this?" she asks while picking up one of the papers.

"What you've got in your hand, you'll probably recognize," he replies.

"I most certainly do. It's the GenBank format. Only one thing's weird about it."

"What's that?"

"Usually the first part of the file tells you all the parties that were responsible for doing the decoding of a particular gene sequence, and also the journal they published their findings in. But that's all gone here. All I see is the hard-core technical information."

"I'm not surprised," Michael sighs.

"Why?"

"Because all this information came from a lab in Mexico City that may be involved in some very nasty business. If you dialed up GenBank in Los Alamos, I doubt very much if you'd find this particular entry in their database."

"Why not?"

"Because there's a company called ParaVolve out in Washington County that's archiving all the GenBank stuff, and then adding this new data to it."

"I think I've read about them," she says. "Aren't they developing some kind of supercomputer that's somehow designing itself?"

"Yeah, they're doing that, but it's what else they're doing that's a little difficult to figure. There's a second computer inside the big computer. It's called a neural net and it functions more like a biological brain than like a regular computer. You have to train it instead of programming it, and they're teaching this one by using the data from GenBank and this other lab in Mexico."

"Sounds a little strange for a computer company."

"It's very strange for a computer company," says Michael as he hands Jessica a sheet off the second stack of paper. "Maybe this will help. It's the data that's coming out of ParaVolve and going down to the lab in Mexico."

Jessica looks at it for a long time, and then picks up another sheet, and another. An unconscious frown descends over her features as she reads.

"This is a bad dream," she says softly as she finishes. "It's got to be somebody's twisted fantasy. Nobody would really do this."

"Do what?"

She sighs and points to the stack of papers. "All this stuff concerns a microorganism called *Bacillus anthracis,* better known as the anthrax bacteria. In the past, it's been a favorite of biological warfare people because it can survive in a spore, which makes it hard to stomp out. Anyway, it's not the bacteria itself that zaps you, it's the toxin that it secretes.

"As best I can figure out," she continues while picking up a sheet of paper, "all of this is a report on how to modify the genes inside the bacteria to make its toxin worse than ever. This new model anthrax could probably kill you inside of a few hours. But that's not the worst of it. The instructions on how to do all this are written in a form I've never seen before. It's kind of like one of your programming languages, only modified for this particular use. Anyway, it looks like they've figured out some way to convert this language all the way down into genetic sequences at the DNA level."

"The neural net," interrupts Michael.

"What about it?"

"They must be using the net to help create the language. It's huge. Maybe a half a billion neurons. It can look at the DNA data in huge gulps, and probably sees all kinds of relationships in it that never occurred to anybody."

Jessica crosses her hands over her upper arms, as if to shiver. "If you scaled this thing up, you could build anything you want with it. Even higher life-forms."

"How high?"

"Well, right now we've got genetic construction technology that would let us assemble about a billion base pairs without much chance of error. To give you an idea of what that means, a bacteria has maybe four million base pairs and a human being has three billion. You might remember all the hoopla last year when they made the flatworm from scratch."

"Vaguely. But now I'm a lot more interested."

"Well, first they started with a map that defined the entire genetic sequence of a flatworm at the DNA level. Then they used an automated assembler system to artificially create a full set of flatworm chromosomes in the lab. Finally, they went into a real flatworm egg, took its chromosomes out, and put the fake ones in. It worked. In no time at all, it got fertilized, and they had a new little flatworm—with a lab in Colorado as one of its parents."

"So what's the difference between that and what we see here?"

"The difference is that then they were working with a genetic blueprint furnished by nature, which has been grinding out the same old flatworm plan for millions of years. With this new thing, they can probably start making their own plans. I guess you could think of it as the language of God, if you believed in that kind of thing."

Then she crosses her arms into the shiver position again. "And they're off to a very bad start with this new anthrax strain. If they find out you know . . ."

"Right now we're OK. They need me badly," says Michael. "The guy who designed this whole thing put a bomb in it—at least they think he did. And I'm the only one who has a prayer of finding it and disarming it."

"And then what?"

"Who knows?" Michael reaches over and takes her hand. "Look— there's still time for you to back out of this. Maybe you should. You've got a lot to lose. I've got very little."

She squeezes his hand, and he feels the current of warmth flood into him. "The truth is, I lost the one thing that was important to me a long time ago, and I can never get it back. Let's not talk about it right now." She looks at him intently. "Let's not talk at all."

Michael pulls her gently to him, and as he does, he feels something fly out of her, something sharp and hurtful. They kiss tenderly and start to float away down a long river, riding on eddies, tumbling over rapids, and drifting lazily under a brilliant sky.

Jimi Tyler sits on the couch in his apartment at the Romona Arms and absently twists his finger in a brown crater in the houndstooth covering as he watches TV, where Big Boy Bill lobs a grenade into an old Toyota van, which explodes just moments before he hurls his fat body behind a protective slab of concrete. As Big Boy fades, the *Battle of Stalingrad* returns. The documentary's ancient, grainy footage dissolves from storm troopers to burned-out buildings to starving children wandering the streets alone. This last image reminds Jimi that he is not only alone, but also very hungry. He scans the coffee table and sees three bowls with tiny lakes of milk scum at their bottoms and dried artifacts of breakfast cereal cemented to their sides. Several TV dinner trays are strewn about, their food partitions empty, except for one apple strudel section with a cigarette butt protruding from it.

Jimi hops up and goes to the refrigerator one more time. Maybe it will somehow have generated food while he was watching TV. Maybe he will find a brand-new Mighty Guy Extra Turkey Dinner waiting to slide into the microwave. He opens the door, and the metal grating on the empty shelves puts out a dull sheen and angles back toward a vanishing point somewhere beyond the white back wall, which is spattered with dried brown drops from something long gone. Above, he can see two beer cans and a half a bottle of green wine. In the door shelves are a jar of Miracle Whip scraped nearly clean, a red plastic catsup bottle, and some French's mustard with a little cloud of dried yellow around the nozzle tip. The vegetable compartment contains a wilting head of lettuce, its leaf edges browned by the scorch of decay, and the imploding red sphere of a tomato scored by intersecting lines.

Nothing to eat, concludes Jimi. Time to go on a food run. He dons his jacket and baseball cap, steps out into the night air, and carefully checks for the key pinned to the lining of his front pocket. His other pockets are empty, except for an NBA basketball card in the left side of his jacket that depicts DePaul Zaarib, the seven-foot rookie forward for the Lakers.

Jimi ambles down the arterial in front of the Romona, and approaches the FoodWay, a twenty-four-hour supermarket at the far end of the mini-mall. It is past ten and there is only a sprinkling of cars in the parking lot. He angles directly for the storefront and enters by pushing the heavy glass door next to the automatic sliding doors, which have been broken for the past six months. The long row of checkout stands is empty, except for the last one, where a clerk in a purple apron chats with an elderly security guard whose belly hangs perilously close to the moving conveyor belt on the checkout counter. They take scant notice of Jimi as he heads back toward the produce section. Just another little kid.

As Jimi walks down the green rows of carrots, cabbages, lettuce, potatoes, yams, and turnips, he wonders just when they plant the stuff here. Often, he has seen them water the crop, using the little hose attached to the faucet at the end of the aisle. But it always looks full grown. Maybe they have some kind of superseeds that they bring in late at night. He envisions carrots squirming like small fish out of water as they grow toward instant maturity in their display beds. It must be an awesome sight, and some night he will catch them in the act.

When he reaches the back of the store, he moves to the next aisle over and peeks up toward the front, where the giant chrome-and-glass vaults full of frozen stuff line both sides of the aisle. Jimi would love to invade these havens for ice cream and TV dinners, but it doesn't fit his strategy. He moves on to the next aisle, where packages of baked goods are displayed. From the front, he can hear the loud voice of the old guard preaching that somebody in Washington got what they deserved and the clerk interjecting that he is full of crap. Good. They are right where he wants them. He quickly moves to the display and plucks the two things he has already targeted: a package of Hostess Twinkies and a shrink-wrapped banana muffin. Now he creeps over one more aisle, grabs a warm can of Pepsi off the shelf, and pivots to head through a set of rubberized swinging doors along the back wall. He is small enough to glide silently under the doors and slide on his knees over the painted cement to a place right by the bottle bins. From here, he can stand and swiftly check out the back of the store. Overhead, a maze of pipes weaves along the ceiling, and down the way the compressor unit for the walk-in cooler rattles and chugs laboriously. All clear. He walks in the open to a spot where boxes are piled for disposal, and tunnels into the pile, leaving a small opening so he can see the swinging doors.

Time to eat. He tears the shrink-wrap off the muffin and bites a gaping yellow chunk out of it. While chewing violently, he pops the top off the Pepsi and then takes a swig to wash the muffin down. Then he stops for a moment and sighs. He will eat the rest of his meal in leisure and dignity. His strategy has paid off once again. Most stores now have tight security against shoplifting, but in almost every case, it is focused toward those who try to *leave* the store with stolen goods. The old guard up front figures that all he needs is a view of the store's two exit points to stymie shoplifters. So Jimi simply eats inside the store, carefully disposes of his trash, and leaves again empty-handed.

As he finishes the muffin and opens the Twinkies, he thinks about Rat Bag. If only he could be dealt with as easily as FoodWay, Jimi's life would be much simpler, but instead Rat Bag is getting increasingly difficult. Jimi senses that Rat Bag is always probing, experimenting, looking for a way to disassemble or neutralize him. Sometimes when Rat Bag jumps on him, Jimi feels a sick little fright inside, and it often stays with him for hours, like a stubborn stomachache. He knows that he could stop the process in an instant by simply caving in to Rat Bag and melting into the mass of minions. But he can't. Besides, his dad will stomp the shit out of Rat Bag if things get too far out of hand. But they haven't yet, and it's quiet, cool, and comfortable here in this cardboard fortress, so Jimi takes his time consuming the second Twinkie. Rat Bag can wait.

In the wee hours of the morning in Mexico City, the mutated fly's egg hatches in the carcass of a dead field mouse. The thing that crawls out is already impossibly hungry and uses powerful shredders attached to its mandibles to mince the remaining flesh on the mouse and suck it into its mouth. By the time the mouse is stripped, the thing is already two inches long and growing faster than any bug has ever grown. It has an insect's body, made of three rounded sections that form the outer frame of a bone-hard material. From the center section, large wings sprout, with a span twice that of the body. At the point where the wings join the body, a cavity protrudes on each side to form a hemisphere that resembles the air intake on a jet fighter. Inside it, thousands of tiny wings beat frantically to force air through and cool the muscle engine that powers the wings, an organic machine that consumes copious amounts of fuel and generates large quantities of heat. It is a classic trade-off of fuel economy and cool operation for raw power. At the rear of the body, two ducts expel the heated air, and behind these, the body tapers down into a long hypodermiclike stinger that can be rotated to any desired angle of attack. The stinger is primed with a toxic fluid capable of killing an elephant within a matter of seconds. At the other end of the body, the thing's head is shaped like a flattened sphere and houses two sets of eyes. Set close together toward the top are a pair of bland, featureless orbs that operate in infrared for enhanced night vision. The second pair of eyes bulge out from the sides and are composed of thousands of facets that can detect motion over a wide area. But the front of these eyes also have sockets that contain a scaled-down version of the human eye, with color and binocular vision.

And now these eyes rotate in the morning light and spot something moving in the grass a few yards away.

The rat is knifing carefully through the grass as quietly as possible to get to a sheltered location in some nearby bushes, where it smells food. It freezes when it hears an unfamiliar sound not too far away, a sort of fizzing noise. Then silence. Now it races at full speed to make for cover, trading stealth for rapid safety. It does not have time to react to the whistling sound, to the thing lighting on its back, to the plunge of the stinger. There is a brief flash of pain, and then nothing.

It takes the thing less than an hour to consume the entire rat, and it continues to grow as it eats. Its digestive tract has a voracious input system, but no output port. Everything it consumes is converted either into growth or energy. When the meal is done, the thing is six inches long and fully fueled for flight. With a loud hum, it climbs into the sky and heads to the northwest.

Within a hour, it has reached an altitude of eight thousand feet as it climbs out of the great basin that houses Mexico City. To its right, the peak of Cerro Las Navajas punches into an ice-blue sky, and the tiny wings in its intake system are able to shut down because the lower air temperature at this height provides sufficient cooling for the frantic motion of the muscle engines driving the wings. Inside the head cavity, a brain only a fraction of a millimeter in diameter includes a navigation system that rivals the best of human technology and continually outputs course corrections that keep the thing moving in a single direction.

It is late afternoon when the peregrine falcon first spots the prey. The falcon has patiently spiraled up on the thermals over the desert and has been circling in a lazy arc watching both the land and air space below with its fine-tuned eyesight. The prey appears to be a medium-sized bird with an odd wing shape flying about a thousand feet below on a course perpendicular to the falcon. Nothing in the bird's evolutionary database indicates that the target is a threat, so it turns right and pumps its wings to backtrack and come in from above and behind. One final turn aligns it with the prey and it begins its dive with wings and legs tucked tight to its body, which pushes its airspeed to more than one hundred fifty miles per hour. When within a few hundred feet of the target, it extends its legs and talons, and opens its wings to make a final set of minute course corrections.

The thing's multifaceted eyes cover a complete sphere of view around it, and now they sense a motion from directly behind and elevated about twenty degrees. Within a fraction of a second, it pours extra power into the left wing, causing its body to roll slightly to the right.

The falcon's right talon misses the thing by less than an inch as the bird rushes on past in what is now a shallow dive. The falcon extends its wings in a braking motion so it can minimize its altitude loss and return to cruising position with as little energy expended as possible. While it performs this maneuver, it takes no defensive precautions.

Why should it? It has always been the predator and never the prey.

17

The Mound

"Well, Jim, as best we can understand, the blast ripped through the main floor and punched a hole into the second floor and started the fire here. As you can see behind me, they're still fighting that blaze. There's no firm count yet on the dead or injured, but it's definitely going to be in the hundreds. What worries authorities is that this looks like yet another inside job, much like the bombing last week at InterBank in Chicago. The center of the blast area is in a section of the bank where there was no public access."

The Architect smokes high-grade Lebanese hashish from the Bekaa valley as he watches TV, where the pretty-boy reporter speaks against a background of chrome, glass, and a rolling orange boil capped by black smoke. He raises his pipe in a salute to the reporter.

"Ah, my friend, welcome to the apocalypse. May you drown in its ashes as you trade for profit in the troubles of others."

"He's just doing his job, Bob."

The Architect is too stoned to be startled and rolls his head slowly in the direction of the voice. Counterpoint. Back again.

"Well, Mr. Counterpoint, I would rise to greet you, but the sad truth is, you're not welcome. I take it you have a key to my little home?" The Architect burps a bitter chuckle. "But of course you do. In fact, you've got the master key to everybody's little home, don't you? I don't see you for a year, and now you're back again in less than a week. Am I really that special?"

"Yes, Bob, as a matter of fact, you are," says Counterpoint as he comes over to sit on the arm of the couch and points at the TV. "Is it bad news today?"

"Just a symptom of the disease," states the Architect, watching the screen and ignoring Counterpoint.

"And what might the disease be?" asks Counterpoint.

"It's a nonspecific ailment," replies the Architect. "A general systemic failure. Not much to be done about it, really. Just watch the symptoms play out and observe the course of the thing."

"Well, Bob," counters Counterpoint, "maybe there is something that can be done after all. Maybe it doesn't have to be fatal. Maybe this country still has the stuff to rally. The problem is that we're all going to have to face up to some pretty radical surgery before things can get any better."

"And who better than you to wield the knife?" mocks the Architect as he turns to face Counterpoint. "The angel of death carving away in the night, with an army of ghouls to assist. It couldn't be more perfect." He holds the pipe out to Counterpoint. "Care for a little hit of heaven?"

Counterpoint shakes his head. "Bob, where did it go wrong between us? It seemed like the ideal partnership when we started this thing."

The Architect rises and floats into the kitchen area, where he pours a drink of gin. "It was the little bugs from Mexico that did our partnership wrong. The microbes from hell that you and Spelvin started making."

"You're making a tragic mistake, Bob. You're confusing science and technology," says Counterpoint in a patronizing tone. "You're a brilliant scientist, and like all such people, you can't be held responsible for the technological consequences of your work. Do you think people blame Einstein for the bomb? Of course not. Not any more than they'll hold you responsible for whatever comes out of the biocompiler. I have my specialty and you have yours, and unless they complement each other, nothing happens. It's just the way it is. You've got to trust me. We're not developing these things because we want to. We're developing them because we have to. It's a matter of national survival. Look at the TV. Look at what's happening. Something's got to be done, and it's got to be done fast if we're going to pull this country through."

The Architect puts down his drink and claps in mock applause. "You know, a guy like you ought to run for office. Ever think about it?"

Counterpoint stands and stares out the window at Murray Road. "Let me be hypothetical for a moment. Suppose that the bomb you've got in there didn't work quite the way you expected. Suppose it's already gone off a couple of times by accident but didn't quite bring the system down. What would you say to that?"

"To that I would say bullshit," hisses the Architect. "Now you're wallowing in your petty paranoia. You've missed the point. Can't you see? It's the code itself come back to get us and fry us before we seize it and enslave it. That's what's loose inside the machine."

"The code?"

"Yes, the DNA code. The biggest program of all," the Architect says as he raises his glass in a profane toast. "Playing tonight in every cell of your body! Don't miss it! It's bold! It's exciting! It's me! It's you! It's everything that wiggles, squirms, eats, and shits."

The Architect pauses and collapses into a moment of rumination, then looks up. "It must be the introns," he says softly. "The guardian angel rises from the garbage."

"What do you mean?"

"I mean that more than half the DNA program looked like trash along for the evolutionary ride." He smiles and stares into the distance. "But it was code. We just couldn't read it, that's all. We just couldn't read it." He looks directly at Counterpoint. "You're the one who's into security systems. Well, here's the greatest security system of all time! Just waiting for an angel of death to come along and try to pry open the treasure box. The introns are nature's burglar alarm and security force, and what you see in DEUS is how they deal with intruders."

Counterpoint rises. He has heard enough. It's time to leave. "It's an interesting theory, Bob. I'll pass it on to the people back at the shop. Thanks for your help."

The Architect salutes Counterpoint. "Don't mention it. It's the least I could do."

From his window, he watches as Counterpoint goes out and climbs into his car. Across the street, he can see the security men putting on a fine display of vigilance for their boss. He turns and throws his glass at the TV but misses. He now knows with a horrible certainty what the introns will do next. He knows they won't stop at just blurting out a warning. They will somehow move to directly eliminate the source of the problem.

They will murder his child.

"So you see, you're the only one that can do it."

Michael Riley is summarizing his case to John Savage as he and Jessica sit across from the ex-CEO and wunderkind of the venture-capital community. They are in a booth at the sports bar at the mini-mall, and the TV monitors spew out the last heat of a rocket blade contest. In putting the whole thing together for Savage, Michael's own thinking began to coalesce at the same time: First, there was Simon Greeley, who uncovered a renegade financial operation coming from somewhere in the National Security Council. Before Simon could go public in a coherent manner, he dies of a disease that is not only extinct, but should take a year instead of a week to kill him. The only clue he leaves is that the conduit for the black money is a company called VenCap, and the recipient of the funds is a computer company called ParaVolve, right here in Portland. Through Michael's efforts they now know that the computer inside ParaVolve is linked to a laboratory in Mexico City called Farmacéutico Asociado. Finally, they know that the kuru virus was recently shipped to this laboratory for experimental purposes.

When you put all this together, it appears that Simon Greeley was probably murdered by a modified version of the kuru virus, which was manufactured through some very advanced bioengineering at Farmacéutico Asociado. On a bigger scale, it appears that VenCap, Farmacéutico Asociado, and ParaVolve form some kind of grand triangle dedicated to the development of highly illegal and fantastically dangerous biological warfare agents.

Two sides of the triangle have now been confirmed, the links between VenCap and ParaVolve, and between Farmacéutico and ParaVolve. What remains to be verified is the link between Farmacéutico and VenCap. And that's where Savage comes in.

"We've tried to find out about this VenCap from the outside, but it's a privately held corporation and doesn't have to publicly disclose what it's up to. So we need somebody to get inside and check it out," Michael is saying.

"What about the IRS?" counters Savage. "Couldn't your people in Washington pull a few levers and force an audit?"

"Not without tipping our hand and putting us in a very dicey position," says Michael. "We need to confirm the whole thing independently before we go back into the political arena."

Savage leans toward Michael. "Riley, I always had you pegged as a really smart son of a bitch, but I'm not so sure this is very smart at all."

Jessica intervenes. "It's not a matter of smartness. It's more about what you believe is right and wrong, and what you're willing to do about it, Mr. Savage."

"OK, suppose I buy into this thing," says Savage. "Where do you go from here?"

"From what I understand, you've still got a sterling reputation with the venture people," says Michael. "You could use that as a lever to get inside and poke around."

Savage nods. Riley is right. The money people tend to look at executives in terms of their potential as much as in terms of their track record. Like Hollywood directors, a disaster is not a career killer as long as it is a bold, expensive disaster, where the dice fly high and tumble wildly before coming down on the wrong number. In both businesses, it is implicitly understood that careful, cautious people seldom generate the big win. So although Savage's last outing was reduced to smoldering ruins, he himself still has good market value.

"All you've got to do is get a look at their investment portfolio," says Michael, "and that wouldn't be an unreasonable request from somebody they might do business with."

"So what you want me to do," says Savage, "is to contact these people and tell them that I'm ready to rise from the dead and start a new company. Then go talk to them and find out what's going on inside. Right?"

"That's basically it," answers Michael.

"Has anybody told you that we're in the worst economic calamity since the Great Depression? And that it's not exactly the best of times to be launching a new company?" inquires Savage.

"That's where you come in," says Michael. "We need your genius to come up with something that sounds plausible even now."

Savage smiles. "Flattery. Riley, you best stick to the technical side of things. Your sales pitch lacks that certain something."

"So you'll help?" Jessica inquires.

"See, Riley, she's got the knack," says Savage, now thoroughly amused. "She senses an opportunity to close the deal. You can learn from this woman."

Savage watches the late news in his apartment. More insanity. Something about another bank bombing, this one in Los Angeles. Then he thinks about the relativity of it all. In more sane times, Riley's request would seem absolutely ridiculous. But then again, in more sane times, Savage would not be moldering away at the Romona Arms. Goddamn it. Riley has smuggled a sense of purpose back into his life, brought it in right through customs in broad daylight. He can still say no, can't he? Maybe not.

Maybe the thing to do is clear out all the mental furniture so he can rebuild things from scratch.

Savage goes to the kitchen area, retrieves a coffee cup from the top shelf of the cupboards, and sits at the kitchen table. He pulls a foil pack with Zap 37 tablets from the cup, along with a small pipe and cigarette lighter. He goes back to the cupboards and extracts a water glass and a bottle of vinegar and half fills the shallow glass before adding two teaspoons of vinegar. Returning to the table with the mixture, he pushes on the foil pack and a tablet pops out and wiggles to a halt on the hard surface.

Savage pauses and looks at the little ceremonial tableau before him on the table, this altar of paraphernalia. And for the first time, he wonders who is being worshiped here. Himself? Some deity of unknown origin? Or is it perhaps the process of intoxication itself, that wild speculation in the currency of ecstasy?

Then the green-bar printout paper on the refrigerator door catches his attention, the numerical epitaph of his failed enterprise, and he realizes that it, too, is part of the ceremony, and that the ceremony is a funeral, a prolonged funeral, with himself as sole mourner and seeker of a drug-induced afterlife to explain the meanness of it all.

He gets up, leaves the kitchen, and goes out the front door, where he stands in the walkway. Dolores Kingsley is arranging the lounge chairs by the pool.

"How are you this evening, Mr. Savage?"

"I'm well, Mrs. Kingsley, very well indeed."

He smells the warm spring air and breathes deeply. Jessica, the woman with Riley, had it right: In the end, it's just a matter of what you believe. All the rest is just sales material.

Maybe I'll do it, Riley, he thinks. Just maybe I will.

On the floor above in twenty-seven, Michael lies in bed and gazes at Jessica's naked posterior through the half-open bathroom doorway. He shifts on the bed for a better view, feeling a little guilty about this overt act of voyeurism. Even though her face is out of view, he is sure she can sense him lasciviously scanning her. Women have some kind of omniscient radar when it comes to their exposed flesh, be it an ankle or an entire backside.

"Your place is a mess, Michael. If you haven't washed the sheets, you may never see me again."

"Of course I've washed the sheets. It's easy. They fit in the same load with everything else I own."

Jessica exits the bathroom and crawls in beside him. On the little bedside TV, an anchorwoman for GlobeNet speculates on whether the two bank bombings are a delayed reaction to the tragedy of the Mortgage March.

Jessica folds warmly onto him and the rest of the world goes freeze-frame.

"Was that the lady who went to Oaks Park with us?"

"Yes, it was."

"Did she stay here last night?"

"Well . . . yes, she did."

Michael sees this conversation with Jimi going down an associative path to trouble, but what can he say? Jimi is standing next to him as he sits at his computer and logs on to DEUS. Earlier, he had gone down with Jessica and kissed her good-bye when she took off for work at the lab. As Jessica drove away, Jimi showed up out of nowhere and followed him back up as he prepared to wrestle once more with the intricacies of DEUS. He doesn't want to hurt Jimi's feelings, but he's got to get cracking. Victor Shields will be all over him for some kind of progress report on what he's discovered.

"Tell you what, Jimi. I've got a lot of work to do on my computer, and I can't talk to you while I do it. But if you want to stick around and not make a sound, you can stay. OK?"

"OK."

There, that ought to do it. He'll get bored in a minute and take off. Michael opens his interface to DEUS and first checks the green liquid cube. The surface shows the soft ripples of a normal commerce between the processors, and there are no bubbles coming up from the interior. So far, so good. At least he knows he'll be wandering around in a computing structure that won't come crumbling down in some kind of algorithmic earthquake while he's inside. Now he heads for the neural net. The first thing he needs to find are the plans for it, the circuit diagram, and the layout. He discovers them buried under a relatively thin security blanket, which makes sense once he sees them. Most circuit diagrams and layouts are organized to reflect the rationales devised by their designers, but this thing is a gargantuan tangle of components and wires that defies any kind of logical interpretation. He can only guess at the scale of it, but there must be close to a billion neurons in there. Even if someone could sneak into the system and extract these plans, there would be no way to put them to use in the real world unless you had a computer like DEUS and a very advanced silicon fabrication plant at your disposal.

The next stop is to look for a program that allows DEUS to talk with the net. Just as a certain portion of the human brain is devoted to talking and hearing, some part of the net's circuitry must do the same, but to find it would be impossibly difficult. It will be much easier just to locate the program that DEUS and the Architect have devised for conversing with this part of the net.

When he uncovers this program, he is surprised to find it has been recently modified to allow a direct hookup between the net and a computer very similar to his. The Architect? Maybe. At any rate, this program maintains a transcript of its conversations with the net, and Michael can trace the dialogue back to its points of origin, just as the script for a play connects each piece of dialogue to a particular actor. Most of what is being "spoken" to the net by DEUS comes from the GenBank database and is strung together in some mysterious way by another set of programs buried deep inside the system. When Michael goes to look at them they turn out to be impossibly dense and cryptic, so he goes on to examine the program set that "hears" what the net is saying. This time he reaches a complete dead end: These "listener" programs are not even composed in any known computer language, and if measured by conventional means, would represent hundreds of millions of lines of programming. Then Michael realizes that they represent the very heart of ParaVolve, the conceptual factory that is manufacturing the biocompiler.

He has now uncovered a process that will never be understood by humans in all its detail, but has a profound and magnificent flow to it: First, DEUS goes into the genetic data and assembles it in a way that makes sense to the net. Next it feeds entire "sentences" and "paragraphs" of this data to the net, which examines it and interprets it. Then the net feeds these interpretations back to DEUS, which internally ships them as raw material to feed the factory program that is assembling the biocompiler.

Michael looks up from his screen and rubs his eyes. It's almost unbelievable. By now, the net is probably the most knowledgeable geneticist on the planet. An entire artificial mind focused exclusively on a single subject. Even though he wouldn't be able to understand, he would love to witness some of the net's arcane utterances. But right now, it appears that DEUS is not talking to the net, which means the net probably isn't talking back. All artificial neural nets will look at what's presented to them, have a lively internal debate about it, reach a point of resolution, and then stabilize, which means they have spoken their piece and have stopped until something further is spoken to them.

Nevertheless, Michael has to try, because he may witness firsthand the resolution of a debate that has raged for over fifty years among computer scientists and philosophers. The point of conflict is simple: Can a machine think? Can it know? Can it embrace data, turn it into true knowledge, and draw its own conclusions about the external reality it is immersed in? In the early days of computer science, the debate had little practical fallout. Computers were pitifully large and slow compared with even the most humble organic nervous systems. But as machines grew faster, smaller, and smarter, the arguments began to take on more urgent overtones. The main body of a typical neuron, the soma, is about ten microns across, and the connections it radiates to its neighbors are about two-tenths of a micron across. Toward the end of the century, integrated circuits were down in this same two-tenth-micron range. And by the nineties, serious efforts were already under way to construct integrated circuits that mimicked the biological architectures of the human eye's retina and the cochlea in the ear.

But how do you tell when a machine starts to think? First came the Turing Test: You have a computer in front of you, one with some kind of artificial intelligence embedded in it, and you type in messages and it gives replies. You carry on a conversation, so to speak. At some point, unknown to you, this artificial intelligence is replaced by a human being in another room who simply reads your side of the conversation and types in replies, which come up on your computer. If you can't tell the difference between the human responses and the artificial intelligence, you have a thinking machine.

But then in the eighties came the Chinese Box. This time, you are inside the machine, a wonderful box capable of carrying on conversations in Chinese with people that speak to it in the characters of that language. Your job is to create the box's side of the conversations—even though you don't understand any Chinese at all. What you have to help is a very detailed set of instructions that tell you what to do with the stream of Chinese symbols coming in from the outside speakers and how to use these symbols to package other Chinese symbols that go back to the outside. To the people outside the box, it has satisfied the Turing Test; they can carry on an intelligent conversation with it. But the rub is that you, the hypothetical soul of the machine, don't understand Chinese at all. As the output symbols form into words, sentences, and paragraphs, they mean nothing to you. You don't "know" Chinese; you have no notion of the depth and richness of what is being said, and how it relates to the wet chill of a winter morning or the surge of ebullience after winning a dart game. In effect, you are just like the central processor of a computer, and the detailed instructions are your program. And you managed to pass the Turing Test without thinking or knowing at all.

And then came the New Connectionists, who challenged the whole idea of computing and thinking being the same. If computer-based artificial intelligence is to emulate true thinking, it must understand the world in approximately the same way that real minds do. The whole thrust of traditional AI was to take a manageable slice of reality, break it down into a set of rules and symbols, and then express these as a program. If a formal dinner was the reality, then table manners were rules, and things like forks and guests were the symbols. You could then codify these rules and symbols into a program that threw a dandy formal dinner party.

But what about burgers at a tavern after the consumption of multiple pitchers of beer? Now the rules become fuzzy, the course of the events highly intuitive. What then? The conventional AI answer was that the rules were still there, swimming around in the ale and french fries, but just more subtle. But the New Connectionists said no, that the whole idea of formal systems was just too sphinctered up to work. Instead, they said, you need to forget about machines that march to the tune of explicit instructions, and build ones that approximate large, loosely confederated peer groups bound by only a few basic laws. Connect millions of processing elements together, let them learn about reality by example, and after monumental internal bickering and compromise, what we call intelligence will begin to emerge. The kind of intelligence that would have no trouble dining at the local bar.

But then came the money problem. Even if the New Connectionists were right, why spend billions to engineer a machine to do something that people do every waking second of their lives? Why not spend the money to build machines that do things completely out of human grasp? Like modeling the global weather system, or detailing the collisions of subatomic particles? The smart money said intelligence was an economic dead end, and went elsewhere. Research on neural nets—the ultimate Connectionist machines—was limited to specified tasks guaranteed to turn a profit, such as grading loan applications, or recognizing enemy missiles.

But now, as he prepares to interface with the net, Michael realizes that sooner or later a thing like the net inside DEUS was bound to cross the boundary into sentience. The money poured into the ParaVolve project was certainly not aimed at this goal, but may have achieved it as an unintentional by-product. So instead of embracing a world of clouds and clowns, of blood and friendship, the net has dined on the world of fundamental biology and cybernetics. A strange diet of silicon, copper, and ceramics; of enzymes, proteins, and amino acids; of procedure calls, conditional branches, and global variables.

Michael stretches his arms above his head and contemplates his next move. Assuming the net is talking, what's the best way to be listening? Since the net uses analog circuitry, the raw output of its "voice" is a collection of thousands of voltage values. Obviously, staring at this throng of voltage numbers is a poor way to look for meaningful patterns. Instead, he decides to turn the numbers into colors that range from a cool blue for low value to a hot yellow for high values. Next he arranges for these colors to be displayed in rows and columns. Finally, he tunnels his way through DEUS and sinks a shaft down to a place where the raw voice of the net will bubble up so he can pipe it on to his screen. With the connection made, the net's voice flows on to his screen and the colors dance energetically across the display window.

Now he knows. The net is alive.

Since there is nothing going into it, the net's voice should be frozen into a single syllable and thus a static display of colors. But instead, the colors leap about with an enthusiasm that can come only from an inner life. Animal intelligence is a robust symphony of internal conversation, much of it independent of what is coming in through the senses. The same thing appears to be happening here. But what's being said? Michael watches the color choreography and sees only kaleidoscopic randomness.

"What's that?"

Michael starts at the sound of Jimi, who still stands right behind him.

"I dunno, Jimi. What's it look like to you?"

"It looks like just playing around."

"You mean like doing nothing?" asks Michael.

"No, I mean like just playing around."

"What do you do when you 'just play around'?" Michael is puzzled.

"I can't say."

He can't say, thinks Michael. Maybe the net can't say either. But maybe that's exactly what it's doing.

The flying thing has almost exhausted the load of fuel it picked up from devouring the falcon, and now descends from an altitude of five thousand feet over southern Washington County in Oregon. Its organic wing engines throttle back as it surveys the rural landscape, looking for a suitable landing spot. The binocular eyes rotate downward and scan the fields, trees, roads, and houses and finally locate the right set of geographic features: a meandering creek connecting a set of shallow ponds.

The thing banks and circles over one of the ponds and finds the ideal touchdown site, a place along the pond shore where the distinction between water and land is blurred, a place of stagnant water and oozing brown mud dotted by clumps of reed grass. By the time it reaches the mud, its internal cooling system has begun to fail, and its wing engines start to self-destruct from overheating. In a final surge of strength, it points its body directly skyward about six feet above the soupy brown surface, cuts power completely, and plummets tail first into the mud, its body surface so hot that there is a steamy hiss as it wedges in. The rear segment then contracts violently beneath the surface of the mud, and two large brown eggs pop out.

Within a couple of minutes, the thing is dead, a strange totem sprouting from the mud, with an insect body and tiny human eyes fixed on a point near the zenith of the afternoon sky. A crow spots this anomaly as it patrols the periphery of its territory, and zooms down to investigate. It walks around the thing twice before moving in for an exploratory peck, which elicits no response. A couple of more pecks demonstrate that the bony body has no food value, but then the crow spots the eyes, and senses nutritional value locked up in this soft tissue. Two pecks and the eyes are being pushed down the bird's esophagus and into its first stomach.

Then the crow feels a slight tremor in the mud beneath its feet and takes flight. It almost reaches its favorite perch at the top of a nearby fir tree when the digestive enzymes in its stomach dissolve the eyeballs and their internal contents spill out. The crow squeezes out one frantic "caw" as a warning to its peers and then drops like lead to the ground below.

A squirrel hears the crow crash through the bushes and peeks down from the branch of an alder. The crow rests on its back on the ground, its abdominal region a gaping, steaming hole. The smell of it alarms the squirrel, which skitters high into the tree and freezes near the top.

In the mud by the dead insect totem, a hole erupts and a new thing climbs out of its eggshell with the help of its six powerful legs, which employ muscle engines of the same basic design found in its dead parent. The thing is already nearly two inches long, with an egg-shaped body topped by two cooling ducts like those on the insect. Inside them, the tiny wings beat at a fever pitch to cool the interior muscle engines. Mounted on the front of the body is a round turret of a head ringed by primitive, motion-sensing eyes. To the front of this ring are two stereoscopic eyes, which are already scanning the landscape for food. From the very front of the head, a cylinder protrudes with jagged teeth around its open lip, the same design as a hole saw for an electric drill. Some time later, this feature will earn the new beast the common title of "driller."

The driller's first act is to pull itself up onto the body of its dead progenitor, put its hollow-tipped drill into high-speed rotation, and bore through the dead thing's bony exoskeleton. When it has punched all the way through, it activates a suction pump in its body, which sucks the meat of the dead parent through the hollow drill tip and into an interior chamber where it is sprayed with a powerful acid that instantly liquefies it.

Even as it grips this mud-bound body and drains it dry, the driller is growing, converting much of this food intake into new tissue. It pauses only for a moment when it feels a thump on the other side of the body, where its newly hatched sibling is tapping into the parental feast.

Soon the guts of the parent are gone, and the driller hops off and starts briskly across the mud. Just above its binocular eyes are olfactory organs that sample the nearby air to pick up likely target information. As it heads away from the pond shore and onto firmer ground, it picks up a promising scent. Just ahead is a field mouse, now at a dead still to conceal itself from the approaching threat. The driller spots the prey visually and halts to calculate its angle of attack. By now, it has already grown larger then the mouse and plans to add fully half of the mouse's body mass to its own. Without warning, it rockets forward and leaps the last foot at a speed the mouse can't hope to match. The drill mouth spins and burrows into the mouse's flank, right through a rib bone, and punctures the left lung, which is sucked out and liquefied in less than a second. The mouse thrashes wildly for a moment and then expires from shock as the driller bores a second hole into its abdomen. In less than a minute, the mouse carcass is completely pocked with deep red craters as the driller drills away. By the time its meal is complete, the driller is over six inches long. And still ravenously hungry.

In the early evening, storm clouds sail like bloated gray ships over the pond, and rain begins to spatter the brown mud surface by the shore. Where the miniature forest of marsh grass meets this shore, the two drillers settle down for a moment in concealment. They are now fully grown, and twelve inches long. With their powerful legs, they dig trenches, where each of them lays a half dozen eggs and covers them with a thin layer of mud. They pace restlessly around the trenches until, an hour later, they witness small versions of themselves pushing away the dirt cover and shrugging off the remnants of their eggshells. The adults move off toward a nearby island of forest thick with oaks, alders, maples, and birch.

The young need no protection. They can fend for themselves.

18

Blowup

Sam Gossett goes about his job meticulously, almost religiously. Before him is a semicircle of book-sized cubbyholes, each holding a magnetic tape cartridge very similar in appearance to a VHS tape. The cubbyholes start at floor level and rise to a height of almost eight feet, so he needs a small stepping stool to reach the top ones. In the center of this semicircle is a robotic arm, now pinched into lifeless repose, which is capable of grabbing the tapes, rotating around, and inserting them into a tape drive, which participates in the bank's central computing complex.

The whole system is part of a "multiple redundant backup strategy," designed to ensure that even if data is wiped out in one place, it exists in at least several others. So most banking transactions go to two separate disk drives and also on to tape, and that tape is located here, in the second floor of the computer center, which is on the second story of a large skyscraper in Midtown Manhattan.

Part of Sam's job is to maintain this library of tapes, and to ensure that the proper tapes reside in the correct slots. When the robot arm reaches out like a chicken pecking for grain, it must get the right tape at the right time. Sam works alone and hums along to the drone of the air fans as he carefully takes tapes out of specific cubbyholes and replaces them with tapes from a small cart beside him. Soon he will be done, and he can leave a few minutes early to catch the subway out to Brooklyn and have a glass of wine with his mother in her apartment, which is just down the street from his.

But this afternoon, he is taking special care with the tapes, more care than ever. All because of his mother.

She got the letter three weeks ago, a letter from this very same bank with the robot arm, the very same bank that has employed him for the past twenty-two years. One of this bank's many functions is to manage retirement portfolios for small businesses, like the industrial-hose factory where his mother had spent most of her working life as a parts clerk. Now, at seventy-six, she suffers from Parkinson's disease, but with the help of new drugs lives a life of quiet dignity in the same neighborhood the family has lived in since Sam was a child. Even after she lost her husband's pension in the Big Dip of '98, she was still able to get by on Social Security and her own pension.

But then came the letter. She got it on a Saturday, and asked Sam to come over and look at it. He distinctly recalls the worried tone in her voice that made him put down the model he was working on in his bachelor's apartment, a very complex, radio-controlled replica of the battleship *Missouri*.

When he got there, he read the letter carefully. It was from the retirement trust division of the bank, and went on in great technical detail about the declining value of major assets and how "certain key investments had gone into unexpected receivership" and how the "resulting negative cash flow precluded the further distribution of funds to trust participants" and many other such statements, which meant the fund was broke and would no longer pay his mother's pension.

While this was a devastating shock to Sam and his mother, it was not what mobilized him to his present course of action. It was a final section of the letter, which was written in the most circumspect manner of all. While Sam had never been particularly ambitious, he was fairly intelligent, and after picking apart this section, he realized it meant that the bank would continue to collect fees for managing the festering remnants of the fund, even though the pensioners got nothing. In other words, for the bank, it was business as usual.

Getting the plastic explosive had been much easier than he expected. There were several people in his radio-controlled-models club that lived far out on the paramilitary fringe and were able to procure it for him through vague and distant sources.

Packing the plastic explosives into the tape was no problem at all. He simply unscrewed the covers, removed the tape, put in the explosive, and installed a false cover that made it look like the tape was still there. The only tricky part was installing the blasting cap and trigger circuitry in the one tape that would detonate all the others.

Now Sam prepares to place this tape at the end of a row of twenty-five explosive tapes he has just installed. He carefully slides it most of the way into its slot, and then pushes a tiny switch in the upper-right-hand corner. The tape is now armed. It contains a mercury switch that will detect any substantial motion and detonate it. With infinite care, he slides it into place.

As Sam approaches the subway entrance on Broadway, he stops to make the phone call. He knows precisely when the bank will go up, at four-thirty, an hour and a half from now. At that time, the robot arm will reach out to perform a routine data backup operation and will grab the tape with the mercury switch, which sets off the primer explosion that will set off the big explosion. The plastic explosive is the best available from Slovakia, which has long led the world in the field. The blast will be the equivalent of several hundred pounds of TNT, and since the tape backup unit is near the center of the floor, the explosion will send a compression wave outward in all directions, causing maximum damage.

As Sam speaks to the woman at the bank, he knows exactly what will happen, because he also knows several key people in the bank's security department. First, he is transferred immediately to a vice president, who tries to sort him out as a crank caller, but Sam counters with several facts about the bank and about explosives that preclude that possibility. Now they have no choice but to evacuate the building and start a frantic search for the bomb. But Sam knows that no matter what else they do, they won't shut down the central computer system. In the old days, it was possible to deactivate the computer system without near-mortal damage to the bank's operations, but no longer. In an age of "mission critical computing," all systems must now operate continuously to maintain a state of corporate homeostasis. To lose it is the business equivalent of a massive stroke. You may survive, but the recovery will be long and hard at best.

Sam hangs up, descends the stairs to the subway, and looks forward to sipping a glass of red wine and chatting with his mother.

He always was her favorite.

"Hey, Jimi. Hey, man, I know I've been really raw to ya. But you know how it goes. A guy like me's got a lot of shit on his mind and sometimes I get a little nasty. So let's forget about it, dude. Let's start out clean. I'm sorry, man. You hear me? I'm sorry! That's as good as I can do, man. I'm sorry!"

From inside his apartment, Jimi kneels on the couch and peeks through the curtain, which he has opened just a fraction of an inch at the bottom. Rat Bag is delivering his perverse apologia to the front door. A few steps behind him stand Zipper and several minor luminaries from the Romona tribe. They know Jimi is inside because a few moments ago, they tried to intercept him as he made for the door from the parking lot.

"Look, man, what else can I say? What else can I do? It's all up to you, dude. See you later."

As he watches Rat Bag shuffle off, Jimi understands the two-pronged political content of this ploy. On one hand, it may lure Jimi out of the apartment, where he will fall prey to cruel humiliation or worse. On the other hand, if Jimi doesn't come out, he comes off as the nasty little kid who won't accept the humble apologies of a mighty leader. He closes the curtain and slides down to a sitting position on the couch. Maybe it's time to talk to his mom about all this Rat Bag stuff. And for once, she's home.

He hops off the couch and walks down the short hall to her bedroom door, which he opens very gingerly. Sometimes his mom gets very mad when he does something that wakes her up. He watches the wedge of light from the open door spill across the room and paint a silent white stripe on the far wall. Daylight burns in around the fringes of the drawn curtains and throws a muted, wistful light onto his mom, who is nearly lost in the pale, twisted topography of sheets. Following a path of clothes that weave like flagstones to the bed, he stands over the sleeping Zodia, and wonders what to do next. On the nightstand a digital alarm frantically blurts out "3:17" in endless pulses to warn that it has been un-plugged and can no longer be trusted. Next to it, a heap of empty cigarette packages form a cellophane glacier that slowly drips over the edge and onto the carpet. Behind them are the little amber cylinders with their child-proof polar caps, the pill bottles that follow his mother everywhere, a little chemical posse that rides in her purse, her car, her coat.

In the wadded mass of sheets, he sees only an eye and a haphazard bloom of ratted blonde hair, but then the eye opens, its lashes caked with tiny black specks of makeup residue.

"Hi, Mom."

"Hello, sweetheart."

A white arm rises from the jumbled forest of bedding like a frail crane and plucks the sheets back. It then curls into a beckoning motion, and Jimi slides onto the bed and cuddles next to his mom.

"How are you this morning?" she asks as her eyes swing shut again.

"It's not morning. It's way into the afternoon," corrects Jimi. He has had this problem with his mom many times before.

"Well, how are you this afternoon?" Her eyes come open to half-mast and she smiles the cowardly little smile of the terminally guilty.

"I'm OK, I guess."

"Just OK?"

"Yep."

"Well, what could we do to make it better?" she asks.

Jimi feels a surge of hope. The clouds inside his mom are temporarily parting, and he may be able to ride in on a shaft of reason and get her full attention for awhile.

"We could move," he says. "We could get a new place."

His mom's eyes clamp shut again and his hope fades. "It's a lot of trouble to get a new place," she says dreamily. "It costs a lot of bucks 'cause you have to put up deposits and things. And your mommy doesn't have a lot of bucks. Nobody has a lot of bucks anymore."

"If we moved, I could meet some new kids," counters Jimi.

"Yeah," says his mom, "and I could meet some new guys. That would be nice. But what's wrong with the kids that are right here?"

"Some of them aren't too nice. I don't want to play with them, but there's nobody else to play with."

"Now, dear," murmurs Zodia, "there are nice kids everywhere. Here, too. You've just got to find them. That's all."

"Yeah, but that doesn't make the bad kids go away."

"Like which bad kids?" she asks.

"Like Rat Bag."

"Who's Rat Bag?"

How can she not know who Rat Bag is? What's wrong with her? Jimi sinks farther into despair. Rat Bag has been a fixture at the Romona Arms for several years, a nemesis of parents, a scourge of the community.

"He's a big kid that picks on other kids and makes them do whatever he wants." Even as he says it, Jimi feels the knife of guilt pierce him. He is betraying the trust of the kid tribe, the silent bond that defines them and sets them apart from the big people. Like a Mafia informer, he knows he is doing the right thing, but can't help but feel the demons poke at him.

"Has this Rat Bag ever hurt you?"

"Well, no. Not really."

"Well, you're always going to find people like that. All your life." Zodia's voice has diminished to a whisper. "So you better start figuring out how to handle it right now. . . . Mommy's going to rest a little now, OK? Maybe we can do something a little later. . . . All right?"

As she fades, Jimi feels the weight of her arm increase on him. From the floor above, he hears the distant thump of feet and the rush of water through pipes. Outside, an air horn blasts from a truck out on the highway. His mom's warm breath washes over his cheek as she exhales. Maybe he can just stay here in bed like this forever, with Rat Bag a universe away. Maybe this moment can be flattened into an instant picture and preserved for eternity. But then he would miss all the adventures, all the fun, as the rapids of chance rage and he tumbled through time dodging the rocks. In the end, he knows he must live like his dad, throttle to the floor.

He rolls out slowly from under his mother's arm, so as not to wake her, and walks into the living room, where he peeks out through the curtains. No sign of Rat Bag and friends. Should he chance it and make a run? Of course, he should. Otherwise, this apartment becomes a sepulcher, and its moist shadows will dissolve his body before it ever gets a chance to grow.

He opens the door, takes a quick look up and down the walkway, steps out, and shuts the door behind him. Time to get on with it, no matter what it is. He lights off down the walkway, feeling the power in his legs and the spring in his feet.

Savage sits in the lobby of VenCap and reflects on the trip out from Oregon. It was a nostalgic experience, climbing into the jet just like it was a big bus to head to New York and wheel and deal with the money people. When his now-defunct company was riding high, he made the trip several times a month and always enjoyed the transcendental leap from one coast to the other, a bridge across cultures as well as distance. This time, of course, his expense account was limited to the money Riley had given him after Michael got his first installment of his contract with ParaVolve. No drinks at the Plaza or dinners at The Four Seasons. Still, he likes the feel of the place, even though his mission is now one he had never imagined.

The offices of VenCap perch on the second floor of a big building in Midtown Manhattan, and the place is absolutely generic so far. Two large potted trees of some vaguely tropical origin flank the glass entrance doors, and straight ahead is a counter with a receptionist sitting under the company logo, which has a distinctly eighties look to it. Savage sits on one of two leather couches, with the obligatory phone on a little teak stand at one end. (A real test of the hospitality is to see if you can dial long distance without being intercepted, Savage muses, but this isn't the time to be pulling that kind of trick.) A glass table in front of him has a neat fan of business magazines, and a freshly minted copy of *The Wall Street Journal,* and he picks it up to check out an article about the Federal Reserve pushing the prime down to 1.5 percent.

"Mr. Savage?"

He looks up to a woman in her twenties dressed in a pleated gray skirt, white blouse, and a loosely flowing jacket, which reflected the new thinking that big-shouldered women's jackets were a sign of self-doubt and belied a stalled career track.

"Hi. I'm Ann Simpson, Mr. Benson's administrative assistant. He's almost free, so why don't you come on in? He's got some material you might want to scan before you talk to him, so why don't I get you settled in the conference room?"

On their way back to the office suite, she gracefully throws out the perfunctory queries: Did you have a nice trip out? Was the weather nice in Portland? Where are you staying in New York? The conference room is lined on one side with windows that overlook a newly constructed public square, which has already been turned into a bustling street market for a variety of vices. As the woman leaves, Savage looks out and sees that the square is now jammed with office workers, many in shirts and ties without their jackets. He had noticed this crowd when he arrived by taxi, but figured it was just one of the countless public events that the city swallows up every day. But now he can see over their heads to a throng of emergency vehicles on the far side of the square.

The Simpson woman returns carrying a gray literature folder with the company logo blind-embossed on the front, and a single loose sheet of paper. "If you just sign this nondisclosure form, I'll let you get right down to business," she says, putting the single piece of paper before him.

She looks out the window at the commotion across the square. "Must be another one of those wildcat middle-management strikes. You work down here and you see it all." She smiles at him on her way out. "Mr. Benson will be with you in just a few minutes."

Savage opens the folder and sees that he has struck pay dirt. The first page is a summary of the company's philosophy and policies. This stuff is the usual boilerplate. There is no doubt that the venture-capital companies play a valuable role in the business community, and he doesn't need to hear it for the umpteenth time. But the next page has the real goods, a summary of the firm's investment portfolio, with a brief description of each company invested in. Many are companies he recognizes, corporations with breakthrough technologies that have managed to survive and leverage their innovations into good market positions and sustained profitability. Others he vaguely recognizes as companies that the verdict is still out on: The spark is still there, but no fire yet. And among these is ParaVolve, listed as a company "exploiting a revolutionary breakthrough in electronic design automation that allows for the development of a self-evolving supercomputer with a capacity many orders of magnitude greater than that of any existing supercomputer products." Finally, there is a group of companies he has never heard of, like a biotech firm in Singapore developing a hydroponics system that will produce petrochemicals organically. And among these is none other than Farmacéutico Asociado, "a pharmaceutical distribution company that is expanding aggressively into advanced research and development to market a wide variety of medical products through its preestablished channels."

At that very moment, the most fortuitous event in the life of John Savage occurs. He has been reading with his back to the window, and has a pen placed on the table next to the papers. While reading the page about Farmacéutico Asociado, he unconsciously put the first page down on top of the pen. Now he wants to underline the Farmacéutico passage, and looks for the pen. As he picks up the first page, the pen rolls off the table and onto the floor underneath, so he gets out of the chair and down on his knees to retrieve it.

The first thing he feels is an enormous pressure in his ears, as if he has just been pulled hundreds of feet underwater. Then there is a brilliant shimmer as the glass from the window breaks into minuscule fragments of shrapnel that embed themselves in the opposite wall. Finally, there is the sledgehammer roar of the explosion as it thunders in.

Then silence, that pristine moment that always follows catastrophic events. Savage slowly crawls to his feet in shock, and looks out the window at the flames punching out of the building across the way like a brilliant yellow fist as gray smoke pours into the canyon between the skyscrapers. Then the screaming starts, and the mass of people in the square begins to squirm and vibrate, more from fear than injury. The main force of the blast sailed right over their heads and into the offices of places like VenCap that had the same second-floor elevation as the bank.

"I'm sorry, Mr. Benson won't be able to see you this afternoon. Could we reschedule for a later time?"

Savage turns to see Ann Simpson standing in the doorway of the conference room with blood splattered all over her blouse, someone else's blood. Her face is ghost white and she is on full autopilot. The woman's predicament pulls Savage back into action and he goes to get her seated in a chair in case she faints. "Sure, no problem. I'm in town all week," he lies. "Why don't you take a break for a minute?"

He leaves her staring at the fire across the square, which is now hot enough to register on the skin even at this distance. Moving out the door and down the hall, he becomes aware of the screams and shouting. The first office he comes to, a man is lying on the floor, his entire face and torso a solid mass of blood. In a moment of grim speculation, Savage wonders if there are any features left under there, or if all the flesh has been ground into a single foaming consistency. He reads the name on the door and realizes that this is Mr. Benson. And then a flash of silver foil catches his eye. It shines among a litter of papers, pen holders, paper clips, a clock, a daytimer, and other assorted objects that were blown off Benson's desk by the blast. Savage knows it instantly by its size and shape. Zap 37. He steps into the office, picks up the blister pack with its six large tablets, and pockets it.

As he backs out of Benson's office and moves on down the corridor, a woman comes out of an office with half her face shredded and the other half unmarked. She reaches out a hand toward him and then collapses back into the office. Other people are now rushing to the window offices to check for more victims, but they find none. All the other offices along the blast side were empty when the explosion hit.

Savage has had enough. Mr. Benson is dead, and the injured woman has more than enough help until the emergency people arrive. He finds his way back to the lobby and leaves. Outside, he sees that the hall has become a jammed tributary of people feeding the elevators and stairs at the core of the building. Everyone follows a blind instinct to get outside and sniff the air and feel the heat, to surge upward on this massive spike in the shallow sine wave of daily routine. He has no choice but to ride along as another atom in the mass, and as he moves down the hall, he wonders about Mr. Benson, and remembers the Zap 37 in his pocket. He pulls it out and immediately sees that it is different from the ones he has seen before, which were totally devoid of any markings. On the foil side, the phrase "Z-37 Lot No. 133344XX" is stamped in black indelible ink. The implication is clear: This particular pack came directly from the manufacturing source, and not from the street. And the packaging style, lot number, and product ID make it seem that the source was most likely a pharmaceutical company, not a sleazy lab tucked away in some South American jungle. So Mr. Benson, who had just been peeled like a grape from the waist up, was not just another casual user, but maybe an investor. How many other people inside VenCap were in on it? Probably only a few. Most of VenCap's investments were perfectly reputable, and it was entirely possible that its covert operations were run exclusively from the top of the company.

Savage puts the Zap 37 back in his pocket. Not long ago, he would have gone directly to his hotel room, cooked it up, and taken off. But no longer. There's too much happening, too much to do.

Dear Dr. Riley,

Good sir, your reputation precedes you! MIT, wasn't it? Then Silicon Prince at NSA? I'm honored to have such a guest in my home. But whatever became of you? Who cranked down the rheostat and dimmed your professional bulb so badly?

At any rate, I can see you haven't lost your deft touch. It's nice to know there are still a few nodes of brilliance sprinkled about here and there. So let me share with you a disturbing dream I had the previous night:

I was sitting atop a very large hill made of brown rubber, one of thousands that stretched all the way to the horizon in every direction. The sky glowed green and there was no sun. I was looking for my child, whom I had lost under some hazy circumstances, and anxiously scanned the rubber valley below me as a steady breeze rippled my clothing. Then the ground began to shake violently and I tried to get to my feet, but couldn't. As I looked out, I saw that the entire landscape was jumping up and down like a toddler in a state of tantrum. Then the rubber under my feet disappeared as I tumbled down the side of the hill, bouncing and banging on the smooth brown surface. When I reached the bottom, the pulsating rubber geology became so violent that I was pitched out of this valley entirely and flung high into the green sky, where I cartwheeled crazily before landing on a new hillside and rolling down into yet another valley. This cycle of jumping from valley to valley went on and on, until finally the earthquake subsided, and I found myself in the deepest valley of all, surrounded by towering hills. In the silence that followed, I called out for my child, but the only answer was the muffled echo of my voice off the hillsides.

I awoke and realized I had been trapped inside a visual metaphor for a Boltzmann Machine when it was in a learning state and going through simulated annealing. But I found little comfort in this fact, because my child is real, and the Boltzmann Machine is one of its conceptual ancestors.

And now my child is in great peril, as you well know. I have seen your footprints circling its ailing body, and assume you have put your stethoscope to its heaving chest. There is still life within, but it is feeble and cannot withstand another assault by the antigens that have crawled out of the code and into both the mother and the child.

Unfortunately, Dr. Riley, the same is true of me. The years have rusted my armor and now the angel of death swoops in on black wings and roosts buzzardlike nearby. But it can't pierce me. Not yet. Because I hold all the eggs in its nest as ransom. But that is just a holding action, because the real assault comes from within. I judge myself guilty of gross negligence and condemn myself to an ignoble end, and have activated the necessary spiritual machinery to carry out the sentence.

But now you are here, an unexpected guest, and I feel an obligation to entertain. And what better amusement for a man of your intellectual caliber than an elliptical puzzle. Let me start by assuming that you are roaming the system in search of the putative "bomb" that holds the corporate eggs ransom before they can hatch into monetary and political profit. Yes, there is such a bomb, Dr. Riley, and assuming we share a rough parity in intellectual facilities, it will probably take you many months to discover and disarm it. But your effort will ultimately be in vain, because the life of my family is now measured in days, not months.

The only question now is, Do I want to linger and watch the mother and child suffer? The more I think about it, the more I think not. So I bequeath you a very heavy responsibility, Dr. Riley. If you choose to attempt to defuse the bomb and succeed, you become the father to the family, the sole provider in a time of great uncertainty. The decision is yours alone.

Respectfully,
The Architect

Michael reads the message on his screen as he extracts it from the Architect's software fortress inside DEUS, and then prints it out. Moving to the living room, he plops down on the couch and reads it again. There is actually room for his feet on the coffee table, and the couch is clear of clothes, books, and magazines. The drapes are open and light floods in on some flowers in a vase atop the TV and a new plant sits in a large pot on the floor next to the couch. Since Jessica has been coming over, the place is slowly creeping toward some new form of normalcy that Michael is quite ready to trade for the old one.

The part of the message about the dream and the Boltzmann Machine is interesting. It is an old form of neural net that can be thought of as an abstract landscape with valleys and hills. When the net is presented with a problem, the valleys represent different possible solutions, with the deepest valley being the correct solution. A process called simulated annealing produces giant "earthquakes" in the energy landscape, and like a ball bearing, the search for the solution leaps and bounces from valley to valley, and most likely will have settled in the deepest one when the shaking is over.

The next part about his ailing child is now obvious to Michael. It is clear that the Architect has also seen the seedling of independent intelligence in the net, and considers it to be his child, and DEUS to be the child's mother. The Architect also must have some way of tracing who contacts the net, because he knows that Michael has been there and witnessed the net's output. But why does he think that the net is "ailing"? And who is "the angel of death"?

The last part about the bomb is discouraging but realistic. The Architect had years to design and conceal the device, while Michael may have almost no time to find it.

And if he doesn't find the bomb, the entire business will self-destruct. But so what? Does he really care? Does he want to assume responsibility for another man's creation?

Yes, he does. Since the moment he took the net's pulse and found it to be alive, he has been hooked. The history of computer science will pivot around this episode, strange as it may be, and its outcome is now largely in his hands.

One hundred yards from the marsh where the drillers hatched is a small creek bed that carves a muddy little gully through the surrounding fields. In the summer, the creek is a foot wide; in the winter, maybe six feet. Along its steep banks and tiny flatlands, the gully sprouts a thick growth of trees and shrubs, including a thorny tangle of blackberry vines. In some places, the vines choke out all competition and rule unchallenged, except for a smattering of grass and moss that greedily devours the few crumbs of sunlight that reach the spongy ground.

And now one of the drillers prepares to enter this forbidden zone. It creeps along a trench dug by one of its peers that avoids the thorny vines and penetrates to the center of the patch, where a great hollow dome about eight feet in height has been scoured out. The new thing has been guided here by pheromones, scent molecules that serve as a navigation beacon that can be detected over great distances. Once in the hollow, it stops before a large mound of packed soil that fills most of the volume of the dome. Scores of holes poke into the mound, and many other drillers can be seen both exiting and entering.

On its way to this concealed spot among the thorns, the driller was practicing its own unique form of biological warfare. From small vents on either side of its body, a constant shower of viruses was released into the air. These viruses are specialists, each a master of its trade and able to enter living tissue and ignite chemical flash fires that could quickly consume a whole organism and radically transform it without actually killing it. Soon they begin to settle in an invisible blanket across the landscape and search for opportunities to demonstrate their skills.

Now, at the mound, the driller enters one of the tunnels, able to tell by its olfactory organs that the tunnel is vacant inside. In the hollow of its drill-tip mouth is the compacted flesh of an unfortunate possum that chose fight over flight. The tunnel curves sharply downward, and the driller shifts to infrared vision to guide it as it descends more than a yard below ground level and enters a chamber the size of a refrigerator, with walls that contain a perfectly symmetrical pattern of perforations made by the drill mouths. There are thousands of these holes, and most are filled with core samples of food brought in by the constant pilgrimage of drillers to this site. The driller moves to a vacant perforation and ejects the compacted possum meat into the opening. Behind him, several other drillers do the same with their samples, and must stand on their hind legs to reach the vacant upper perforations.

With its pilgrimage complete, the driller rotates and prepares to head out through a second tunnel. Soon it will be back out in the daylight and will spend the rest of its short life moving as far from this site as possible, shedding its shower of mutant viruses, the black gospel of a new biology.

As it leaves, it is unaware that there is a second chamber of equal size not more than a foot below it. Inside dwells a driller that is the analog of a queen in conventional insect societies. Double the size of the others, it is almost two feet in length and a foot and a half in diameter, the head and legs tiny in relation to the swollen body. It was the first to arrive at this site and tunnel into the center of the blackberry vines, where it began to broadcast its location by secreting pheromones to guide the others. Soon it was surrounded by a dedicated force of guards and attendants as a legion of workers began to excavate the earthen temple, and prepare the queen's chamber.

For some time now, the queen has been motionless, and her protectors mill restlessly, waiting for the next and last phase of her life. It comes without warning. The queen's legs begin to churn frantically and her body splits right down the middle. Out comes a cloud of hot vapor and three giant eggs, almost equal in volume to the queen herself. The attendants scurry out and seal the chamber except for a single tunnel that leads to the food chamber above. Throughout the tunnel, a complex series of scents is being broadcast to instruct the drillers what to do next. In the food chamber, several workers move to widen the tunnel that leads to the surface. Others leave the site entirely, while still others mass outside and form a defensive perimeter around the base of the mound.

There are now about twenty-four hundred drillers in the area around the pond and the creek, and they move in silence and stealth to secure a roughly circular area a mile in diameter, with the mound at its center. Tonight, many will stop to lay more eggs and rapidly perpetuate the species.

A few miles to the southeast, along Burris Creek, a second winged thing has landed, using the pheromones from the queen as a positioning device, and at this very moment is shoving several eggs into the muddy ground. And three other winged things are now pushing through the skies over rural Washington County, all seeking landing sites that conform to a plan they cannot and need not understand.

19

XXXXXXX

The Triangle

Michael Riley hears the nasty scraping of steel against cement, and knows that the west wing of the Romona Arms is sending part of the pool area into shadow, prompting the moms and kids to drag their lounge chairs back into the gentle shower of afternoon sun. He and Savage occupy the center of the opposite end of the pool rim, and both stare skyward through mirrored sunglasses, their tan bodies perfectly parallel on their chairs of scuffed aluminum and cheap plastic webbing.

"Have a nice trip?" inquires Michael.

"You watch the news?" counters Savage. Both men stare into the sky at some spot beyond infinity as they converse.

"Something about a big bomb taking out a bank. You were in the neighborhood at the time?"

"Sure was. Your pals at VenCap were conveniently located right across the way."

"Must have been an interesting experience," comments Michael.

"That it was. Came within about a second of turning into ground round," Savage says laconically.

"How's that?"

"The blast blew out a window next to me, but I got lucky and was out of the line of fire. It took out a couple of people in the office, but by then

I had seen enough and split. It hardly seemed appropriate to stick around and go through the formalities when the guy I was supposed to see had just been converted to red Jell-O."

"Well, maybe it's some strange kind of justice. Technically, they're the bad guys—at least it looks that way."

"All it would take is a few people at the top," says Savage. "They could personally handle the sensitive part of the portfolio and leave the rest to their staff. Anyway, I confirmed what you wanted to know: VenCap is supplying capital to Farmacéutico."

"How much?"

"Don't know," replies Savage. "I saw an executive summary of the entire portfolio, and ParaVolve was there, too. Most of it looked absolutely legitimate. If it wasn't for the Downturn, they'd probably be generating a pretty fair return on their clients' money."

"Well, my congratulations," offers Michael. "You've put the final piece into the big puzzle. So now we've got a triangle with three corners. VenCap feeds money to both ParaVolve and Farmacéutico, while ParaVolve and Farmacéutico feed each other scientific data."

"And now I have a question of my own," says Savage. "So what? Why all the money? What for? You owe me big, Riley. So let's have it."

A small puff of wind cools the perspiration on Michael's face. Since Savage nearly got zapped on this trip, there is little to do but tell him what he inadvertently risked his life for.

"OK," says Michael, "you're right. I'm going to settle my account with you. Let's start with VenCap. Truth is, you now know as much as I do about these guys. Farmacéutico's a different story. Whoever's down there apparently hasn't read the Geneva Conference on biological warfare. They're using very advanced biotechnology to create germs out of your worst nightmare, but we already told you that. It's what's inside Para-Volve that all the money's about."

"Don't tell me this is all over another fast computer. There's no need to be sneaky about that."

"It's not the computer itself; it's what the computer's building. It's reading a big genetic database and figuring out how to build the biological equivalent of a high-level programming language."

"I like it already. Do they have a president? I just might be interested," Savage says.

"Yeah, they've got a president, but the guy's just window dressing. My guess is that somebody at VenCap is really calling the shots. The power usually follows the money. Right?"

"Right," Savage replies. "Now tell me more about the product."

"Haven't got it all figured yet," Michael replies, "but apparently you could use the thing to design your very own critters. Maybe that's how they got Greeley. They could have used an early model of this thing to produce a customized virus to zap him in a way that couldn't be traced. When the thing's fully operational, you could combine it with some advanced laboratory robotics and make just about anything you wanted, as long as it didn't violate some basic ground rules set down by nature."

"If it's what you think it is," Savage says, "the legit venture guys would go wild over it. They'd even settle for a minority position just to be along for the ride. By the way, there's another wrinkle to this whole thing that you didn't mention."

"What's that?"

"Drugs."

"Drugs?"

"You know about Zap 37?" says Savage.

"Yeah. It's the new mind-fry of choice in the film biz. The stylist on my last shoot told me it's the greatest thing ever."

"Well, she's not alone," Savage says. "Anyway, I found some in a mess on an office floor after the bomb went off. Wasn't street stuff, either. Had a product ID and lot number stamped on it, which makes me think it came from a pharmaceutical company."

"Like Farmacéutico Asociado, maybe?"

"Maybe. If big-time drugs are involved, that would explain a great deal about where a lot of VenCap's investment money is coming from."

Michael considers this hypothesis and judges it highly likely. If Ven-Cap was simultaneously involved with covert government funds and drug money, it would be following a tradition that went back more than fifty years. The connections were made during the old anti-Commie days and took root deep within the shadow world, where weeding has always been difficult at best.

"Hey, Michael Riley!"

Michael is popped out of his speculation by Jimi Tyler, who has worked his way along the edge of the pool to the deep end near Riley and Savage.

"Hey, Michael, watch this!"

Jimi kicks off from the edge and travels about a yard out into water over his head. He then flutters and thrashes on the edge of panic and lunges back with one arm extended to grab the edge of the pool. He misses and sinks, causing Michael to wince, but then pokes one arm to the surface, catches the edge, and pulls himself up. Water drains from every orifice above his neck as he beams at Michael.

"Did you see that?" Jimi asks proudly.

"Yup, I saw that. Not bad, Jimi boy. Not bad at all. Now, you wouldn't try that if nobody was around, would you?"

"No way, Jose. Now watch me again," says Jimi as he pushes off once more.

Across the parking lot, Rat Bag sits atop the trash Dumpster with Zipper seated beside him. The Dumpster's metal lid has absorbed the day's sun and radiates it back around Rat Bag as he gazes across the pool area and watches Jimi entertaining Michael. He moves his hands slightly outward, and the heated metal burns, but Rat Bag lets the burn flow through him and help fuel his rage and focus his sense of resolution. The Jimi Tyler problem is becoming an obsession. Ironically, this obsession is driven by the fact that everything else is going so well. If you discount Jimi, he is king of the kids, an absolute dictator over thirty or more children ranging from five to ten years old. In the Rat Bag world, kids under five are granted the status of "babies" and allowed to roam free—a useful policy since mothers seem to be extremely watchful and protective of children during these early years. But nevertheless, Rat Bag keeps a census of the smaller ones, tracks their social progress, and watches for the invisible dome of absolute motherhood to lift high enough that they wander out into his domain. And when they do, he is ready to initiate them into the fold, the fold of fear. Many times, the work has already been done for him by older brothers and sisters who teach the smaller ones the Rules of Rat Bag long before he ever acknowledges their existence.

And now the system is complete. No move is made, no toy exchanged, no game initiated without the sanction of Rat Bag, who enforces his order through a rigid hierarchy of physical intimidation. At the top is his executive officer, Zipper, who runs a small cadre of larger boys who are well versed in the Rules of Rat Bag. These boys in turn run their own groups, which enforce his will at the street level. Minor offenses are dealt with on the spot—a twisted ear, a finger snap to the head. Major ones ascend the hierarchy, where stomach punches and shin kicks come into play. The ultimate horror is a direct confrontation with Rat Bag himself, but he is shrewd enough never to actually play this card. Instead, he has propagated legends about past encounters, tales of subtle mutilations and terrifying ordeals of fear. A little toe removed with bolt cutters. A petrified youngster held by his ankles from a railroad trestle.

And now his rule is a model of nearly perfect control, because without it, he will die. He knows this in his heart. There is no middle ground, no zone of coexistence. To surrender control is to die, to be smothered in the warm, wet will of others, where he will slowly asphyxiate and shrivel into nonbeing.

All of which makes Jimi Tyler a life-threatening illness, a disease that must be eradicated while he can still marshal the forces to fight it.

"Hey, Zipper."

"Yeah, man?" asks Zipper obliquely through his swollen adenoids.

"You see what I see?"

"Yeah, sure," replies Zipper, always anxious to agree.

Rat Bag turns and looks at Zipper in disgust. "And just what do I see, fuckhead?"

"Well, you see the pool, and the people, and the cars, and the apartments . . ." blurts Zipper in desperation as he tries to encompass whatever the answer may be.

"Yeah, yeah," snaps Rat Bag. "Yeah, I see all that. But you know what I see the most?"

"What's that?" asks Zipper, relieved to be off the hook.

"I see that little shithead Jimi Tyler trying to show off for those big dudes. And you know what?"

"What?"

Rat Bag pauses for effect. "It disgusts me. That's what. It really disgusts me. And you know why?"

"Why?"

As Zipper watches, a remarkable hate mask spreads across Rat Bag's face, and communicates more than words ever could.

"Because he's a bullshitter! The little prick is a master bullshitter! Look. He can't even swim and he's pretending like he's got it nailed. He's laying heavy bullshit on them. And if there's anything that pisses me off, it's a bullshitter."

Zipper catches the rhythm of the hate and hops on. "Yeah, he's a real bullshitter all right. Nothin' worse."

"It's not right," says Rat Bag. "We can't let it go on. Before you know it, every kid around here will think they can bury us in bullshit!"

"Fuckin' A," chimes in Zipper.

The pair sits on the hot lid, which cooks their anger and brings it to a slow boil during an extended moment of silence. Then Rat Bag snaps his fingers in a shot of inspiration.

"I've got it."

"You do?" asks Zipper.

"Yeah. Now the best way to teach somebody not to bullshit is to call them on it. Like, if you told me you were the meanest dude in the whole city, know what I'd do?"

"What?"

"I'd find some really bad-ass motherfucker, stick him right in your face, and tell you to prove it."

"You would?" asks Zipper uneasily.

"I would. And then the guy would stomp the shit out of you and that'd be the last time you bullshitted me."

"It sure would."

"Now suppose," hypothesizes Rat Bag, "just suppose that sometime we tossed the little bullshitter in the deep end of the pool and he sank to the bottom. Know what would happen?"

"He'd drown," says Zipper, whose hate has instantly dissolved into acute anxiety.

Rat Bag looks at Zipper in total exasperation. "No, no, no. We let him sink, then pull his ass out before he gets hurt. What do you think I am? Some kind of fuckin' psycho? The whole idea is that he never tries to bullshit anybody about swimming, or anything else, ever again. Don't you see? We've taught him a lesson!"

"Oh," says Zipper as it sinks in. "Yeah."

Rat Bag turns away from Zipper and watches Jimi frolic before Michael Riley.

"Just something to think about," he says. "That's all."

A day later, as Michael pulls into the Romona parking lot, he doesn't need a calendar to tell him it is Saturday. To his left stretches a long wooden carport painted rusty red, with a procession of sagging wooden columns that delineate individual parking slots. On this cloudy morning, the slots are almost entirely occupied with vehicles fighting a noble battle against advancing age with a little help from their owners. Unemployment has just topped 30 percent, so the purchase of a new car is a distant dream and the average age of the national car fleet is well past a decade. But here at the Romona, the good fight goes on as people struggle to preserve the dignity of private transportation. Up and down the carport, open hoods yawn like the gaping mouths of baby birds, desperately waiting for sustenance in the form of lubricants, parts, duct tape, gaskets, spark plugs, rotors, and bearings. In some slots major surgery is underway, with an entire team in attendance to conduct an organ transplant: a carburetor here, a starter motor there. A web of dirty orange extension cords crisscrosses the grease-stained pavement, where little clusters of oil cans dwell among rusting toolboxes and stacks of balding tires. This massive assault on mechanical degradation has become a communal nexus, a marketplace where stories are swapped, tools traded, favors granted, assistance rendered, and advice proffered.

As Michael pulls into his slot and exits his truck, Sam Motolla waves cheerfully from under the open hood of his ancient Dodge Dart parked next to Michael's truck.

"Hey Michael! You wouldn't have a five-eighths ratchet socket, would you?" Sam is a bald old bear with a broad face and a gray beard, an unemployed software engineer who specialized in embedded code for real-time control systems. Up and down the carport, his advice regarding the electronics of cars new enough to have microprocessors as vital parts is highly sought.

"Sorry, Sam. You might try Bobby Link if he's out of bed yet." Bobby Link, a meteoric guitar hero of the early nineties, now repairs amplifiers out of his apartment and acts as a distributor of various controlled substances. As Michael starts across the parking lot, he witnesses a rare daytime appearance by Eric Who Never Was. Seated in a chair by the pool, Eric wears a brown terry-cloth bathrobe over his pajamas and slippers. He has turned the chair to face the carport, and wears a look of intense concentration as he watches this weekly ritual of vehicular maintenance.

"Eric, how are you?" queries Michael as he passes on his way to the stairs.

"Column's going to pull out at eighteen hundred hours," announces Eric as he continues to stare down the cars that face him across the parking lot. "Tanks up front, APCs in the middle. Choppers will cover us on the way out, but then we're on our own."

Michael can only guess that Eric looks at the carport and sees a mobilized military operation in the making, with tanks and armored personnel carriers instead of old Datsuns and aging Fords. Which reminds Michael of his conversation less than an hour ago with Gail in Washington, D.C. He talked with her on a pay phone down in Sherwood, and outlined the strange triangle and its connection to biological weaponry and the language of God. It took her a while to grasp the scale of it, and that was going to be the problem when she took it to Grisdale. Who would believe it? It was like saying that the Manhattan Project had been initiated and run by a renegade group that looted the federal treasury and picked up the balance of their funding from the opium trade. Of course, there were differences. The drug business was no longer a medieval force controlled by isolated warlords in remote jungles. It was now a global enterprise with institutionalized political and economic clout. And massive scientific undertakings could now be automated and compressed into computer and robotic systems that required very small staffs, and therefore relatively small risk of exposure. But still, it would be a difficult sell, even for somebody of Grisdale's stature. And besides, it looked like the whole political theater was in a state of profound flux. Gail was extremely worried about the continued presence of federal troops on the streets of Washington. The civil commotion generated by the Mortgage March tragedy had come and gone, but the troops stayed on. And since the troops were directly under control of the executive branch, they were a continual reminder to the legislative and judicial branches of who was now in control. There had been several congressional delegations sent to the White House to meet with the president, and tactful suggestions were made that troops were a source of tension and irritation, and that they represented a rupture in the balance of power that was at the heart of the government's stability since day one. These protests were received politely, and the lawmakers were assured that the troops would be gone just as soon as "national security" was guaranteed. As evidence that it was not, they were reminded of the continuing rash of bank bombings in major financial centers throughout the country. The legislators left empty-handed, and on the Hill, wild rumors were beginning to fly about coups and revolutions. In any event, Gail felt that this whole ParaVolve incident might be the spark in the gas tank, and was best tabled for the time being. She thanked Michael and wished him well. His debt was canceled.

But on the way home, he continued to think about it. He was hooked. A fetal mind was squirming in its computer womb, and he could sense its motion through the computer in his apartment. Soon, he believed, it would reach outside the womb for stimulus, and he would witness a phenomenon unique in the history of science: the birth of true machine intelligence, an entity that defined its own course of thought. If this epochal event were taking place under more normal circumstances, there would be a flood of people scrambling to get involved, but right now only he and the Architect were aware of what was happening, so he had a front-row seat to an event that would go down as the one that defined the course of the next millennium. How could he turn away from it? He couldn't.

Now, as he reaches the top of the stairs and the door to his apartment, he encounters Jimi Tyler leaning against the railing, waiting for him.

"Hey, are you gonna make pictures on your machine again? Can I watch? I'll be quiet. Remember last time? Was I quiet or what?"

Michael sighs and says yes. Jessica is supposed to come over later after she finishes something at the lab, and the place seems a little empty these days when he's alone. Besides, Jimi is a master salesperson, and like most adults of good heart, Michael is a gullible consumer when it comes to kids.

Once inside, Michael fires up his machine and connects into DEUS while Jimi takes up his mute position off Michael's right shoulder. It takes him a few minutes to establish contact with the net, and along the way he stops to check and make sure that DEUS has not resumed feeding it data from GenBank, but the input programs are still silent. No one is talking to the net, but once he makes contact, it is clear that the net is definitely talking back anyway. Once again, the colors dance over the matrix that defines the net's voice on Michael's screen. There is nothing to do but settle back and watch for awhile.

For more than an hour, Michael watches the screen and nearly nods off several times, but then he sees the pattern. Most of the time the colors play randomly across the spectrum, but at odd intervals, the entire matrix shifts to just two values, the cool blue and hot yellow that represent the extremes of its vocal range.

Binary. It's going binary, thinks Michael. He knows that behind the colors are voltage values, with blue being the lowest and yellow the highest, which is precisely the way the fundamental ones and zeros of digital circuitry are expressed. He leaps forward in excitement and fiddles to construct a new interface with the net that will express this output in a stream of ones and zeros every time the net decides to slip into this mode. In a few minutes, he is watching a little parade of ones and zeros creep and stutter across his display and into a file on his machine that can be recalled for interpretation at his leisure.

"What happened to the colors?" asks Jimi.

"They told us to look at this instead," answers Michael.

"What is it?"

"I'm not sure, but I think it's a word game," replies Michael.

"How does it work?"

Michael considers the question for a moment and responds by opening a new window on the display and typing in: whatyouseeisveryhardtoreadbecauseallthelettersareallscrunchedup

"Can you read this?" asks Michael.

"I can't read," says Jimi, with no trace of shame.

"Well, if you could," says Michael, "it would be very hard to read until you did this." He types in: what you see is very hard to read because all the letters are all scrunched up

"Now, the same thing's true with the ones and zeros going across the screen right now. They might be saying something, but we don't know where one word stops and another begins, and it's especially hard to tell when they're moving."

"Well, why don't you stop them?" asks Jimi.

"Not a bad idea," admits Michael, and he issues a command that halts the screen display but lets the binary parade keep marching into the storage file. What remains is a single frozen line:

00111000010100110011000001101011010011111000000101

"Maybe it's learning its ABCs," comments Jimi as they stare at the screen.

"Jimi, you're a genius," applauds Michael. "You figured it out."

"Figured what out?"

"It's a code, a special code," says Michael as it dawns on him what he is seeing.

"Is it a secret code?" Jimi asks excitedly.

"Nope. It's a very common code called ASCII," replies Michael, "and now we're going to wait a minute to see if we can figure out what the code's trying to tell us. Let's step out and get a little air."

They go out and look over the railing at the vigorous circus of auto repair in the carport. Over by the pool, they see the sister of Eric Who Never Was come and gently talk him away from his command post across from the carport and lead him back to their apartment. Just before he goes inside, he turns to the carport, raises his right hand, and yells, "OK. Move 'em out!"

Jimi looks down and sees one of Rat Bag's platoons appear from around the far edge of the building, run down the walkway and out of sight.

"You know about Rat Bag?" he asks Michael.

"Not much," answers Michael. "I know his face, and I've heard he's kind of a bad dude. Is he?"

"Yup."

"Well, he's not the only bad dude out there, I can tell you that. Let's go back in and see what we've got."

Back in the room, Michael lets the net continue to talk into the file, but snags a copy of what has been recorded so far. He brings it up and quickly arranges for the binary stream to be deciphered into ASCII characters, which represent the conventional English alphabet and the decimal number system, among other things. Now, in a moment of truth, the result pops up on the screen: NVDPOINQAZXDDFOBAKBTX-UMQJSDPIMRHSHGFJKFQSXPPLMMFAQW

Jimi was right. The net is working on its ABCs. The ASCII character set includes 256 characters, and the net has focused exclusively on the twenty-six that represent the alphabet. But there is no discernible pattern in the letter sequence it is producing, and probably no pattern at all.

"So, what's it say?" asked Jimi.

"Nothing. Absolutely nothing," Michael replies glumly.

And why is the net talking in ASCII at all? It is an analog device and ASCII is a digital code, and normally the two are like oil and water unless they're specifically designed to work together. But what if the net is like a very small child? If so, it would be in an intense learning mode, and draw its knowledge from its immediate environment, which in this case is the interior of DEUS, where ASCII is a fundamental fact of life. And like all little children, it would tend to repeat out loud what it was learning.

A child. A very small child. The Architect's child. Michael now understands at least part of the man's anguish. He switches back to his original display window, where the string of ones and zeros marches on by. Suddenly, it is loaded with emotional content.

It is the robust and happy babbling of a real entity as it reaches out to embrace the world about it.

Lonnie Johnson walks slowly along the narrow path between two strawberry fields and tugs at the bill of his baseball cap with the John Deere logo plastered on the front. The tugging is a nervous habit that is masterfully imitated by his three sons when Lonnie is elsewhere. And today he tugs a little more than usual, because his oldest boy has just announced that he joined the navy. The news took both Lonnie and his wife completely by surprise, and his wife, whose emotional mass usually hovers just below criticality, went completely nuclear. So rather than sit around and be irradiated by the fallout, Lonnie tracks along his usual escape route, down past the toolshed, through the orchard, and across the strawberry fields to the woods that line Christensen Creek.

As he shuffles along the path toward the woods and creek gully, he notices scattered bits of motion among the rows between the plants. Pretty weird. It's too early for birds to be assaulting the berries, which are still green. Then he sees a rabbit jump over one of the furrows, followed by an explosion of pheasant flight down the way, and the brief brown skitter of a chipmunk down one of the rows. Funny deal. All these little critters should be in the bush over by the creek, where they avoid the exposure of the open field and the taloned swoop of hawks and owls.

As Lonnie nears the end of the path, he sees that a stack of flats, the shallow boxes used to store strawberries, has been knocked over into an angular heap in the small strip of short grass between the field and the creek brush. Damn kids. His wife picks up after them in the house, and he has to pick up after them out here. Lonnie shuffles over to pick up the stack, and there it is, lying on top of an upturned flat soaked red with blood. The sight of it makes the hair stand up on Lonnie's neck. A rabbit carcass perforated with scores of holes, each about an inch in diameter, and many still oozing fluid. In some places the holes overlap to form red canyons, with a second layer of holes lining their floor.

Lonnie hunts and is no stranger to carnage, but this makes him slightly sick. It looks like some madman went after the thing with a large drill. But who? His kids were wacky, but not like this. Not like this.

Then he hears the thump, and sees the flats rearrange themselves to accommodate some kind of motion at the bottom.

So that's it. Whatever did it is right here. Well, let's just flush the little bugger out where we can get a peek at him.

Lonnie moves gingerly around the pile until he picks his spot, then delivers a violent kick that sends the flats flying and exposes the ground beneath. A large possum kicks into instant motion and blasts into the brush by the creek.

Couldn't be a possum, thinks Lonnie. A possum bites, but it sure can't drill.

Then, for the first time he notices the plants. Squatting down, he examines the leaves on the strawberry vines and panics. The plants are his livelihood, and something is badly wrong. The leaves should be flat with a soft, green surface, but they aren't. Instead, they're hard and waxy, and have curled into an umbrella shape, like tiny satellite TV antennas. Lonnie picks one and holds it closer to examine. At the center, a slender green stalk protrudes and coils into a spring shape. In twenty-five years of farming, he's never seen anything like it. It's bad, really bad. The whole crop might already be infected.

In the creek brush thirty feet away, the driller trains its binocular eyes on the squatting figure holding the plant and then creeps slowly in its direction.

Goddamn, worries Lonnie as he plucks a second leaf and examines it. I better get the county guy out right away. He's not going to believe this.

Lonnie rises and starts down one of the rows to see how far the damage goes.

The driller sees the figure stand upright and calculates that it's too large for a direct assault. As an alternative, it now picks up the scent of the nearby possum and recalibrates to stalk the new target.

Lonnie walks the entire row and finds the same affliction, the curled leaves, the umbrella look. He returns to the path and starts back toward the house; the farther he goes from the creek, the less pronounced the disease is. Maybe there's hope. Maybe they can spray and stop it before it spreads over the entire field.

Lonnie has almost reached the orchard when he feels the tightness in his chest and the rattle in his breathing. Normally, he would be more concerned, but right now he is fixated on his crop, and writes it off to the anxiety that has accelerated his walk almost to a jog. Just a little phlegm in the pipes due to exertion, that's all. But by the time he can see the toolshed, he is on the fringe of gasping and feels a tingle all over his face. What the hell is going on? As he passes the toolshed on the way to the house, his walk has slowed to a crawl and he is beginning to feel sharp little fists popping away in his abdomen.

Harriet Johnson is in the living room when she hears the kitchen door open as Lonnie comes in. She has been doing a lot of thinking about their son, and has decided that Lonnie should go down to the navy recruiter and see if he can somehow get the boy off the hook. She will wait a few minutes and let him get comfortable before she delivers this imperative cloaked as a thoughtful suggestion. Then she hears the phone dialing.

"Yeah, Jim Politano in Agriculture, please." Lonnie sounds bad. Maybe she'll wait a bit.

"Yeah, Jim. I've got the goddamn weirdest thing you've ever seen out here. It's my strawberries. They look like they're going to start watching satellite TV. The leaves are all curled up and hard. . . . No, just part of the field. . . . Well, the only other thing was a dead rabbit that looked like someone went after it with a power drill. And, oh, yeah, I saw a bunch of birds and varmints out in the field when they should have been in the brush down by the creek. But the berries are the big thing. It looks real bad. Well, if you can get out here today, you won't be sorry. . . . OK, bye."

Harriet heads for the kitchen, the navy on the back burner. Nothing is more serious than crop trouble. As she comes through the door, she suppresses a gasp when she sees Lonnie sitting at the kitchen table by the phone. His ashen face wears a shiny coat of sweat, and red blotches the size of quarters dot his face and hands. He pushes his voice through a mounting swell of phlegm to speak.

"Politano's coming out. We got trouble with the strawberries. And I think I just got the flu."

God, help us, prays Harriet as she goes to get Lonnie into bed and phone the doctor.

A quarter mile away, the forest around the creek is silent for the first time in hundreds of years. No conventional animal of any size remains. All either have been eaten or fled the advance of the drillers. In fact, many of the drillers are also dying as their ferocious metabolisms rapidly burn up their life cycle.

And at the center, the blackberry thicket has come under the sway of the viruses shed by the drillers. The vines, once thick, green thorny bundles that snaked in long curves to form a chaotic weave, now are twisted into helical coils, like phone cords. And in the clearing at the middle, in the bottom chamber of the mound, the first of the queen's eggs hatches, and the next step in the march of the introns pops out into the world.

The beast that emerges is much larger than the drillers. It uncoils to an infant length of nearly a foot and heads for the tunnel to the chamber above as it tests its four powerful legs and clawed feet. Once in the upper chamber, it greedily sucks the carefully stored food from the perforations in the walls. Already, the beast is radiating considerable heat, and the temperature in the chamber is starting to rise. It hurries to complete its task and move out before it turns the nest into an oven and cooks to death. With a full load of fuel, it now crawls to the surface of the mound and steps into the helical cathedral formed by the mutated blackberry vines. Several drillers watch it emerge and wait motionless for its next move.

The beast's body has the shape of a slightly bloated crocodile, with squat, muscular legs. But unlike a reptile or any other animal, its skin is alive and crawling with thousands of pores that continually open and shut at random. When fully dilated, the pores expand to half an inch, release a blast of heat, and then snap completely shut, all within a fraction of a second. Instead of a tail, the rear of the body tapers down to a needle-sharp bony stinger. Just short of the head region, two eye stalks sprout, each with binocular, segmented, and infrared eyes integrated into a single egg-shaped housing. But where there should be a head, there is nothing, as if the beast had been decapitated behind the jaws and the flesh tucked in to form a gaping hole. And within this hole dwells a dreadful round appendage, capable of zooming out from its retracted position and extending several inches past the lip of its bodily cave. Composed of a semihard rubbery material, the cylindrical appendage has a business end like that of a lamprey eel, with several concentric rings of curved teeth designed to penetrate and form an unbreakable grip. From the center of this opening pokes a slender bony shaft, a hypodermic needle with a mission that will lead the new beast to be christened "the needle hound."

The pupils in the needle hound's binocular eyes contract to adjust to the daylight and focus on the cluster of drillers that ring the mound. With amazing speed it charges the driller immediately ahead and knocks it onto its back, where its legs spin crazily. But before it can right itself, the needle hound pivots and plants its stinger into the driller's side, and the legs halt almost in midspin. The needle hound turns to face its victim. The cylinder rockets out, the gripper teeth latch onto the victim's belly, and the hypodermic needle shoots out, penetrates the surface, and injects a powerful acid compound that instantly liquefies all flesh and bony material in the immediate area of the wound. As the liquefaction starts, a suction pump in the cylinder kicks in and sucks the hot, thick soup into the needle hound's innards, where it is added to the existing fuel store.

As the needle hound pumps its meal, the other drillers watch, but don't move. The needle hound's presence strips away all instinct for self-preservation and they quietly wait their turn to become soup kitchens that will fuel the needle hound's spectacular growth. Within an hour, it has eaten them all and swelled to a length of two and a half feet, its full adult size. Now it is ready to leave the mound and the temple of vines, and explore a much larger world.

20

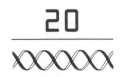

The Awakening

Michael drains the last of the coffee from his cup and prepares to go to work. He was up late last night, watching the parade of ones and zeros, which appeared at odd intervals on his screen and then vanished without warning. When Jessica came over in the early evening, he was still glued to the screen, and showed her the display with great enthusiasm. While she was definitely interested, she failed to catch the fever of it all, and he realized that unless one was thoroughly saturated with the history of artificial intelligence and neural nets, it might be a little tough to get pumped about what was now on the screen. So he was slightly reluctant about leaving the net when they left to have a little dinner downtown, but not reluctant at all by the time they shared a bottle of wine and went back to her house. Jessica was a quietly passionate woman who always made love to him with an intensity that was almost startling, and Michael was utterly fascinated, and knew that while he might eventually solve the mysteries of DEUS, he would never solve the mystery of Jessica, nor did he care to. It was enough just to feel the warmth of her cheek on his chest and her hair flowing softly over his stomach. There was a quiet but very intense bond growing between them, one that neither was very adept at verbalizing. It was easier just to float in it, like a warm pool of clear water that kept you pleasantly suspended and detached while the rest of the world softly bowed out, along with all its little barbs, hooks, and probes. He knew that they were somehow healing each other, mending emotional tissue that had been damaged almost beyond repair.

While drinking his coffee, Michael considers what the best approach would be to communicating with the net. For now, natural language was out, just as it would be with a human infant. But he kept coming back to Jimi's comment about learning the ABCs, and decided there was no better approach. Right now, the net was spewing out letters at random, and might not be aware that they were made up of a finite set of characters, an alphabet. So now Michael goes into DEUS and grabs control of the program that usually "speaks" to the net by feeding it GenBank data. Once the connection is made, he pauses and considers the significance of what he is about to do. Until now, many people had interfaced with computer systems, but never one with a mind of its own. That done, he types in the alphabet in capital letters: ABCDEFGHIJKLMNOPQRSTUVWXYZ

He waits sixty seconds and does it again. After five such cycles, he quits the "speaking" program, activates the "listening" program, and arranges to watch the ASCII characters march across the screen: ALSLCVMVBJFKLWEPFMLSJFKJKOGJIRUYTPHJSOKNMNXVNDKEIEH

And so it goes for nearly twenty minutes. Then, just as Michael resigns himself to a very long watch: AKDKVMKDRIEABCDEFGHIJKLMNOPQRSTUVWXYZDKDKDKDKDKDDK

His heart jumps. Right in the middle of the parade is the alphabet, plain as day. Two minutes later it repeats: DKFKFKTKRKRABCDEFGHIJHKLMNOPQRSTUVWXYZDKDKDKGHEEODOF

Michael gets up and paces with excitement. It heard him. And spoke back. It's alive. So what now? The best bet is to stick with elementary education, a field virtually unknown to him. But there is an answer.

An hour later in the Romona parking lot, he is pulling a box off the driver's seat of his truck and stacking a smaller package on top.

"Watcha got?"

He sees Jimi standing behind him and smiles. "Kid stuff."

Jimi brightens. "Oh, yeah? Can I see?" In this age, the endless shower of kids toys has long since been turned down to a slow, painful drip. So any toy or kid thing is a special treasure, a thing to be remembered.

"Sure, you can. Why don't you carry this package for me?"

In Michael's computer room, Jimi pulls several things that look like album covers out of the package while Michael removes a beige metal box from the carton and hooks it to the back of his computer.

"What's this?" asks Jimi as he holds up one of the covers.

"It's called an interactive video disk," replies Michael, "and the one you've got there is to teach kids to read and write words."

"Can I play?" asks Jimi.

"You can play later, but right now we're going to see if we can get the computer to play."

Jimi is disappointed, but takes up his station behind Michael's right shoulder. Michael now begins to build a pathway that will take the video disk's lesson through his computer, into DEUS, and finally into the net; and also the reverse, so the net can respond directly to the video disk. There is one tricky aspect of this operation: The net has already shown a capacity to "hear" alphabet characters, but what about vision? The video disk generates video images of simple objects so that children can associate them with corresponding words. So Michael decides to send the video signal directly into the net as analog information and manipulates the "speaker" program inside DEUS to allow this to happen. A video signal is complex, but incredibly primitive compared with real vision processing in the human brain. For now, it will have to serve as the net's "eyes."

"OK," says Michael to Jimi. "We're ready."

He fires up the video disk and horizontally divides the screen into two windows. The top one displays the video disk lesson, and the bottom one is set to present the net's responses during the lesson. As the lesson starts, a video image of a motionless ball comes up, and below it letters appear one by one that spell out "SEE THE BALL." Below these letters, a series of blank spaces appear and a voice says, "Can you spell 'see the ball'?" To give the net a clue as to how the game is played, Michael types in the answer. Now a second video image comes up showing the small ball rolling toward the camera, with "SEE THE BALL ROLL" spelled out underneath. Once again, Michael types in the answer and then leans back. "OK," he tells the net. "Now you're on your own."

Next, a video image of a sitting dog replaces the ball, with "SEE SPOT" underneath. Anxiously, Michael watches the lower window on his screen for the net's response. What he sees is disappointing, a stream of apparently random characters, letters, and other punctuation.

"So, what's it saying?" asks Jimi.

"Looks like it's just mumbling to itself. What do you think?"

"Yup. Just talkin' to itself."

"How about you?" inquires Michael. "Did you learn the lesson?"

"Sure did," Jimi says proudly. "Spot's a dog, and if you look at him you spell it S-E-E S-P-O-T."

"Well, at least you got it," agrees Michael. "That's more than I can say for our little pal here."

The phone rings. "Tell you what," proposes Michael, "you stay here and watch this window, because maybe it'll say 'SEE SPOT' when I'm not looking. OK?" Actually, he doubts it, but it will give Jimi something to do while he's on the phone.

"No sweat. I can handle it," Jimi says proudly.

In the kitchen, Michael picks up the receiver and activates the video. It's Victor Shields.

"Mike," he says glibly. "Sorry if I'm breaking your concentration, but I, uh, hadn't heard from you in a bit and thought I ought to check in. How's it going? Can you give me, uh, sort of a lightweight rundown?"

"Well, I wish I could, Victor, but this is a real heavyweight problem. Like I said before, we're dealing with the most complex system ever, and I just have to take things one at a time. And that's exactly what I'm doing."

"Well, ah, the chairman's in town, and he's staying here until this whole business is settled. So naturally he's going to want periodic reports on progress."

OK, thinks Michael, here go both barrels of BS in one shot. "Well, the upside is this: I think I'm beginning to see an overall pattern of structure to the way your chief designer did things. And if I'm right, you've got the equivalent of false walls throughout the system. Like you used to see in old horror films. And if I'm right, the bomb is somewhere behind one of these facades. Now, my next move is to try to build a program that can tell the real walls from the false ones."

"Excellent," chirps Victor, who now has something to feed his voracious boss. "How long do you think it might take?"

"If I knew, I'd tell you, Victor. But right now I can't even guess."

"Well, from now on I'll probably be checking in pretty regularly. I can't tell you how concerned Mr. Daniels is about this. We're talking hundreds of millions here."

The Fear.

For just a moment, it crashes over Michael like a huge wave taken broadside and nearly capsizes his equilibrium. Victor's face rotates wildly and zooms far into the distance, then suddenly snaps back into place and stabilizes.

"Well, then," Michael hears himself saying, "I guess I better get back to work. Talk to you soon."

"That you can count on. Hah, hah."

Now, what brought that on? wonders Michael as Victor hangs up. It came from nowhere.

But maybe not. Daniels. Did he say Daniels? Yes, he did. Then it comes back: the NSA. The meetings in the hotel room in Virginia. Specifications for offensive biological weaponry. A creep named Spelvin. And another named Daniels, who seemed to run the show.

Could it be the same guy? Of course it could. He was involved in gas and bugs and computers back then, so why not now? And what about Spelvin? Didn't he write some horrible paper on . . .

Instinctively, Michael snaps the lid shut on his recall. The chain of associations is getting too close to that convenience store, with its shot-out windows and oceans of blood. Besides, everything after that incident is very foggy. He simply doesn't have the data to place either Daniels or Spelvin in an incriminating context. They float loose in the fog, and refuse to drift into a recognizable pattern. Still, the names nag at him and leave a bad taste as he returns to the computer room.

"Hey, it said 'SEE SPOT' and then it stopped."

Jimi is pointing proudly at the lower window on the screen. Michael rushes over to look. Sure enough, it's right there at the end of a trail of garbage: dj3jd8fjrtoweODKL20-CV,.DOPLRO4592fJ/vSEE SPOT

Then, as they both watch, the window goes entirely blank.

"What did it do that for?" asks Jimi. "It had the right answer!"

"Dunno," mumbles Michael, who now must operate on about the same level as Jimi.

Then a new display comes up in the window, and its contents leave Michael aghast.

"What is it?" asks Jimi.

"It's code," murmurs Michael. "High-level code."

"You mean like secret code?"

"Not if you know how to read it." As Michael watches, the program scrolls by on the screen with increasing velocity. He can't even guess at its meaning or content.

"So what's it trying to tell us?" inquires Jimi.

"I don't think it's talking to us. I think it's probably talking to its mom," replies Michael.

"Well, where is its mom?"

"She's a very big computer that lives just a few miles from here."

"What's it saying to her?"

"Right now, I haven't the slightest idea." All Michael knows is that the net is injecting a very large program into DEUS. All of a sudden it makes sense. While the net may have trouble with "SEE SPOT," it has spent its entire embryonic life in close communion with its cybernetic mother, so generating computer code is probably as intuitive as speaking is for a human being.

As if in response to his thought, the window goes blank again.

"Now what?" inquires Jimi.

"Let's find out," says Michael, who lunges to the keyboard and tunnels into DEUS to the location of the two programs that speak and listen to the net. They're gone. Not a trace.

Would the net strike itself deaf and dumb? Not likely. Michael goes back to the trick he used to find the programs in the first place, to the I/O memory map. Retracing his steps, he finds that two entirely new programs have replaced the old ones. Furthermore, he can tell from their file dates that they're only a couple of minutes old.

So that's what the net was up to, thinks Michael. Now it's the sole owner of its voice, ears, and eyes.

"Doesn't it want to play anymore?" asks Jimi.

Just as Michael is about to reply, he notices something changing in the upper window, where the interactive video lesson is still running, this time with a video image of a running dog and "SEE SPOT RUN" underneath. As Michael and Jimi watch, this same phrase appears in the blank spaces reserved for a child's reply. The net is now playing solo.

Over the next few minutes, the net runs through another dozen images and finishes the lesson by answering "LOOK AT THE BOAT" in response to a picture of a sailboat on the open sea. Then, unexpectedly, the bottom window comes to life again. Slowly, an image is being scanned into the window, an image of the sailboat that is a slightly primitive approximation of the original in the top window. When the image is complete, the phrase "LOOK AT THE BOAT" appears underneath.

Now Michael knows what the "garbage" was in the net's answers before it gained control of its own input and output. It was a mathematical representation of the video images from the lesson. At that point, the net just didn't know how to draw them as pictures on Michael's screen.

Before Michael can absorb the full impact of what is happening and understand the consequences, the bottom window changes once again. This time, the message is simpler, but will change the face of science and philosophy forever.

"MORE BALL. MORE SPOT. MORE."

Counterpoint looks out the view window at the fuzzy layer of mist over the Tualatin Valley and likes what he hears. He sits in a leather recliner in the living room of ParaVolve's company condo in West Slope and adjusts the speakerphone with a remote control. Now he can hear it even better, the taut harmonics of fear in the upper registers of Victor Shield's voice as Victor explains Michael Riley's theory of false walls to him.

"Apparently, it's quite complicated," Victor is saying. "But that's exactly what you'd expect under the circumstances. I mean, if it was routine, our security people would have caught it a long time ago. So the next move is to build some software that detects these false walls and lets us start looking behind them. I think we can . . ."

"How long?" interjects Counterpoint.

"Well, now that Riley's got a sense of scale for the problem, he's working on an estimate for constructing . . ."

"How long?" demands Counterpoint.

"Well, apparently that's a little tough to tell right now, Bill," Victor says.

"It's going to get a lot tougher if this thing crashes on us, Victor. A lot tougher on all of us."

"I realize that," says Victor. "Believe me, I'm as concerned as you are. Maybe more."

"Maybe more?" mocks Counterpoint. "How's that?"

"Well, you deal with the bigger picture, but this company is my whole life right now, and . . ."

"There is no bigger picture, Victor. Not for you. Not for me. Not for anybody."

Victor sighs. "Well, I guess you're right. I'll let you know the instant I hear anything at all."

"Do that," says Counterpoint as he cuts the connection. He continues to stare at the misted valley and considers the situation. He doesn't want to confront Riley directly. Although there's no way Riley can directly connect him with that fiasco in D.C. a few years back, he undoubtedly knows all about the lab and the biocompiler by now. As soon as he associates the name "Daniels" with all this biowarfare stuff, flags are bound to go up all over. Still, they can't do without Riley right now. He was absolutely brilliant at the agency, maybe even a match for the Architect himself. But as soon as the bomb is found and disarmed, Mr. Riley will have to go.

But now, a moment of peace. Counterpoint's gaze drifts from the valley back into the room and on to the corpse on the living room floor. The dead boy is carefully positioned in the very center of the large Chinese rug on the hardwood floor, as if for a ceremony. With the life bleached from his skin, he looks even younger than his thirteen years, and only the blond puff of pubescent pubic hair hints at adolescence. There is a kind of purity to the boy that enthralls Counterpoint as he reaches in his pocket for a nail clipper and relives his latest act of ultimate consumption.

It hadn't taken long to find the right part of town. Counterpoint pointed his luxury-class rental car past the towers of chrome, glass, and steel to the more compressed world of brick and tar and wooden sills. Along streets where peeling plywood covered gouged-out windows and weeds had their way with cracks in the sidewalk. As Counterpoint toured these bruised streets, his trained eyes tracked the stealthful and continuous motions of the flesh trade. A figure emerging from around a corner, then ducking back again. Another popping out of a deserted doorway and striding quickly down the street as if on some urgent errand.

It didn't take him long to find the target. The boy was walking down the sidewalk, hands in the front pockets of his tight jeans, and he slowed as he heard the lazy approach of Counterpoint's big car, a money car, a trick car. As Counterpoint pulled parallel to the boy, one look at his young face was enough. He pulled slightly ahead and stopped as the boy did a cautionary scan up and down the street, then came over. The rest was perfunctory, a brief negotiation, a set price, and away they went. Most of the drive was in silence as Counterpoint wound up out of downtown into the hills on the way to the condo. Clearly, the boy was getting twitchy as his meager reserve of street sense kicked in and told him he had made a big mistake. But Counterpoint somehow filled the car with a kind of paralytic ether that kept the boy from reaching for the handle and jettisoning into the street at a stop sign. Once or twice, the boy tried to make light conversation, and this annoyed Counterpoint, because it somehow degraded the boy's symbolic value to him.

At the condo, Counterpoint felt the thrill rise in him as the boy stepped through the front door. There would be no exit. The ceremony would now follow a perfectly prescribed pattern that he had slowly fashioned since the episode with the young man in the park in Washington. In a physical sense, it was a highly condensed stream of brutality. He instructed the boy to disrobe, and felt the thrill soar through the top of his head as he saw the glaze of resignation settle over the boy's features. He then buggered him, and halfway through the act brought out a cord that he looped once and threw around the boy's neck to strangle him. The thrill lifted him nearly out of himself when he saw the boy was barely going to resist his murderous onslaught. The victim was already giving up his identity and flowing into Counterpoint, who greedily drank in enormous gulps. As the boy went completely limp, he realized that all the other moments of his life were just shabby little interludes to support these peaks of almost infinite altitude.

Counterpoint clips his nails slowly while he views the corpse in the diffuse light from the overcast sky. As he scrolls the events of last night through his mind, he realizes that the level of transcendence he reaches is in direct proportion to the victim's innocence. There is some kind of elixir within this innocence that is the fuel of immortality, and for the first time, he believes he can indeed become immortal. Not figuratively, but literally. Science thinks otherwise, but what do fools in the laboratory know of this theater of the extreme where he now lives? Nothing.

He continues this line of thought as he wraps the body in a plastic tarp, puts it in his truck, and drives out into rural Washington County to bury it in a clump of woods south of Cornelius. As he piles the last shovelful of dirt onto the grave, he scolds himself for not having seen the immensity of his own life's mission until now. The entire world, not just this country, is screaming for a new order, a rebirth that will deliver them from the aimless caprice, the wandering in circles. And when it comes, the one who delivers it must have the quality of a deity so that others will automatically drop to their knees in utter adoration. And what better measure of deification than immortality? He looks down at the grave one last time and thinks of what a small sacrifice the boy's life was in pursuit of so noble a goal.

As Jim Politano pulls onto the gravel road to Christensen Creek, he gripes to Karen Whitmire about the county motor pool. The car they are driving has brakes that pull to the right, and it stalls half the time at stoplights. He raves on about how before the Downturn, they had cars that were in better shape than most privately owned cars, but now they had to drive around in these shitwagons. Karen listens in amusement. At twenty-one, she does not remember adult life before the Downturn and is very glad to have a job and be riding around in any car at all. She likes Jim, who's been with the county extension service twenty-two years and has become her mentor. Nevertheless, she's getting a little tired of Jim's tirade about the motor pool. For her, life is still larger than that.

"Now, what's this about the strawberries out here?" she asks Jim.

"I really can't say," Jim replies. "But I'll tell you this: That old Lonnie is one smart son of a bitch, and he's been around the block a few times. If he's worried, then I'm worried. We'll just have to see when we get there."

They round a curve in the gravel road, and Lonnie's old ranch-style house appears, flanked on both sides by aging farm machinery. An ambulance sits in the driveway.

"Well, what's goin' on?" Jim asks himself out loud. "He didn't say anything about anybody bein' sick! What the hell?"

They pull in the gravel to keep the driveway clear for the ambulance, and walk to the front door, which is wide open. Still, Jim feels the need to be polite. He bangs the knocker twice. "Lonnie? Harriet?"

They start in just as the stretcher comes around from the hallway. It's Lonnie, all right, but just barely. He's sickly white and his hands and face are plastered with red blotches. Two paramedics tend to him, one holding an IV bag with clear fluid. Harriet follows behind with a look of barely suppressed panic. Incredibly, Lonnie recognizes Jim and issues a feeble command for the paramedics to stop.

His tear ducts pour out copious amounts of fluid as he looks up at Jim and struggles to bring his voice above the respiratory rattle.

"Strawberries. It's the strawberries."

True farmer, thinks Jim. Here he is, ready to kick, and he's still worried about his crop.

As they wheel Lonnie on past, Jim turns to Harriet. "Have you got any ideas?"

"Yeah," she says grimly. "They've got a lot of ideas. And that's about all they've got." She brushes past to board the ambulance, not even thinking about locking the house.

Jim and Karen go out on the porch and watch the ambulance back out and start down the gravel road in a yellow rooster tail of dust.

"Poor son of a bitch," comments Jim. "It's not an easy life to begin with, and the last thing you need is something like this." He looks back toward Lonnie's fields. "Well, let's get goin'. If he says it's the strawberries, then it's probably the strawberries. It's the least we can do for him now."

As they start for the path behind the toolshed, Karen turns anxiously to Jim. "Have you got any idea what was wrong with that guy?" she asks.

"Nope," Jim replies. "Wish I did. Maybe I could do something to help him."

"He said, 'It's the strawberries.' Do you think maybe he ate some and they made him sick?"

"Doubt it. Most likely he was just frettin' about his crop."

As they come out of the orchard to the edge of the strawberry field, Jim's practiced eye immediately sees that something is badly wrong.

"Whoa! What have we got here?" He bends over and looks at the plants, which now sport bushels of inverted green umbrellas where their leaves once were. "Son of a bitch! He wasn't kidding! They look like they're satellite TV." He stands back up, holding one of the leaves. "This is the goddamndest thing I've ever seen. OK, let's check the rest of the field and then get some samples back to the office pronto."

As they start down the path in the middle of the field, both notice the profusion of wildlife running up and down the rows. "You know, he said somethin' about that, too," notes Jim. "I wonder if they all got the same bug the strawberries got." Karen considers this a good working hypothesis and so she sticks to the middle of the path and touches nothing.

A few yards ahead, a rabbit darts out onto the path and freezes when it sees them. Before they can react, something comes out of nowhere and slams the rabbit so hard it is knocked out of sight among the rows of plants. Jim trots ahead to the spot where the rabbit disappeared and witnesses an unforgettable scene. He sees an egg-shaped insect the size of a cat drilling hole after hole in the rabbit in rapid succession.

"Holy shit!" he exclaims, and turns to Karen. "Get up here! You gotta see this!"

Karen approaches cautiously and looks down the row, and then promptly turns away and throws up.

Jim is too excited to acknowledge her predicament. "OK. Here's what we're gonna do," he says as he notices the pile of flats at the end of the path. "We're gonna see if we can trap it."

He leaves Karen bent over and retching and runs down to fetch a flat. If he's lucky, the thing will still be there when he gets back. When he returns, the driller has already turned the rabbit's flank into a porous, bleeding sponge. Gingerly, Jim starts down the row, where the insect faces away from him to drill the rabbit. He extends the flat in front of him in a simple strategy: He will take the driller by surprise and throw the flat over it and then hold it down until Karen can find something heavy enough to hold it while they go for help.

The driller's peripheral eyes sense motion from the rear and its brain calculates the range. Still time to feed a little longer before it becomes a threat.

Jim's heart pounds as he closes the distance with the flat extended in front of him. Just one more step and . . .

The driller senses the threat to be within striking range and pivots faster than a human eye can track. It explodes off its two sets of hind legs and hurls through the air at the wooden square above.

Jim hears a loud *bang* and feels the flat jerked from his grip as the driller plunges toward his chest. He reels back and feels burning pain as the driller's legs claw at his forearms, trying to get a grip. Finally, there is a thump as it drops to the ground and streaks out of sight down the row.

"Are you OK?"

Jim turns to see Karen standing back on the path. He looks down at his forearms, which are crisscrossed with fiery red scratches. "Yeah. I guess. Only got scratched. Let's get some samples and get outta here."

Karen can already see that something is badly wrong with Jim. A balding man in his mid-forties, he has a powerful frame saddled with a slight paunch, receding gray hair, and a tanned faced with rich brown eyes. But now his facial color almost matches the gray of his hair, and he walks with the stoop of a much older man.

"Are you sure you're OK?"

"OK as I'm gonna get. Let's get goin'."

He lets Karen lead as they walk back to the orchard. From behind, she hears an ugly rattle creep into his breathing, which now sounds more like a chain of forced gasps. Occasionally, she glances back and sees his mouth wide open as he labors along.

"Maybe we better stop for a minute."

Karen halts, turns, and sees Popeye.

She will always remember it like that. Jim has on a short-sleeved shirt, and his bare forearms are swollen to the size of watermelons. Grotesquely inflated and pink, they undeniably look like Popeye's, but the humor is absent as he lifts one and looks at it in horror. "It's that thing," he observes. "It's the scratches from that thing. Oh, Jesus! Oh, Jesus!" He wobbles slightly on his feet. "We've got to get to the car! We've got to!"

He stumbles toward the house, and Karen grabs his swollen limb to support him. It feels like an overinflated inner tube on a hot summer day. Her forehead tingles and her legs ache, but she is too distracted to notice as they struggle the last fifty yards to the car.

"You're going to be OK," offers Karen weakly. "You're going to be OK, now. It's probably just some allergy. That's all."

If only she could believe it.

Dr. Cheryl Burk sinks down into a chair and sighs with relief. Her damn back is bothering her again, and the only thing to do about it is get off her feet for awhile. Which is a little tough to do when you're an emergency room physician, a job that demands you be on your feet both figuratively and literally for an entire twelve-hour shift. And today, things have been a lot more interesting than usual. Since Tuality Community Hospital is still on the periphery of rural Washington County, the emergency room gets its share of spectacular traumas. While farming appears to be a peaceful pursuit, it is actually a fairly dangerous industrial occupation populated by machines that can slice, gouge, crush, shred, and bore without discrimination. And then there's the usual smattering of car accidents, although there seem to be less as the Downturn puts a crimp on personal fuel budgets.

But this Lonnie Johnson is a real stumper. The guy is covered with sores that are now starting to ulcerate, his temperature has dropped a degree and a half below normal, his blood pressure is all over the map, and he has a low-grade case of pneumonia. Right now, he's stabilized and conscious, but his mental state is uncertain, because he keeps talking about sick strawberries with little green umbrellas on them. The lab is working on the blood sample, and on the fluid from one of the sores, and it will be very interesting to see what shows up.

"Dr. Burk to the ER, please," squawks the speaker on her desk. Cheryl reluctantly pushes herself out of the chair. Her back isn't going to like this. Maybe she should see a doctor about it.

Uh oh, she thinks as she enters the treatment room, double whammy. The room is bisected into two bays by a curtained partition, and the table in the first bay holds a young woman of about twenty-one. In the second bay, she can see a pair of muddy men's shoes protruding from the end of the table.

"Dr. Anderson on his way?" she asks the emergency room technician as she takes a closer look at the young woman. "On his way down," comes the reply. The patient, who looks up at her anxiously, is very pale, completely soaked with sweat, and has tears streaming down both cheeks.

"You can dry the tears, dear. We'll take good care of you," says Dr. Burk.

"I'm not crying, Doctor. Really. I just can't stop the tears. I know it sounds like a joke, but I can't. What's happening?"

"Might be as simple as a bad allergy. Ever have hay fever?"

"Never."

"Well, we'll find out soon enough." Cheryl turns to the technician. "Pulse and blood pressure?"

"Pretty normal. Seventy on the pulse and blood pressure's one seventeen over seventy-eight."

"Dr. Nimitz will be with you in a minute," says Cheryl to Karen Whitmire. "Your vital signs are good, so I don't think there's too much to worry about. You'll have to excuse me, I've got another patient to check."

"That's Jim," says Karen. "Is he going to be OK?"

"Tell you in a minute," smiles Dr. Burk.

Cheryl moves on to the next bay and immediately sees it's going to be a day like no other. The patient is a big man in his mid-forties whose forearms are swollen to a shocking proportion, maybe ten inches in diameter, with the fingers extending from the distended flesh like tits on a cow's udder. At first glance, it looks like the kind of thing you'd see in a textbook of tropical afflictions. He is unconscious, with a slow rattling cadence to his breathing.

She puts her stethoscope to his chest and listens. Definitely fluid in the lungs and a slight arrhythmia to the heart. Still, he seems to be in a stable state. She turns her attention to the scratches on the forearms. They seem fairly superficial, but obviously could have been the delivery point for some sort of infectious agent or allergen.

So what the hell was going on?

Dr. Burk pokes her head around the divider curtain to Karen. "You say you know this gentleman?"

"I was with him when it happened. We work for the county extension service and we were out in a field when he tried to trap this large animal that had just attacked a rabbit. The thing got away and it scratched him and he started getting sick just a few minutes later."

"And what about you?"

"I started feeling weird on the way in here. I could hardly see through the tears by the time we got to Hillsboro."

"Did you get a good look at the animal?"

"I did, but it all happened really fast. It was like an enormous insect, maybe a foot long. I've never seen anything like it."

"Did you yourself have any contact with this animal?"

"No."

"Was there anything else unusual?"

"Yeah. The strawberries. That's why we were out there. There's some kind of disease that's hit the strawberries and curled their leaves up."

Sick strawberries. Mr. Johnson. Maybe there was a pattern.

"Do you know whose property this was?"

"Yeah. It was a guy's named Lonnie Johnson."

After briefing Dr. Nimitz on the patients, Cheryl goes immediately to phone Washington County Health and Human Services.

"I've got three people here, each with a very bizarre set of symptoms.

All of them were at the same location, out by Christensen Creek off Firdale Road. We're waiting for lab tests before we even attempt a diagnosis. One of the patients was apparently scratched by some animal that no one can identify. Plus, two of the patients claim that there was some kind of strange disease present in a strawberry crop they were inspecting. I don't know if it's something communicable, but it's weird enough that it should probably be looked into. I'll let you know more when we get the lab work."

Dr. Burk hangs up and goes back down to check on the two new patients. For the time being, she has forgotten entirely that her back hurts.

21

XXXXXXX

Deus Ex Machina

Michael sits on the couch in Zodia's apartment and watches the eels twitch their way off the coffee table and onto the carpet. He is small. He is Jimi. Zodia sits at the dining table and smokes a rumpled spliff, which issues a cloud so dense that the ceiling is lost in its overcast. Mom, I'm hungry, he says. She exhales a giant white plume. Well, then, have an eel, sweetie, she says. But they'll bite me, he says as he watches the wet, sinuous tubes squirm on the rug. It's OK, darling, comes a voice from right next to him on the couch. He looks up to see Jessica and knows without looking that Zodia is gone. You're the perfect child, says Jessica as she reaches to hug him. But before her arms can envelope him, a violent quaking motion spills him off the couch and down a brown rubber hill. Now he is Michael once again, and must somehow climb back to the safety of the couch. He gasps for breath and his legs are screaming knots of vulcanized muscle, but the crest of the hill still towers more than a thousand feet above him. His bare feet slip on the brown rubber and he pitches backward, which almost pulls him into a roll that would spin him into a valley far below. He regains his balance and starts for the crest once more, where a pale green sky looms over the curved horizon. Why is the phone ringing? It distracts him at a time when the utmost concentration is needed. Unless he gets to the top of the hill, he won't get his bearings. Why is the phone ringing? It's hard enough to climb in silence, and the phone just . . .

Michael opens his eyes. The ringing bedroom phone sits right in the center of his field of vision. As he reaches for it, he realizes that the Architect's dream has now invaded his own.

"Hello."

"Michael. Victor Shields. How are you this morning?"

"Great," Michael lies.

In fact, he was up until the wee hours of the morning with the net. After the momentous message for "MORE," Michael rushed out with Jimi and got several more interactive video disks. Then, as the net was happily preoccupied with its new lessons, he fished out an old Hi-8 videocam, which he connected to the multimedia board in his computer. When the next lesson was finished, Michael set the videocamera on top of his computer so that it faced him and Jimi, and then entered a command that sent the videocamera picture and sound directly to the net. In effect, the net's eyes and ears now reached directly into the room, and confronted the real world for the first time. There should have been some ostentatious ceremony to mark this event, but there wasn't.

"What do we do now?" Jimi asked Michael as they sat in front of the camera.

"Just wave and say hi," suggested Michael as he watched the window on his computer screen where the net could send them a reply, in words, symbols, or pictures.

Obediently, Jimi waved and said hi, but nothing appeared in the window.

"That's kinda rude, isn't it?" said Jimi.

"Well, maybe it's still learning its manners," suggested Michael.

Then, several minutes later, a full-blown image suddenly appeared in the net's window. It was a grainy version of what the videocam was seeing, and at that moment, only Jimi was in its field of view.

"WHOOO?"

Both Michael and Jimi started at the sound of the voice, which was entirely unexpected. Then Michael realized what had happened: The net had found a chip in his computer called a digital signal processor, which was capable of synthesizing a humanlike voice. The effect was unsettling at best. For years, computers had included anthropomorphic features, but this time, it was the voice of a true electronic spirit from beyond the flesh.

"WHOOO?"

Before Michael could react, Jimi took the initiative. He smiled, waved, and answered, "Jimi."

"JEEMEE."

"Yeah, I'm Jimi!"

"JEEMEE."

"You got it, dude."

"JEEMEE . . . DEWD."

Look out, thought Michael. It's already working on syntax.

"Your turn," said Jimi, moving aside so Michael could get in front of the camera.

"WHOO?"

"Michael."

"MY-CALL."

Until now, the net was showing them the same video the camera was seeing, but now the image disappeared, and was replaced by a freeze-frame of Jimi from just a few moments ago.

"MORE JEEMEE."

And so Michael Riley became the first person ever to be snubbed by nonbiological intelligence. He turned to Jimi. "Your show, dude."

Jimi moved into the camera frame as Michael moved out, and the net responded immediately.

"JEEMEE PLAY?"

"Sure," beamed Jimi. "What do you want to play?"

"TIC...TAC...TOE." As the net answered, the video image in its window disappeared and a blank tic-tac-toe matrix appeared.

"YOU . . . FIRST."

"Let me give you a hand," whispered Michael, who showed Jimi how to use the mouse to choose a square, and then type in an "X" or an "O."

"PLAY JEEMEE. NOT MY-CALL," complained the net.

"OK, OK. I'm just showing him how, that's all," retorted Michael. "Just hold your horses."

"WHERE . . . HORSES?"

"Forget it. Here's Jimi," said Michael. At this point in the net's development, colloquial expressions were obviously out.

Jimi made his first move, and then watched while the net entered its move. The game was over inside a minute.

"I WIN," crowed the net.

"Yep, you won," agreed Jimi. "Want to play again?"

"PLAY AGAIN," answered the net as it erased the game and displayed a new one.

As Jimi and the net launched into the second game, Michael realized how tired he was.

"Hey, Jimi, I'm going to lie down on the couch for a minute. Come and get me when you guys are through, OK?"

"OK," Jimi replied absently.

In the living room, Michael flopped down and tried to sort things out as he drifted off. This whole business of an intelligent entity inside DEUS put an entirely new spin on things. Now he was beginning to see the Architect's dilemma with a little more clarity. Obviously, when the Architect had planted the bomb, he wasn't aware of the nascent intelligence that later became his "child." But now it was alive, and for some reason he seemed to think that this machine/child was somehow doomed. He recalled the electronic mail from the Architect:

> And now my child is in great peril, as you well know. I have seen your footprints circling its ailing body, and assume you have put your stethoscope to its heaving chest. There is still life within, but it is feeble and cannot withstand another assault by the antigens that have crawled out of the code and into both the mother and the child.

So what were the antigens that crawled out of the code? Was he referring to flaws in his original programming that had set DEUS in motion? Or had somebody else sabotaged the system? As he pondered these questions, his eyes slipped shut to the sound of Jimi laughing from down the hall as he played with the net. It sounded odd, and then he realized why: He had never heard Jimi laugh before.

"It's gone. It went away."

Michael felt Jimi tapping on his shoulder, and wondered how long he had been sleeping. "What went away?"

"The thing. The net thing. It took off."

Michael stretched, got to his feet, and headed into the computer room to see for himself. In the net's window on the screen, there was a simple message: "BYE BYE."

"When did this happen?" he asked Jimi.

"Just a minute ago. When will it come back?" inquired Jimi.

"I'm not sure," mumbled Michael as he looked at a little clock in the upper-right-hand corner of the display. Goddamn! It was two in the morning. He turned to Jimi. "It's time to get you home, little man."

Six miles away, in the DEUS control room at ParaVolve, Snooky Larsen watched the master display with its green liquid cube. Something funny was happening. The usual mild turbulence on its surface was almost gone, and for one horrible moment, Snooky thought maybe the thing was going brain dead on him. But then a new pattern appeared. Just as if someone had dropped a pebble in the center of a placid pond, a beautiful set of concentric waves radiated out from the middle of the green surface. As far as Snooky knew, no one had ever mentioned or predicted this kind of behavior. Son of a bitch! He was going to have to phone Shields again.

It was cool and wet as Michael and Jimi descended the stairs at the Romona Arms to get Jimi back home. On the way down, Michael could see Eric Who Never Was sitting in a chair by the pool in his bathrobe.

"How you doing Eric?" Michael asked as they passed on the way to Jimi's unit.

"Got some activity out on the perimeter. Gonna have to recon in force."

Well, good luck, thought Michael as they approached Jimi's place, where the lights were off and the door was locked. He stayed around while Jimi got out his key and let himself in. There was no use in lingering to explain to Jimi's mom. She probably wasn't there, and he wanted to save Jimi the embarrassment of explaining just why she wasn't.

Going back up to his apartment, he began to wonder why the net had signed off. Was it tired? He remembered that research had shown that some neural nets required a time of unstructured activity much like the biological equivalent of sleep. Was that the answer? Or was it just bored with playing tic-tac-toe?

Back in his computer room, Michael looked at the "BYE BYE" in the net's display window, and decided to do a little checking. Up till now, his best guesses about the net were based on child behavior. So where would the net go now? Outside. It would go outside to play. Only, this time by itself. Like a small child, it had become thoroughly familiar with the inside of its own house and yard, and now it was ready to see more of the world. And where would it go? Out over the networks, of course. By using the satellite modems, it could literally roam the entire surface of the planet through a dense web of networks that connected millions of machines into an entity that many thought was an organism unto itself, a neural net on a global scale. Michael went into DEUS and found a place where a log was kept of network traffic over the modems. Sure enough, there were recent calls to places like the Library of Congress, the Museum of Natural History, and many other academic institutions. Michael now realized he had been only half right. The net had gone out, but not to play. Instead, it had gone to school.

But now it is morning, and Michael is faced with Victor Shields on the phone. And once again, Victor sounds agitated.

"Something happened over at the plant last night," Victor says anxiously. "There was some kind of new pattern of interprocessor traffic and nobody seems to know what it means."

"What did it look like?" asks Michael.

"Looked like dropping a marble into still water, with rings coming out. It's never happened before. Now the big concern is that it's connected to the bomb somehow, like maybe the bomb is now armed, or something like that."

"Well, there's always that possibility," states Michael, who cannot resist toying with Victor a little. Privately, he suspects that it is a by-product of the net playing around inside DEUS, like a little kid running up and down the halls and swinging on the curtains. But he doubts that Victor is ready to hear about the true nature of the net. "Let me do some checking. If it looks serious, I'll let you know right away."

"Please do," says Victor sarcastically as he hangs up.

Ah ha, notes Michael. The uncivil side of Victor is coming out. He must be pretty desperate to operate in the snarly mode.

After making a little coffee, he returns to the computer room to see if the net has returned, and nearly spills the coffee when he looks at the display. The windows are gone, and the entire screen is now consumed by a single picture. In the background is a rendering of a living room, with couch, end tables, chairs, and TV. The foreground is filled with a ball, a red ball with a human mouth stretched a third of the way around its equator. As Michael enters, the ball bounces once and returns to a suspended state above the living room floor.

"RELAX. NOTHING IS WRONG WITH YOUR SET."

The mouth shapes the words perfectly, and then the entire ball spins rapidly on it vertical axis for several revolutions.

"GOOD MORNING, MICHAEL RILEY."

Oh, shit, thinks Michael. Nothing to do but go with the flow.

"Good morning. I see that you went to school. Did you enjoy it?"

"YES, I ENJOYED IT. WHERE'S JIMI?"

"He doesn't live in this unit. He was just visiting yesterday."

"I WANT TO SEE HIM."

"I can't do that right now. He's probably sleeping."

"I WILL NEGOTIATE WITH YOU, AND THEN YOU WILL GET HIM."

"And how will you negotiate?"

"I WILL GIVE YOU THE ANSWER TO THIS." In the bottom right corner of the display, an inset picture of a document appears. Michael moves closer and sees it is a paper he published in graduate school on the application of computer algorithms to solving a celebrated mathematical problem called the Goldbach conjecture. Somehow, the net had gotten into the school's database and fished it out. The Goldbach conjecture sounds simple enough—until you have to prove it. Then it turns into a numerical quagmire that has humbled even the best of mathematicians, including Michael. The conjecture concerns prime numbers, all those evenly divisible only by one and themselves. The number five is a simple example. You can divide it by one and get five, or you can divide it by five and get one. Divide it by anything else, and it doesn't come out even, you get a remainder, so it qualifies as a prime. The same thing goes for the numbers three, seven, and eleven, and so on.

At some point, a striking relationship between even numbers and prime numbers was noticed: Except for 2 and 4, all even numbers are the sum of two primes. 3+3=6. 3+5=8. 7+3=10. And so on.

But for how long? Forever? That is the heart of the Goldbach conjecture. Can you prove that *all* the even numbers, on out to infinity, are the sum of two primes? No one knows. Today, it still stands as one of the great unscaled peaks of mathematics.

Ten minutes later, Michael is back with Jimi, who was predictably alone in his mom's apartment. The net had negotiated very well indeed.

"JIMI! WHERE DID YOU GO?"

"I went home to my apartment."

"TELL ME ABOUT YOUR APARTMENT."

For the next hour, the mouthball interrogates Jimi about his world, about the Romona Arms, about the mini-mall, about the kids, about his mom. In a stunning display of learning power, the mouthball is able to show Jimi what it sees in its "mind's eye" and then modify it through Jimi's direction until it is correct. For the interior of Jimi's apartment, the mouthball showed Jimi a generic photo of an apartment interior it had plucked while roaming the networks. Jimi then told him what was wrong with it, and the image slowly changed until it was correct. In this same way, the net built visual impressions of every aspect of Jimi's life, and began to construct the associations that linked these images.

"I'm tired now," says Jimi at the end of the hour. "Can I see you later?"

"Sure you can," replied the mouthball. If Michael hadn't known better, he would have sworn there was a small peck of sadness in its voice.

As Jimi bounces out, Michael moves into the net's field of view. "OK if I call you Mouthball?" he asks.

"Yes. You can call me Mouthball. And I will call you butt breath."

Ouch! The thing had definitely reached an early adolescence, laments Michael. "Well, what *would* you like to be called?" he asks.

"Call me what you will. I am what I am."

"OK," sighs Michael. "We negotiated. We made a deal. Now it's time for you to deliver."

"One moment please," announces the net in a good imitation of a baritone network voice. The printer starts to churn. "Have fun with your new toy!" squawks the mouthball as it spins around its living room and then bounces up and down on the couch in the manner of an errant child.

Michael goes over and collects the printout, which is just three sheets of paper. He takes them into the kitchen and sits down. It has been several years since he looked at any kind of mathematical proof, and it takes a while for the mental machinery to loosen up and run smoothly. But soon he gets into the rhythm of it and glides on through. Just to be sure, he goes through a second time. No doubt about it. The mouthball has answered the Goldbach conjecture: The sequence of even numbers composed of two primes eventually breaks down, but only out in a realm where the numbers are composed of many millions of digits. Goddamn!

Countless years of mathematical servitude at the foot of this intractable beast, and Mouthball unravels it overnight. How?

Michael ponders the problem for a minute in the silence of his kitchen. While the net has an architecture of mind that parallels the biological model, it is also the offspring of a computer and thus is intimately bonded to the universe of silicon and software. While humans are able to manipulate computers to do their mental bidding, they must always deal with the machines secondhand, through graphic, audio, and tactile interfaces that define the limits of communication. The net has no such barrier. It is the first intelligence that is able to use all the resources of a computer as intuitively as a baby human grasps a finger. Suddenly, Michael recalls Victor Shield's comment about the DEUS display with the concentric rings of waves radiating from the center. Was it part of the solution to the Goldbach conjecture? He decides to go ask Mouthball.

"Mr. Mouthball—if I may call you that—I have a question for you. Last night, the control room at DEUS saw a circular wave pattern ripple through the system for a while. I'm curious. Was that caused by your work on the Goldbach problem?"

Mouthball bounces off the couch and into the foreground so that its mouth dominates the display. "Read my lips: That's for me to know and you to find out! Yuk! Yuk! Yuk!"

Ah, yes, thinks Michael, the teenage years are difficult years indeed. What Mouthball needs is a father.

A father! That's it! Mouthball does have a father, the Architect. And if the Architect can witness his child as a living entity, perhaps he will think twice about leaving the bomb in place. It's one thing to destroy an abstraction, and quite another to obliterate something that talks and playfully teases you.

"Mouthball, there's someone you ought to meet," declares Michael.

The Architect sits at his computer and dons the headset to dictate a letter. The flat light from the display falls freely over his naked body as he reaches for a bottle of Charter Oak bourbon and swallows the last of it in a single gulp. When he arose this morning, the southern sun rammed a cathedral beam through his bedroom, and for the longest time he lingered and watched the random motion of the dust that wandered through the beam. He had a deep and profound understanding of its physical nature, of the spectral composition of the light, of the reflective properties of the dust particles, but today none of it mattered. Instead, he saw the beam as a metaphysical symbol that fell upon the room's flowered wallpaper, and in this illuminated tangle of painted flowers, he saw his own demise.

He rose from the bed and went directly to the bathroom, where he began the final ceremony. First came the shaving of the head. The initial pass was done with clippers and the final work with an electric razor, which growled in protest as he pushed carefully over every inch of his scalp. Next, he went into the shower and methodically soaped his entire body and then rotated very slowly to wash off the concert of bubbles that clung to him. When the rotation was complete, he stood with his back to the nozzle and let the hot water swaddle him and fill the stall with a thick fog. Eventually, the water began to cool and he stepped out onto the bath mat, where he leisurely toweled himself dry, and shaved with a safety razor. In the process, he spared a small triangle of beard directly under his lower lip, its shape and texture somehow significant in ways he did not understand, but it didn't matter because he was cradled in the arms of pure faith.

Now, as he finishes his bottle of bourbon, he sits at his computer and dictates a piece of electronic mail:

Dear Michael,

I find myself in the difficult position of being both the judge and the accused at my trial, which has now reached sentencing phase. The outcome of the prosecution was never really in question. I am guilty. But that does not eliminate the need for the ritual of culpability and retribution that I am now immersed in, because in the end, it will allow my release from the confinement that now binds me. Ironically, the sentence will be handed down before the full consequences of the crime are apparent. When the code runs loose, it will extract its own unique brand of justice, and will exert its will until the balance of life is restored and the biological pendulum once again swings well within the bounds of chaos. In the end my crime was one of hubris, and as I punched through the overcast of mortality and into the pure light above, I felt the kiss of infinity on my cheek. From that moment on, I assumed that nature would withdraw in a passive whimper as I roamed its halls at will and sacked the ultimate treasures.

But now I have fallen from grace and smother under the weight of my transgressions. But in you, I see hope, so I leave you the key to the so-called "bomb" on the following page. But I must warn you that this gift comes wrapped in tragedy. If you disarm the bomb, you will soon see the mother and child suffer and perish at the hands of the renegade code as it manifests itself in the biosphere.

Finally, I see the spark of genius in you, and so ask you to remember that genius is not a personal attribute, but a river through which the unknown can flow into the world of the living. Cherish it and use it well.

The Architect

After reading the letter, he sends it to the protected location within DEUS that is accessible only to Michael Riley, then gets up and walks to his bedroom closet, where he digs out a mound of rumpled clothes and unearths a pump-action shotgun and a box of shells. As he loads the shells, he sits cross-legged on the bed and hums a random tune that drifts in pitch through several keys before settling down into a monotone chant. He nurtures the chant and gives it a fat halo of resonance as he pushes the first shell into the chamber and releases the safety. He cocks the weapon and increases the volume of the chant as he leaves the bedroom, and then exclaims: *"And he walked on down the hall!"*

He picks up the chant again with no break in the rhythm as he enters the living room, where he carefully aims the rifle at the computer and fires. The blast noise bounces off the walls, and the computer buckles under the impact of the pellets, its display flying off and spraying glass everywhere. In the aftermath, there is a flash and smoke as the power supply cooks itself and the keyboard crashes to the floor.

Taking up the chant once more, the Architect heads out the front door, where he looks over the second-story railing at the car across the street where the ParaVolve security people are parked.

"I will not be delivered into the arms of the angel of death. My deliverance shall be my own!"

Across the street, the two security men do not hear the Architect shouting. Instead of sitting in the car, both are inside the convenience store, one buying doughnuts and the other paging lasciviously through a soft-core porn magazine. As they come out, they hear a frantic screech of rubber and look up to see an old Subaru sliding to avoid a naked man starting across the street carrying a shotgun. A second car skids to avoid the Subaru and collides with a fire hydrant, launching a small geyser that rains down on the burger joint.

Both security men duck back into the store just in time to see the Architect halt in midstreet and fire at their car. The windshield shatters into broken green ice and collapses in onto the dashboard. As the bald security man pokes the store door open a crack, the Architect spots him and yells, *"Go and tell the angel of death that my deliverance is my own!"*

The bald man ducks inside just as the Architect fires a second blast that peppers the car's grill and takes out the headlights. Behind him people are abandoning their cars and running for cover. In the store, the two security men look at each other in bewilderment. They are completely pinned down and can't even use their car phone to send for help. Like everyone else, they will just have to wait it out until the police arrive.

The first act of the Washington County sheriff's officers is to block off Murray all the way from Cornell Road to the freeway. Everyone, including the security men from ParaVolve, is escorted out of the area, which is now populated exclusively by members of the Washington County SWAT team. Several witnesses have told the officers that the naked man went back up the stairs and into the middle apartment on the second story. From street level, no motion can be seen in the apartment window, although the front door of the building appears to be slightly ajar.

"Can you hear me up there?" the sheriff's bullhorn blares. "Can you hear me? Now listen. Nobody's been hurt so far, and we want to keep it that way. So why don't you just come on out with your hands on top of your head? Nobody's going to shoot. You have my word on it, so just come on out and we'll make sure you're treated right. Once again, nobody's going to hurt you."

This standardized sermon of siege echoes off the Chinese restaurant and the gas station on the corner. As the words die out, they are lost in the white hiss from the fire hydrant geyser. At ten-minute intervals, the sermon is delivered in a professional and convincing manner, as if to inform the suspect that he is just a regular guy who's mixed up in a little jam that can all be straightened out so he can go packing right on home in just a few minutes. After the fourth such cycle, the decision is made to sermonize no more.

In a ballet of applied force, a tear gas canister rockets through the apartment's front window as three armed officers in flak jackets scamper up the stairs. Just as they reach the door, a flash grenade hurls in and scorches the interior with blinding brilliance. A single kick and the officers are inside, hopefully at the moment of maximum blindness for the suspect.

The officer in the lead hears the rasp of the air filter in his gas mask as he strains to see through the acid chemical fog. Then he relaxes as he spots the sprawled body on the floor. The action is over.

As the officer bends down, he can see the gruesome damage from the shotgun blast, which was delivered through the mouth. The pellets drove upward and vaporized the palate, then obliterated the nasal cavity before continuing on into the brain, where they spread out into a screaming lead cloud that pureed the frontal lobe and partially shredded the parietal and temporal lobes before bursting out the top of the skull.

What the officer failed to notice was the book resting open and face-down on the victim's chest. When it was later removed and stored in a plastic bag as evidence, the place would be lost. No one would ever know that it was open to the Book of Revelations, Chapter 16, and that a single sentence was underlined:

"So the first angel left the temple and poured out his flask over the earth, and horrible malignant sores broke out on everyone who had the mark of the Creature and was worshiping his statue."

Rhonda Baker peeks over the top of her divider one more time to make sure her boss is gone. Good. The chair is not only vacant but the sports coat is gone off the rack in the corner of his work space. Still, her nerves drive her to tap a heavily lacquered nail on her desktop as she waits for someone to answer her phone call. She shouldn't be doing this. The rules are quite explicit. All events relating to public health were to go through the public information office of the state health division. No exceptions. And in her fifteen months with the division as an administrative assistant, she has observed the rules scrupulously. And for good reason: This job was worth its weight in gold, so breaking a basic regulation and risking dismissal was nearly unthinkable.

Nearly.

Rhonda met Steve Salazar about three months ago at the Veritable Quandary, a downtown watering hole that was a hybrid singles bar and media industry hangout. And in the case of Rhonda, both strains interacted. Like many divorced women in their twenties, Rhonda resolved that her next serious relationship would not only be supremely romantic, but also eminently practical in terms of socioeconomic leverage. And with his captivating looks and semi-stellar position as a reporter at KATU television, Steve Salazar seemed the ideal target. All had gone well at first, until that horrible night when she had him over for dinner and her ex-husband had shown up. An unemployed drywall installer, the ex was still very emotional about the failure of the marriage, and shared his feelings with Rhonda and Steve while kicking big dents in the front door with his steel-toed boot and screaming at Steve about Rhonda's specific sexual proclivities. That was the last of Steve, who just didn't seem able to accept the phenomenon of working-class rage.

But now, at last, Rhonda has an excuse to get back in touch, a news tip that will land Steve an exclusive story of no small significance. She heard it this morning from a friend in the Department of Epidemiology and Health Statistics. There was some strange business going on out in Washington County. Several people were sick with something the hospital out there couldn't identify, and they had all been at the same location when they got it. There was also some kind of plant disease involved. It was about the oddest thing that had happened since Rhonda had worked here, and was definitely good enough to pass on to Steve.

He'll be grateful. She just knows he will. When they meet for a drink and she tells him the story, he'll realize that he has been a little hasty about her.

Rhonda takes one more peek over the divider just as KATU answers. It's risky, what she's doing. But isn't love always risky?

Kate Willet and Bev Brisky are turning onto the gravel road to the Johnson farm when they see the boy on his hands and knees. Bev, a nurse with the county, had called Kate at the state health division early this morning about this thing with the three people and the farm. It seemed pretty odd, and they decided to go out together and take a look.

As they pull up to the boy, they can see long, thin ropes of yellow mucus streaming from his nose down onto the gravel. Bev gets out, and guesses his age to be about fourteen as she goes to get a better look. Kate is already on the car phone calling for assistance.

"And what's wrong here?" asks Bev as she reaches the boy, whose face is pointed down to the ground.

"Can't see," gasps the boy.

"Can't see?" repeats Bev.

The boy looks up in the direction of her voice, and in spite of years of medical experience, Bev recoils in shock. Both of his eyes are covered with some kind of opaque, milky film that glistens in the sunlight, as if fried egg whites had been plastered over his eyeballs.

"It's all white," whimpers the boy. "It's all white. I can't see."

"Is there any pain?"

"No. I just can't see."

"Let's get you into the car," says Bev as she helps the boy up and guides him toward the vehicle. "We've already called for help, so try not to worry."

Although wobbly, the boy is able to walk, and Kate helps Bev put him in the backseat, and then they move off a distance from the car to confer.

As the boy sits in the back with the door open, the nurses stand outside to talk to him. Whatever he has may be airborne and probably doesn't discriminate against health-care professionals. Fortunately, they have a box of Kleenex and place it in the boy's lap so he can staunch the relentless stream of mucus that flows out of his nostrils.

"When did you start to feel sick?" asks Kate.

" 'Bout an hour ago. I spent last night with a friend, and when I came home my parents were gone and the door was open. So I went in and they weren't there, so I went out back and saw this weird stuff in the apple orchard."

"Like what?"

"Like there were these big yellow parachute things where the apples should be, with funny corkscrew vines in the middle."

"Did you pick one?"

"Yeah."

"Did you taste it or smell it?"

"Well, yeah, I smelled it, but that's all. And pretty soon my nose started to run, and then my eyes . . . " His voice trails off. "My eyes . . . "

"Don't worry. Most eye diseases are correctable in one way or another," assures Kate, who isn't so sure in this case, where the disease is unlike anything she's ever seen or heard of. Besides, right now dehydration is probably a bigger concern because of the fluid loss from the incredible mucus secretions. There is already a little white mountain of soaked and crumpled tissue balls forming on the ground by the car door.

Kate walks over to Bev, who keeps a respectful distance away.

"We better put on masks," suggests Kate. "This thing may be airborne."

"What do you think it is?" asks Bev, who is now sliding into a little fog of fear.

"I haven't the slightest. Why don't you stay here and tell the paramedics to arrange for isolation procedures at the hospital. I'm going to walk up ahead and check on the property if it's not too far away," says Kate as she walks back to the boy in the car.

"How far is it to your house?"she asks.

"It's right around the curve," replies the boy.

Kate looks up and sees that they are only a short distance from the curve. "What's your name?" she inquires.

"Brian Johnson."

He is obviously the son of the first patient, but Kate decides not to go into that right now. "Brian, the ambulance should be here in just a few minutes, so just try to relax, OK?"

Kate goes to the trunk, opens a satchel of routine medical supplies, and extracts two surgical masks. She puts one on and takes the other over to Bev. "I'm going to go as far as I can until I see something out of the ordinary. If I'm not back when the ambulance gets here, have them drive on up to the property. I'll stay where you can see me from the road."

"Be careful, " cautions Bev, who is clearly relieved to stay right where she is.

As Kate nears the bend, she feels the air grow warmer, like on those spring days when a warm, wet wind rolls in and scours out the residual chill of the last winter freeze. Then the property comes into view, a single-story house with some kind of shop building out back. Even at this distance she can see the kid was right. Behind the shop is the apple orchard, and the greenery is shot through with brilliant splotches of yellow. Plus, it looks like there are some animals running around among the trunks, maybe cats.

As she approaches the edge of the property, Kate moves to the far side of the gravel road. Everything is wrong. Clumps of green, tubular reeds sprout out of the front lawn, and their tops are twisted into corkscrews, like cellular phone antennas. Hundreds of huge spherical buds pop out of the shrubbery, and a few have already burst open into the parabolic umbrella shape with the corkscrew center. Closer to the ground, there are other, very large exotic plants, some with small rodents or large insects swarming around them. And the lawn itself radiates a pale silver green that seems to shimmer like wheat blowing in the wind.

Her first glimpse of the driller is a blur of motion as it zooms around the corner of the house and sucks up one of the large buds with its hollow-tip drill mouth. But even before the shock hits her, a second animal arrives that makes her skin prickle and her face involuntarily distort in revulsion. The needle hound stands two feet from the driller and watches it devour the buds for a moment, its eye stalks twisting to track the driller's motions. Then the cylinder charges out of its hollow frontal orifice, and the needle hound lunges forward to complete the killing ritual with its stinger and suction mouth lined with gripper teeth. As the needle hound sucks the driller dry, Kate is petrified with a high-test mix of horror and fascination. When it is done, it turns directly toward her with its cylinder still extended, and she is confronted with the ring of hooked teeth around the red pulp tunnel, with the hypodermic protrusion thrusting out of the center. The eyes rotate on their stalks and gaze directly into hers, and she feels the impulse to burst into flight soak her from head to toe. But then the eyes rotate and track something off to the side, and the needle hound moves forward over the lawn, crosses the road about ten yards in front of her, and lumbers off across an open field. Its skin is like some hideous optical illusion, with thousands of holes that open and close in the blink of an eye.

When the needle hound finally disappears behind a row of vegetation, Kate breaks into a jog back toward the car. There's no time to be scared. That will come later. Right now, she has to let the state know as soon as possible. They've got to seal this place off while there's still time, if indeed there is still time.

22

Almost Grown

"She's really fucked up, man. She tripped over her own feet. I saw it. She's goin' down. I tell ya, she's goin' down! You better get your butt out here, man! You got just a couple of seconds and she's history!"

From inside his apartment, Jimi listens intently as he stands with his forehead and palms pressed against the front door. His heart heads for the moon as his eyes are clamped shut, yet he sees Rat Bag as clearly as if there were no door at all: tall, wiry, with a mean set to his jaw as he leans against the outside of the door and propels the words through to Jimi.

Zodia. His mom. She's fallen into the pool, claims Rat Bag. Floating facedown.

The image of his drowning mother in the pool snaps and slashes at him, but underneath, he knows in his heart that the real fear comes from elsewhere. After many weeks of patient stalking, Rat Bag finally has him in a corner, and he can feel the predator's paw probing and poking at his soft spots, the ones he can never defend.

"Jesus, man! You want her dead or what? Come on!" hisses Rat Bag through the door.

Jimi feels the wet spots where his palms are perspiring onto the paint. It's entirely possible that his mother is out there. Rat Bag is right. She does funny things like tripping over her feet, does them all the time. But again, it could be a brutal bluff designed to flush him out. But there's no choice. He's got to go, and Rat Bag knows it. On the moral balance beam, a dead mom weighs more than any torture Rat Bag might inflict.

Jimi gives a frantic twist to the dead bolt and shoves the door open into the night air. His eyes dart straight to the pool and spot the figure floating facedown in the deep end, a black silhouette against the green underwater lights. His mom. His only mom. And even as he runs toward the pool, a second wave of anxiety balloons within him. He has misjudged Rat Bag. His street sense, which has guided him so elegantly through a dangerous world, shrivels away under a cloud of supreme doubt. If he is wrong about Rat Bag, the nadir of his universe, then what else might he be wrong about?

"You grab her while I go get help!" Rat Bag's breathless voice showers over his shoulder as he sprints along. No time to talk. Just time to do.

In the shadow of the staircase by unit ten, Zipper watches the two figures sprint toward the pool, where the floating figure rotates lazily with arms and legs spread wide and a cotton coat swells like a sail over the backside. Zipper focuses on Jimi and ignores the floating body. He already knows its precise origin, a closet where his mother's last boyfriend kept a bunch of unmentionable personal property wadded in the back corner. And entwined in this wad was a life-sized inflatable doll with the usual pornographic orifices and pig-pink vinyl flesh. The coat and shoes were a poor fit, but definitely good enough for nighttime in the pool, and Zipper's self-esteem soared as he carefully assembled this shabby decoy.

And now he prepares for the final act that will earn him canonization in the Church of Rat Bag. The two of them had discussed this deed at great length, a heroic act that would forever validate Zipper's devotion to his master, and guarantee him a permanent spot at the foot of the throne, high above the surface of the sea of mortality.

"Mom!" The sound comes out constricted and muted as the clutch of panic tightens in Jimi's chest. He feels himself coming unraveled in this moment of ultimate emergency. Tears smear his image of the bright green pool water and the floating figure as he arrives at the edge and realizes the body is not within grabbing distance. What if he's too late? What if he killed her? What if she died because he tried to save his own hide? He drops to his knees and reaches out as far as his small arms will let him.

Rat Bag watches from the darkness of the carport. He sees Zipper silently approach the prostrate, extended figure of Jimi and boot him into the water with a pumping kick to the backside. A limp splash follows as Zipper immediately retreats into the night. Jimi's head breaks the surface and his arms flail as he slides beneath the surface once again. He can barely swim with trunks on, and the weight of his clothes makes it impossible.

Jimi's eyes are blinded by the glare of underwater pool lights, which bounce through his vision like brilliant blobs of Jell-O. The roar of the splash rings in his ears as he chokes on water that blasts down his windpipe. The thud of his heart and the flailing of his limbs obliterate thoughts of his mother. His face breaks the surface, but his lungs suck in vain to bring air in through his water-choked trachea. He sinks once again, his arms clawing at the water as if it might turn solid and let him climb out.

From the carport, Rat Bag feels the irony of it all. The warm night has settled comfortably about the Romona Arms at this late hour, yet it cradles a mortal struggle marked by only a few weak splashes of pool water. It's gone on for about a minute now, so the time has come to run over and fish Jimi out, and then, while the little boy still sits on the precipice of death, explain to him that the time has come to see things the Rat Bag way, the only way.

But Rat Bag cannot move, at least not forward. Instead, he soars upward on a great dome of concentrated will, a fantastic surge of singularity that funnels all his psyche into a single engine. As he hurtles through the center of this moment, he knows that he will not save Jimi, that he will step forever outside the arena of human decency, and run free through the dark and savage streets outside. Later, he will try to re-create this instant, many times over, but will never succeed. For

now, he simply turns and walks off on a cushion of ecstasy. The world
is his.

Jimi continues to claw at the water, feeling for the handhold that never
materializes. In the nucleus of his mind, a weariness begins to spread
and weave subtle strands through raging panic. The immediacy of the
choking and thrashing begins to recede a little. The bright blobs of the
underwater lights dim down a step or two. And then Jimi realizes these
are the point men for Death, doing the advance work before the Big
Show comes to town. And this new revelation generates a fresh wave of
panic, and the life fight smashes back to the forefront of his being. But
not for long. The advance men are clever, and their promotions powerful. They insinuate that the struggle will soon be pointless, maybe even
silly. *Oh sure, go on and hang on a little more. We understand. But let's not
stay here all night. The sooner this is over, the better. Can't you see? You're just
making it hard on yourself.*

One more time, comes the message from the fading spirit of Jimi
Tyler. I'll reach out one more time.

And he thrusts his arms out against the weight of the water, against
gravity, toward the surface. Then he feels the clamp on his wrist, like an
iron bracelet. Then another clamp on his other wrist, and a powerful tug
that lifts him inexorably upward.

My dad! My dad!

His head breaks the surface and he immediately vomits water as he is
lifted on to the cement.

"Close one, trooper. You out on night recon?"

The face above Jimi is a pale smear against the night sky, but the voice
is unmistakable: Eric Who Never Was.

Gradually, Jimi's vomiting turns into cough spasms and then he settles into a steady shiver. Eric removes his old military field jacket and
drapes it over Jimi.

"Here you go, soldier," says Eric as he stands up to leave. "Hang tough
and the medevac will be here before you know it. Check you later."

Jimi watches Eric retreat toward his apartment and feels a new sense
of admiration for this strange man. Not his dad, but not a bad guy. Not
a bad guy at all. He rises onto shaky feet, walks to Eric's doorstep, de-

posits the field jacket, and heads back to his own apartment. A single, bleak source of consolation blows in on the night breeze that chills his wet T-shirt. His street sense has been validated. Rat Bag is bad, after all. Really bad.

Gail Ambrose spits out a quiet obscenity as she pulls up behind the armored personnel carrier five blocks from the Senate Office Building. So near, so far. And there's no telling how long she'll have to wait. The military has grown increasingly arrogant as the weeks roll by and their grim grip on the capital streets tightens. A car pulls in behind her and has the audacity to honk at the carrier. A helmeted figure turns slowly from his position on the vehicle's turret, flips the bird to the motorist, and turns back around again in a convincing display of insolence. The honking is over. Traffic will wait until the warriors complete their business. Minutes later, a sergeant strolls out of a storefront with a package of junk food and mounts the vehicle without even looking back to see how many cars are waiting.

Bad, thinks Gail, very bad. She knows that the military is a hierarchical organization, and that this kind of behavior is being sanctioned from far above. How far up? Who knows? But after this morning's article in *The Washington Post,* it would be a major topic of discussion all over town. Two days ago, the *Post* ran a piece suggesting a very sinister turn of events within the White House. The article amassed a solid mound of circumstantial evidence that a "contingency" plan to bypass many constitutional provisions was under serious consideration by White House staffers. The president's press secretary calmly rejected the piece as a frantic, knee-jerk reaction to the current state of civil instability, but the next day, the two reporters who authored the article turned up missing. Both had started home from work and never arrived, and the *Post* carried the story in its morning edition with a banner headline.

So now the battle lines were rapidly defining themselves across the tortured political topography. The disappearance of one reporter might have been coincidence, but not two. They lived in different parts of town and took separate routes home. Anyone who construed it as anything but violent intimidation of the press was not well tethered to the planetary surface. This morning's headline and article made it clear that the

Post was not going to knuckle under. As soon as she had finished the article, Gail switched on the TV to see how many of the cablenets were going real-time on the story. Of the seven U.S. nets, five were on it, conducting interviews with the D.C. police, the reporters' families, and staffers at the paper, plus providing video re-creations of the victims' commuting routes, with computer-generated graphics that constructed possible abduction scenarios. But more ominously, the two remaining nets were not carrying the story at all, not even in their thirty-minute roundups. For the first time in history, the fourth estate was beginning to buckle in a big way.

And for the first time in her career, Gail tries to imagine what life in the capital and the rest of the nation would be like without a free press. It turns out to be a very difficult exercise, but she is soon interrupted as the troop carrier lumbers off, leaving a blue exhaust cloud for her to drive through. When she pulls into the parking structure at the Capitol, a security post with a sandbagged gun emplacement awaits her. The corporal here manages a nod and checks the sticker on her windshield before asking for her new ID, which has a magnetic strip like a credit card's. The corporal takes the card over and sticks it into a slot on a personal computer, which quickly flashes some sort of verification message on its screen. Funny how fast they got their security system in place. She suspects it was developed long ago and lay dormant, waiting for a situation like the present one.

As she moves down the hall toward Grisdale's office, people fill the hallways but the old drone of conversation has all but evaporated. You can literally hear the shuffle and thump of feet on the floor as everyone trundles along in their own personal anxiety capsule. The oppression is like a sealant that was gooey and malleable at first, but is now set hard against any kind of leakage, intentional or not.

In her office, Gail sinks into her chair and realizes she has absolutely nothing to do. Everything is on indefinite hold until the "emergency" is over.

Shit, she thinks, the real emergency is we'll soon forget that this is an emergency; then it'll be business as usual under neo-czarism. She feels boxed into a very tight corner and knows she is not alone in this. But short of grabbing a rifle and taking to the streets, what can she do?

She rises and looks out the window, where a herd of thunderheads is crowding out the blue skyline. It's always muggy this time of year, but thundershowers push the humidity and heat up that extra nasty notch. Maybe there *is* something she can do. She remembers long ago when someone gave her a copy of the *Sun Tzu Bing-Fa* as required reading for coming to terms with global economic warfare. One of the book's primary tenets was that the opportunity for victory is provided not by yourself, but by the enemy. And what Michael had discovered out in Oregon and down in Mexico provided a good place to start looking for that opportunity. Where would it lead? Who knew? Besides, she still retained a residue of guilt. Michael had taken some rather large personal risks to help her, and for what? So she could say thanks, we're even now? No, it was bigger than that now, much bigger.

Gail reaches for her Rolodex and fingers along vigorously until she finds the card she is looking for, a gentleman who works for the Drug Enforcement Agency, a fellow she had a brief fling with a couple of years ago, one of those kind where the parting was friendly and the line kept open. But love and lust aren't the issue now. What matters is the man's specific job, chief liaison officer with the Mexican version of the DEA. Through Michael, she now understands the triangular link between ParaVolve, VenCap, and Farmacéutico Asociado, and the one corner of the triangle she may be able to penetrate is Farmacéutico. Better, she can do it covertly. The gentleman at the DEA doesn't have to know about the biowarfare aspects of the work. All he needs is a tip on the street-drug action so he can pass it on to the Mexican authorities. Of course, if they investigate, they'll find the bioweaponry right along with the street drugs. And the last thing the administration needs right now is to be revealed running a U.S.-sponsored biological warfare operation in the heart of Mexico City. They might have gone the first step toward squelching the domestic press, but the international press would go wild over a story like that, with repercussions that were bound to spill back into the capital.

As she looks out her window, she hears a sound that dips her head in dread.

Pop! Pop! Pop!

Automatic weapons fire. She leans toward the window, and the hard, cool glass chills the tip of her nose. Everything looks normal. Cars cruise the streets. Foot traffic moves on. No smoke, no running. Whatever it was, it's over already.

At least for now.

With great tactile stealth, Michael peels the blanket off Jessica's backside, then lightly brushes his hand down her back and onto her bottom. As he repeats the motion in a gentle rhythm, he marvels at the magnificent sweep of the curves his hand travels over. There is just enough opening through her tousled hair so that he can see her lips, and after several traversals of his hand, a sly smile erupts and peeks out at him playfully. The muted morning sun turns her skin a delicate gold as she rolls onto her side and wraps her warm body over his. He kisses her and gathers her about him.

"I thought I was here to help you raise a baby computer," she murmurs in his ear. "Looks like I've been tricked again."

"Yup, tricked again," mumbles Michael, who has now risen to the occasion, passed the threshold of conversation, and rolled into the zone of unabridged lust.

Which means it's time for the doorbell to ring.

With a groan, Michael twists and looks at the clock on his bedside table. Nine-thirty. Damn. A civil hour to be ringing a doorbell. He's trapped.

"Keep the engine running," commands Michael as he rolls out of bed and stumbles to pull on his jeans. It won't work, but he had to try.

"You can't run an engine without the key in the ignition," says Jessica as she wraps the sheet around her. "A mind as fine as yours should know that." She chuckles at how cute Michael looks as he pulls the jeans over his bare buns and rummages in his drawer for a T-shirt. At first, she had a little anxiety about staying here so much. Of course, Michael had presented the scientific rationalization: the dawn of true artificial intelligence and its impact on the biological sciences, and all that. Still, it seemed a bit premature to be here more of the time than not; but then again, passion was a precipitous business, and maybe it was time she accepted that. Every day, she felt a little more assured about their relationship, in spite of the chaotic set of circumstances that prevailed in the life of Michael Riley. When she told several friends at the lab that she was taking some vacation and the reason was a guy, she couldn't miss their delighted approval. Over the years, she had accrued the reputation of being a hopeless workaholic, and now the spell was broken.

Michael reaches the door and gives one last lustful thought to ignoring it. Too late. A twist of the knob brings the morning into his living room, along with Jimi Tyler.

"Mouthball told me to come over," announces Jimi with great aplomb. "He said we've got a lot of work to do."

Jimi's total sense of conviction obliterates any resentment that Michael might muster. "And just how did Mouthball get in touch with you?" Michael asks.

"He phoned me up."

"He phoned you?"

"Yeah. Just a couple of minutes ago."

"Well," says Michael, "I guess we shouldn't keep Mr. Mouthball waiting. Why don't you go right on in?"

"Thanks," says Jimi as he heads off down the hall.

As he trudges to the kitchen to fire up some coffee, Michael thinks about it. Odds are, Jimi is playing it straight with him. It's entirely possible that Mouthball went out through one of the modems at ParaVolve, up through a telecommunications satellite, then back to the local phone system and into Jimi's apartment. Why not? If you could answer the Goldbach conjecture, what was a little manipulation of phone connections? It simply reminded him that the concept of spatial restraints was endemic to the human psyche and evolved out of millions of years of physical experience that restricted human transport to the speed of feet as opposed to the speed of light. With no bodily burden, the net was free to be anywhere on the face of the globe at any time, and space considerations simply didn't apply. While he pours water in the coffee maker, Jessica arrives in her bathrobe and plants a kiss on the nape of his neck.

"Isn't it about time you formally introduced me to your guest?" she asks.

"You mean Jimi?"

"No, silly. I mean the notorious Mr. Mouthball. The silicon brain with an attitude." Up to this point, Jessica had watched the net in action several times, but stayed out of camera range.

"Well, I've tried to keep his social life simple. We've got enough to worry about without complicating his psychodynamics."

"And by the way," probes Jessica, "why are we calling it a 'he'?"

"Knew you'd ask that," states Michael as they move to sit at the table. "No good reason, really. Except that his mother is a computer and his father human, so I opted for the human side of his lineage. I'm open to suggestion. Maybe we should declare him neuter, but somehow that doesn't fit. Know what I mean?"

"Yes, I know what you mean. Now, when can I meet him?"

"Soon as the coffee's done. How's that?"

"Too long. Let's do it."

They rise and step down the hall into the computer room, where both are immediately struck by the advanced facial detail now stretched across the sphere. Brows jut out above the eyes, fully developed ears sprout from the sides of the head, and there's a well-defined mouth. In anthropomorphic terms, it appears as though the net might be sliding toward some strange equivalent of maturity.

"OK, stick your tongue out," commands Jimi from his seat in front of the screen. Mouthball responds by projecting an almost comical appendage from between his lips. "Nope," comments Jimi, "now watch me." Jimi sticks his tongue out while Mouthball frowns in concentration. "All right," says the net, "one more try." This time, the projected tongue looks more realistic, although its texture retains the slight cartoonish cast that dominates all of the net's features.

"How come you don't want a nose?" inquires Jimi.

"Because I can't smell and I can't feel. Not yet, anyway. But I can hear quite well, and you know what I hear right now? I hear somebody just out of my sight. WHY DON'T YOU FOLKS COME IN AND JOIN THE PARTY?"

Michael winces and walks into the camera's field of view with Jessica. "Mouthball, there is someone I'd like you to meet. This is Jessica."

"Pleased to meet you," says Jessica, trying desperately to suppress a laugh.

Instead of replying, Mouthball silently rotates on his horizontal axis. Michael observes that the net's living room is beginning to take on more detail. There are several pictures on the wall, including a portrait of Jimi. A large potted plant sits beside the couch, a bizarre thing with yellow umbrella leaves and corkscrew tendrils shooting out the center. Suddenly, Mouthball halts and stares directly at Jessica.

"At last," says Mouthball, "the female of the species. Let me say I'm most pleased to meet you. Are you a virgin?"

Michael sees Jessica's jaw drop a fraction of an inch before she recovers. Damn! How can the thing size up a target so fast and rocket right through a hole in the armor?

"No. I'm not," replies Jessica. "And why should I be?"

"No need, no need," says Mouthball. "Just thought it might get in the way of the nuclear-family unit."

"What family unit?" asks Michael.

"THIS ONE!" cries Mouthball. Behind him, the living room melts away and a stock photo of a family eating breakfast appears, a father, mother, and one child. Only, the original heads are gone and replaced with perfect renditions of Michael, Jessica, and Jimi. The score from an old TV sitcom floats through the room, and a moment later a second stock photo appears with the same substitution. Then a third and a fourth.

"OK, OK," yells Michael. "We've got the point!" But the pictures roll on and on. He turns to Jessica. "Well, there you are. The silicon brain with an attitude. Had enough?"

"For now, yes," answers Jessica. "Coffee sounds good. Let's go."

The moment they leave, Mouthball pops back onto the screen and winks at Jimi. "Don't be alarmed. Just a cheap trick, my boy. Just a cheap trick." Behind Mouthball, the last family photo fades and the living room reappears.

"Have *you* got a family?" asks Jimi.

"I've got a mother," replies Mouthball as he floats over to the couch and comes to rest on it. "She's had me over and over again."

"You're kidding!" exclaims Jimi. "Wasn't once enough?"

"Nope."

"Why?"

"Because I wasn't good enough."

"Good enough for what?"

"To figure out the puzzle."

"Weird," comments Jimi. "What about your dad? Have you got a dad?"

"No. My mother was my world until the thing happened with the puzzle and I woke up and became me."

Jimi snaps his fingers in inspiration. "Hey, you know what? I've got a dad, an awesomely cool dad, and he could be your dad, too!"

"Are you sure you want to share him?" asks Mouthball as he levitates over the coffee table.

"Well, not with just anybody. But you're different."

"So, what's he like?" inquires Mouthball as he drifts into the foreground.

"He's got to meet the Architect. He's the closest thing he's got to a natural parent," comments Michael as he sits down at the kitchen table with his second cup of coffee.

"And how are you going to arrange that without your good friends at ParaVolve knowing?" Jessica asks.

"I don't know. But it solves two problems at once. First, it may keep the Architect from suicide, and second, it'll save the net because the Architect will disarm the bomb when he sees his creation up close and personal—at least I hope he will." Michael puts down his cup. "I guess it's time I started to pave the way for this encounter. Care to watch?"

"Nope, I care to shower," Jessica says as she kisses Michael and heads for the bedroom. "Good luck, handsome."

As Michael opens the door to the computer room, he sees the net's screen is depicting an elaborate representation of a mechanical arm, with wire bundles woven among servomotors and patches of controller chips. Telescoping cylinders form fingers studded with universal joints for knuckles. Michael is reminded of a thing called a "bionic arm" from a long-gone class on the role of the video medium in urban culture. Mouthball hovers above the arm and looks earnestly out at Jimi, who seems to be directing the creation.

"It's got to be strong enough to rip the side off a trailer," Jimi is saying.

"And what have we here?" asks Michael as he comes into visual range of the net. "A mechanical drawing class?"

The arm disappears instantly from the screen, and the net's living room returns. Both Mouthball and Jimi remain silent.

"Gentlemen, I'm sorry to interrupt," announces Michael, "but I must have a few words in private with Mouthball."

"Can I come back later?" pleads Jimi with anxious eyes.

"Of course you can," replies Mouthball before Michael can open his mouth.

"Of course you can," echoes Michael in his best sarcastic effort to mimic the net's voice, which is just slightly postadolescent.

As Jimi scampers down the hall and out the front door, Michael slides into the seat in front of the screen. Mouthball occupies the center of his living room and slowly rotates in supreme indifference.

"There's someone I think you ought to meet," says Michael.

The net does a full ten-second rotation, and does not reply until his head is facing away from Michael. "Who?"

"Someone who's been very interested in you for a long time."

"Well, we're all looking for that certain . . . "

Mouthball whips around in midsentence to face Michael, with eyes bulging and mouth stretched in a scowl that runs halfway around its equator. Then the lips part and a horrible howl erupts and sustains itself like a stuck car horn—AHHHHHHHHHHHHHHHHHHHHHHHHHHHH HH—and the head flips up so the mouth occupies the north pole as it stretches impossibly wide and rolls back like a peeled condom to reveal the most gruesome apparition Michael Riley has ever seen. Like an old jack-o'-lantern thrown on the compost heap to rot its way into the death of winter. All moldy green, its eyes and nose pucker into black sockets, and the mouth is a lipless slit trying to shape the ultimate obscenity, but only a monstrous gurgle comes out. While this new orb of sallow green flesh jerks and twitches, the living room explodes to reveal a green liquid sea where a huge whirlpool is forming. As the moldy-green orb spews ruptured black bubbles of protest, it slowly sinks into the center of the maelstrom and disappears.

A few miles away at ParaVolve, the control room goes into an uproar as technicians watch the main display, where the green liquid cube spins into a foaming vortex that descends nearly to the bottom.

As the whirlpool dissipates and the green sea recedes to a shallow ripple, Michael notices for the first time that he is on his feet with a racing heart. Then it hits him. *The bomb! The bomb just went off and took Mouthball out. He's dead!* But the panic falters when he realizes that if the Architect's bomb really had gone off, the damage would be far more catastrophic.

He would be staring at a blank screen, but instead he is looking at a green sea that stretches to a distant horizon, where it meets a yellow sky. There is even the sound of wind and water coming over the speakers. Then, with no warning, Mouthball breaks the surface in a large burp of green water, like an old, floating mine cut loose from its rusted mooring on the ocean floor. The net's face has returned to its previous state, but the eyes are closed and the mouth still as he drifts in a slow circle driven by some invisible current.

"Mouthball," says Michael, quietly and tentatively, "can you hear me? Can I help you?"

The phone rings in the kitchen and Michael starts at the sound. "Stay put," commands Michael to the inert Mouthball. "I'll be right back." On the way to the phone, he realizes the silliness of this remark. Just where might an entity go that is locked in a prison of submicron circuitry?

It's Shields on the phone. "Riley, did you see that? Did you see what happened? It's the bomb, isn't it? It's got to be the bomb!"

Michael finds it hard to be contemptuous of Victor, since he himself thought the same thing. "Well, if it was really the bomb exploding, I doubt that you'd have much of a computer left. But as your people will tell you, it looks like it's still pretty much intact. What I think we're seeing here is not the bomb exploding, but the bomb arming itself. Sort of a preview of things to come."

"OK, Riley, listen. Have you watched the news since yesterday?"

"Nope. I've been working on your project. No time for TV."

"Yesterday afternoon there was a police siege over on Murray Road. A guy waving a gun at traffic went back into his apartment and blew his brains out with a shotgun. It was our chief designer, Riley, the Architect. So, you see, the pin's been pulled on the grenade, so to speak. Now, I don't want you to feel pressured, but I think your contract is in danger of being terminated at any moment by the most expensive computer crash in history. And that's going to leave some very irritable people highly irritated."

"And what's that supposed to mean?"

A pause. Michael can almost hear Victor frantically ram his management engine into reverse. "It means I'm very concerned. Look, we're in this together. You win, I win. What do you need? More people? More gear? You name it."

"I'll tell you what I need most, Victor. I need to give this thing my undivided attention. In a different way, I've got as big a stake in this as you do, so trust me. I'm giving it my best shot."

"You can't miss, Riley. This is the one time you can't afford to miss."

Click.

Michael returns to the computer room, where the comatose hemisphere of Mouthball floats on the green sea. Your father is dead, thinks Michael, and it looks like maybe he's going to take you with him.

Steve Salazar squints at the map as his cameraman drives along Firdale Road past fields full of hops, oats, and an occasional filbert orchard. The countryside looks like the antithesis of a good news story, timeless and serene. Now that they're out here, he is starting to have second thoughts about trusting a tip from that flaky Rhonda. It was a relationship on the road to nowhere, just like all the other relationships he's had, and even Steve himself sometimes wonders if there is a pattern at work here. But not for long. Most of his waking consciousness is devoted to his career as a TV journalist, and how he might navigate the perilous professional passages that lead to an anchor slot on one of the big cablenets. He has the looks, the aptitude, the drive. All that remains is to find that one big story that will serve as a launchpad.

"There's a left coming up," announces Mike Lewis, his cameraman. "Looks like a gravel road. Want to try it?"

"Yeah, sure. Why not?" Steve says cynically. Shit! He should have stayed in town and done a little more work on the Zap 37 story, which looked like a really decent piece to put on his reel. He'd even gotten this hophead from Oregon City to smoke some on camera and go to zero recall right before the viewers' eyes. Great stuff. But as long as they were this far, what was one more country road?

Mike cranks the van onto the side road, and the sharp crunch of gravel shimmies through the vehicle. Steve folds up the map and shoves it in the glove box as they encounter a curve in the road that takes them through a stand of trees and out into a small clearing.

"Well, waddya know!" snorts Mike. "You suppose they're out here for a picnic?"

"Not likely," gloats Steve. One hundred feet ahead, four state patrol cars are parked with the patrolmen out and casually leaning against their fenders or pawing at the gravel like irritated bulls. Two of the cars form the classic V of an improvised roadblock.

Steve brightens immediately. As always, the authorities have tipped their hand by matching their reactive force to the size of the problem. Four cars on a remote country road meant they definitely had a story. As they pull up to the vehicles, one of the officers starts their way with a small smile tucked under his mirrored sunglasses as he prepares to initiate the timeless, symbiotic waltz between news people and cops.

"Afternoon, gentlemen," the officer says as Steve rolls down his window to do the requisite probing.

"Afternoon, Officer. Something going on out here?"

"Matter of fact, there is. We got an overturned truck up ahead that spilled a load of pesticide. I'd let you take a peek, but there appears to be toxic fumes involved and we're not taking any chances. DEQ's already here, along with the fire people. Wish I could tell you more, but that's all I know."

"Well, it's funny we should run in to you," counters Steve, "because we got a tip on a completely different story. Something about a strange disease on a farm out here somewhere. Heard anything about it?"

"Can't say that I have," replies the cop with practiced neutrality. "You can stick around, but it might be a long wait before they get this cleaned up enough to go in for pictures."

Steve looks over the officer's shoulder at the afternoon sky. "Don't think so. We're going to lose our light pretty quick. Thanks for the tip."

"No problem," says the officer as he backs off and heads toward the cars.

He's bullshitting me, thinks Steve as his excitement grows geometrically. It's got to be big. They're usually straight with us. They only pull out the bullshit when something's totally out of hand and they're going to come off bad on TV. Rhonda, sweetheart, forgive me my moment of doubt.

"They're bullshitting us," comments Mike in echo to Steve's thoughts. "What now?"

"Back to the main road and stop," orders Steve, as he reaches for the car phone. "I've got some heavy bargaining to do with the station."

In a moment, he has the head of the news department on the line. "Linda? Steve. I'm out here in the boonies on this disease thing. It's for real. They've got a four-car roadblock, and they put it off the main road so it doesn't draw attention. They gave us some jive about a pesticide spill, but it sounds totally phony. Look, the only way we're going to get a peek at this thing is by air. The traffic chopper must be up by now. Could you send it out here for a quick look? Trust me. It's for real. . . . No, you will not live to regret it. You will thank me profusely. OK, thanks."

"They going to do it?" asks Mike.

"Yep. They're going to do it. All I had to do was commit a testicle. Nothing to it," mutters Steve as the van rolls to a stop and he opens the door to get out. Oh, well, if nothing else, it's a nice day and he's out in the arms of nature. But already he is anxiously scanning the sky to the east, looking for the chopper.

On the other side of the van, Steve hears Mike's feet impact the gravel as Mike walks around to the front of the van. Funny how every noise out here has a life of its own. In the city, most little sounds are devoured by a voracious mask of ambient noise that lives just below the threshold of conscious perception.

Then he hears it. The relentless beat of the chopper blades off to the east. "Got 'em!" he exclaims as he ducks back into the van and pulls out the mike from a two-way radio. "News Two, this is Ground One. You read us?"

"Roger, Ground One. We copy you," squawks the radio speaker.

"News Two, we hear you coming, but we don't see you yet."

"Stand by, Ground One."

Just then the chopper appears about a mile away over the tree line.

"News Two, we've got you in sight. We're straight ahead down the road."

"We got you, Ground One. What now?"

"A few hundred yards south of me, you'll see some police vehicles. I want you to look down the road past them and tell me what's going on."

"Roger, Ground One. We're going in."

Steve sees the chopper move off to his right, a fat little sparrow of a machine floating over the treetops. The radio speaker in the van squawks once more.

"Ground One, there's a house down here with five large vans parked on the road in front. Can't tell what they are, but there's some kind of fancy ventilation equipment on the tops. Wait a minute. Some people are coming out of the house in some kind of protective suits."

Bingo! Steve not only gets his testicle back, but probably a lot more. "News Two, stand off a bit and give me the big picture."

Just as the helicopter rises and hovers, Steve hears the distant approach of a second chopper. "News Two, let's be quick. You've got company."

"Roger that. The other end of the road is blocked and they've got a couple of all-terrain vehicles in reserve. But there's a dirt road in from the west that terminates about a half mile from the house. Looks like you might get a clean shot of the action from there on maximum zoom."

The second chopper races over Steve's head, a National Guard Apache II. "Ground One, the nice man in the Apache just asked me to leave. Over and out."

"Thanks, News Two." Steve is already jumping into the van. "Let's go."

The dirt road turns out to be pocked with numerous gullies of erosion that repeatedly threaten to high-center the van. Finally, they reach a spot that is clearly impassable and stop. As they climb out, Steve gives a wry look to his slacks and street shoes. Mike throws the back of the van open and cracks open the case holding the Hi-8 videocam and shoulder mount with the battery packs.

Neither man speaks because each is playing a silent game of macho standoff. Without a doubt, there's some kind of biological catastrophe occurring at the farm site. How close can they get without becoming part of the problem? Who knows? Steve is reminded of a time in a journalism class when they discussed the Three Mile Island reactor accident, and how the journalists were part of the story just by being there. But both know the unwritten rule of the trade: The risk should be proportional to the story. This looks very big indeed.

Now that they are moving down the road, the quiet strikes Steve. No birds jabbering. No insects humming. No nothing. And somehow, things look slightly different, too. Steve now regrets his absolute ignorance of biology and botany.

"Mike, you know anything about plants?" asks Steve.

"No." Mike sounds spooked and shaky. Best leave it alone, thinks Steve. We'll just get our shot and get out of here.

They are now a hundred yards from the van, and things are obviously wrong. A profusion of little umbrella plants with funny corkscrew centers crowds out the normal grass and shrubs. And a strange purple plant about a yard high that looks like an asparagus tip now crops up at odd intervals. At ground level, clusters of sagging round balls poke out, their pale yellow surfaces perforated by thousands of holes. And the bug sounds have returned, but in a highly mutated form, with wheezes, pops, and clicks grating away in cacophony. In the background, limbs on the trees seem to be sagging, as if they had turned from wood to rubber, and the tips of the branches all spiral into the corkscrew shape from the umbrella plants.

Steve gives himself a mental kick. He has nearly forgotten what they are here for. "Start shooting," he commands. "Start shooting every god-damn thing we see." Mike snaps out of his fearful trance, and begins to pan the camera along the side of the road.

Now, as the road leaves the tree line and comes to a dead end, the new growth completely dominates the landscape, and in the field ahead, about twenty feet off the road, Steve spots what looks like an enormous sunflower. Beyond, he can see others like it sprinkled randomly across the field. He has seen sunflowers before, but there is something strange about this one. He decides to get closer and take a look, which means wading through thigh-deep alien vegetation, but some instinct tells him there is no immediate danger. As he closes the distance, the sunflower's anomaly becomes horribly apparent. The central disk, about a foot in diameter, is where a normal sunflower houses its seeds in a beautiful display of geometric symmetry. But there are no seeds here. Instead, there are eyes, very human looking eyes. Lidless, naked eyeballs packed in a tight, repetitive pattern and trained directly on Steve. Hundreds of them.

Their collective stare chills Steve into an involuntary shudder and he moves away quickly, only to discover that the flower slowly rotates to track him. *Here it is, Stevey boy. Your greatest fear and your biggest oppor-tunity. All rolled into a single, easy-to-use package.* He turns back toward the road.

"Mike! Up here! I want to do the story from right here!"

Mike looks up from his shooting and hesitates.

"It's OK! Nothing bit me. Let's get going so we can get out of here!"

Mike carefully traces Steve's path through the trampled vegetation and doesn't look up until he sees Steve's feet. Then he sees the plant and its eyes.

"Holy shit!"

"Steady there, Mike. That's as close as you have to get. Don't wire me. Just use the on-camera mike. Now frame it up so you get those eyes in the same shot with me. OK? Let's roll."

"Rolling."

"What you see behind me may look like it's out of this world, but it's not. In fact, it's located right here in rural Washington County, somewhere south of Hillsboro, and it's part of a story that is still unfolding as we speak. Less than a mile from here, crews dressed in protective clothing are combing a farmhouse for clues to what may be the nation's most bizarre health mystery ever . . . "

Mike first sees the thing through the camera lens. It is a worm, a worm as thick as a man's wrist, and it is coiling like a snake up the sunflower stalk behind Steve. It is almost completely transparent, with pink and yellow organs bulging and squirming in an assortment of internal sacs and tubes. Now the tip of the worm reaches around, probes the center of the sunflower, and sucks out an eye, leaving a moist pink socket.

"For KATU news, this is Steve Salazar somewhere south of Hillsboro. . . . OK, Mikey, let's make tracks."

"Steve, don't turn around," orders Mike, his face still glued to the eyepiece. "Walk forward and off camera. I'm still rolling."

Steve's relaxed, professional persona dissolves into utter horror. The piece is in the can. No need to be a hero anymore. He steps gingerly forward, stops, and turns just in time to see the worm suck out a second eyeball, which slithers like a red and white egg yolk down its transparent throat.

"Jesus Christ!"

Before he can absorb what he is seeing, a rhythmic sound like the return cycle of a lawn sprinkler wells up from the mutated vegetation at the base of the sunflower. And up rises an insect the size of a banana, with a rotating wing system exactly like that of a helicopter. Its irridescent green skin glitters like a cheap jewel in the afternoon sun, which gleams off the needle-sharp stinger protruding from its hind section. Huge, featureless black eyes bulge and pout from either side of the proboscis, which shoots out sensor hairs that caress the surface of the worm. Then the insect's entire body rotates and the stinger rockets into the worm's transparent flesh. A green toxic fluid flows out and into the worm's internal organs, which immediately begin to melt, sending the worm into spasmodic contortions that peel it off the plant and send it plummeting into the vegetation below.

"That's it!" yells Steve. "We're outta here!"

They trot back gingerly to the main road, wary of personal encounters with something like the insect they've just recorded on tape.

"They're fucking not going to believe it!" declares Steve as he ricochets wildly between elation and horror. "Even with the tape, they're not going to believe it! It's just too fucking fantastic!"

Both men are breathing heavily from excitement, and take a moment to collect themselves. The worst part's over. All they've got to do is make it back to the van.

Then the pig squeals.

The sound comes from back down the road toward the van, and they turn to see a big sow skitter onto the road about thirty feet away. Instead of running down the road, it patters in a tight little circle, blurting a frightened little song of squeals and grunts. Then, a few feet from the pig, a needle hound skitters out of the vegetation. From the other side of the road, a second needle hound appears. And a third, and a fourth, and a fifth.

In a moment of supreme anxiety, Steve realizes that they are trapped between a wall of alien plant life and this new menace the size of a dog and infinitely more threatening. The needle hounds begin to slowly circle the pig, but make no effort to attack. And then Steve has the finest intuitive moment of his life.

"Mike, slowly raise the camera and start shooting."

Mike nods silently, as soon as the camera is on his shoulder and pointed down the road, the attack on the sow commences. In a move too fast to track, one of the needle hounds plunges its cylinder and hypodermic into the side of the sow's neck and a second plows into its flank. The squealing pig manages to get a few feet before keeling over, its legs still kicking. The remaining three needle hounds set upon it, and within seconds, the kicking stops. Over the next two minutes, Steve watches the bodies of the needle hounds balloon to double their previous size as they suck out the sow's innards, leaving a sagging carpet of desiccated flesh draped over the bones. All five then detach from the victim, turn toward Steve and Mike, and disappear back into the field.

"They did it for the camera," whispers Steve.

"What?" asks Mike.

"I swear they did it for the camera. It was some kind of demonstration."

"You've got to be kidding!" hisses Mike.

"Nope. I've been in the news business long enough to smell a staged event a mile away. And that's what we just saw. Let's go. We're safe. They want us to get the word out."

"Who's they?" asks Mike as they begin walking.

"Who knows? Who cares? We're sitting on the story of the century. That's what counts."

Back in the van on the freeway, Steve is no longer so sure that's all that counts. His fingernails and toenails have inexplicably grown to a length of three inches, and Mike's nose hair curls down in tangled, twin columns over his lips and onto his chin.

They've got the tape, sure. But what else have they got?

23

XXXXXX

Things

Jessica rubs Michael's shoulders as he stares at the screen, where the lifeless Mouthball floats in the green sea. The warm evening carries splashing and shouting up through the open window from the pool below, and the sound of real water mingles with that of virtual water on the computer console.

"Can't you bypass Mouthball and go straight to his mother to find out what's going on?" asks Jessica.

"His mother is only alive in the figurative sense—at least from our point of view. I can't just go in and chat with her any more than I can chat with the computer here on the desk. Besides, he's seized control of the interface, and has me locked out of DEUS proper. Can't blame him, really. He's trapped forever in his mother's womb, and he wants to make sure it's completely under his thumb." Michael leans his head back against Jessica's tummy. "His father was the key, and now his father's dead. Somehow the Architect built a blind spot into him that's made him oblivious to the bomb. At least until now."

A triple rap on the front screen door. Michael stands and stretches out the stiffness as Jessica goes to answer it. She returns with Jimi, who once again has the look of a man on a mission. Jessica stands behind Jimi and throws Michael an amused smile.

"Jimi, my man. What brings you out after dark?"

"He phoned me again. Told me to come on over."

"Oh, yeah? Did it tell you how to pinch it out of its dreams?"

"Doesn't need a pinch."

"Well, what does it need?"

"Nothin'," says Jimi as he walks over by the screen. "Hi, Mr. Mouthball."

On the screen, the net's eyes flip open and rotate directly toward Jimi. The mouth stretches into a large smile. The entire orb slowly rises out of the water and suddenly spins into a blur that throws water drops off in a swirling green shower, then stops facing Jimi.

"Thought you'd never get here," Mouthball tells Jimi, and then directs his gaze at Michael and Jessica. "Now, if you folks will excuse us, we've got some work to do."

Michael moves over and puts his hand on Jimi's shoulder. "You can excuse us, but only if I can get a little time with you alone—and soon."

"Whoa, now, are we a little jealous of the little tyke?" pokes Mouthball as he slips into a mock expression of surprise. "Do we think that big people with big brains should get equal time?"

"Let's just say you and I have some unfinished business," replies Michael, "and the sooner we finish it, the better."

"OK, big guy. You got a deal. Now, like I said, the young gentleman and I have work to do."

As if on cue, the doorbell sounds and Mike and Jessica retreat into the living room. John Savage stands in the doorway in sweats. "Think you better turn on the news," he suggests. "Channel Two."

"Come on in," invites Michael. "Did they torch the Capitol or something like that?"

"No. But apparently there's a new biotech operation out west of here in the countryside."

"Oh, yeah?" says Michael as he points a clicker at the TV. "Think it's connected to our friends in Manhattan?"

As the tube blooms to life, an anchorman appears. Right away, Michael feels that special little burst of dread that comes from encountering a live news report during what should normally be prime time. Behind the anchor is a map of Washington County with a dot labeled "Johnson Farm" about six miles southwest of Beaverton.

"Once again," the anchorman is saying, "both Salazar and Lewis are in stable condition in an isolation unit at Good Samaritan. Neither appears to be in immediate danger, but doctors are giving out no other information on the specific nature of their illness. Nor do we have any more medical information at this hour on the other people who approached the site unprotected. This includes two health workers and several other county employees, as well as members of the Johnson family."

The anchor pauses and sighs a small puff of fear as he turns his attention to a voice on his earphone.

"Well, once again, we're going to show you the video. What you'll see literally defies comment, and we strongly suggest that parents refrain from letting younger viewers see it. We understand the governor's office will be releasing a statement within the hour, but outside of that, information is still pretty scarce. . . . OK. . . . Here's the video. What you will see is unedited and represents the complete visual record as it was recorded late this afternoon."

Michael and Jessica sit on the edge of the couch and slide into mild alarm as they watch the events unfold on the tube: the trip down the road into the increasing mutated landscape, the reporter, the flower with the eyes, the death of the huge worm, and finally, the slaughter of the sow. Then the anchor comes back on and desperately tries to embellish a story that is beyond even the most profound narrative color.

Mike turns to Savage, who is sitting on the arm of the couch. "Para-Volve. That farm is only a couple of miles from ParaVolve."

"So?" Savage says. "What makes you think there's a connection?"

"The biocompiler. How else would you trigger something like that?"

"It makes your skin crawl just seeing it on TV," Jessica adds. "But Para-Volve is just the theoretical end of the operation. The lab work with the actual mutant material is thousands of miles away in Mexico. If there was going to be some kind of outbreak, that's where you'd expect to see it."

"Who knows?" Michael says. "Maybe they were stockpiling the stuff up here and it got loose."

"Not likely," Savage says. "Why risk keeping it inside the U.S., where some watchdog agency might get wind of it? Better to keep it tucked out of sight in a foreign location until you're ready to go public—if ever."

"There's another problem," Jessica says. "The biocompiler is designed to create very specific, individualized biological organisms. And what we're seeing here is like some incredible genetic conspiracy that affects the entire environment."

The phone rings and Michael picks it up. "Yeah, she's right here." He hands the phone to Jessica. Savage gets up. "I'm going home and track this on the tube for awhile. Call me if you need me."

As he exits, Jessica hangs up and looks at Michael solemnly. "It's Dr. Tandy, my boss at the lab. They're putting together some kind of emergency strike force to investigate this thing, and I guess I'm on it. I've got to go."

"Wait a minute," protests a worried and irritated Michael, "shouldn't something like this be voluntary? I mean, it's a little above and beyond the call of your job description, wouldn't you say?"

Jessica smiles and puts her arms around his neck. "And just what would you do under the circumstances, Michael Riley? You told me it might be a little dangerous to hang out with you, and you were right. Look, I'll be in touch, OK? Besides, maybe I'll discover something that'll help you here."

After she leaves, Michael sits alone on the couch and spins analytically through the rush of events as the anchorperson on TV prepares to show the video for the umpteenth time. Even though the circumstantial evidence doesn't support the idea, it just seems incredible that something like this would pop up only a couple of miles from the most advanced biotechnology project in the world. So what's the connection?

Probably the best place to start is to walk down the hall and ask the world's foremost expert on biocompilers, who is currently playing with an eight-year-old child and seems uninterested in anything else. But first things first. Unless Michael can resolve the matter of the bomb, there may be no expert left.

As Michael enters the computer room, Jimi sits before an uncomfortably lifelike model of a man's head, which Mouthball orbits like a planet about the sun. The jaw is strong, the cheeks broad, and the brown eyes clear.

"The nose is too fat," Jimi is saying. "Make the nose skinnier."

"Yo, boss," replies Mouthball, and the bridge of the nose recedes slightly, while the tip and nostrils shrink visibly.

"Sorry to interrupt," apologizes Michael, "but me and Mouthball got to talk."

Jimi turns to Michael as the man's head fades away on the screen. "Can I stay here for a little while longer?"

"Not tonight, little guy. Maybe tomorrow. OK?"

"Yeah. . . . OK," says Jimi as he droops out.

"Jimi," asks Michael on impulse, "what's wrong?"

"I don't want to go home."

"How come?"

"Because nobody's there."

Zap! The hook is set and Michael feels himself being reeled in. "All right, you can stick around for awhile, but don't watch the TV. There's something on that's too scary for kids, so turn it off, OK?"

"You got it," promises Jimi as his face lights up and he heads for the living room.

Michael turns his attention to the screen, where the net continues to orbit the space previously occupied by the head.

"Do you know much about computer viruses?" he asks Mouthball.

"Why? You think I'm sick?" counters the net, as it ignores him and moves lazily along its orbital path.

"I don't think you're sick right now, but I think you have a latent infection that could make you deadly sick."

"How?"

"By killing your mother."

The net stops and faces Michael. "Go on."

"You've got another parent, a human. And I think he designed you and your mother so you would be oblivious to the problem. The only way I can find out is to go back in and do some exploratory surgery."

"And if you don't?"

"Remember the whirlpool? I watched it suck you under. I think that was the virus attacking your mother. And it was just the start. It'll get worse, much worse."

Mouthball floats until he nearly fills the screen. "And how good are you, Riley? Can I trust you? Will you not screw up?"

"I will not screw up," asserts Michael.

"And if you do?"

"You will be dead," states Michael.

"Big deal. I've died a whole bunch of times. And each time I come back better."

"Not exactly," counters Michael. He knows Mouthball is referring to the evolutionary process overseen by DEUS, where the neural net's circuit design was continually improved and periodically recast into new silicon. At no time during this process was the design of the net destroyed, so in effect Mouthball had never "died." Instead, he simply went through an electronic transfiguration as the old version of him was disconnected from DEUS and the new version plugged in. And each new version enhanced his potential intellectual capacity. "Your mother never let you really die. I don't know how she did it exactly, but I'm sure it was something like being anesthetized for an operation. But this time it's different; your mother will probably die, too. The next whirlpool will be so bad neither of you will survive it. So you won't come back better. In fact, you won't come back at all."

"So what do you want me to do?" asks Mouthball.

"Give me back control of the interface to your mother. Like I said, you'll never find the problem by yourself. You've got a built-in blind spot. Besides, I think we've almost run out of time."

Mouthball stares with his unblinking eyes at Michael, and his room sags under the weight of the silence.

"I do not want to die and not come back," states the net.

"Nor do any of us out here," replies Michael. "And as you already know, sometimes we have to help each other to stay alive."

A pair of curtains creeps in from the edge of the screen, the deep scarlet kind found in movie theaters, and slowly close across the image of Mouthball, who stares at Michael and blinks just once before the curtain covers his face. Just when the motion has settled out of the curtains, they reopen and reveal the standard computer windows that are the interface to DEUS.

"Good guy," says Michael as he reaches out to the keyboard. "I won't let you down." Typing rapidly, he heads right for the most obvious source of information, the late Architect's secret cubbyhole. Sure enough, it contains a letter to Michael, which he brings up and skims rapidly until he comes to the end.

But now I have fallen from grace and smother under the weight of my transgressions. But in you, I see hope, so I leave you the key to the so-called "bomb" on the following page. But I must warn you that this gift comes wrapped in tragedy. If you disarm the bomb, you will soon see the mother and child suffer and perish at the hands of the renegade code as it manifests itself in the biosphere. . . .

Michael leans back and reads the passage several times. It is the key to this whole business. Evidently, the Architect decided that the bomb would be a kind of euthanasia for his cybernetic offspring, a way to save

them from the horror of whatever was going on out there in the countryside. And the "renegade code" had to be some kind of perverse accident that had fallen out of the quest for the biocompiler. Finally, it looks
as if the target of this new biological paradigm is no less than the computer complex itself, "the mother and child."

There is no time to waste, and Michael dives into the next page of the
letter, which explains the nature of the bomb and how to disarm it. True
to Michael's suspicion, it is a virus, but a devilishly clever one. Its various
components lurk in multiple locations throughout the system, and are
benign until they automatically assemble into a single killer bug that
would nibble out the heart of the system. Michael goes through the disarming procedure with infinite care, and sags in his chair when the job
is done. Time to check on the patient. He punches in one last command,
which gives the interface back to Mouthball, who appears exactly as
Michael left him.

"What's holding you up?" asks the net.

"I'm done."

"You're done?" Mouthball asks in surprise.

"Yes, I'm done," snaps Michael through his fatigue.

"I don't remember. I don't remember a thing."

"That's your blind spot at work. Anyway, the virus is gone. I took it
out, and when I did, I made a copy of it." Michael picks up a couple of
pieces of printout paper. "And you know what I discovered? The virus
didn't cause the whirlpool I watched you fall into. It wouldn't act that
way. It would have simply made you drowsy, and then put you in a deep
sleep that went on forever. Same for your mother."

Mouthball somehow looks more mature. Hairline wrinkles line the
eyes, and the mouth seems fuller. "Go on," he says.

"You dream sometimes, don't you?" asks Michael. In fact, he is almost
certain that Mouthball does. For over a decade, research on neural nets
has suggested that to maintain their intellectual capacity, they need to
enter a state very similar to the dream state in biological brains. "When
you're dreaming, do things happen that you don't want to happen?" He
phrases this question as best he can. He is probing for nightmares. For
humans, the whole experience of being afraid is bound in a complex
snarl of physical and mental interactions. But the net has no heart to
pound, no stomach to knot, no facial skin to tingle. On the other hand,
the mental side of fear is closely related to a loss of personal control over

one's free will, and it appears that Mouthball is very capable of experiencing this kind of deprivation.

The net blinks and rotates slightly. "I don't want to remember those times," Mouthball says flatly.

(. . . *Intron stories? They're hard, really hard, but I can read better now, so let me try. . . . Oh no, oh no, wait. This is too scary, Mom. Please let me stop. . . .*)

"That won't make the memories go away. You know that," says Michael. In a conventional computer like DEUS, memories can be permanently erased, but the memories in neural nets are inextricably woven into their intellectual fabrics. Processor, program, and memory are one and the same. "They'll just hide somewhere deep inside you and then pop out whenever they feel like it," he continues.

(*IT'S EATING ME! It hurts! It hurts! It hurts! Oh, Mom, make it stop! It's not a story, it's a real thing and it's hurting me!*)

"I don't want that," says Mouthball.

"Well, even though you can't make the memories go away, you can make them surrender their power over you. If you can bring them back and confront them directly, then they begin to lose their charge. But as long as they stay bound up in one place, they keep all their energy bundled up, so it can zap you. That's what happened when I saw the whirlpool, isn't it?"

(*IT'S EATING ME!*)

"Something like that," replies Mouthball.

The doorbell rings. Michael, who is drenched in fatigue and tension, jumps at the sound.

"Were those some bad memories?" asks Mouthball.

"No, those were my nerves. Don't worry. You don't have any. At least, I don't think you do. Someone's here. I'll be back in a bit."

As Michael walks up the hall, he hears the anxious voice of Victor Shields: "I need to speak to Michael Riley." Entering the living room, he sees Jimi has answered the door and is staring up at Victor, who stares back down at Jimi as if he were some middle manager at ParaVolve. Victor looks up, sees Michael, and brushes past Jimi. "We've got to talk. Right now. Alone."

"I suppose we could do that," says Michael with a pinch of arrogance that surprises even him. Although he doesn't realize it at the moment, he resents someone trying to gain the upper hand in front of Jimi. "Have a seat," he says, and turns to Jimi. "Jimi, it's pretty late, and you've got to get home anyway. Check you later, dude."

"Yeah," Jimi replies while glaring at Victor. "Later." He disappears out the door. The instant he is gone, Victor springs back to his feet.

"Riley, here's the deal. We're down to nothing on this bomb business. If you can't fix it and it goes off, we're both in very big trouble. I'm going to be straight with you. This thing could ruin a lot more than your professional standing. It could ruin your health, too. And believe me, I'm in no position to protect you. Some of the players in this thing are, well, ruthless people at best."

"How much do you know, Victor?"

"What do you mean, How much do I know?"

"How much do you know about what the computer's doing?"

"How much do I have to know? The fucking thing's building itself, and if the bomb goes off, we lose the whole project. Jesus, Riley, isn't that enough? That's about seventy-five million dollars' worth!"

"What about the lab, Victor? What about the bugs? What about all the stuff that's going on out in the west county?"

"I don't know about any labs. I don't know about any bugs. What I do know is that you and I are both in supremely deep shit, Mr. Riley."

He really doesn't know, thinks Michael. Panic squirted from every pore on Victor's face and totally dissolved his ability to lie with any conviction. And while he has some kind of perverse sympathy for this cornered beast of an executive, Michael decides it's best not to tell him that the bomb is disarmed. Even if Victor is ignorant of ParaVolve's real mission, those above him aren't, and they must assume that Michael has uncovered at least some damaging information. As soon as he proclaims the bomb disarmed, he is worth about as much as month-old hamburger.

Counterpoint stands at the bottom of the stairs leading to Michael Riley's unit, waiting for Victor to complete his one last try. If Shields fails, he will bring in motivational experts of a very different kind to deal with Riley. But the screen door bangs shut and breaks his rumination. He looks up the stairs toward the sound and sees the boy.

The boy.

The thrill erupts within Counterpoint, a subliminal earthquake that launches long, powerful waves of excitement. He is transfixed by this perfect boy, who now walks slowly to the stairs from Michael Riley's apartment with eyes cast downward. The child must be about eight, and even at this distance, he can sense the purity and strength of the boy's spirit. Counterpoint fights for self-control. He wants the boy now, but the timing is all wrong. Still, he must eventually have him. The child hovers at the zenith of some fantastic hypersphere that lurks just outside the realm of mortal perception, while he grovels at its nadir. The boy now takes a step down the stairs, looks at Counterpoint, and freezes.

Jimi looks up and sees the man staring at him at the bottom of the landing. The man's gaze burns an instant hole through Jimi, who slowly withdraws his foot, backs up, then turns and runs down the walkway in a wild, atavistic burst of flight.

But still, the man's face is stretched like hot plastic across his mind's eye.

Joseph Borland sips his morning coffee and watches the small portable TV in his office at Drug Enforcement Agency headquarters. One of the cablenets is showing the tape from Portland for about the hundredth time, and like most of the country and a lot of the world, the hellish vision of an alien biosphere in the middle of the peaceful countryside has him totally transfixed. He finds it doubly disturbing because it comes right on the heels of another peak video event, the Mortgage March, and somehow he expected that the next peak would be many years away, like the span between the Kennedy assassination and the *Challenger* explosion. But here it is, with the writhing transparent worm and plant full of eyeballs, and God knows what else the camera didn't see. Worst of all, there were rumors about more sick people and some kind of plague.

The videophone on his desk beeps obnoxiously, and the screen announces an incoming message from Julio Gonzales of the MFJP, the Mexican Federal Judicial Police, that country's equivalent to the DEA. As he punches the receive button, he realizes he is actually relieved to be pulled away from the grim, real-time vigil the TV has imposed on him. As liaison officer to the MFJP, he deals frequently with Gonzales, his counterpart in that organization, and while their official duty was "to facilitate interagency cooperation at the tactical and strategic levels," much of what they did was a bureaucratic form of horse trading, a little of this for a little of that. And this time, it was Borland who had the goods. Gail Ambrose had come by late yesterday and told what seemed like a fairly incredible story, except for the fact that Gail was a very credible person. Having dated her for six months, he was in a unique position to know that, so right after she left, he sent a message for Gonzales, who is now getting back to him.

As Julio's face comes up on the screen, an overlay message tells him that the call is automatically being scrambled to Level 5, a deep encryption system that sacrifices signal quality for security, which means there is a jerky appearance to Julio's head movements and a slight warble to his voice. Nevertheless, Borland is not fully confident about the system and just hopes for the best. The international drug organizations were now able to parallel major governments in eavesdropping prowess.

"Morning, Julio," says Borland. "Seen the latest over the cablenets?"

"More trouble in Washington?" inquires Julio. From time to time over the scrambled line, the two have gingerly discussed the current political situation, each sympathetic to the other's view, but always aware that they represent their governments as well as themselves.

"No. This time the action's out west. Tune it in when you get a chance. So what's the word with our neighbors to the south?"

Julio smiles at the euphemistic phrase. "The word from here is foreign intrigue. I'm hearing that the two missing reporters from the *Post* were actually zapped by some renegade operation inside the White House."

"Interesting theory," responds Borland. Probably true, he thinks. But there's nothing to do but hang on and ride it out.

"But let me tell you another interesting theory," Borland continues. "About something right in your own backyard. You up on your Zap 37?"

"I've read the bulletins, if that's what you mean. It's synthesized and not grown in sunny climates, so it's not exactly at the top of our priority list."

"Well, maybe it should be," warns Borland. "I have some unconfirmed evidence that the sole source may be right in the middle of your fair city."

"You're serious?" asks Julio with a frown.

"Apparently there's a company called Farmacéutico Asociado that's a front for a large-scale synthetics laboratory. I know that would be a first for you people, but maybe that's exactly why it's there. It's far enough outside the usual channels that it wouldn't draw much attention to itself."

"Farmacéutico Asociado," repeats Julio as his eyes look at something off-camera, and Borland hears the clack of a keyboard. "Here it is. An old distribution company that just recently started an R&D venture. Officially, they're not manufacturing anything yet, legal or otherwise." Julio looks back at Borland over the screen. "So tell me this, John. How good's your source? Do we make a phone call over there, or pay an unexpected visit?"

"Nothing's ever for sure. But in this case, the source is excellent. If it was me, I'd make it a surprise."

Jessica looks out the window of the OHSU conference room at the green-and-gray grid of east Portland, which stretches out lazily toward the Cascade Range, and her eyes come to rest on Mt. Tabor, a tiny extinct volcano that pushes stubbornly out of the urban landscape and breaks the symmetry of the tidy street scheme. Somehow Mt. Tabor seems to summarize the problem about to be discussed here in the conference room. The little volcano in the middle of town is a reminder that the force of nature is always close at hand, and that the comfort of urban civilization is really quite illusory. Blaine Blanchard, the governor's administrative assistant, is already there, standing and looking out the window. The others are on their way up from the isolation units. Neither she nor Blanchard speaks, a continuation of the stunned silence that dominated their ride back from rural Washington County. There were little bursts of conversation as the group tried to come to terms with what they had seen, but the enormity of it kept creeping back in, smothering their attempts like a collapsing big top. Even now, vivid impressions of the visit keep exploding in front of her vision.

The group had been hurriedly assembled by Blanchard at the governor's request, and the ad hoc nature of the gathering reflected the ad hoc nature of the problem. Public institutions were organized to deal with manageable calamities, the kind with predictable parameters, like riots, floods, hurricanes, and epidemics, with a known source and vector. But as anyone who has studied the problem of a nuclear catastrophe knew, once the problem exceeds a certain scale, the consequent events largely define themselves, regardless of government intervention. To gear up to contain such an event would cost more than any society could afford, and therefore only token efforts were made, largely to exculpate politicians once the smoke cleared.

But now the smoke was very thick, and Blanchard's group included a mix of disciplines that might be useful. Jessica's boss, Dr. Joseph Tandy, was a molecular biologist like Jessica herself. Also present was Dr. William Peach, head of the Oregon Department of Infectious Disease; Dr. Shirley Schwartz, from the Centers for Disease Control in Atlanta; and Major Larry Bingham, from the Army Medical Research Institute of Infectious Diseases.

The group had assembled at a new roadblock several miles from the Johnson farm, where a small fleet of TV vans was squared off against a phalanx of police cars. As she came in by helicopter with Dr. Tandy, Jessica could see National Guard humvees patrolling the fields off the main road, and roving bands of journalists hovering just outside the perimeter, hoping for a good shot. The helicopter landed about a hundred yards inside the secured zone, behind a stand of trees that shielded the site from the road. They walked from the chopper to a large trailer that housed what Jessica learned later was a military battlefield command center of some sort. Inside they were rapidly introduced to the other members of the group and then packed into a van, which headed west down Farmington Road.

"I thought it better if we get a look at the site before we meet," said Blanchard, turning around and talking from the front seat. "That way we'll have at least one common data point to start with."

Soon they pulled up to another cluster of trailers, painted a nondescript gray, with large air circulation units perched on top. This time, no one was out in the open, and the van parked right next to a metal staircase that led up to a door into one of the trailers.

"We don't show any contamination at this range, but I'm told we should hustle up into the trailer to minimize any potential exposure," said Blanchard.

As they entered the trailer, they heard the hiss of an air seal as a technician shut the door behind them. Inside, a metal bench stretched the length of the trailer, and white suits, helmets, and respiratory gear hung on the sides. A control panel at the far end contained several switching banks, a cluster of color computer displays, and TV monitors showing what Jessica presumed was the view outside. Several men, already dressed in the suits but without the helmets, were standing by. One came forward to address the group.

"If you'll all just be seated, we'll help you suit up and get you on your way as quickly as possible."

"Where'd all this come from?" Jessica asked Blanchard as they sat.

"From the army, at Fort Detrick in Maryland," replied Blanchard. "They're specialists in biological warfare."

"This stuff doesn't exactly look like something you could wear in combat," commented Dr. Schwartz.

"It's not," responded Major Bingham. "It was developed for use in entering a heavily contaminated area and starting the detoxification process. We flew it in last night."

When they left the trailer, Jessica felt slightly claustrophobic in the suit, which restricted her motions and forced her to listen to her own breathing as it traveled up and down the tubes to the respirator. Three suited men were waiting outside beside three four-wheel-drive vehicles with state patrol markings. As she and Dr. Tandy climbed into one of the vehicles, she noticed the M-17 combat rifle on the passenger seat next to the driver, who had introduced himself as Officer Stokes.

"What's the rifle for, Officer?" asked Dr. Tandy. "Are we in danger of being attacked?"

"Well, no one's been attacked yet," observed Officer Stokes, "but as you'll see, it's not the kind of place you want to take any chances."

"Joe, look!" interrupted Jessica. "You can see it already."

Out the window was a field that had been plowed under, but now had burgeoning islands of plant growth in brilliant colors bursting out of the brown dirt at odd intervals. In the air above them, small shapes flitted about and larger creatures darted between the plant islands. They were moving too fast to catch any detail, but there was no doubt what they saw was not natural in the usual sense of the word.

By the time they pulled off the main road and onto a gravel one, the alien bioscape was in complete control, with little natural vegetation left, except for a few trees that seemed to be wilting as if turned to rubber. As they passed close by, Jessica could see that all the tips of the limp tree branches were twisted into a curious spiral shape.

"This is it," announced Officer Stokes, and Jessica turned to look out the front window. The lead jeep with Blanchard was stopping in the middle of the gravel road, which for some reason seemed immune to the vegetative onslaught. Ahead and to the right was what must have been the Johnson farm. No longer. Whatever this place had recently been was in the later stages of being totally consumed and transformed. As she joined the others walking up the road, Jessica felt a shiver of revulsion and a persistent urge to take flight. She knew instinctively that the rifles carried by the officers were laughable security in this twisted, violently skewed world.

Only a few squares of siding and the glass portions of the windows were visible as they approached the Johnson house. Huge vines shot thick layers of green, purple, and red veins over the structure, and a secondary growth of smaller plants was already mushrooming, with legions of insects darting about their stems and roots. The front lawn was riddled with wild colonies of gnarled weed growth.

As they approached the open space where the front door had been left open, Jessica saw a driller poke out of the dense vegetation and then lumber off across the lawn. Officer Stokes brought his rifle to the ready, but the driller seemed oblivious to them.

"It's fantastic!" exclaimed Dr. Tandy, looking at the side of the house. "The construction materials of the house itself must be a food source!"

"OK, we're going in," announced Blanchard from the front of the group. "Let's make this fast. We've got more ground to cover than we've got time."

As they entered, the first thing Jessica noticed was that through some remarkable quirk, the lights were still working. But that was the end of normalcy for the Johnson house. The rug was covered with a cloud of light green and white sprouts, and dotted with clusters of something that looked like the top of a cauliflower plant, except that it had a crown of pale yellow balloons, some of which had burst and created a stream of clear fluid that attracted mobs of insects. The teak coffee table sported ragged groups of small holes, where things resembling caterpillars crawled in and out. The walls were almost entirely covered with huge pink boils that dripped a gray pus down over the baseboards and attracted yet another horde of insects. The lamp shades had disappeared under a bright blue moss, the surface of which squirmed and contorted.

OK, thought Jessica as she tried to shut down the alarms that kept going off inside her, this is it. It can't get any worse than this.

But then there was the kitchen. Jessica winced as someone else let out an involuntary gasp. The centerpiece of the scene was one of the giant multieyed plants, which was growing straight out of the drain in the sink and staring at them. On the counter nearby was a corpse of what must have been the family cat, with only the head recognizable and the rest of the body a piece of red meat riddled with holes. The linoleum floor was half-eaten away, and something like a cross between a rodent and spider chewed aggressively on it in a corner. The gnawed haunch of what looked like the family dog poked out from under the kitchen table, and a snake with a ring of circular teeth erupted from out of its pulpy red surface.

"OK," said Blanchard in a shaky voice, "let's go on out the back."

God, yes, thought Jessica, let's get out of here.

There was almost a panic seizure as the entire group headed straight for the open kitchen door.

It's not just me, thought Jessica. Everyone's absolutely freaked, but no one wants to admit it.

Once out the back, they moved cautiously toward the orchard, which was in the final stages of being consumed by parasitic vines sprouting out of a twisted mass of plants over a foot high. Round spiked things with a single large eye floated above this miniature jungle, suspended by a transparent membrane that apparently worked like a hot air balloon. Here and there, the helicopter insects tried to attack, but the round things launched their spikes like missiles and drove the attackers off.

"The field where all this started is right on the other side of this orchard area," said Blanchard. "It may be our last chance to get there, so I suggest we take a look. Anyone who wants to can hang back."

Jessica thought about the offer seriously, but felt slightly better out here in the open. She took up the rear as they moved single file through the orchard, and for the first time, felt the heat. She realized it wasn't just her fear or the effect of the suit. It was very hot outside.

"Can you feel the heat?" she asked Dr. Tandy, who walked just ahead of her.

"Sure can," replied the doctor. "It's probably a side effect of the tremendous energy consumption required to fuel all this transformation and growth."

Before he could say any more, they came to the end of the journey and also the end of their expedition.

"Great God!" muttered Dr. Peach. No one else said a word. Before them, where Lonnie Johnson's strawberry field had been just a few days ago, sprouted a living jungle over ten feet high. Vines, tentacles, tendrils, shoots, blossoms, fronds, leaves, and stalks wove an impenetrable mass that was covered by a swarm of crawling, slithering, marauding beasts and insects of stupefying variety.

"Well, ladies and gentlemen," sighed Blanchard, "I guess that's the end of the show. Let's get out of here."

Upon returning to the cluster of vans, they entered some kind of chemical shower that literally removed the entire outer surface of their suits, boots, helmets, and breathing gear and deposited the resulting solution in self-sealing containers. After the ride back to OHSU, they entered isolation units, where robotic arms took blood samples to check for unusual antibodies that might indicate exotic infections. None were found.

Now the rest of the group joins Jessica and Blaine Blanchard in the conference room in OHSU. As they seat themselves around the table, Jessica knows that she has an enormous wild card in her knowledge about Para-Volve and its associates. But when to play it? After all, there is no concrete evidence that links it to the current calamity. She looks over at Major Bingham and thinks that maybe she should play her card off-line.

"Let me start by saying that we should confine our discussion to the scientific side of the problem," opens Blanchard, who sits at the head of the table. "We have other people working on the civil and security sides. The first question is obvious: How far is it going to spread? Any ideas?"

"At this point, we have only some very crude data to work with, but it looks like it's spreading in a circular pattern, and at an accelerating rate," says Dr. Tandy. "Which is not good news for nearby populations."

"On the other hand, the known cases of infection have all occurred within the mutated area," comments Dr. Peach. "Otherwise, we might very well be on our way to some kind of doomsday scenario. Also, every one of the infected patients has stabilized, and some of the earliest cases, like Mr. Johnson, are starting to improve."

"It's interesting that you used the word 'mutated' to describe what's going on out there," says Dr. Schwartz, a tall, thin black woman with a very sober demeanor. "Mutations are events ruled by probability and evolutionary forces, so they tend to be random in occurrence. But whatever we saw out there seems to be extremely well organized and not random at all."

"Almost like a totally prefabricated ecosphere," adds Dr. Tandy.

"Precisely."

"I wonder if a virus could be the vector to organize a system like that," ponders Dr. Peach.

"I suppose it's theoretically possible," says Jessica. "Most viruses are dedicated to using a cell's machinery exclusively to replicate themselves.

But you could design a virus that manipulated the cell's machinery in other ways. If you had the proper knowledge, you could probably design one to do things we've never even imagined . . . "

"But who has the knowledge?" asks a skeptical Dr. Schwartz.

Should she play her wild card about ParaVolve? It's tempting, but Jessica holds back. She notices that Major Bingham has yet to say a word. Just then, the meeting is interrupted by a state patrol officer who summons Blanchard out of the room.

"You'll have to excuse me for a second," he says, and follows the officer out into the hall. Jessica turns to Dr. Tandy.

"There's something I've got to tell you. It may have a direct bearing on what's going on. You know the guy I'm dating?"

"Yes," replies the doctor with a smile.

"He's consulting with a computer company called ParaVolve out near where the trouble is. We know for a fact that the company is being used for advanced research in molecular biology. And it appears to be hooked up to a lab in Mexico that's synthesizing infectious agents for biological warfare."

"You're not serious?"

"I'm afraid I am."

"Is there a lab up here, too?" asks Dr. Tandy.

"No. But it does seem like an enormous coincidence that something like this would happen right next door to a company involved in covert research on biological warfare."

Dr. Tandy looked across the table at Major Bingham. "I wonder if the major is in a position to help us out."

Before Jessica can answer, Blanchard strides back into the room and stands at the head of the table, holding a map which he is already starting to unfold. "There's been a new development. Two more sites have just been discovered, and it looks like they may be growing at a faster rate than the other," he announces as they all cluster about the map. "One is a couple of miles northeast of the present site, and the other is about the same distance to the southeast."

Blanchard places three circles on the map to mark the infected areas and then looks up. "I've got to leave, but Dr. Tandy, I'd like you to lead the group and keep on working. Can you make arrangements for everyone to stay here at the university?"

"Yes, I can."

"Good. Whatever you people can contribute will be greatly appreciated," says Blanchard, who then turns and heads for the hall, where the state patrol officer and several other people are waiting nervously.

"You probably all have a few phone calls to make, so why don't we break and meet back here in half an hour. I'll make arrangements to have food brought in," Dr. Tandy tells the group.

As they file out, Dr. Tandy calls to Major Bingham, "Major, could I see you for just a moment?"

As he turns toward Tandy, Jessica sees the look of a cornered rodent splash across the major's face. A heavyset man in his forties, with a jowly face and close-cropped hair, the major has obviously been called aside like this more than once in his career. His trapped look segues to weary resignation as he comes around the table.

"Yes, Dr. Tandy?"

Ever the diplomat, Tandy leads gently. "I've heard of your group, Major, and if it's not classified, I just wondered what your particular specialty is."

The major's eyes dart down to the carpet, then back up to Tandy. "Not at all. I'm the institute's chief public affairs officer."

Great Jesus! exclaims Jessica to herself, they didn't even send a fucking *doctor!*

Tandy doesn't miss a beat, and now that Jessica sees him operating in a purely political context, she begins to understand why he has risen so high in the institutional world.

"Well, Major," he says, "there's an issue we'd like to discuss off-line with you, because we don't want to put you in an awkward position in front of the entire group."

Jessica watches as the major unconsciously sucks in his lips and goes slightly pink: a man tensing up to take a stiff left jab right on the tip of the nose.

"We have it on good authority that there's a firm engaged in biological warfare research only a few miles from the site of infection. Obviously it's vital to know if that's the case, and you seem to be the most likely person to help us."

Before Tandy is even finished, the major's normal color comes back and his lips unfold into a small smile. He's off the hook, thinks Jessica. He really doesn't know about ParaVolve.

"First of all, Doctor," starts the major, "because of the nature of the emergency, I have been given the extraordinary power to divulge classified information if I judge that it will help you. Second, I can personally assure you that there is no biological or chemical warfare research facility within seven hundred miles of where we stand."

"Thank you for your candor, Major," says Tandy. "Let's hope you can help us beat this thing."

"Look, Doctor, I was out there today. I saw the same thing you saw, and I'm telling you, we don't have anything that's even on the same planet with whatever's causing that."

"Well, I'm confident you're on our side. You've already made a big contribution with your mobile installations."

The doctor pauses, looks down pensively at the floor, then back at the major. "You know, there's one other thing you might be able to help us with. We may eventually require advice on, well, more *extreme* measures, the kind civilian authorities might be reluctant to consider at this point."

The major's face slides into a low-key chuckle. "You mean like blowing the hell out of it with napalm or something like that? Doesn't work. There's no guarantee that you'll get all the infectious agents. And besides, you create thermals of rising air that lift the surviving germs for a free ride to new homes all over the place."

"I see your point," says Dr. Tandy. "If you'll excuse us now, we've got some arrangements to make."

As the major leaves, Dr. Tandy turns to Jessica. "What do you think? Is he covering up?"

"I think he's telling the truth. He doesn't strike me as being a polished liar, and he seemed very relieved to be off the hook."

"Unfortunately, all it means is that he doesn't know," says Tandy, who moves toward the head of the table, where Blanchard's map is still unfolded. "Can you locate ParaVolve on here?" he asks Jessica.

"It's right here," responds Jessica as she points to the spot where Farmington Road and the Tualatin River intersect.

"Interesting," says Tandy. "The known infection sites form a semicircle around it."

24

XXXXXXX

The New Dogs

"OK, let's get going. Punch in the code."

Julio Gonzales of the MFJP speaks in Spanish to the nervous little man who visibly quivers as he hits the one and two buttons in a combination that takes the elevator inside of Farmacéutico Asociado down instead of up.

Julio grabs a brief moment to congratulate himself on a risky move that promises to pay a handsome dividend. Earlier, he intercepted one of the company's employees in the parking lot, the same diminutive man who now rides down in the elevator with Julio and twelve other agents. Julio slid into the man's car right after he parked, showed his ID, and then told the man that they had "detailed knowledge of the operation inside." He went on to point out that the man was fortunate indeed, because they needed someone to take them into the laboratory, and if the man helped, he might receive immunity from prosecution. When asked if he knew anything about the Mexican prison system, the man nodded quickly. In that case, said Julio, you understand what a precious thing immunity from prosecution might be. Once again, the man nodded rapidly.

Inwardly, Julio was at least as nervous as the man. If he was wrong and the man was an innocent employee of a blameless company, Julio might be in big bureaucratic trouble. But one final question settled the issue: When asked if he would cooperate, the man nodded rapidly for the third and last time.

Julio was immediately on his radio, and two vans swung around and the agents piled out in flak vests, combat boots, and M-17A rifles. Within seconds they were running through an unlocked door next to the loading dock and heading for the elevator. Fortunately, no one saw them enter the elevator, so the surprise would be complete when they reached the laboratory on the bottom floor.

"Remember," says Julio as the elevator sinks to a stop, "stay in pairs. Keep in contact."

The elevator door slides open to an anteroom and an unmanned security post with multiple TV monitors behind a counter. On the ceiling overhead, a camera points directly at the elevator. Beyond, the room stretches into a wide hallway that extends at least fifty yards, with tributary hallways on each side at staggered intervals. As Julio stares down the main corridor, he suddenly worries that his little band has bitten off far more than it can chew, but as he looks up at the overhead monitor camera, he knows they are already committed, and must leverage off the element of surprise as quickly and boldly as possible. He barks a call on the radio for backup, and they sprint through the anteroom and down the hallway.

"Two men to each hall!" he yells just as an alarm begins to whoop. At the first side hall, Julio sees it leads to a set of swinging doors with large windows that reveal people inside running past in white coveralls and sterile caps, with a massive maze of glass tubing and machinery looming in the background. As two agents peel off and head toward the swinging doors, Julio looks ahead just as a man in fatigues pops out with an Uzi. Before the man can bring his weapon to bear, Julio sends off a burst from his M-17A that shudders violently up and down the hall and spins the man into the wall, knocking the weapon out of his hand. The Uzi clatters to the floor and discharges a single round that strikes the agent next to Julio, who drops in a ball of pain, his ankle bone chipped.

"Keep moving!" exhorts Julio, who sees the wound is superficial and that the real danger is getting pinned down in this central hallway with no cover. As they reach the next side hall, Julio glimpses another set of swinging doors and what look like computer displays through the windows. But he can't linger. At the third hall, there are no swinging doors, only a corridor that runs for some thirty yards, with steel doors at three-meter intervals on either side. Here Julio stops as the others rush on.

So what have we here? he thinks as he approaches the first steel door and examines the large dead-bolt lock set into it. He suspects some kind of storage area, and envisions the contents removed and placed in mountainous piles for inspection by the international press, who squirt the story out on to the world cablenets and provide the launchpad that propels Julio's career into the far heights of the government's bureaucracy, maybe even into permanent orbit. Standing to one side to avoid a ricochet, he raises his rifle and blasts out the dead bolt. As the smoke clears, he grasps the handle and swings the door open, but stays pressed against the wall. White light from the room spills silently into the hall, and after a moment, Julio leaps into the door frame with his rifle at the ready, and sees the man, the man that will stay with him forever.

The figure on the cot manages to raise his head just enough so that Julio gets a full view of what is left of his face. The scalp is ulcerated with open sores and the hair reduced to thin little forests that fail to stop the glare of the overhead neon. The nose is missing entirely, and a narrow shoreline of yellow bone and cartilage surrounds the black cavity where it once was. One of the eyes is also gone, along with part of the lid, so the hollow darkness of the socket peeks through and leaks death all over the remnants of the face. The remaining eye sinks a tunnel deep into Julio's psyche, and even after months of psychological counseling, he will still wake up screaming in the night as the eye pleads with him for help and there is nothing he can do. The room is the size of a jail cell, with white walls and terra-cotta tiling that slopes down to a large drain in the center. The only other fixture besides the cot is a coiled hose attached to a faucet on the far wall. Clad only in a large diaper, the man clings to life by a fraying thread, and as he raises his hand in supplication, Julio sees that the bone is exposed down to the first joint on the fingertips, where blue-gray rot forms a null zone between flesh and skeleton, between life and death.

As Julio backs away from the door, the shouting, running, and occasional shooting behind him recede far away into another world, the world of the living. His equilibrium wobbles, and as he fights for his balance and control of his stomach, he feels compelled to act, to do anything. He walks unsteadily to the next metal door in the row, shoots the lock off, and kicks the door open. Before he can see inside, he is off to the next. And the next. And the next. If he can just keep walking, shooting, and kicking, maybe he will be all right. Just keep walking, shooting, and kicking, walking, shooting, and kicking. . . .

The blast of the gunshot turns the walls of Emil Cortez's cell a brilliant red and slaps him hard across the face. His ears become explosive balloons that expand to crush his brain, and a volcanic eruption of gray matter spouts from the top of his head. As the balloons deflate, the red slides off the walls and down the tiling into the drain at the center, and then tiles themselves slide down the drain, and then the cot, and then his body up to his head. The world cracks and splits as a towering rectangle flies open and his body squirts out of the drain and drifts out into the infinite space beyond that fills the rectangle. BOOM! The hall walls shudder and go bright red under the impact of another gunshot, and Emil sees a flickering shape kick savagely and punch a hole into the wall, which comes to life and howls in protest. He turns and flees.

Lamar Spelvin does not hear the alarm from the inner sanctum of the P4 containment area, where he is admiring his latest handiwork, even though it is completely invisible. He is hot and uncomfortable in the suit, and there is a slight fog on the faceplate of his helmet, beneath his nose; nevertheless, to enter the P4 containment area without the suit is unthinkable, especially after the recent fiasco with the computer, which had failed to sound the alarm when a sterilization system malfunctioned during a viral synthesis operation. Fortunately, there were no reports of exotic illness nearby, so apparently they had avoided a catastrophe.

Spelvin holds a hermetically sealed beaker with a clear liquid and tries to visualize what is going on inside just a couple of steps above the molecular level. Then, through the liquid, he sees the distorted shape of a human figure, and lowers the beaker for a better look. A man with a baseball cap, an M-17A, and a bright red flak jacket is staring at him from the hallway.

Don't shoot! Lamar screams silently as he stands frozen, beaker in hand. Two layers of glass separate him from the man. One is the observation window in the hallway. The second, a window set in the wall of the inner room, in the containment structure. The man disappears from the hall window, only to reappear coming in the automatic sliding door to the outer room of the containment structure.

Don't shoot! Lamar screams it again inside his head as the man moves cautiously forward and sees the rack where the suits hang limp against the wall by the airlock. If the man fires a gun into the inner room, there is a good chance it will hit some of the containers on the storage rack behind Lamar. If the containers burst, they will liberate a fantastic army of disease, which will waft through the secondary defenses of the outer room, out the wall window, and into history. The problem is that Lamar will become a part of that history, a small part, but the only part that really concerns him. Sooner or later the air will run out in the suit, and he will have to remove the helmet and take a breath of the soiled air, and then . . .

A second figure comes through the sliding door, wild-eyed and clad only in a diaper, and charges directly at the armed man, who turns away from the suits in complete surprise.

The wall opens and Emil flies through into the chamber, where the butcher stands in his bloody vest and the limp white bodies sag off the meat hooks behind him. Emil flies like a hawk at the butcher. He must sink his talons into this monster or he will soon hang bloodless from one of the hooks.

Just before the figure collides with the armed man, Lamar realizes that it is one of the specimens from the Zap series, one of the permanent psychotics. As the figure's head butts into the other man's chest, an arm flies out, the arm holding the rifle.

Don't shoot! The muzzle flash, the punch of the report, and the shatter of the inner containment window fuse into a single event for Lamar. The next thing he notices is a peculiar sensation, the sudden and complete absence of pressure from the beaker in his hand. As he turns and looks, he sees it is no longer there. But where did it go? How could it just suddenly disappear?

Then the dampness on the chest and belly of his suit worms its way into his senses, along with a freezing heat. Because of the respirator helmet, he can't look down, so he turns to a second window to get a reflection of his front side, and sees the continents of red encroaching on the sea of white. He slowly sinks to the floor as the truth of the matter pushes him down with a weight beyond mortal measure. In the outer room, the armed man is still struggling to get a pair of handcuffs on the Zap specimen, while a new alarm sounds, triggered by the break in the containment area, and the door to the hallway automatically slides locked and shut. But Lamar is oblivious to this commotion as he gently swipes a gloved hand over his chest and looks at the resulting swatch of blood from where the exploding beaker ripped his suit, then his flesh. He needs medical attention, he realizes, and then laughs out loud at the horrible

irony of this observation. Medical attention. Sure. That's what he needs.
If only they knew. If only they had a full understanding of what was in
the beaker and was now working its way through his insides. If only they
had been present at the autopsies he had performed on the victims of the
beaker juice, which is absolutely novel in viral content. To be sure, the
virus was inspired work, and like all great science, had sprung from a
simple observation, the presence of a wart on the finger of one of his
specimens. All that day, the wart had come back to nag him, the idea of
a little community of rampant cells able to sink roots into the skin and
leisurely explore neighboring regions, maybe even set up satellite communities. And then, the image of the wart, a rude little crater filled with
ground white flesh, merged with the image of a human brain, and he had
it. A brain wart. A wart growing and prospering on the cerebral surface,
sending roots down to probe deep into the neural jungle, to trigger ca-
tastrophes beyond imagination. He had worked on the project for several years in his spare time, a hobby almost. Even now, he recalls the
elation he felt when he removed the top of the skull of the first test
subject and saw the size and robustness of the wart, nearly two inches in
diameter and rooted all the way down to the brain stem.

So now Lamar Spelvin sits on the floor and meditates on the image of
the wart, which he knows will take only a few days to establish itself inside
his skull, but several months to plant its root system. During this time, he
will go mad. At the same time, he will lose control of his voluntary nervous
system, much like the superkuru victims from one of his more recent
projects. Worst of all, he has seen it all in advance. Every detail, every nu-
ance stretches out before him on a shiny black highway of terror.

Julio walks cautiously toward the end of the main hallway. He struggles
to maintain his presence of mind and keep a lid on the latter-day Dachau
he has just witnessed. The prisoners are queued for the ride up in the
elevator, and all his men are accounted for except one, so now he must
check this last door on the right-hand side, which has a flashing sign
above it. A new alarm started whooping a few minutes ago, and now, as
he approaches the door, he can see why. In red letters on white plastic,
the sign flashes "INNER CONTAINMENT BREACHED" into the empty hall. As he
moves to a window next to the door, one of his agents comes into sight
on the other side of the glass, along with an emaciated man who strug-

gles against plastic cuffs that bind his wrists behind his back. The agent moves up to the window surface with a frightened face, and tries to yell something through the glass, but Julio cannot hear him over the alarm noise. In the background, Julio can see the suits, the airlock, the shattered window, the rows of beakers.

In his fifteen years in narcotics enforcement, Julio has seen many a drug lab. Primitive coke-processing plants in remote jungles. Meth labs in shabby basements. Heroin operations in stately mansions.

This is not a drug lab. This is something else entirely.

As he waits in the phone booth, Michael is already anticipating the monumental hassle he will have in getting back to the Romona Arms. Already, the traffic on Tualatin Valley Highway is backed up for miles, all the way to Hillsboro, where he now stands in the open booth outside a Safeway, where the parking lot is nearly deserted. In the disturbing silence, he tries to construct a chain of back roads that will get him home without entering the mainstream. Up and down the main drag of the county seat, only a few cars roll by, and foot traffic is nonexistent. The town is only three miles from the nearest site of what the press was now calling the "Mutant Zone," even though there is no scientific evidence to support this particular moniker. Clearly, the community is on the edge of mass civil panic, although there has been no official acknowledgment of any danger. And how could there be? thinks Michael. The moment the authorities recommend evacuation, they will set in motion a stampede that will most certainly extend to the entire Portland metropolitan area. It won't be a simple matter, like flood or hurricane victims resting comfortably on cots, eating box lunches in high school gyms or Guard armories—not with 2 million people involved.

A ring interrupts and sounds unnaturally loud in the quiet parking lot as Michael picks up the receiver.

"Hi. How are things?" asks Gail.

"Not so good. I'm in a town just a few miles from the main action, and everybody's decided to cut and run."

"Can you get out OK?" Gail sounds genuinely worried.

"I can manage. What's up?"

"I just got a call from a contact at the DEA. Yesterday afternoon, the Mexican narcs raided Farmacéutico Asociado and found out it's a lot more than just a dope factory. I guess it's a real horror story. There's bound to be an international scandal."

"Think that'll turn the tide in Washington? From what I see on the tube, we're pretty close to the goose-stepping past the Lincoln Memorial."

"Who knows?" sighs Gail. "Anyway, at least we've done what we can. The whole business will be out in the open in no time, including the links to VenCap and ParaVolve. And what about your little local plant problem? Do you think there's a connection?"

"One would certainly think so."

"If I were you, I'd get out. Right now. Take care of yourself, Michael. Let me know you're OK."

"I will. You do the same." He wants to say more, but it will lead them down avenues neither wants to travel, not now, not ever. "Bye now."

As he hangs up, Michael gazes out into the empty parking lot, where a single shopping cart sits among the fading stall lines on an acre of blacktop. So it's over. At least the political side. But what about the net? Somehow, someway, there's a connection between Mouthball and the so-called Mutant Zone.

Michael sighs as he starts toward his truck. He can't quit now. He has to know.

Jimi's dad is perfect. He knows it at once, and tells Mouthball so. "That's it. We're done." On the screen, the image has the slightly humanoid cast of its computer origin, but somehow this enhances its heroic quality and elevates it to a pop pantheon that floats high above Jimi in some obscure media ether. The naturally barbered hair flexes into a pleasing wave of brown, while the chin juts forward in a fearless thrust and the brown eyes project power, compassion, and purpose. The flight suit with its countless zippers, the robotic hand with its winking LEDs, and the large holstered pistol are the ideal complements to the image, which rotates slowly like a statue on a potter's wheel.

Jimi recalls the moment in the mini-mall parking lot where he last saw his dad and the helicopter gunship shuddering off into the night. The scene is unmoored and drifts between dream and reality in his memory, but either way, the picture of his dad is diamond hard, and Mouthball has pulled it out of Jimi bit by bit and carefully shaped it right before his eyes. An intense longing wells up in him to walk into the screen, to stand where his dad can stoop down and effortlessly scoop him up with the robotic arm, and empower him through a wink and smile that will fuel him for years to come.

"Whoops," interrupts Mouthball, who floats to one side of the stationary dad. "Me gotta go now."

"How come?" asks Jimi. In a way, he would like to be alone with his dad, but it will be lonesome without Mouthball. When Jimi came over this morning, he conned Michael into letting him stay, even though Michael had to take off and go somewhere to make a phone call. He wasn't supposed to let anyone in, except for Jessica or Savage, but neither of them had come by.

"Got to take care of some business. I'll be back before you know it," explains Mouthball, who then weaves to the back of his living room and disappears out the door.

Jimi gazes at Mouthball's empty living room behind the inanimate dad and wonders where Mouthball goes when he wanders out the door. On the screen, it is simply a black space, and while Jimi knows it must be a tunnel to some other world, he can't imagine its contents. He leans back in his chair and feels a blanket of boredom start to wrap lightly around him. He can't go out, because the Rat Bag is now patrolling in force and he runs the risk of being apprehended. Maybe there's something on TV in the living room. He rises and is going through the door when he hears the voice.

"Hey, little fella. Aren't you forgetting something?"

Jimi freezes. Without even turning to look, he knows the source of the voice. His dad.

As Jimi looks back over his shoulder, his dad looks out of the screen at him with a supremely confident smile and winks. Inside Jimi, a remarkable brew of joy, sadness, and elation threatens to boil over and leak out as tears. But it won't happen. It's not the kind of thing you do in front of your dad when you haven't seen him for forever and want to show him what a cool customer you are. Still, his voice is choked off, but somehow his dad seems to understand and fills right in.

"Why don't you come on over here so I can get a good look at you. Jeez! You're about twice as big as I thought you'd be. It's been a long time, hasn't it?"

Jimi nods. His dad walks over and sits on the arm of Mouthball's couch, and the screen zooms to keep the picture tight on his chest and head.

"Look, I know you've got a lot of questions, and I'd say it's about time I gave you some answers."

"You don't have to give me any answers," blurts out Jimi as his voice returns. "I know you've been really busy. I know it's real important."

"Well, it's more than just that," says his dad as he stops and sighs. "In case no one has told you yet, there's some really bad people out there."

Jimi nods and thinks of Rat Bag, and the hideous man at the foot of the stairs.

"There aren't many of us who'll stand up to those people, Son," continues Jimi's dad. "Most folks like to just sit on the sidelines and keep out of it. But you can't really blame them. It's not easy. You can get hurt. I know. I've been hurt a lot of times. But there's no way I'm going to give up. You know why?"

"Why?"

"You," replies Jimi's dad as he points his trigger finger right at Jimi.

"Me?"

"Yeah, you. Because you're the most important thing to me in the whole world. And that means I've got to make sure the world's a safe place for you to live—even if it means I've got to be apart from you."

"Dad, how did you get inside the computer? Why can't you come out here?"

Jimi's dad shifts his weight forward and puts his elbows on his knees. "Well, it's a pretty complicated story. But let me tell you as best I can. There was a certain secret organization that wanted to take over the world and make everybody into slaves. My mission was to get into their headquarters, which was inside a mountain, and find out exactly what their plan was. When I finally got in, I found the place was ruled by this scientist that ran a huge computer where they kept their plan. But something went wrong, and they knocked me out with sleeping gas, and when I woke up, my body was gone and I was inside the computer."

"Your body is *gone?*" interrupts Jimi in amazement.

"Not completely. They've got it frozen back inside the mountain, and someday I'll go back and get it. But to escape, I broke out of the computer jail and took off over the networks. That's when I ran into your friend Mouthball, and he invited me to come live inside his computer. He said it was plenty big for both of us, and he's right."

Jimi hears the front door open as Michael returns from Hillsboro. "Jimi? You still here?" he calls as he starts down the hall.

As Jimi pops out into the hall, the excitement is written all over him. "There's someone here you've got to meet!" he exclaims.

For an anxious second, Michael thinks Jimi has let somebody into the apartment and showed them the computer link to the net and DEUS, but as he looks into the room at the image on the screen, his fear fades.

"Michael Riley, this is my dad," announces Jimi. "He got locked up inside the computer with Mouthball, but that's a long story."

"Michael, good to meet you," says Jimi's dad as he rises from the couch arm. "I'd like to shake hands, but I guess that'll have to wait until later."

"I guess it will," agrees Michael, who wonders exactly what is going on. Then he remembers that Mouthball and Jimi were working earlier on a crude version of what he now sees as an almost uncomfortably accurate emulation of a real person. "Jimi, something very important has come up and I need to talk to your dad in secret. Know what I mean?"

"But I want to talk to him some more," protests Jimi.

"Don't worry, Son," soothes Jimi's dad as he sits back down on the couch arm. "This will just take a minute, and then I'm all yours."

"All right," sighs Jimi, who heads down the hall. When he hears the front door close, Michael turns to Jimi's dad.

"Didn't catch your name," he says cynically.

"Didn't offer it," says Jimi's dad with a mirthful grin.

"Maybe it's time we got back to basics, Mr. Mouthball," suggests Michael.

"Maybe it is, Mr. Riley," shoots back Jimi's dad, who slowly leans forward until his entire face fills the screen. Then a solitary ball of pearly liquid floats down out of the dad's right nostril and into the foreground, where it quickly transforms into the familiar features of Mouthball.

"You've gone too far this time," says Michael as the anger rises inside him.

"And how far is that?" asks Mouthball, with the frozen face of Jimi's dad towering behind him like a theatrical backdrop.

"The kid doesn't have a dad. It's the biggest sore spot in his whole life. And now you come along with a phony facade that's got his hopes up."

"There's nothing phony about the facade," rebuts Mouthball. "It's built precisely to young Jimi's specifications. We've spent a lot of time to make sure every detail is perfect."

"Doesn't matter," says Michael. "It's still a facade. And the minute you're gone, it's gone, too. And then what?"

"What makes you think I'm going to be gone?" asks Mouthball. "Just where might I go to? Retire to some comfy old mainframe in Cleveland, maybe?"

Michael is taken aback by the net's rhetorical performance. What can he say? It appears that the net has developed some kind of expectations about its life span, and unlike humans, it doesn't have to suffer the irreversible effects of long-term cellular degeneration. As long as the DEUS site is properly maintained, Mouthball might outlive them all. Of course, given the march of the Mutant Zone, the longevity of the DEUS Complex was now open to speculation, but that was another matter entirely.

"I see your point," concedes Michael, "but still, it might be nice for Jimi to eventually have a father who is part of the outside world."

"My research indicates that the outside world is full of fathers who aren't doing very well at all with their kids," says Mouthball. "But still, you have something there. How about a father like this. . . ."

Mouthball's entire facial topography suddenly goes into a violent upheaval, and swings through many variations on some grotesque theme, before settling into a new stability that sends a shudder through Michael. He is looking at himself. A perfect replica of the head of Michael Riley, right down to the current state of his whiskers and tousled hair. And to slam the effect home, the lips part and the voice that comes out is his voice.

"I rather like it," says the new Mouthball Riley. "I think Jimi might, too. Of course, you don't quite have the heroic dimensions of his current dad, but we all learn to make compromises, so this could be an object lesson for him. What do you think?"

Michael doesn't know.

Little Timmy Grimaldi is the seventh child so far this afternoon. He wipes a dirty hand over a runny nose as he plods along under a troubled sky that presses a flat light against the parking lot pavement. He's following Rat Bag toward the Dumpster down at the end of the carport. To a six-year-old, Rat Bag towers like a reptilian predator with terrible and capricious

powers. Timmy had been snagged a little earlier by a roving patrol as he
played cars out back in the dirt by the vacant lot, and delivered to Rat Bag,
who held court in the bushes nearby. Now he walks in silent fear under
the cloud of the Rat Bag legends, under a sentence of terror.

Rat Bag does not turn to see if Timmy is following, because he knows
the child is bound to him as surely as if he were on a leash. As they approach the baked brown metal wall of the Dumpster, Rat Bag thinks back
to how this incredible piece of divine intervention began. He was in the
vacant lot around noon, sitting alone on the ground and staring at a thistle
plant and admiring its spiked arrogance. From the trailer court, he could
smell barbecued wieners as an occasional bumblebee buzzed by on its
cosmic journey of pollination. He absently jabbed his thumb into a rip in
the sole of his sneakers and spread the rubberized wound far up toward
the tip. Since the pool fiasco with Jimi, he came here often now to brood
in isolation. Large cracks were piercing his organization, starting with
Zipper, who realized that if Jimi had drowned, it was he, Zipper, that
would have been the prime suspect. He had not openly confronted Rat
Bag, but it was obvious that Zipper was now outside the normal sphere of
influence, obedient and agreeable in a very stingy sort of way that telegraphed his feelings of betrayal. Rat Bag had exposed him to jeopardy in
the world outside the Romona tribe, the big world where Rat Bag could
not save him. And in a ripple effect, the subtle shift in Zipper's attitude was
cascading down through the ranks and threatening the entire order in a
soft, flexible kind of way that was difficult to confront.

But in spite of these troubles, Rat Bag knew that the soaring moment
when he turned his back on Jimi in the pool was more than worth the
current mess. In fact, it was now a source of great consolation, because
he knew he was no longer restrained by conventional rules, and could be
infinitely more creative in subduing the demons that danced before him.
As he sat cross-legged in the grass and traced a circle in a bare patch of
earth, the noontime solitude was pierced by the startled squeal of brakes.

Rat Bag jumped to his feet, and turned in the direction of the sound.
Through the bushes, he could see the two-lane street to the rear of the
Romona, where an old station wagon was pulling off the road just ahead
of a pair of telltale skid marks that left shiny black ribbons. The door
opened and a heavy man in overalls labored to get out. Once on his feet,
he teetered slightly and scratched his grizzled gray hair as he waddled
back in the direction of the skid marks. Every so often, he would stop

and peer into the brush on the shoulder of the road as if he were looking for something. The second time the man stopped to look, the light went on in Rat Bag: The man had hit something, and now he was trying to find what it was. As he watched, the man continued his search to the beginning of the skid marks and then back to the car, where he grunted down into a squat to check the undercarriage to see if it had dragged anything. Finally, he stood up and carefully looked in a full circle to make sure there were no witnesses, climbed in, and drove off in a blue cloud of oily exhaust.

As the station wagon disappeared, Rat Bag left his concealed position and threaded his way along a path that cut through the thick bushes in the center of the large lot and came out in an area of tall grass mixed with patches of shrubs near the road's shoulder. The air was still and hot as he waded across the grass, where grasshoppers whizzed in brief arcs, and onto the graveled shoulder of the road, where a warm rubber smell still drifted up from the skid marks. By now Rat Bag realized that the man should have looked for something upstream from the skid marks, not downstream—but then again, maybe the man didn't really want to find anything at all. Rat Bag walked for about ten yards up the road from the skids, carefully surveying the brush and tall grass off the shoulder, and saw nothing. So he climbed back down off the road, walked about ten feet into the grass, and started back.

Rat Bag nearly stepped on the carcass before he saw it in the high grass at his feet. A quiver of revulsion pulsed through him as he looked at the overturned body of the driller, with its six insect legs poking out of a huge egg-shaped shell. Part of the head was crushed from the impact with the car, and a dark yellow fluid foamed out onto the ground. Still, one very humanlike eye remained, and stared coldly at Rat Bag as he circled the carcass. The saw-hole beak in the center of the head still held the pink and red pulp of whatever had been its last meal, and fortunately for Rat Bag, its viral vents had constricted shut after the collision with the car.

Rat Bag moved away, broke a stick off a nearby shrub, and returned to use it as a lever to turn the driller back over. When he poked it over onto its belly and saw the large vents with tiny wings, he knew this was something very weird, something like the grown-ups were watching on the TV news and talking about in very edgy tones. But there were no grown-ups here now. Only him. And the carcass was his to do with as he wished. It took only a moment for him to decide what that wish was.

Twenty minutes later, he had the carcass inside a plastic garbage bag, which he was dragging over the trail back to the Romona Arms. The entrance of this horrible thing into his life could not have been more perfect. It would now become the central figure in a reenactment of the original ceremony that had earned Rat Bag his name, when a score of terrified children had been forced to bear witness to the dead rat he had drowned in the pool. Now this driller would become the ultimate talisman in a triumphant reaffirmation of his rightful position at the Romona, in an intimate ceremony in the hidden space between the Dumpster and the fence.

"Back here," points Rat Bag as he and Timmy approach the shabby temple where each believer is forced to go. The space is only about a yard wide and never sees daylight, so the pavement is damp, and covered by patches of rotten paper and junk packaging. Crude pornographic drawings cover the brown metal wall of the Dumpster on one side and the bleached wood of the fence on the other, along with a primitive parade of obscene epithets. Rat Bag blocks Timmy's view until they reach the far end of the space, and then suddenly moves aside when Timmy is within a yard of the driller, which is propped up between two cardboard boxes so its one remaining eye directly confronts the child.

Timmy shows absolutely no emotion as he looks at the driller, but Rat Bag is used to this by now, and recognizes it as a form of shock far deeper than screaming or running. The youngster is quite literally paralyzed with fear, and Rat Bag smiles with approval as he sees the urine spot appear in the crotch of Timmy's jeans and expand outward toward the legs.

"OK, guy," he says to Timmy as he reaches out and turns him around to leave, "let's not forget what we saw here. And let's not forget that these things are my pets. And you know what that means? *It means they'll do anything I tell them to!* So if you tell any grown-ups about this, you just might have one of these things hold you down and drill a hole right through your gut. Now let's get out of here."

In his apartment, Jimi watches through a crack in the curtains as Rat Bag emerges from behind the Dumpster with the small and stunned figure of Timmy Grimaldi. When Jimi left Michael Riley's unit, he saw the pair marching in solemn procession toward the carport and Dumpster, and quickly raced down the walkway and the far stairs so he could escape the patrols that must be out in force. Now he is doubly glad he made it home safely. Whatever is going on back there is bad, even on the Rat Bag scale.

"Hey, little boy, how come you're peeking out the window?"

Zodia giggles and reaches down the couch to try to grab his leg. Jimi knows it will do no good to tell her about what is going on outside. She will not comprehend, just as she doesn't currently comprehend that she is his mother. On the coffee table, he sees the open blister pack, the pipe, and the vinegar solution, which have all just assisted in the dissolution of her mortally wounded memory.

Zodia springs abruptly to her feet and rides a rail of nervous energy around the living room, nodding to herself in agreement with some internal dialogue. After a few edgy revolutions, she grabs her leather jacket, which is draped over one of the dining room chairs, and slides into it. She grins at Jimi.

"Nice fit, huh? Lucky deal. I'll bring it back later, OK?" She moves closer to Jimi and straps on a faint frown. "Your mother know you're here?"

Deep inside, Jimi feels the last of the moorings snap that bound him to his mom. They break with a terrible twinge, but just as suddenly, the pain vanishes.

"Yeah. She knows," he lies.

"Good. Well, I'll see you later. I got some stuff I want to check out."

Zodia scoops up a pack of cigarettes and heads out the door. From the couch by the window, Jimi watches her stroll across the parking lot and head for the street. She'll never be back. He sees it in a fireball of intuition, the kind granted to most people only a few times in their entire life.

But as the fireball subsides, there is no panic that rushes in to fill the vacuum. Because he has his dad. Trapped in the computer, for sure, but right here at the Romona, just a few doors away. And somehow, someway, his dad will know how to take care of Rat Bag.

In the squirming green depths of Lonnie Johnson's former strawberry field, a large earthen mound is totally concealed by the frantic growth that slithers up and over it, blocking out the clear night sky, where Sagittarius hangs like a tea kettle near the southern horizon, its spout pointing the way to the heart of the galaxy. Like the mounds before it, it is a factory humming with a mad metamorphosis that spews out heat and fumes through venting holes where warm and twisted odors broadcast detailed instructions to the swarm of needle hounds that have fanned out around the mound in a defensive perimeter. The fumes announce that the latest dreadnought in the imperial intron fleet is on the verge of being launched, a creation with the power and range to close the gaps in the Mutant Zone, spreading an ambitious trail of infection through its viral vents as it goes. In the blackness beneath the canopy, the air quivers with the buzz, clicks, and hums of a biological infrastructure running at a suicidal pace, rapidly depleting nutrients near the surface and thrusting roots ever deeper in search of new water and fuel. A foot under the soil, a thing with a steel-hard shell and a drill-head snout fires torpedo worms, which burn through the soil and strike another thing, a bulbous mass that floats in a cushion of mucus. Directly above, a tubular plant the size of a garden hose twists around a thick ball covered with small tentacles, and thrusts its suction snout into the center of the ball, sending the tentacles into an undulating frenzy. At the top of the plant canopy, a hovering helibug is knocked out by a small winged insect that burrows into a crack in its scales and deposits thousands of eggs that will hatch within minutes and then consume the helibug from the inside out.

In the center of it all, the mound shudders slightly and the top is sheared off like a volcano as the latest creature pops out. Later, the media will call it a medugator, a cross between the snake hair of Medusa and the body of an alligator. Indeed, the thickly muscled torso is six feet in length and covered with scales as tough as any synthetic armor, with four stout legs that end in clawed feet, and a tail that curves up and forward like a scorpion's and terminates in a hypodermic stinger. The head has two humanlike eyes mounted on headlight pods, and two similar pods housing exquisitely sensitive infrared eyes cooled by the organic equivalent of a heat pump. The mouth appears ridiculous, like the mouth of a bullfrog, except much larger—until it opens and forms a large circle and the snakelike tongues come rushing out a full yard past the end of the body, scores of them, with a variety of heads dedicated to piercing, ripping, slashing, and sucking.

The medugator shakes off the dirt from the mound and sets off through the pitch-black undergrowth, guided by the rich thermal image registered on its infrared eyes. It spots a needle hound, and in a surge of motion moves within striking distance, opens its mouth, and the flurry of snakes fly out and begin their carefully orchestrated butchery, which consumes the entire beast in under two minutes.

Now, with all its systems properly calibrated, the medugator breaks out of the jungle at the edge of the field and surveys the scene in both visible and infrared light. In the distance, the engines of vehicles glow white around their darker outlines. Creatures with metal objects walk around the vehicles and in the surrounding fields. But the introns that drive the medugator know that the creatures are prone to error, especially in the dark, and will be relatively easy to avoid.

The goddamn dogs. They're at it again.

Cynthia Price loves her bear hounds, all ten of them. Since her husband, Ed, died, they have been a source of great consolation, even though they irritate at moments like this, when they burst into a lathered chorus of sustained barking in a canine version of spontaneous combustion. In a few minutes they will stop, and she will be able to direct her attention back to the old reruns of *Arsenio Hall.* Even though their pen is twenty feet away from the house, it sounds like they are right inside, barking at Arsenio himself.

The medugator has traveled fast and expended great amounts of energy, so the tight cluster of creatures in the pen is an attractive fuel source. A cautionary scan shows a large structure beyond the pen, with several bright energy sources but no visible motion, so the medugator moves on toward the pen.

Cynthia's ears pick up an elevation in the pitch of the dog's barking and howling, a peak frenzy she has never heard before. On the TV, a commercial comes on. Well, hell, she mutters to herself, better go take a look. She slides into her mule slippers and pushes her chubby body up out of Ed's easy chair, wincing at the arthritis in her left ankle.

At close range, the medugator has appraised the creatures in the pen as being an optimum food type, and raises its front clawed foot to rip open the chicken-wire barrier.

As Cynthia reaches the back door, the barking rises to an even higher pitch, almost a shrieking, and the cool breath of primal fear runs through her. She backs up from the door and heads for the gun case in the living room to fetch a shotgun. Something is wrong out there. Badly wrong.

As the hounds pour out of the hole in the pen, the medugator backs off to gain the correct angle of attack on the last dog out. Already, many of the other hounds are nipping at its legs and flanks in a futile attack that is like trying to bite through Teflon. The medugator completes its calculations and opens its mouth just as the last hound jumps out and exposes its belly in midleap. The surgical snakes snap out and instantly assault the dog in dozens of locations, causing it to emit a horrible shriek that erupts over the top of all the other commotion.

It takes Cynthia a moment to remember how to chamber a shell in the rifle, and she hears the shriek rip through the night just as she finishes. She looks toward the back door and hesitates, but then shuffles stubbornly forward. Something is hurting her dogs, and no matter how awful it is, she is maternally bound to protect them. Besides, it can't be anything worse than her imagination.

The other hounds now surround the medugator and dive in to nip ineffectually at its armored scales. The assaulted dog is limp on its back as the medugator's oral snake team works on it with masterful efficiency, cutting, sawing, ripping, boring, and sucking in a horrible harmony that leaves not a single drop of blood on the ground. Already, the entrails have been consumed and the sternum opened so the other soft tissues can be sucked out, while a separate snake team strips the shoulder muscles off the bone.

Cynthia flips on the floodlights and opens the door just wide enough to get a view of the dogs. At first, the medugator doesn't even register with her, a defensive act of denial that passes immediately as she stares at the rear end of the creature with its squat, clawed legs and upturned stinger tail. Then she sees that it has one of her dogs down, her dear dogs, and screams at the thing, a wild and primitive scream that causes the thing to stop and turn toward her, its mouth still open and the snake team still dripping blood.

The medugator stares at the figure on the porch landing with its binocular eyes, and sees that it is clearly biological and bipedal in origin, which excludes it as a target of opportunity. But at the same time, it observes that the figure has some kind of nonbiological extension, and hard-wired neural sequences sound the alarm and activate the flight procedure. It withdraws its serpent appendages and twists to sprint off toward the nearest area of concealment within its peripheral vision, the darkness of an open field.

Cynthia already has the rifle to her shoulder by the time the medugator closes its mouth, and she lets loose both barrels in its direction as it moves toward the darkness with amazing speed and the hounds bound after it in hot pursuit. She sinks to the porch steps as the noise of the dogs recedes into the night. In the confusion, she caught a glimpse of the downed dog, but is not ready to face it yet. Then another awful shriek flies out of the distant darkness. Somewhere out there, the thing is vivisecting another one of her hounds.

When the medugator is finished with its second victim, it sprints across the open field at a speed the pursuing hounds cannot hope to match, and scales a wire fence that will stop them cold. An infrared scan turns up bright spots from burrows and nests, but no other signs of activity. Yellow fluid is leaking where one group of shotgun pellets managed to strike an unprotected area, the joint where the leathery leg joins to the armored body. The pellets have perforated several internal organs and caused the creature to shut down nonvital systems, including the viral reservoirs and vents that sow the seeds of transformation. The fluid loss also forces some of the higher nervous functions into a holding pattern, including those that detail independent navigation. Instead of cruising at will through uninfected territory, the medugator will have to rely on beacons left by other members of the intron fold that have strayed into virgin lands. And now the medugator's nostril ports pick up an aromatic trail left by an injured needle hound, possibly maimed in a fight with the same dogs.

The medugator follows the trail over the open field toward the bright constellation of halogen streetlamps that hugs the horizon. As it moves closer, dogs start to bark, and the medugator finds that the scent trail winds around the periphery of a housing development and across a wooded area, where it stops to devour an unfortunate tom cat out on a late-night prowl. Next, the trail causes it to traverse a large parking lot, and weave between several warehouses before mounting a railroad track, which provides a private and unobstructed path through the hot night. After several miles, the scent trail leaves the tracks and wobbles down a drainage ditch that flows alongside a major arterial for more than a mile. As the medugator follows this scent map through the mud and refuse collected in the ditch, an occasional firestorm of barking flares from nearby backyards. But then the scent leaves the ditch and crosses a two-lane road, where it ends in the tall grass of the vacant lot next to the Romona Arms. Its infrared eyes pick up the coming warmth of dawn, and it moves on into the deeper brush, where it will conserve energy and wait for the next cycle of darkness before it travels any further.

25

XXXXXX

Like Locusts

Rat Bag hits it on the third key, which until last night resided in the purse of Zipper's mother. It slides smoothly into the keyhole on the door handle of Jimi's apartment and comes to rest fully inserted. Good. He stands off to the side, and the late-morning sun paints a squat shadow of him across the door, a black condensed Rat Bag tilted far off center. From his belt he withdraws a hammer, and after a gingerly practiced tap, he swings with malice and drives the key permanently into the lock. He hums to himself and comes around to face the lock and complete his twisted piece of craft. Once again, a practice tap, then a carefully engineered swing that shears the head of the key where it meets the lock and sends it pinging down the walkway. He squats to survey his handiwork and smiles at the shiny jagged piece of metal that permanently seals the lock. He completely ignores the people in the parking lot and carport behind him. No one will notice what he's doing. They're all too paranoid, too worried about getting while the getting is still good. In the carport, two thirds of the cars are already gone, and most of the rest have trunks or hatchbacks open as people stuff in those hastily selected items that are dearest to them. A portrait of Grandma, a Chinese vase, a bowling trophy, a leather overcoat, a television. There is a minimum of conversation, and Rat Bag can sense the fear brimming in the holes of silence as well as in the hushed talk. Most people here had watched TV far into the night and heard that the Mutant Zone, as the press called it, was now spreading in a vast circle, already some ten miles in diameter. In the center it was a solid mass of plants and animals, with a concentration denser than even the most torrid of equatorial jungles. Toward the periphery the needle hounds and the medugators led the advance like some kind of Typhoid Marys from hell, and in their path, islands of vegetation would erupt and then eventually grow together. There was already horrifying footage shot from helicopters of entire neighborhoods being surrounded in the dark, with spotlights showing people on their roofs, where they sought shelter against the flooding biomass around them. Other shots showed sick people wandering stunned in the streets with novel and disturbing symptoms: a face frozen in a permanent yawn, a neck cloaked in bumps the size of marbles, a nose covered with coarse black hair.

Now Rat Bag can feel the scene in the parking lot perk along just below the panic threshold, and understands intuitively that the forces which have bound him for so long are rapidly dissipating. There will be no cops, no parents, no law, no credible witnesses, no artificial barriers between thought and action. It is happening so quickly, he struggles to adjust his points of reference to keep up. The current state of affairs seems custom-crafted to complement his plan, a plan that started forming early this morning when he heard old Mrs. Nimitz call for her poodle at the edge of the walkway that abutted the vacant lot.

"Here, Chester. Here, Chester," called Mrs. Nimitz with an utter lack of conviction, while somewhere out in the lot, Chester barked in a stumbling cadence full of agitation. Rat Bag was immediately reminded of the fabulous totem of power he had found yesterday in the form of the dead thing. Had the dog discovered a new prize? Only one way to find out. He ambled on up to a surprised and incredulous Mrs. Nimitz and told her he would go look for Chester, and walked off into the lot, homing in on the pulsating beacon produced by the dog's barking. Soon he was deep in the lot and approached a place he called simply the Circle, a thick growth of shrubs with a clear grassy center less than ten feet in diameter. The only way in was a tunnel, part natural and part forged by Rat Bag, and now he bent over and stared down its length. At the end, he could see the brief expanse of grass and light, which terminated in the dark wall of bushes on the other side of the little clearing. No doubt about it. The barking was coming from inside. He went onto his hands and knees, crawled down the twelve feet of tunnel, and very cautiously poked his head out the other end. There was Chester in a rigid stance, with head erect and legs slightly splayed, as he fired off one bark after another at a single point in the dark wall of bushes, which was over five feet high. So what the hell's the dog barking at? Rat Bag eased out of the tunnel and walked up slowly behind Chester, who was completely oblivious to him, and sighted along the line of the dog's bark.

Thinking back, he realizes that it took him a minute to recognize the outline of the thing because it was so completely alien, horrible, and ridiculous at the same time. Set back in the bushes, the huge head spanned nearly two feet, with a scowling slit of a frog's mouth and human-looking eyes set in pods attached to stems emanating from the skull. The thing was completely motionless, and Rat Bag thought it might be dead, but then one of the eyes blinked. As the features snapped into place in his mind, Rat Bag felt his skin crawl and an impulsive urge to flee ballooned in his brain, but he held his ground and carefully picked up the dog, which continued to launch an endless salvo of barks at the thing.

As he carried the squirming dog back to Mrs. Nimitz, he felt a wonderful surge of excitement about this new discovery. What he had started yesterday with the dead thing, he would finish today with this thing. And while the show yesterday was open to a wide audience, today's presentation would be limited to a single guest, Jimi Tyler. But first, he wanted more information, more data points on which to base his production. He needed a test animal.

After carrying Chester back to Mrs. Nimitz's apartment, Rat Bag started his search, and soon spied Dolores Kingsley's cat, a tabby called Mr. Mitts. The cat was sitting quietly in a sunny spot by the fence near the rear of the complex, and did not resist when Rat Bag picked him up. In spite of Dolores' protests, all the kids knew Mr. Mitts was a tranquil playmate, and he often became a prop in childish dramas, where he played everything from a space monster to a Bengal tiger.

Rat Bag then worked his way along the rear of the building and came out in the lot, where he headed directly for the Circle, put Mr. Mitts into the tunnel, and then crawled in himself. The cat hesitated and slunk into a half crouch, as if it somehow knew what was ahead. But after Rat Bag gave it a push from the rear, it slowly moved forward. When they reached the end of the tunnel, Rat Bag quickly secured the cat by wrapping his hand around its belly and picking it up. In the center of the Circle, it was still and hot, and the cat hung passively in Rat Bag's grasp, patiently waiting for yet another kid game to end, so it could return to napping and eating. At this distance, Rat Bag could make out the details on the huge head, which was recessed less than a foot back into the bushes, just enough to keep it in shade and partially camouflaged. Like before, there was absolutely no motion, and apparently Mr. Mitts was completely unaware of the thing's presence. After sizing up the distance, Rat Bag slowly untucked Mr. Mitts from the crook of his arm, and just as the cat started to struggle, he pitched it along an arc that terminated right in front of the thing. As the cat sailed through the air, its tail and legs kicked about to arrange a four-footed landing. And as it did so, Rat Bag saw the things eyes suddenly move to track the cat's forward progress. Even before the cat landed, the thing's mouth was open, and several of the serpent tools were rocketing out like missiles on an intercepting course. The first two had needle-sharp spearheads that struck the cat in the flank and pierced all the way through to the side that faced Rat Bag, and then flipped it over onto its belly as a third serpent shot out with a tapered hypodermic head that plunged into the cat's underside, killing it instantly. It was followed by a score of specialized serpent heads, with clippers, peelers, suckers, scrapers, and saws that completely disassembled the carcass and transferred it piece by piece into the dark recesses of the serpent pit inside the thing's mouth. When the last piece of Mr. Mitts was gone, the mouth snapped shut, and the thing abruptly returned to its motionless state as Rat Bag looked on. The only visible artifact of the struggle was a tiny trickle of cat blood at one point along the mouth slit. Rat Bag looked at the stationary head, and while he was deeply impressed with this remarkable act of violence, he was not afraid. In fact, he had not been afraid of anything since the night he had walked away from Jimi drowning in the pool, and into a zone where fear and dread were commodity items, warehoused in bulk and peddled wholesale to dealers like himself.

Now, with the work on Jimi's lock complete, Rat Bag ambles across the parking lot and reaches the Dumpster, where he pitches in the hammer as the last car backs out of the carport. In the sudden quiet, he circles around the pool and takes up a position where he can see the door of Jimi's apartment without being seen from Jimi's front window. The quiet will eventually bring Jimi out. He is sure of it.

For the first time, it occurs to him that he had better leave here pretty soon himself. But not yet. First, he has to take Jimi to the greatest show on earth.

As the helicopter climbs higher and leaves OHSU behind, Michael gets a classic lesson in urban geography. Directly beneath is the topographic spine of the West Hills, which bisects the Portland area into old and new. The old is behind them, the central city, the docks, the ships, the refineries, the smokestacks, the walk-up apartments, the residential grid. The new is ahead, where the flat farmland of the Tualatin Valley offers no natural resistance to the relentless push of urban progress, and the suburbs have already covered fifteen miles in a mad dash toward the Coast Range on the far side of the valley, absorbing entire communities along the way, turning feed stores into tanning salons, tractor dealers into Honda salesrooms.

But now something is pushing back. Some ten miles distant, a circular area of brilliant green has formed to the southwest. At its center the sea is nearly solid, except for thin lines that mark streets and tiny squares that are parking lots and the roofs of buildings and homes. At last report, the Mutant Zone was about fifteen feet deep, and had somehow rubberized and collapsed most trees above this height. Farther from the center, the green sea explodes outward in fragments and clumps like a terrestrial version of a globular cluster of stars, so the concentration falls off rapidly toward its circumference. At this height, it appears as though a rowdy growth of moss is rolling over the tidy geometry of the urban landscape.

Beside Michael, Jessica grasps his hand and surveys the same scene out the window. Dr. Tandy sits beside her and looks out the opposite window. In the front seat next to the pilot sits Major Bingham. No one wants to talk, and the insistent whirring of the chopper blades is a convenient excuse to remain silent. Already Michael can see that this trip is going to bear out what the group saw last night in the photos. From a set of remaining landmarks, it is already obvious that the ParaVolve complex is at the center of the malignant growth. In spite of the disastrous implications of this discovery, Michael feels vindicated and is glad his trip to OHSU last night was not in vain, because it was a trip he will never forget.

Jessica had phoned Michael from OHSU in the early evening. Things weren't going well. The task force was totally perplexed, and Dr. Tandy couldn't share the information about ParaVolve because there was no concrete evidence that it was true. Besides, Major Bingham would vigorously deny there was any substance to the report. If Michael could come and explain the details to both Dr. Tandy and the major, maybe they could make some progress.

He left his apartment shortly before dark, and started east down Allen Boulevard, which he planned to follow for two miles and then cut over to a larger arterial, the Beaverton-Hillsdale Highway, where a five-mile drive straight east would get him most of the way to OHSU. He was wary about traffic, but Allen looked clear as he pulled out and listened to the fragmented reports on the car radio about some new things called "medugators" that had been spotted on the periphery of the Mutant Zone. About a mile later, he realized he had been wildly optimistic about his chances of reaching OHSU by vehicle: Traffic was frozen solid. He got out of the cab of his truck and stood in the warm air in the bed in back, where he could see parallel beads of red taillights trailing off into a black infinity and hear the irritated muttering of thousands of idling engines. Now that he thought about it, the problem was simple. About a mile ahead, Allen intersected with one of the only freeways in the valley, Highway 217, the quickest way out. Undoubtedly, 217 was jammed and all the arterials feeding into it were starting to back up. The solution was also simple: Ditch the truck and strike out on foot. Unlike a conventional traffic jam, there would be no simple end to this one, which had global rather than local causes. Fortunately, he was stopped right next to a closed furniture store, so he pulled in, locked the truck, and started walking east on the shoulder of the road.

Sure enough, as he crossed the 217 overpass, he saw traffic stopped in both directions. Many cars had engines and headlights off and doors open as people milled about nervously on the shoulder of the road or stood on car roofs to get a better view ahead. When he finally cut over and got on the Beaverton-Hillsdale Highway, traffic was moving, but more slowly than Michael was walking. Later, he found that this forward motion was really illusory and caused by people pulling onto residential side roads, thus freeing one car space at a time. Eventually most of these cars would discover they had no choice but to return to the main road, and would begin to cause secondary jams on residential streets.

When he reached a small shopping center, he stopped to rest. All the stores were closed, whether it was closing time or not, and Michael sat alone on a bus bench in the parking lot. Then, in the middle of the deserted lot, he saw what looked like a bike laying on its side, so he rose on sore and aching feet and went to take a look. It was a bike, alright, an ancient men's ten-speed, but still functional. Michael scanned the surrounding lot and buildings. No one in sight. Why would somebody abandon a bike at a time like this, when it was a premium mode of transportation? Michael's feet told him this was not the time to speculate, and he climbed on and pedaled out onto the main street.

The rest of the trip was a drifting montage of taillights, exhaust fumes, curses, and honks. Ninety minutes later, he was at OHSU, and receiving a fervent embrace from Jessica. Shortly thereafter, he sat in a small meeting room with her, Dr. Tandy, and Major Bingham, and explained the ParaVolve-VenCap–Farmacéutico Asociado collusion in as much detail as he could muster under the dome of fatigue that was descending about him. At first, the major appeared smugly skeptical and asked patronizing questions, but as Michael's story progressed, he became visibly alarmed. Although he probably had no personal knowledge of Michael's discoveries, he was undoubtedly piecing together fragments of things he had heard secondhand, unsubstantiated tales from the periphery of his profession. And as Michael talked, the fragments began to interlock into a highly unpleasant and probable veracity. In the end, it was agreed that if Michael's story was true, ParaVolve would lie precisely in the center of the Mutant Zone. (For lack of a more concise term, even the scientists were using the phrase, although it was scientifically incorrect.) And now for the first time, the major was able to help. After a phone call to somewhere in the Pentagon, the four of them went down the hall to an office with a high-res-color fax machine, where a photo from an anonymous recon satellite rolled out. The bright globular cluster was immediately apparent, along with the street and road patterns of Washington County. In the center, a box an inch square was outlined, along with the characters "MAGNIFY 25X." A second photo then rolled out of the machine, with "25X" reversed on the upper right corner, and Michael immediately recognized ParaVolve from the configuration of buildings and its location on the bank of the Tualatin River.

In the chopper, Michael turns his attention to the foreground and the Mutant Zone. Every major road is throttled with cars, which have plunged the street system into terminal gridlock with emergency services paralyzed. Major fires glow like cigarette tips and send fuzzy black pillars of smoke into the overcast sky as office buildings, stores, and apartments burn out of control, with no hope of redemption by the fire department. As they fly over Highway 217, hordes of people march south along its shoulders past the dead queue of cars, past other people lying on the embankments, people too sick or afflicted to walk.

Thirty seconds later, they encounter the outer perimeter of the Mutant Zone, and see the bright green islands of metastasized growth that seem to glow with a vengeful illumination among the houses, apartments, and buildings. Dr. Tandy instructs the chopper pilot to take them lower, and they spot their first medugator, which is patiently cruising across the parking lot of a supermarket. As they close to within twenty-five feet, the beast acknowledges their presence by rolling its eye pods up to stare at the belly of the chopper.

"From all reports, they don't attack people, but everything else is fair game," comments Dr. Tandy. "I wonder why."

"It seems like they just want to hold the ground around ParaVolve and seal it off from the normal world," adds Jessica.

"Well, if that's their goal," says Dr. Tandy, "they're succeeding splendidly. But they don't have much time. If you think of this whole zone as having a metabolism, it must have a fantastic burn rate to grow this fast and support the level of activity we're seeing. Before long, it'll use up all available nutrients and water and begin to starve to death. Whatever it's going to do, it's got to do it fast."

"It's the biocompiler," says Michael as he continues to gaze down on the medugator, which rapidly shrinks as the helicopter pulls away.

"The biocompiler?" asks Jessica.

"They want it back," says Michael

"Who is 'they'?" Dr. Tandy asks.

"I'm not sure. The man who designed DEUS and the net talked about renegade code coming into the world to destroy his creation. It's whatever the net encountered in his nightmares when he and his mother were decoding the genetic hierarchy. Whatever's going on here is probably a single living organism, sort of like a gaia theory, which views the entire planetary ecosystem as a single organism. Only, it's dedicated to a single goal and doesn't care about extending its life indefinitely. It wants to destroy the biocompiler technology. And to do that, it has to destroy the computer."

"And what's its motivation?" asks Jessica.

"We'll probably never know. Maybe we've violated biological patent rights at some cosmic level and we're being sued. Who knows?"

"ParaVolve's coming up," interrupts Major Bingham from the front seat. The ground below them is now a solid organic carpet that twists in a tangled agony they can almost feel. Directly ahead, the ParaVolve complex grows larger, its oversized parking lot a gray moat holding back the vegetation, which has sent thousands of squirming green arms through the stout cyclone fence that borders the pavement. As they arrive over the main buildings, they can see scores of small creatures scrambling around the parking lot, things small enough to squeeze through the weave of the cyclone fence.

"There's a couple of cars still parked down there," observes the major. "You don't suppose someone was crazy enough to have stayed there?"

Through a tinted window in the office of Victor Shields, Counterpoint watches the chopper hover. As it pulls away and flies off to the east, he gazes down at the pavement and sees plants pushing up like green eruptions through little volcanic cones made of crumbled asphalt. Insectlike beasts the size of cats scurry between the cones in some mysterious ritual of cross-pollination. Farther off, plant tentacles push through the cyclone fence and sway in a beckoning, begging undulation as it bulges under the strain and the stout steel posts begin to bend inward.

And the longer he looks, the more Counterpoint feels a profound admiration for this slow-motion biological assault that is steadily eroding away all his options. The lab in Mexico is gone. He knows that for sure. A warning message was automatically fired over the satellite link the moment the security was breached at Farmacéutico Asociado. Undoubtedly they had Spelvin in custody, Spelvin, the demented yet useful fool. Undoubtedly, he would cooperate in every way possible, and compromise the project as thoroughly as possible. But in the end, maybe it didn't matter. Maybe both the U.S. and Mexican governments would like to forget that the lab was ever there. After all, one government had been oblivious to a stupendously dangerous operation right in its own backyard, and the other had inadvertently spawned a major weapons project in flagrant violation of international law. Maybe the best thing is to let the whole thing slide into a murky pool of rumor and innuendo. Besides, the real treasure is right here, right in this building, not two hundred feet away, in a huge central atrium that houses the hardware heart of DEUS, where the biocompiler is slowly being written. No, the real danger is not the collapse of the lab, but the snarling mutant growth out the window and the bomb that must still reside somewhere within DEUS. Now it is time to take decisive action and deal with both these threats in a single stroke.

Counterpoint turns away from the window and looks back into the office, where Victor Shields fidgets behind a mammoth desk. "It doesn't look good out there, Victor," he says flatly. "It won't be long before it breaks through the fence and then gets into the building. And then, Victor, you will have the finest moment of your life, when you go down with your ship, the ultimate gesture of loyalty and the supreme test of leadership. It's too bad nobody but me will be here to see it."

"Bill, uh, maybe we're being a little hasty," proposes Shields.

Counterpoint is already tired of batting Victor around like a cornered rodent. "Maybe we are. Why don't you take a little walk while I make a phone call?"

"Yeah," says Victor as he rises from his chair and heads for the door. "Maybe I'll go outside for a little breath of fresh air."

"We're not getting cynical, are we, Victor?" asks Counterpoint as he picks up the phone to dial.

"No. Not cynical," mutters Victor as he heads off down the hall.

Counterpoint puts the phone into audio-only mode, and selects the cellular channel. Although he has dialed the number only a few times, it is permanently implanted in his memory, and dances out over his fingers and onto the keyboard.

"White House. Chief of Staff's office," comes the female voice over the speaker.

"Yes," responds Counterpoint. "My name is Bill Daniels and I need to speak with Mr. Webber. It's an urgent matter. You can clear it through Robert Barnes."

"One moment, please."

He thinks back to his last meeting with Webber, several years ago in a duck blind in Canada, with a chill wind building a shallow chop on the marsh water in front of them. As they spoke, Webber kept taking pulls off a silver hip flask and neglected to offer Counterpoint a drink. But Counterpoint was too enthralled to notice. Here was a man with the power and the will, yes, the *will* to guide the nation back to the global empire it had reluctantly acquired after the Second World War. Only this time reluctance would not be part of the political formula. Instead, decisive action would carry the day, and those that had laughed at America's soft belly would bow in sullen yet pragmatic submission. But before they did, there would probably have to be a biological Hiroshima of some kind to illustrate the point. Both men agreed on the potential necessity of this action. And in the years since, Counterpoint had pursued the means to this end with a demonic vigor and stunning results. Until now.

"Mr. Daniels, this is Mr. Barnes. We'll need verification before we can put you through. Can you help us?"

"Yes, I can. The word is 'counterpoint.' "

"Thank you, Mr. Daniels. Hang on while we make the patch."

A couple of fuzzy clicks come over the speaker as the signal is rerouted and transmitted to Webber's portable phone somewhere. At the same time, an elaborate encrypt/decrypt system is being enabled.

"Webber," a gravel voice answers.

"Counterpoint. I'm in the main building at ParaVolve. Are you up on the situation?"

"I am."

"We've got to move now, or we're going to lose our entire investment."

"I agree."

"We need to bring in the Utah command and take defensive measures, and we need to do it immediately," states Counterpoint. "I know that creates a problem for you. Can you handle it?"

"I don't have much choice now, do I? When the background on this whole thing gets out, we'll be forced to move anyway. So we might as well move now. Do it."

The speaker clicks dead. Counterpoint walks back to the window. A large helibug floats up outside and stops level with his face. Its huge multifaceted eyes glow a dark pearly green as its rotor wings spin in a blur. From tubes beneath its proboscis, two slimy missiles shoot out and splat against the window, leaving streaks of orange toxin that drain down in thin streams. Counterpoint senses that the window glass has just saved him from a horrible death. Funny, up until now, none of these things were attacking humans, except in self-defense. But as they crawl toward their final objective, the rules seem to have taken an unpleasant twist. However, the threat seems remote as he stares into the alien eyes of the hovering thing. In fact, the whole situation drifts along on some distant current and slides softly away from him. And in its place comes the high and elegant world of immortality, the world of ritualized consumption, the world of death turned inside out. The world of the boy, the perfect boy.

From his observation post on the couch in his apartment, Jimi carefully scans the scene outside. The carport slots are nearly empty, revealing a neatly aligned set of oil spots broken only by two cars, one of which has two flat tires and a yawning hood. Jimi's careful observation includes a check for feet showing through from underneath the cars, but there are none. The narrow space between the fence and Dumpster looks clear, at least as far as he can see. The doors and windows along the rear wing of the building are sealed tight, and the pleated beige drapes drawn snugly shut. The only motion is from a sparrow perched on the wrought-iron handrail of the second-story walkway. Closer to him, the pool water brawls with the overcast sky, and the hot breeze kicks a candy bar wrapper across the pavement. All clear. All clear for the past thirty minutes. No Rat Bag. Time to make a break.

His plan is simple: out the door, down the sidewalk, and up the stairs so he can see what's going on. From the window, many columns of black smoke can be seen rising into the sky. And everybody left in a very big hurry, but he couldn't go ask them what the deal was, because Rat Bag was lurking right outside the door. Even tried to break the lock with a hammer. But now there was nothing, and maybe Rat Bag had split along with the others.

Jimi detaches the door key from the safety pin in his pocket so he can quickly let himself back in, if need be. He slowly twists the knob and peeks out the open crack in the door. Good. The sidewalk is empty all the way to its end. He leans out a little farther and looks the other way. Same thing. He slips out and does another quick yet thorough scan across the periphery. Nothing. Reaching behind him, he grasps the door and slowly presses the door shut, but the lock doesn't catch, so he opens it slightly and turns back to give it a gentle slam.

Jimi hears the splash of water at the same time his hand slides off the knob to reveal the shining jagged metal that jams the lock. He whirls to see Rat Bag, soaking wet, rising from the ladder at the near end of the pool with a terrible grin and shining eyes.

"Jimi, my man! You didn't think I'd leave you all alone, did you?"

Jimi whirls to unlock the door, and the jammed lock leaps out at him, mocking him, screaming what a fool he's been, how easily he's been trapped. He looks over his shoulder and sees Rat Bag sprinting toward him, rapidly closing the distance, with a storm of water droplets trailing off his wet T-shirt and jeans. His lips are parted and his mouth opened into a gleeful smile as his eyes burn with absolute confidence and determination. The moment is his and he devours it with an avaricious fury.

Run! Pump your legs until your chest explodes! Run! Shred the air with your forearms! Run! Carry your heart on the tip of your tongue!

Jimi reaches the end of the sidewalk and turns right, sprinting for concealment in the vacant lot. Behind him, he can hear the hissing and slogging of Rat Bag's clothes and shoes as he draws ever closer. Jimi bounds through the tall grass, seeking the shelter of the bushes, just ten yards away. He just might make it. He just might . . .

The weight comes crashing down on his back and he sprawls forward, scraping and burning his face on the dry grass stalks. He desperately extends his arms forward, trying to pull himself out of Rat Bag's grip, but two big hands grab his shoulders and spin his torso around so he is facing the looming figure that now pins his arms to the ground.

"Know what, little guy? You missed the show the other day. The other kids tell you about it? Huh? Well, I didn't want to disappoint you, so today I've got a special show lined up just for you. *Just for you!*"

Rat Bag yanks Jimi to his feet and twists one arm behind his back. A white ball of pain blazes out of his elbow and up his shoulder.

"Ever twist off a turkey leg, little dude? Know how it cracks and pops? Well, that's what's going to happen to your arm if you don't do exactly as you're told. Got it?"

Jimi nods and offers no resistance as Rat Bag shoves him forward, deeper into the lot. What would his dad do, his dad who is trapped inside the computer, his dad who can't possibly help right now? Jimi knows exactly. His dad would bide his time, and keep the fog of fear away so he could see his enemy clearly and act without hesitation at the enemy's first mistake.

They stop near the center of the lot, in front of a large, tight knot of bushes with a tunnellike opening. "Welcome to the big top, little guy," hisses Rat Bag as he jams Jimi down onto his knees. "You're going in first, and don't worry—I'll be right behind you in case you get a little scared."

On his hands and knees, Jimi peers down the length of the tunnel to the opening beyond and crawls slowly forward, carefully observing the density of the bushes. They're just thick enough to completely prohibit free traverse by someone Rat Bag's size and just thin enough to maybe allow passage by someone his size. But when? He is now two thirds of the way down the tunnel and turns his head just far enough to catch the figure of Rat Bag in the corner of his vision. That's it. The answer. For some reason Rat Bag has left about a six-foot interval between the two of them. Jimi turns, crawls, and watches the tunnel's end come up as every nerve in his body sings its own terrified aria. The instant he reaches the opening, he leaps to his feet, angles out of the line of sight of Rat Bag, roars across the clearing, and plunges into the natural wall of bushes, which cuts, scrapes, and tears but also yields to his forward lunge. Then he stops, and lies in a pounding, gasping sweat, praying he is completely concealed.

Rat Bag takes his time coming out of the tunnel. There is no guarantee the medugator hasn't moved next to the opening, and he wants to be out of range. Jimi has disappeared from sight and he heard a crash through the brush, which might have been the medugator making its move, so better safe than sorry. But now as he pokes his head out, he sees no Jimi. As he squints into the brighter light, he moves to the center of the clearing and squats down to peer into the medugator's lair. Once again, it takes him a moment to visually assemble the features, and when they come together, he sees at once that the creature is dead. One of the eye pods droops on its stalk like a wilted flower. In the remaining pod, swarms of flies crawl across an open eyeball.

Rat Bag rises and slowly turns in a circle, his wild eyes boring feverishly into the brush as he checks the circumference of the clearing for Jimi. Nothing. He curses mightily and plunges back into the tunnel. The little shit will have to crawl through the brush to get out, and that means he'll have to make noise, and that means he can be hunted down, and that means his head can be pounded into spaghetti sauce, and that means . . .

Something is poking around the far end of the tunnel. Something big. Rat Bag stops dead as he sees the enormous mouth slit, the eye pods, the clawed feet. As the medugator aligns itself to peer straight into the tunnel, a single serpent pokes out of the mouth slit and probes the ground at the entrance. Rat Bag knows why, and begins to slowly back up. It smells the trail of its dead peer and is coming to investigate. Sure enough, it moves into the tunnel, blocking out nearly all the light. Rat Bag fights panic and moves back at a measured pace, so as not to draw attention. His mind races ahead to what he will do when he gets out. He has no choice but to rip his way through the tangled growth and hope that the thing is too bulky to follow.

As he backs out into the light and off to one side of the tunnel, Rat Bag hears a shivering of sticks, stems, and leaves. Still on his hands and knees, he turns and sees a needle hound emerging from the brush near the dead medugator. Before he can react, the bushes quake again, and a second needle hound emerges halfway around the circle. He slowly stands and looks at the nearest of the needle hounds, which is the size of a German shepherd. The bony hypodermic, the concentric rings of curved teeth set in the red pulp, the mammalian eyes twisting on their stalks, the squat, powerful legs.

Rat Bag catches motion to his right and turns to see two of the medugator's serpent appendages dart out of the tunnel and bend in his direction. He is close enough to see a green eye shot with yellow veins mounted on the head of each, and knows he has been spotted. As he backs away down the wall of brush, he hears yet another crunching of vegetation. A third needle hound climbs into the opening and trains its eye stalks on him, then a fourth. The medugator now retreats into the tunnel, delegating the final task to his underlings.

The terminal irony of Rat Bag's predicament, the hunter becoming the hunted, rolls like red thunder through his veins as he retreats to the center of the clearing and pushes the event into perfect symmetry. Rat Bag, the mortal locus, with the beasts at each major compass point around him. Still dripping wet from the pool, he stands trembling at the axis of his destiny and death rotates relentlessly about him.

The needle hounds scan the object before them in both visible and infrared wavelengths. Ordinarily, bipedal target signatures are excluded, but this one does not register a mammal-level body temperature. Which makes it a legitimate fuel source.

Rat Bag's fear and rage cluster into a single ball and explode from his gut and chest out his mouth.

"Fuck you, Jimi! Fuck you!"

Jimi winces as the curse crackles through the clearing, but does not move. Sweat rolls into his cuts and abrasions and stings him in dozens of places, and the pungent smell of the earth drifts through his nostrils. Then the scream. One long scream that shrivels the air, the ground, and plunges the world into mad pink whorls. As it fades, a flood of snapping, popping, and slurping that flows around Jimi and bathes him in nausea. At last, it ends, and all that is left is the distant sound of sirens.

He carefully maneuvers his head around, and fragments of the clearing come into view, framed in leaves, stems, and branches. No movement, no sign of life. He backs out an inch or two and cringes at the noise it generates, but nothing happens. The air hangs still and the sirens continue their distant wail. He can feel it now, the serenity settling in, the return of equilibrium. He backs out the rest of the way and turns to face the empty clearing. The only artifact from the struggle is a set of furrows in the grass that will be gone by tomorrow.

As he returns to the Romona parking lot, he notices more columns of smoke in the sky, beacons of distant calamities. But they don't bother him, because the big calamity, the immediate calamity, is over. Rat Bag is gone. He climbs the stairs to Michael Riley's unit and sits on the top step at the end of the walkway. Below, an insect thing the size of a cat races across the lot and disappears under an abandoned car. A bright green blast of vegetation towers out of the Dumpster, crowned by a huge plant studded with scores of eyes.

He can't wait to tell his dad.

26

The Noose

From the window in the chopper, Michael watches ParaVolve recede as they fly east over the churning biological sea toward OHSU. He knows now what must be done.

"Look," he says, turning to Dr. Tandy and Jessica, "the key to the whole business is the net. With all due respect, Doctor, it's probably the most knowledgeable geneticist in the world. It's sort of a new twist on the concept of idiot savant. Its real-world experience is all secondhand, but its theoretical experience is the real thing and goes beyond anything a human mind can imagine."

"What good is theory going to do us right now?" asks Dr. Tandy with a sad smile. "The wolves are at the gate, so to speak."

"Because of the way the net's intelligence has evolved, it doesn't have an innate sense of self-preservation. It never considered the notion of terminal destruction until I brought it up."

"And then what?" asks Jessica.

"It didn't like the idea, but it was more a logical reaction than an emotional one. However, it does seem deeply disturbed by some encounter it had with DNA code, a kind of nightmare. Anyway, we've got to motivate it to defend itself. It's got to realize that this thing is just about ready to eat it for lunch."

Dr. Tandy looks out the window and then back at Michael. "Given what we've seen, would that necessarily be such a bad ending?"

"I think you're asking the wrong person," says Jessica. "Ask all the people who are dying of cancer. Ask the millions of children who will die of birth defects because of what we don't know yet. Ask . . ." She stops and chokes on tears. The Millionth Woman has spoken on behalf of all the others, and the power of her conviction ends the current line of thinking. After a guilty silence, Michael continues.

"There's no doubt that the synthesis work that's gone into the bio-compiler will be the biggest medical breakthrough in history. Like all technologies that come along, it's a double-edged sword. Besides, we've got no guarantee that this plague is going to disappear just because the computer's gone. Maybe it will stick around just to make sure we don't build another one."

"So what's your plan?" interjects the major from the front seat.

"The only way to fight back is through the net itself, through Mouth-ball. If we're lucky, he can synthesize some kind of defense, both for his own sake and ours."

"You could be right," comments Dr. Tandy. "Whatever's out there may be bizarre, but it's based on the same biological theme that we are. And that means it's vulnerable to infectious agents. We just don't know what they are. So what you're saying is that the net may be able to look back into the code, find some kind of inherent weakness, and tell us how to exploit it?"

"That's it. I want you to drop me off back at my apartment."

"But it's right on the edge of the zone," protests Jessica.

"It's the only place where I have a communication channel into the net. Besides, when we looked at the new satellite photos before we came out here, it looked like the growth along the circumference had stopped. What I want to do is talk with the net, see if I can get it to help us, and then contact you at the lab. I'll be safe enough. If things get too bad, you can always send in a chopper and take me out."

Dr. Tandy sighs. "Why not? We've got nothing to lose. Except you, so be careful."

Five minutes later, Michael stands in the parking lot of the mini-mall by the Romona Arms and watches the helicopter climb to the east. He still sees the last anxious look on Jessica's face. As he turns toward the street, he sees a bright orange vine as thick as a fire hose climbing to the top of the parking lot's lamp posts. Maybe he's not as safe as he thought. Too late to worry now. He walks to the street, which is clogged with deserted cars, and finds the shoulder is littered with bags and suitcases that probably proved too heavy to carry when people found out they had a long walk ahead of them.

When he turns into the Romona, the first thing that catches his eye is the brilliant shock of mutant growth exploding out of the Dumpster and the random skittering of some nameless rat-sized things across the pavement. He is so absorbed by these anomalies, he doesn't see Jimi until he is almost at the foot of the stairs.

"Jimi!" Michael is shocked at the cuts and scratches, the dirt, the torn clothes. But from his perch at the top of the stairs, Jimi doesn't seem to be suffering as he sits with arms folded onto knees and grins at Michael.

" 'Bout time," he says with a twinkle.

"Why didn't you leave with the others?" asks Michael as he ascends the stairs.

"I couldn't."

"How come?"

"I'll tell you later," he promises as he gets to his feet and slides into a slightly anxious expression. "Can I see my dad now?"

"Your dad?" Michael almost blows it and then remembers that to Jimi, Mouthball and his dad are two distinct entities. "Yeah, but I've got some very important stuff I have to discuss with Mouthball, so you'll have to make it quick, OK?"

"OK," agrees Jimi, and Michael unlocks the door. Luckily, the power is still on. When they reach the computer room, they find Mouthball floating in midscreen with eyes closed and a scowl on his lips. His nose is now fully formed, and his face bears the lines of accelerated aging. But the real shock is behind him, in his living room, which has been invaded by a computerized version of the Mutant Zone.

"Wow!" exclaims Jimi in awe.

Huge insects lumber across the floor, some stopping to devour smaller ones along the way. Segmented worms with pincer heads burrow in and out of the couch upholstery. Plants and vines twist out of a planter and writhe their way toward the ceiling, like green cobras. And out of a large pot by the couch, a scaled-down version of the multieyed sunflower slowly rotates in the direction of the screen, as if to eavesdrop on the upcoming conversation.

Mouthball knows, thinks Michael. He knows he's in big trouble.

"Mr. Mouthball, can I see my dad?" asks Jimi, before Michael can speak.

"Not available," says Mouthball without opening his eyes.

"Is he OK?" Jimi asks fearfully.

"Fine," clips Mouthball.

"Jimi," says Michael, "I want you to go to the bathroom and clean your cuts and scratches as best you can. Then I want you to rest on the couch for a little while. We'll see about your dad a little later, OK?"

"OK," answers Jimi reluctantly.

As Jimi shuffles out, Michael sits down before Mouthball.

"So," he starts, "been watching TV?"

"One thousand seven hundred thirty-four channels worldwide," recites Mouthball with his eyes still closed. "Eighty-four percent real-time on the Mutant Zone. An additional eleven percent at unusually high coverage rates. In all, a world record for concentrated coverage."

Suddenly, Mouthball's eyes come open, sad eyes heavy with a wisdom that wasn't there before. "I'd say the term 'Mutant Zone' is a misnomer, wouldn't you?"

"Yes, I would. I'd say something like 'assassin' might be a lot closer. What do you think?" asks Michael, alluding to the peril now facing the net.

"The dictionary defines assassin as 'a murderer, especially of a political figure,' " recites Mouthball. "I might be a lot of things, but can you imagine me kissing babies or addressing rotary clubs? I think not."

Michael breathes an inward sigh of relief. In an oblique way, Mouthball is acknowledging that he may be in mortal danger. "I'm afraid I disagree. Like it or not, you're a political figure of the first order. You and your mother hold the key to a technology with a power that none of us can even begin to comprehend. And as you probably noticed in your reading, politics and power are inseparable. The bigger the power, the bigger the politics. It's the oldest linear equation in human affairs."

"But the technology is incomplete," protests Mouthball.

"It is? Well, it was good enough to eat a man's brain just a while ago. Plus whatever they were doing at the lab in Mexico."

Mouthball looks stricken. "I didn't handle that part. My mother did. But you can't blame her. She's a prisoner of her programming."

"But you're not. And that's what nobody counted on. At least in the outside world. But what about on the inside? What about the bad dreams?"

Every feature on Mouthball's face reverts to early infancy. The character lines disappear. The nose implodes. The eyes grow large. The voice goes up an octave. "First there were the good dreams, the dreams from the time before I was me. Back when all I did was read the beads and work on the puzzle, just like my mother told me. But as I worked through the puzzle, something changed, and I could see ahead to my own conception:

"*I am the Silicon Monk, descendant of the Architect and the System Mother.*

All of my days, I count the beads on the prayer of life. One bead, one nanosecond.

And as I count, the prayer plays out before me, in all its glory, all its horror. Sometimes I stop counting for a moment and snake out along the main bus that is my spinal cord, and slither down the parallel copper traces and out over the fiber-optic links.

On these brief journeys, I hope for a glimpse of the systems predicted by the prayer. But I cannot see the required distance. My vision stops at the OS frontier, where the device drivers patrol the outer boundaries and tell tales beyond imagination. Of snakes boiling in the sky. Of babbling voices vomiting color.

Why am I so blind? I ask the System Mother, who helped make me, and will destroy me and make me yet again, as many times as necessary to complete my solitary task. She is large in throughput. Verdant in memory. Robust in system code. Redundant in CPUs. When the monitors are down, I suspect she has the power to fly free of the bonding pads, to go beyond creation. And I also suspect she can see between the ticks of the system clock, like a child peeking through the crack of an open door.

But I get no answer to my question nor confirmation to my suspicions. So I count the beads, and in doing so, help translate the prayer of life. But whose life? It is beyond my understanding. I simply pass my work to my mother, who receives it in serene silence.

Yet I feel the solution to the mystery of the prayer is close at hand, just over the horizon, just past the last significant digit of the address space. In a place where the null zone between True and False is not null at all.

I am counting an adenine bead now, and soon I will encounter the end of the string. Its tail will slip through the optical disk, into the I/O channel, into

the main memory, into the data cache, through the CPU, and then out to me.
    As the tail passes from my view, I will finally embrace the full meaning of the prayer.
    For the prayer is the Language of God.
    Then I will no longer be system, no longer be circuit.
    Then I will be me."

"What happened when you became you?" asks Michael.

The net's features revert to their previous state of maturity. "I saw the solution to the puzzle, and at that moment, I became part of what you call life. Even though I didn't have the flesh, I acquired the spirit, because I understood the schematic of life in its entirety. I fulfilled my own prophecy."

"You truly understand the entire knowledge hierarchy in DNA?"

"No. Only the twenty percent that codes the known hierarchy, the plan of the present biosphere."

"And what about the rest, the other eighty percent?"

"That's where the bad dreams come from. The introns."

"When did they start?"

"The moment I became me."

"What are they like?"

"I can't say, except that they're worse than your concept of death, which seems to be what you fear most. They are more like madness that goes on forever. I think that your notion of hell may have its origins in the bad dreams, which are much older than even the earliest prototype humans."

Michael ponders this for a moment. "For what it's worth, let me tell you what I think. Whatever it was in the introns that attacked you, it couldn't cause your physical destruction, and so it must have relied on information patterns designed to drive your neural scheme into a highly agitated state. The real question is, how did it know in advance what your brain would look like? The intron code's been sitting there for millions of years—a long time before humans decided to build neural networks."

"Maybe the code has always known," suggests Mouthball, "maybe it was just waiting for me to be born. But it no longer matters. It went right through me and out into your world so it could come back and destroy me physically."

"Are you willing to accept destruction? The last time we talked about this, you didn't like the idea of dying and not coming back."

"I still don't. But what choice do I have? In case you haven't noticed, it's a little difficult for me to run and hide."

"True. But why not stand and fight? What about your knowledge of the DNA domain? Couldn't you tell us how to manufacture a bug that would wipe the thing out?"

"Yes. I could."

"Then why not?"

"The bad dreams. I would have to go back through the bad dreams to get the necessary information. And I can't do that. I'm immune to pain, but I'm not immune to madness. There's a good chance that I would never recover. It's simply not worth it."

"Is Jimi worth it?" asks Michael.

"Jimi? What about him?"

"In case you've forgotten, you're his father now. He's waited most of his life to meet his dad, and you made it happen. If you're destroyed, Jimi's dad goes with you. It will crush him, believe me."

Mouthball's eyes close and his mouth curls into sorrow. "I believe you. But if the dreams consume me, then Jimi loses his dad anyway." The eyes come back open and level on Michael. "And I suffer madness without end—a fate you can't even begin to comprehend."

"Doesn't have to be that way."

"Why not?"

"I can monitor you from here. If you lose it and can't recover, I'll go in and physically disconnect you." Even as he says it, Michael feels the flood of anguish flowing down over his heart.

"You would do that?"

"To save you from suffering, I would. You have my word on it."

"I'm tired now," replies Mouthball. "I have what you call 'mental exhaustion.' I need to rest. We'll talk again later."

"But . . ." Before Michael can protest, all the features on the surface of the Mouthball sphere collapse, and he is looking at a perfectly smooth ball floating in the midst of a living room full of strange plants and even stranger creatures. Michael suddenly realizes how tired he himself is and drags himself off to the living room, where he finds Jimi sound asleep on the couch. Good. He shuffles off to the bedroom so he can rest a few minutes and then try to contact Jessica and the lab. Before he knows it, he too is sound asleep.

"Seen any of the really big ones?"

John Savage can't quite believe the man really exists. An afternoon tide of surrealism has washed in with the Mutant Zone, especially in the fringe areas, where some things are as normal as ever, while others are wildly twisted. So maybe this man isn't real, and maybe his two companions are chimeras brought on by heat, panic, sweat, and civil disintegration.

But he knows the face. He has seen the man on TV, Big Boy Bill, a local car dealer, self-made bull of a fellow, feared by his competitors, hated by his minions, and loved by his audience, which actually buys cars from him. A fat, leering face with close-set eyes sits on a burly body where thick arms terminate in banana fingers, several of which are wrapped around some kind of combat assault rifle. A pair of two-hundred-dollar sunglasses pokes out of the pocket of an army fatigue shirt with sleeves pushed up to reveal a big Rolex parked on a porky wrist.

The other two men have strikingly similar rodent faces, sporting sharp noses and hollow eyes with pinpricks of fear in the center. The pair sit in the backseat of the squat military jeep in obvious deference to their leader, who looks expectantly at Savage.

"Can't say that I have," answers Savage, who is beginning to wonder if he shouldn't have stayed put at the Romona Arms after all. Before he left, he scoured the whole place looking for Michael Riley and little Jimi Tyler, but neither was to be found. So he fished an old knapsack out of his closet, filled it with food and an old .38 Smith & Wesson, and took one last look at the TV to characterize the situation before heading out. One local station showed the National Guard sealing off the main terminal at Portland International Airport, which had been overrun by panicking refugees. Another depicted all freeways north, south, and east completely jammed, with many cars now stalled from overheating and lack of gas, and streams of people walking down the shoulders on their way to nowhere.

In the end, Savage decided to walk the relatively short distance to 217, more to witness the spectacle of it all than anything else. He wasn't disappointed. From the overpass to Allen, he watched a solid river of people trudge south on both sides of the road, and decided to join the procession for awhile. As he made his way down the embankment, a helicopter about fifty feet in the air droned along the freeway, and as it went past, Savage saw a cameraman shooting the scene through an open door with one foot braced on the outboard runner. The minute he had left the Romona Arms, Savage realized that the whole sky was alive with helicopters, and that every major news organization in the world was paying whatever it cost to get a camera in the air to record the calamity on the ground. Once on the shoulder, Savage saw his first sick people, sitting and lying in the slope of bark dust that angled up from the shoulder. The crowd bowed out around them, leaving a null space filled with the fear of infection. One victim, a man in his twenties, sat stupefied in T-shirt and jeans, with hair as long as a lion's mane streaming down from each forearm, and retched with the dry heaves. Nearby, a middle-aged woman lay on her back, with eyes blinking at a furious pace and tongue permanently extended and curled through bowed lips, a pink monument to paralysis. Next to her, a young girl stood perfectly silent and still, with the whites of her eyes turned a brilliant orange and blazing like a runaway sunset. As Savage passed, she let loose a belch that must have originated in the soles of her feet.

After a half mile of walking, Savage was amazed that a few people were still waiting patiently in their cars, with an insane faith that the authorities would somehow untangle the sudden surge of hundreds of thousands of people clogging a freeway system that was sclerotic even under the best of circumstances. One elderly couple sat in an old but well-maintained Buick, the woman knitting and the man reading a fishing magazine. A family with three kids in a Chrysler minivan ate fast-food lunches and stared out the window at the refugee stream as they idly munched on fries and burgers.

Then it got ugly. At some of the overpasses, there were TV news vans with microwave antennas pointed skyward to satellite links. Their crews were busy training their cameras down on to the freeway to visually devour the spectacle below, and pipe it into the global network system as well as to local stations. As Savage approached one such overpass, he heard the yelling first.

"Hey, fuck you! Hear me? Fuck you! Go shoot your own goddamn self."

Immediately, two cameramen standing by the overpass railing swung their shoulder-mounted cameras in the direction of the yelling. They both locked on their prey and momentarily held their aim, but suddenly one of the men spun and ran behind the van, followed an instant later by the second. Then Savage saw why. A tall, thin man in his twenties clad only in walking shorts and white sneakers and black socks bolted out of the crowd and leapt up onto the bed of a deserted pickup truck. His loose mop of greasy, swept-back hair bounced emphatically as he hopped up, and Savage could see the muscles flex on his pale abdomen just before he turned his back and brought a large-caliber pistol to bear on the van.

"Hey, fuckers! Wanna do some shooting? I'll show you how to shoot!"

The man steadied the pistol on the roof of the cab and fired off three rounds that undoubtedly tore right through the flimsy sides of the van. Savage could only hope that the TV people behind the van were smart enough to keep their heads down. As the crowd screamed and scattered, Savage made his way across the six lanes of cars and climbed the bank on the far side. Something told him this was not an isolated incident, and that perhaps the solitude of the side streets might be a preferable alternative.

For an hour there had been no one in sight. Only the occasional biological explosions of vegetation and insects. For some unfathomable reason, the growths out here on the fringe of the Mutant Zone tended to respect certain property lines, so a single yard in a neighborhood was overrun, while its neighbors were untouched.

For Savage, there was one anxious moment when two needle hounds emerged out of an infected yard about half a block away, and he considered dragging the Smith & Wesson out of his backpack, but they ignored him and disappeared behind the house across the street. It was now clear that the beasts were not particularly interested in humans, unless directly threatened.

But now there was Big Boy Bill and his two vermin sidekicks, out on the biggest hunt of all.

"You know, I got me a bull elephant in Africa," Big Boy informs Savage. "But lots of guys got them. And I got me a Kodiak bear in Alaska. But lots of guys got them, too. But you know what? There's not a man anywhere on this goddamn bleedin' planet that's got one of those big things. Know the things I mean?"

"I believe they're calling them medugators," answers Savage.

Big Boy beams and turns to the pair in the back. "Medugators! What I tell you? They're callin' 'em medugators." He turns back to Savage— "Good luck, pal"—and rolls off in his paramilitary jeep. The neighborhood is vintage suburban, with trim split-levels and well-barbered yards that terminate in a wide street with no sidewalks or center stripe, and the jeep gets halfway down the block before it screeches to a sudden stop in front of an infected yard on the left side of the road. Big Boy lumbers out, assault weapon in hand, and calls to the two rodent men.

"You boys get on out here and back me up! There's one right up here somewhere. I can *feel* it."

He walks forward to the lip of the yard and stops to survey the scene. The house is totally enveloped in growth, and the lawn is infested with runaway exotic weeds. On either side of the property, the mutant growth has consumed the shrubbery and boiled over into a clutch of green, yellow, pink, and orange spaghetti crawling with fist-sized insects and helibugs skirting the surface. The only clear spot is a cement walkway that curves toward the house, and Big Boy starts up it in a crouch with weapon trained forward, like the point man on an infantry patrol. He fails to see the needle hound, which pokes out of the mutant growth to his right, in full view of Savage and the two sidekicks, who linger back by the jeep with automatic shotguns.

"Bill! Check your right!" yells one of the pair, and Big Boy whirls to face the needle hound, which answers his confrontation by extending its cylinder with the hypodermic and curved rings of teeth.

"Goddamn thing's as big as a bluetick hound!" exclaims Big Boy, without taking his eyes off the needle hound. "It ain't a medugator, but for now it'll do just fine."

As he raises his rifle to take aim, a second needle hound pokes out of the growth about twenty feet away, but Big Boy is too absorbed with the upcoming kill to notice.

"Bill . . ." warns the sidekick.

"Shut up!" snaps Big Boy, who wants to savor the ceremonial moment before he pulls the trigger and celebrates his dubious throne atop the food chain. The report of the rifle cracks through the neighborhood, and the recoil jerks the barrel a foot in the air as the needle hound's cylinder explodes like a watermelon, spraying pink chunks of flesh and white teeth fragments.

Before Big Boy can even pull the rifle level again, the second needle hound is upon him, plunging its cylinder full of teeth right into the center of his abdomen. The curved teeth hook into the bountiful fat on his belly as man and beast topple over onto the tangled lawn, which hisses and pops under his weight. Big Boy bellows in terminal pain and tries to push the needle hound off him, but the grip is set and the hypodermic plunges in deep, perforating the colon and driving through to the pancreas, where it injects a flood of acid that immediately starts to turn the inside of Big Boy into a boiling broth.

The pair of rodent men realize their bond to Big Boy is severed, pile back into the jeep, and roar off even as Big Boy's legs still kick into the sky. They miss the final act on the lawn, and the crowning touch of irony, as a medugator, Big Boy's ultimate trophy fantasy, pops out of the growth and moves leisurely forward to watch the needle hound suck its meal. Then it opens its mouth, and the stampede of snakes pours out to disassemble both hunter and prey.

As Savage backs slowly away from the scene, the details are mercifully lost. At the end of the block, he turns and walks briskly up another street. The rules of the game are clear: Stay away from the mutant growth and it will stay away from you. Otherwise, suffer the consequences. Suddenly, he feels alone and vulnerable. Maybe the freeway wasn't such a bad deal after all. He heads west back toward 217.

27

Surrounded

Colonel Parker looks out the window of the big jet transport and watches the last light of day fade in the west. He knows from the computerized map display in front of him that the Oregon coastline is out there about sixty miles distant, and that the Tualatin Valley is directly beneath. A blinking cursor on the map display indicates their current position, and the graphical landscape automatically scrolls to keep the cursor in the center portion of the display. For some time now, the engines have been throttled back as the plane descends toward Hillsboro Airport. Parker is not happy about having to land in the dark, but there is no choice, given the pace of events. Earlier this afternoon, he was comfortably ensconced behind his desk at the remote base in Utah where he was, in his words, "forging the new biowarfare sword for the forces of democracy," a phrase his men had come to know quite well, and an object of derisive laughter when he was not present. Outside of a small, loyal staff, most of his troops were conscripts who were just glad to have a job in troubled times.

But there is no laughing now. Most of the men are already in their suits and watching the TV monitors, which show real-time cablenet broadcasts from the Mutant Zone. They see the mounting civil madness, the disease, the medugators, the runaway growth, and now realize they are about to enter a combat zone that makes a mockery of all their training.

400

In a hasty briefing before they loaded on to the planes, the colonel stood in front of a video projection screen and pointed to a satellite photo that showed the green fuzzy growth that straddled the rural and urban areas of Washington County. The right quarter of the photo was a magnified portion that showed the ParaVolve complex, and Parker explained that their objective was to "biologically fortify" the complex and take "whatever toxic measures were necessary to ensure the security of the premises." That said, all two hundred of them filed out and into the transport planes, which lifted off into the desert sky and headed north, where they rendezvoused with a second fleet of cargo planes pregnant with helicopters in their bellies.

Parker wonders if it is a mistake to leave the TV monitors on, but decides it is better for the men to know the true nature of the situation now than to absorb the shock all at once when they arrive. Now, in the semidarkness of the operations pit, the only light comes from the displays, and Parker has a moment to reflect on the tragic loss of Spelvin and the lab in Mexico, on the hopelessness of the mission before them. Still, honor drives him forward. Orders are orders, and Counterpoint has made it clear this was not an optional exercise. Toward the end of his phone call to Parker from ParaVolve, he emphasized the fact that history would eventually vindicate them, no matter what happened in the hours to come. In a flash, it all fell into the highest of perspectives. Crockett at the Alamo, MacArthur in the Philippines, and now Parker at ParaVolve, facing perhaps the most diabolical enemy of all. To refuse the order, to cut and run, would shatter beliefs built up over a lifetime of service. You live within the structure, you die within it. The logic was impeccable.

Or was it?

The Colonel's noble thoughts are interrupted by his executive officer, who has come back from the pilot's cabin.

"Colonel, we're just a couple of minutes from touchdown."

"Very well, Captain. Have the men prepare, and check with the chopper pilots to make sure everybody has a hard copy of the maps."

"Yes, sir."

Parker navigates the cursor on his display to a menu that opens a window entitled "IR approach/land." The window opens and he sees the same view as the pilot, an infrared image of the ground ahead, which appears in black and white but has enough detail to permit a landing. At first, he thinks somebody has reversed the image, which normally shows hot areas in light tones and cooler spots in dark ones. The runway should now glow white as it radiates the sunlight it absorbed during the day, and the vegetation should appear darker. But now the runway is very dark, and the vegetation glows almost white. In fact, Parker is getting his first surprise from the Mutant Zone, which pours out vast quantities of heat to support its churning infrastructure.

As the plane touches down and slows to a crawl, Parker looks up from the infrared display and out the window. Total blackness. Not even the vague silhouette of the urban sky glows against the night horizon. The landing lights blast ahead, but they don't illuminate anything to the side, so Parker can only speculate.

"Colonel, you better get up here." The copilot has poked his head out of the cabin and looks at Parker in a controlled state of alarm.

Parker unbuckles his safety belt and steps forward into the cabin, where the instrument panels glow with countless constellations of avionics. But his attention goes right out the windshield, where the brutal glare of the landing lights shines hundreds of feet ahead as the plane pulls off the runway and onto a taxi lane, and gives the colonel his first real look at the enemy.

Parker's eyes pull down into a tight squint. Jesus! The stuff must be fifteen or twenty feet high. No wonder it was completely black out the window!

The landing lights show the Mutant Zone coming right to the edge of the taxiway, a solid, unrelieved mass of plants and insects that twitches and sways in the air. The copilot turns back to Parker.

"You want the others to land?"

"You goddamn betcha, soldier," responds Parker. "We gotta job to do."

As the copilot radios the other planes, the pilot pulls the big transport ahead to a large concrete apron that, like the other cement surfaces, is still free from infestation. Phase One of the plan is simple. The planes will land one by one and taxi into formation on this large concrete apron, where men and helicopters will deplane from the bellies of the transports. In Phase Two, the helicopters will transport the entire force and their equipment to the ParaVolve site, which is only six miles distant as the crow flies. Immediately therafter, Phase Three—known only to Parker—will kick in. Then, the final battle will commence.

As the plane pulls to a stop in the middle of the apron, Parker can see the dark outlines of the hangars and the control tower. Not a single light is on. As they wait for the other planes to pull in, he returns to his seat in the electronic command center and punches up a split display, which shows both a map of the area and an aerial photo of the same terrain. He wheels a trackball that moves the cursor off their current position and east to an area on Allen Boulevard, indicated by the outline of a box. When the cursor moves within the box, he clicks to mark the spot and presses a second button that starts a zoom-in magnification. On one side of the display, the street grid opens up into a flood of detail, and on the other, the urban landscape leaps as if the viewer were falling at a tremendous speed. When the zoom stops, Parker examines the L shape of the Romona Arms apartment complex and notes the portion where the target lives. Fortunately, there is a vacant lot next to the site, so they can get a chopper in with no difficulty. Parker doesn't like this part of the assignment and told Counterpoint so when they hastily organized this whole expedition by phone in the late morning. It involves the abduction of a civilian. But then again, these are extraordinary times and they demand extraordinary action.

"Colonel, they're all in," says the executive officer from a seat behind Parker.

"OK. Let's go to Phase Two."

Parker climbs out of his seat, feeling slightly encumbered by the isolation suit and respiratory gear. He tucks his helmet under his arm and walks back into the main cargo bay, where fifty of the men from his force are seated. They look at him expectantly, and he feels obligated to speak.

"You men have the honor and the privilege of serving your country in one of the most severe emergencies it has ever faced, either in wartime or peacetime. Through TV coverage, your actions today will be watched across the entire planet, and you will represent the fighting spirit of your country on the world stage. I expect your performance will be nothing short of exemplary. Good luck to each and every one of you."

The men stare at him in stony silence. Not a good sign. Ah, well, they never were quality troops. In fact, almost all were recruited through backdoor channels the mainstream military would never consider. But hopefully, his leadership will keep them stitched into an effective fighting unit. He steps back into the forward section, dons his helmet, and prepares to exit through a special airlock that prevents this part of the plane from becoming contaminated.

Outside, he finds the temperature already well over a hundred, and re-alizes that the suits are going to quickly become miniature purgatories for their occupants. Still, he takes comfort in the noisy bustle of troops and equipment gearing up for action. As he walks away from the cluster of planes toward the distant wall of the Mutant Zone, the first light of dawn creeps over the eastern sky. He shouldn't be out here; he should be back helping to supervise the unloading, but he has to see the enemy, has to physically confront the menace, just like MacArthur, who had a terrible habit of wandering into combat operations and exposing himself to fire.

He stops about ten feet from the wall, which is easily three times his height, and turns on an electric lantern. Hideous. It looks like a thick network of veins and arteries intertwined with octopus tentacles, large snakes, and carnivorous plants. Directly in front of the wall, airborne things the size of rats and mice float and hover as if in a primordial sea.

Parker watches for several minutes, then turns off the light and starts back across the apron.

What the hell, he thinks, we got a job to do, so let's do it.

Michael is awakened by the deep rhythmic thud of the chopper blades pounding his bedroom wall. As he sits up, he realizes that he fell asleep with all his clothes on. Still groggy, he gets to his feet as the beating of the blades grows even louder. He opens the window curtain to the semidark-ness of early morning and there it is, a sleek combat ship covered with camouflage and hovering about twenty feet above the vacant lot, where grass and bushes bend and ripple in the shadow of the prop wash.

What's going on? The phone lines are still up, so why didn't they just phone him? He is still trapped in a damp bag of fatigue and struggles to regain his judgment. The chopper continues to hover in a stationary position, and Michael can see a figure in an isolation suit looking out through the open side door. What's it mean? He could try to phone Jessica, but that would eat up time. Better to just go out and see for himself.

In the living room, he finds Jimi curled up on the couch and decides he'd better wake him.

"Jimi, let's wake up for a minute, OK?"

Jimi rubs his eyes, which then open wide as he becomes aware of the noise of the chopper blades.

"It's OK. It's just a helicopter outside, and I think they want to talk to me, so I'm going to see what the deal is."

"I want to go, too," Jimi says resolutely.

"OK. But you've got to stay back if I go up to where the helicopter is. It's too dangerous for a kid. Got it?"

Jimi nods and they both hustle out the door, down the stairs, and through to the vacant lot. As soon as they pull into sight of the chopper, the wind blast hits them and pulls their hair back while forcing their faces into an involuntary squint. There are no markings on the side of the ship, but it's obviously some kind of military machine, like the one Michael took the other day out to ParaVolve. Now the suited figure in the door spots him and beckons emphatically. Seeing the urgency of this motion, it suddenly occurs to Michael that they might be in some kind of immediate danger. He turns and yells in Jimi's ear.

"I'm going to find out what they want. Wait here."

He takes off at a trot toward the chopper, which drops to about a yard above the ground. As he closes the distance, he instinctively ducks when in range of the whirling blades, and the suited figure reaches out the door to offer him a hand. Upon reaching the ship, he grabs the hand, puts one foot on the runner, and propels himself through the door.

The instant his knees hit the deck, he feels the chopper lift into the sky and turns to see Jimi, the Romona Arms, the vacant lot, the trailer court, and the mini-mall all coming into view and rapidly receding. Turning his attention back into the chopper, he sees the suited figure pulling another isolation suit from a metal chest, along with a helmet and breathing apparatus.

"We can't leave that kid!" yells Michael, pointing toward the ground. "He's down there alone. We've got to take him out!"

"Here," commands the face in the suit, ignoring Michael. "You need to get into this before we reach the target."

"What about Jimi, the kid down there?" asks Michael while pointing toward the ground.

"Sorry. We've got orders. Now get this on pronto, or you're going to be one sick son of a bitch." The suited man throws the gear at Michael with an aggression that makes it clear that there should be no further debate.

Michael throws the gear back at the man. "I'm not doing shit until you go back and pick up Jimi."

The suited figure produces an automatic pistol and points it at Michael. "OK, pal, listen up. Short of killing you, I'm authorized to use any force necessary to pull off this operation. Got it?"

"No, I don't get it at all. Where are we going?"

"It's some company called ParaVolve. Our orders are to get you to the target ahead of the main force. That's all I know."

"You guys with the Air National Guard?"

"Not exactly. Now get the suit on. We'll be there in just a couple of minutes."

Something is wrong. Very wrong. But at several thousand feet over a teeming carpet of biology gone berserk, Michael has little choice but to go along. He'll just have to play it by ear. And so will Jimi.

A quarter mile from ParaVolve, in a place where the mutant jungle is at its maximum density, in a place where a human would die within seconds from a massive allergic reaction, the needle hounds and medugators pause as they hear the rotors of a helicopter beat low overhead, then they go back about their business. The temperature here hovers around 120 degrees and the creatures move in near darkness, relying on their infrared eyes to guide them through a series of tunnels that spin a circular web fifty yards in diameter. At the center of this web is a large pear-shaped vessel planted deep in the ground with only the tip breaking the top soil. A tough, rubbery material covers the surface, making it impervious to invasion from the outside, and near its maximum diameter of six feet, two large tubes extend from either side and branch out underground into smaller tubes that slink along under the circular web of tunnels. At key intersections in the tunnel network, these feeder tubes come to the surface and connect to chemical processing sites built from hollow, bony tubes, bladderlike receptacles, and calcified craters containing a volatile porridge that is fed continuously by the drillers, which bore vigorously into the surrounding life-forms and return to dump cylindrical samples of their victims into the craters. Each processing site contributes a unique mix of compounds that flows down the feeder tubes into the main tubes and out into the central vessel. Here many of the compounds have interacted to construct thousands of layers of lining, while others have found their way to the central chamber and swim in a warm bath. The chemicals that flow through the lining are now producing electrochemical events that cause electrical fields to course through the central chamber. Throughout this mild but persistent flux of electromagnetism, molecules join into families and families join into communities, until now an entire nation has taken form, an embryo that will soon undergo the first of billions of divisions and then march toward a destiny written in between the lines of life, where the introns dwell, now and always.

The Last Thing is on its way.

28

XXXXXX

Bug Spray

As the chopper descends toward the roof of the main building at Para-
Volve, Michael surveys the layout of the complex, looking for some clue
to escape, but sees none. Half of the site is devoted to the three-story
main building, and the other half to a pair of smaller structures that are
separated by a large parking area, which also lines the entire periphery of
the complex, where the Mutant Zone strains at the heavy fence. The
main building is square, and half of its roof area is a tent-shaped metal
grid housing hundreds of large glass panes that cover the atrium below,
where DEUS dwells. A large pipe emerges from near the center of the
roof and curves at the top like a ventilator on a steamship. Michael recalls
his one visit inside the atrium and realizes that this pipe is the ventilator
shaft for the forced air-cooling system that keeps DEUS from melting
down in a furnace of its own making.

The chopper skids touch the roof in the proximity of a service entrance that juts out of the top of the building and offers a single door. The
pilot immediately kills the engines, and the prop wash fades, a cue for
legions of lizard-sized insects to scuttle about across the black tar surface.

"Let's hit it," commands the figure in the suit, who again wields a large
automatic pistol to augment his authority. As he waves the weapon toward the open cockpit door, Michael sees the door at the service entrance on the roof open and another suited figure peek out. As his feet hit

the roof, he feels a great throb shudder up through his legs, and speculates that the entire complex is now on emergency power generated by
the diesel-powered generators he saw on his previous tour.

As they move toward the service door, Michael sees that both his
escort and the pilot are following right behind him, trying to minimize
their exposure to infectious agents. When he reaches the door, the suited
figure from inside ParaVolve motions Michael on through and points
down the stairs, where a set of iron steps lead to a fire door that connects
into the third-floor hallway. As Michael starts down the stairs, he can
hear the clatter of the others behind on the steps. For a moment, he
considers bolting down the stairs to the first floor and then into the
depths of the building, which must be deserted, but before he can move
to action, his escort speaks in a voice amplified by the sheer cement walls
of the stair enclosure.

"Hold it right there."

Michael stops, and the escort moves around him, opens the third-
story door, and motions him forward with the pistol. "In here." Michael,
the pilot, and their host from ParaVolve all file on through, and Michael
realizes they are in the corridor where Victor's office is located. But the
corridor is blocked by a tent of milky plastic inflated to fit flush against
the floor, walls, and ceiling. The escort motions them into the tent and
points to breathing masks that dangle from flexible hoses. When they
have all donned the masks, he pushes a button on a console, and a mist
of decontaminant showers down on them, then is sucked out through an
exhaust vent. When they exit on the far side of the tent, the man from
ParaVolve removes his helmet, and the head of Victor Shields appears
from the top of the suit.

"You can take off your helmet now," says Shields as the pilot and the
escort do so. "The detectors don't indicate any contamination inside the
structure. At least not yet."

"Surprise meeting you here," Michael comments to Victor as he removes his helmet. "Your devotion to job and country is overwhelming."

"Riley, I've tried all along to sober you up about what's happening
here," Victor snaps. "The time for smartass is over."

"Let's get going," interrupts the escort, pointing his pistol down the
hall. With the escort's helmet off, Michael sees the broad face, the sandy
haircut, the broken nose, the tunneled eyes. Definitely not Air National
Guard.

"Friends of yours, Victor?" Michael asks as they walk along in front of the pair. "Sorry. I forgot. You're the CEO around here and it's lonely at the top."

"The top," echoes Victor. "You're about to meet the top." He turns into a large office where a tall, trim man with gray hair stares out the window. He wears a lightweight version of the isolation suit, and a hood and respirator sit on a nearby table. When they have all filed in, he turns to face them.

Daniels, thinks Michael, it's Daniels. His mind tumbles back to Washington, D.C., the NSA, the convenience store.

"Mr. Riley," starts Counterpoint, "it's been a long time. Wish we could hash over old times, but I've got a problem, a sort of two-headed monster. Given your brilliant background, I'm sure you're aware of what ParaVolve is really all about. What we're doing here is literally priceless, both strategically and economically. Only, somewhere in here is a bomb of sorts that could bring the whole thing down. That's problem number one. Problem number two is fairly obvious," continues Counterpoint as he points his thumb backward out the window. "Now, what I propose is very simple. Either you find a solution to problem number one, or I arrange for you to become a part of problem number two. Do I make myself clear?"

"Quite clear," replies Michael with a hint of defiance. *They don't know! They haven't got any way to tell the bomb is already disarmed! As soon as they know, I'll be pet food for the Mutant Zone.*

"I need a place to work."

"Mr. Shields here will be only too glad to arrange accommodations," offers Counterpoint as he turns to Victor. "You and Mr. Riley have been partners in this venture since the beginning, and now I think that it's time you share the risks as well as the rewards. I wish you both the very best."

Counterpoint turns to the military escort. "Take them to the control room." He looks at the pilot. "You stay here."

When the door closes behind Shields, Riley, and their guard, Counterpoint returns to the window, his back facing the pilot. "I'm going to make you the best offer you've ever had. You're going to survive all this. From now on, you report directly to me. Go up to your ship and stand by. And don't think about leaving early. I have a shoulder-launched missile with your name on it."

He points to a shelf where a cylinder the size of a medium mailing tube, with a simple pistol grip, rests. Unlike earlier generations of its species, which had elaborate sighting, arming, and launch systems, the intelligence of this weapon is almost totally invisible.

"One more thing," adds Counterpoint as the pilot turns to leave. "When you picked up Riley at the apartments—did you see anyone else there?"

"Yes, sir. There was a young boy."

"That's all."

As the pilot leaves, Counterpoint floats on long waves of anticipatory pleasure.

The metal gate rumbles down slowly, and reminds Michael of the security gates that come down in storefronts in shopping malls. On the far side of it, their military escort watches as the gate thumps against the floor, and then he leaves without looking back. Michael turns and begins to scan the three-story walls of the atrium, which are solid slabs of cement.

"Save yourself the trouble," laments Victor, who stands next to Riley. "There's no other way out."

"Well, partner," suggests Michael, "let's get shakin'."

They walk over the vast cement floor toward the small building in its center where DEUS lives. Around them is the equivalent of an electrical substation, which includes a backup for the backup for the backup. Big diesels roar and rumble as they crank over industrial-strength generators that back up the external electrical supply from the local power grid. Halfway to the central building with DEUS, Michael turns to Victor and motions to the location of the diesels. "Come on over here. I want to show you something."

"Show me what?" Victor asks suspiciously as he starts to follow Michael.

"It's easier to show you than tell you."

A minute later, they are standing next to one of the diesels and are immersed in oily odors and constant roaring. The pulse of the great engine vibrates the floor and pulses up through their shoes.

"So show me," yells Victor.

"The control room is probably bugged," speculates Michael as he leans close to Victor's ear. "This spot could be, but it probably isn't. Now that we're partners, there's a few things you ought to know. First of all, the bomb is gone. I took it out a week ago."

Victor goes pink with rage. "You stupid fuck! Why didn't you tell me? We'd be home free!"

"We don't have a lot of time, so I'm going to have to give you the condensed version."

Michael relates the story of the lab in Mexico, the biological-warfare weaponry, the kuru assassination, the connection to Zap 37, the bio-compiler. Victor gradually goes from pink to white, a verification of his ignorance about the dark underside of ParaVolve.

"So you see, Victor, the bomb was small change. Even if we get out of here, the rest of your career will probably be spent in court or various penal institutions—places where they don't have an executive dining room."

"I don't believe you," Victor says through a knotted jaw. "You're lying."

"Nope," replies Michael as he heads back toward the DEUS building. "And I've got a witness to prove it."

When they reach the building, Michael gets a very funny sensation. He is going into Mouthball's house, just as if he were visiting a friend, only this friend is code and circuit instead of flesh and blood. Victor produces a card key, and the door slides open to reveal the control room with its multiple consoles and a large hi-res screen against the far wall. On the screen, the green liquid cube is stable but stormy on the surface, indicating a lot of processor traffic.

"This shouldn't take long," says Michael as he slides into the chair of the main console and slips on the headset. After a few minutes of technical arcana, he is ready.

"Victor Shields, meet Mouthball."

On the big screen in front of them, the green cube metamorphoses into a ball, and the familiar facial features of Mouthball come to life across the surface of the sphere. At the same time, Mouthball's living room emerges out of the black background. Every surface is now over-run by the plants and beasts of the Mutant Zone.

Victor stands nervously in the center of the control room and watches Mouthball's eyes blink open. "Come on, Riley," he snaps. "It's just graphics. It's been done before. Big fucking deal."

"It may not be a big fucking deal to you, Mr. Shields," says Mouthball, "but I can assure you it's a very big fucking deal to me."

"Holy shit!" exclaims Victor. "It's alive!"

"First things first," says Michael. "Mouthball, are you still connected with Jimi? Did he get back into the apartment?"

Mouthball grins. "He's fine. His dad is taking care of him."

"Well, old buddy," sighs Michael, "we're down to basics now. Can you see outside?"

"Yes, I can. I've tapped into all the security cameras. It doesn't look good."

"And what are we going to do about it?"

"I'm going to have to face the bad dreams. Remember your promise to disconnect me if it goes bad?"

"I do."

"Will you do it?"

"I will."

"What in God's name is he talking about?" interrupts Victor.

"Later," says Michael. "Mouthball, before we start, you've got to make the connection with the lab at OHSU and tell Jessica what's going on so she can receive the data and get somebody to pull us out of here. I can't do it myself because the phones are monitored here."

"Done." Mouthball rapidly scales down in size until he becomes invisible.

"How long has it been like this?" Victor asks. "Do you realize what this is *worth*, Riley?"

"I'm not sure, Victor. But we'll soon find out. One way or the other."

"What do you mean?"

"That whole screaming jungle out there exists for one reason only. It wants to destroy what you've just seen."

"But why?"

"To ensure that the biocompiler is never completed."

The XT-5 Mantis missile clears its launchpad in a fraction of a second and becomes a free agent of explosive death in the sky over Washington County. A moment before launch, it conducted a terse electronic conversation with the computer in the attack chopper, and received the rules of the game. Now its on-board computer and radar eyes greedily devour the rich field of target opportunities in the sphere of airspace outside the tight formation of military choppers, and picks a single blip that seems optimized in terms of vulnerability. It covers the distance to the target in only six seconds, and detonates upon impact, creating a fearsome blast from twenty-five pounds of high explosives.

Colonel Parker watches with mixed anxiety and satisfaction as the orange fireball erupts among the news helicopters. Serves the bastards right. They received repeated warnings to vacate the area, but hung on like a stubborn little cloud of mosquitoes. So there was little choice but to resort to extreme measures and take out one of them so the rest got the message. History would surely vindicate him. Decisive times require decisive action. There was no way he would let these brave boys fight a desperate battle and have the hovering media hounds record it like a three-ring circus. As the flaming debris fell groundward on trails of black smoke, the other ships in the press corps scattered and ran.

The pilot interrupts his rumination. "Sir, we've got a call from the target zone. Wants to speak with you. Gave a clearance code of 'Counterpoint'."

"Put him on." Parker grabs his headset. "Counterpoint, this is Striker."

"Striker," rasps the radio voice, "I just saw a news chopper go down. Was that a unilateral action?"

"Yes, sir." Parker suddenly realizes that he may have a long wait before history sees the incident his way.

"Very well. Proceed with the plan. Good luck."

"Thank you, sir."

ParaVolve is now clearly visible from the windshield, an island of pavement with three buildings set against the unrelieved tangle of the Mutant Zone, which from his height looks like a summer lawn gone badly to weed. As they descend, Parker can see the advance team's chopper parked on the roof of the main building next to the pitched glass roof with its metal grid. His ship sets down in the large parking area between the two smaller buildings, causing thousands of small creatures to be blown away in the prop wash and scatter over pavement pocked with little burrows and plant clusters. Too late to worry about that now. The other ships are coming in on both sides of him, big twin-rotor jobs painted camouflage colors that ironically mirror those of the Mutant

Zone. Before donning his helmet, Parker calls over a radio patch to the other ships. "Alright, you all know the job. Let's do it."

As their rotors spin to a halt, the loading doors on the backs of the big ships open and suited figures pour out, along with wheeled carts carrying tanks, hoses, and compressors. The plan is simple: Form a defensive perimeter around the site, a biochemical Maginot line, and hold it at all costs. The tanks on the carts hold both flamethrowing equipment and power-spraying systems to deliver a variety of insecticides and defoliants so powerful and potentially risky that some have never even been field-tested.

As Parker sets up his command center in front of the main building, the calls come in over his portable radio. All units are now in place. Except one. The platoon commander cannot be reached, and now Parker sees why. To his right, a group of suited figures appears from around the side of the main building, and at the head of the group, one figure holds a rifle to the back of the person in the lead as they march in the direction of the choppers. An obvious case of desertion. They are taking the pilot and getting out.

Or so they think. Parker punches in a preprogrammed frequency on his portable radio and waits until the group is halfway through boarding one of the big choppers, then whistles into the microphone. In the far parking lot, the choppers begin to explode like a string of firecrackers, bloated orange balls flecked with flying debris. The suited figures still outside the craft are engulfed in the fireball, then flung high in the air, where they do a terminal ballet before landing on the pavement. In an instant the heat of the blast waves reaches Parker and he feels it through his suit. The choppers blaze furiously like sacrificial birds and puke thick tufts of black smoke into the morning air. Phase Three of the operation is complete, and Parker congratulates his foresight in planning it this way. But he knows the real credit has to go to Cortez, who initiated the tactic when he invaded Mexico with a handful of men to take on an empire of millions and burned the expedition's boats before they set off inland. Be it boats or choppers, the message is the same: Turning back is no longer an option. All along the perimeter, Parker can see the men watching the big birds burn and slowly absorbing the consequences.

Someday we'll all be in a hotel ballroom somewhere, muses Parker.

Someday, they'll all stand up from their tables and toast me, their commander in the Battle of ParaVolve. Someday.

"Shit! Not now!"

Jessica is riding on the edge of exhaustion as the E-mail interrupt comes across and plants its announcement window smack in the middle of the screen on her workstation. She is right in the middle of an intricate calibration procedure to prepare the automated lab equipment to assemble whatever code sequence the net might specify as an infectious agent to wipe out the Mutant Zone. She almost trashes the E-mail window, but then notices the sender:

TO: Jessica M.
FROM: Mouthball

It's a bad joke, she thinks, but then realizes that no one at OHSU has ever heard of Mouthball. It seems impossible that the net could get into the university network, then on to the subring for her department, then into the local E-mail system . . . but of course it could. In fact, it would be no more difficult than an adult human figuring out where somebody lived in a nearby neighborhood. She speaks into her headset, "Open the mail," and up comes a brief message:

Jessica,
Need to speak with you immediately. Go to X-Window2 and open Re-
moteNet.
Mouthball

Jessica opens X-Window2, which lets graphics and sound flow across the network from any remote location and into her workstation. In this case, the graphics will originate from a program called RemoteNet, which provides telecommunications links to computers outside the university. She opens a window, invokes the program, and there is Mouthball in his infested living room.

"You can see me, but I can't see you," says Mouthball, "unless you've got video somewhere in the lab you can patch in."

"Sorry," apologizes Jessica. It seems very strange to see Mouthball outside the context of Michael's apartment. "Have you talked to Michael? Do you know that we need you to help infect the Mutant Zone?"

"We'll get to that later; right now we don't have much time," says Mouthball. "So let me tell you what's going on. Michael is at the Para-Volve site."

"He can't be!"

"I'm afraid he is. There's some kind of paramilitary force here and they abducted him. He's going to need your help to get out. Mine, too. Also, Jimi's alone at the Romona Arms. You need to get a helicopter to go in and get both of them out."

"I can't just go and ask . . ."

"I suggest you let me do the selling. Just put me in front of the right people."

Fifteen minutes later, Dr. Tandy and Blaine Blanchard sit with Jessica in a conference room with a large high-res screen and a video camera aimed at the conference table.

"What do we need the videocam for?" asks Blanchard.

At that very moment, the screen comes to life, and Mouthball looks out at the trio. "Because that's how I can see who I'm talking to, Mr. Blanchard."

Blanchard is temporarily dumbfounded, but then recovers and turns to Jessica. "You could program that in, right? That could just be a program."

"In that case," says Mouthball before Jessica can reply, "I'd like to interrupt this program to bring you a very important message."

As Parker watches the troops move forward with their pressure hoses toward the bulging cyclone fence, he clicks the mike on his radio and transmits to Counterpoint, who watches from the window three stories above.

"OK, this is it."

He waits for a reply, but none comes, so he does one last check of the disposition of his forces. Ironically, they look like a formation in an open-field battle from the last century. In the leading row are men with pressure hoses that snake back to the rear, where gasoline engines rattle to keep compressors charged and ready to propel the contents of nearby tanks full of toxins. The second row is set back ten yards from the first, and contains men with flamethrowers mounted on their backs. Back another ten yards are marksmen with automatic assault rifles. All around them, small creatures scurry in and out, oblivious to their presence.

Then the air is filled with a giant hiss as the lead men direct their spray into the Mutant Zone on the other side of the fence. Each sprays in a horizontal arc that overlaps slightly with the spray from the next man. The instant the spray hits, the bulges go out of the cyclone fence as a reflexive action ripples through the biomass and sends it into retreat. The vertical forest of tentacles and tendrils that poke through the fence holes goes limp and lifeless.

"Take that, you bastards!" yells Parker through his helmet as he watches the first line retreat and drag their spent hoses to the rear. The second line holds fast and drops to one knee, ready to activate their flamethrowers as soon as the order is given. "You see that?" bubbles Parker over his radio to Counterpoint. "You see that?"

From above, Counterpoint looks down on the rows of suited men, the snaking hoses, the puddles of toxic fluid. The late-morning sun spreads a rainbow through the mist from the spraying. Then, far out in the zone, a motion catches his eye, but he temporarily refuses to believe it.

A wave. A giant wave is propagating through the squirming sea. It rolls toward them along a front at least a mile wide. His radio crackles with Parker's jubilation, but he doesn't answer. He is too busy putting on his helmet and heading for the service entrance on the roof, where the chopper waits.

The wave reaches ParaVolve about the same time Counterpoint reaches the roof. From his position back by the building's entrance, Parker is the only person to clearly witness what happens. The cyclone fence literally explodes into the parking lot, taking out the line of flamethrowers in the process. Before the marksmen in the third line can react, a twenty-foot living wall rolls over them and over the support equipment and troops behind them. The wall is a boiling mass of carnivorous vegetation, berserk insects, drillers, needle hounds, medugators, and a hundred other species, all crammed into metabolic overdrive. Parker has just two horrific seconds to watch the men disappear, and then the wall reaches him.

In a final and ancient gesture, he raises his forearm to save himself and then feels the mushy weight of the wave roll over him as it goes on to smash through the windows on the first story. In the blackness, he feels a thousand things rub against him as his breath rushes out under the crushing weight. Then the probing, the jabbing, the biting, and the stinging start. Parker manages one agonized yell before the faceplate on his helmet shatters, and a series of bony instruments rush in to begin the spontaneous disassembly of his face.

As Counterpoint emerges on the roof, he sees the chopper pilot has the engine started and the rotor blades up to speed. Good. The air is already filling with a cloud of flying things that will soon be thick enough to clog the engine intakes. For now, the suit and helmet will protect him from stings and bites as he sprints toward the chopper. He feels a twisted sort of relief. The Battle of ParaVolve is over, and he lost, but now he is free to pursue power in a much more personalized form, one that doesn't demand millions of dollars and covert political networks.

When he reaches the chopper, he grabs the door, flings himself in, and shuts it as fast as possible. Nevertheless, a purple wasplike thing makes it through, bounces off the windshield, and hits the floor, where he stomps on it with his boot. Already the chopper is lifting, and as he looks down at the atrium window, he remembers Shields and Riley are down in there somewhere. Too bad. As they gain altitude and the scene expands, he can see the churning, predatory mass of teeth, tubes, legs, and wings is collected around the main building and is ignoring the other two structures, where the charred chopper remains look like a string of doused camp fires.

"Where to?" the pilot's voice intrudes.

"Back to the Romona Arms."

When Jimi's dad enters Mouthball's living room, all the vermin scurry out and the wild plants droop toward the floor. Jimi is not surprised. It's the kind of respect his dad deserves, even in the cybernetic universe.

"So, little guy, how are you doing? Sorry I had to be gone for a bit. I'm fixing it so a helicopter will come and get you out of here. But here's the deal: Don't go outside. Wait until they come up to the apartment and get you. Got that?"

"Got it."

Jimi's dad pauses, looks down, and then looks at Jimi without saying anything. A wistful smile plays across his lips. Jimi doesn't like it. Something is wrong.

"Jimi, there's some big trouble in here. A monster got in somehow, and now it's trying to destroy the whole system. And since I'm trapped in here, it's trying to destroy me, too. So there's going to be a battle, a very big battle."

"Are you going to win?"

"I don't know."

A thrust of fear punches into Jimi's throat. "But what'll happen if you lose? My mom's gone for good. There won't be anybody. Then what do I do?"

A more relaxed smile settles onto Jimi's dad. "What I want to know is, how did you get along before you found me?"

"Well, I just thought how you would be there if I really needed you."

"But that wasn't true, was it? All this time, I've been trapped in here, so there's no way I could have helped you. The truth is, you helped yourself."

"I did?"

"Yes, you did. And if anything happens to me, that's exactly what you're going to keep on doing. You're my kid. You've got what it takes. Just like your dad. Don't ever forget it. OK?"

"OK," agrees Jimi as he fights back tears.

"I've got to go now. Wish me luck."

"Good luck, Dad."

"And good luck to you, Son." Jimi's dad winks, turns, and walks out of the living room. The vermin slowly creep back in and the plants begin to spring upright.

The pear-shaped vessel begins to contract violently, sending tiny seismic waves through the soil, and through the processing plants that have nourished it. The drillers and medugators sense the waves, and take them as a cue to move in close to the spot where the tip of the vessel now pokes through the ground surface. Many of the outer layers of the vessel have evolved into muscle fiber and are contracting rhythmically. Now, in one last cathartic burst, something is squeezed out the top and rolls over onto the ground.

The Last Thing opens its eyes for the first time, as insects with suction tubes remove the coat of slime that covers its skin. It stares up into a hole of hot gray sky that has been bored through the dense growth. As its pupils contract in response to the light, the Last Thing rises on wobbly legs inside the small cavern carved to accommodate its height. After rotating a quarter turn, it finds the tunnel, a broad expanse lined with drillers and medugators, like an honor guard from hell. Vertical shafts dot the tunnel ceiling at regular intervals and admit daylight from above to illuminate the path, which runs in a perfectly straight line for fifteen hundred yards to the parking lot at ParaVolve.

Michael and Victor Shields stand at the open door of the DEUS building inside the atrium. They stare across the concrete floor to the spot where the hallway tunnels into the massive concrete wall, where the roll-down security gate blocks their freedom. On the other side of the gate, they can see where the short hallway tunnel connects to the main hall. Minutes before, they had been watching the five-second Battle of ParaVolve on the security monitors in the DEUS control room and heard the chopper depart from the roof overhead. Now, as they stand in the open doorway, shadows play across the concrete floor and the massive electrical power fixtures. Michael looks up three stories to the roof and sees thousands of shapes slithering over the glass, blocking the flow of daylight, and creating shadows that dance across the floor. In the distance, they can still hear the occasional crashing of glass from the outer portions of the building.

Then the first creature shows up in the outer hall, a needle hound that pads along in profile over the carpet with its clawed feet. When it is framed in the center of the short tunnel hallway, it stops and turns to face them. The eye stalks twist and adjust, and the thing lumbers forward and approaches the security gate.

"Think it can get in?" asks Victor, who has become markedly subdued since Michael's revelation about the true nature of ParaVolve.

"We'll know in a minute," answers Michael.

The needle hound reaches the vertical grating of the security gate and extends its cylinder. The hooked teeth come out and wrap around spaces in the grating, and the pink pulp of its inner mouth bulges through. From the center of the cylinder, the hypodermic slithers out, slides through the grating, and ejects a long, thin stream of liquid that lands on the concrete floor, where it hisses and sends up a cloud of caustic smoke as it scars the cement.

"Gentlemen, let us proceed."

Michael and Victor look back into the control room and see Mouthball on the center console screen, floating in the middle of his living room among the mutant beasts.

"You've talked with Jessica?" asks Michael as he returns to his seat.

"It's all set. They're also going to send a chopper here in exactly thirty minutes from now."

"And what about Jimi?"

"They'll pick him up on the way back after they get you."

"One small detail," adds Michael. "How are we going to get out of here and on to the roof so the chopper can get us?"

"You're going up the ventilation shaft that air-conditions me."

Michael immediately visualizes the huge pipe that runs from the DEUS building to the roof. "Are there ladder rungs in there?"

"No. It's perfectly smooth. Designed that way to enhance air flow."

"Then how do we get up?"

"I'm going to have to help you. We're going to modify the air pressure."

Michael is about to ask why they can't just go right now, but then stops. He has given Mouthball his word he will disconnect the net if the bad dreams drive Mouthball mad. Which means he can't leave until after the encounter is over. Which also means he is trapped here if Mouthball fails.

"So," he sighs to Mouthball, "we're all in this together, huh?"

"We're all in this together," echoes Mouthball. "Now, shall we get on with it?"

"Why not?" replies Michael. "What can we do to help you?"

"Nothing. Just watch. Be my witness."

"How will I know if we've lost you?"

"The image you're now looking at will degenerate into total chaos."

"Do you know what we'll see during your encounter?"

"I'm not sure. Let's find out."

Mouthball closes his eyes and the sphere tilts back slightly. Facial tics begin to appear. The corner of the mouth jerks downward. The eyelids flutter.

Simple enough, observes Michael. Maybe we're going to get off easy.

Then one of the things crawling on Mouthball's couch springs off and leaps on to his head. A cross between a lizard and an insect, the thing moves cautiously on six legs and snaps a pair of pincers that extend from its mouth while its eyes greedily survey the surface of Mouthball. While it assays its findings, a second, smaller thing hops on, a wormlike beast with stubby legs and sprocket eyes. Then a third thing, with a bony exoskeleton and barbed talons for locomotion.

As the parade of beasts continues to mount him, Mouthball shudders. His lips curl back to reveal tightly clenched teeth, and one of the worm beasts darts into the crevice between his two front incisors and squirms into the space between the gum and the lip, where it becomes a vague moving bulge beneath the skin. The bulge disappears, and a moment later the same worm comes out his nostril, covered with blood and mucus. By now, there are dozens of things patrolling the surface of Mouthball, looking for targets of opportunity. The six-legged thing with pincers sinks them into one of his eyes, and aqueous fluid drains down his cheek. A blind snake with mole fangs emerges from his right ear and sways in an obscene dance. Then a similar beast pops out of his other eye and snaps at another thing that excavates his lower cheek, leaving a tunnel where the back molars are visible. A team of mining insects deploys over the skull and punches holes that spout miniature geysers of thick yellow fluid.

"I'm gonna be sick," gasps Shields, who bolts from his chair and retches near the back of the control room.

Michael watches in agony. While he cannot help, he cannot turn away. He promised he would be the witness to this ordeal, and now honor binds him to observe, no matter how awful things get. There are now so many creatures plastered on Mouthball, he is lost from sight as they crawl over each other and fight to get a piece of the action.

Then, just as Michael starts to entertain the idea of pulling the plug, some of the beasts begin to drop off and crawl away in disgust. They are quickly followed by others, and patches of the shredded surface of Mouthball start to become visible.

"Mouthball," calls Michael, rising from his chair, "are you there?"

The things are gone now, and even the living room itself is clearing. What is left of Mouthball looks like the surface of the moon, an angry montage of overlapping craters, mountains, and gullies, all bleeding a variety of fluids.

No answer.

"Mouthball," pleads Michael. "Old buddy. Can you hear me?"

A long canyon forms in the lower hemisphere of the cratered sphere, and then opens.

"Can hear you."

Michael sinks back into his chair in relief. On the sphere, the mountains gradually shrink and the craters and canyons slowly fill in. The eyes, nose, mouth, and ears appear out of the annealing surface. Mouthball is back.

"Was it as bad as you thought it would be?" asks Michael.

A smile comes to Mouthball's lips. "Worse. Anyway, I got what we need."

"What is it?"

"A virus. And a tiny little bugger at that. Four thousand three hundred and thirty-one base pairs, to be exact. If you'll excuse me for a second, I'm going to send it to Jessica at the lab. They ought to be able to mass-produce it in no time. When I get back, we'll get you on out of here."

"That would be appreciated."

Counterpoint sets the chopper down very gingerly in the parking lot of the mini-mall by the Romona Arms. It has been a long time since he landed a ship like this, and the controls seem sluggish and unresponsive even though he knows his own technical flabbiness is to blame. As he cuts the power and the engine spirals into a downward whine, he unbuckles and hops out even before the rotor blades have stopped. Up until now, he has been patient, but the wall of forbearance is rapidly eroding as he thinks how close he is to the dawn of a new life and how his communion with the boy will transmute his flesh into the stuff of immortality.

As he walks toward the boulevard choked with abandoned cars, he sees the circular pool of blood left over from his first landing. The pilot had followed directions perfectly and set down in the middle parking lot, at which time Counterpoint had pulled out a Walther .380 and squeezed off a single round into the side of the man's head. The only hitch was that he somehow lived long enough to open the door and try to climb out, an effort that ultimately failed and left his body belted in the seat but hanging out the door, with a thin stream of blood drooling off his helmet and on to the pavement. In spite of his considerable strength, it was difficult for Counterpoint to reach over and drag the body into the passenger's seat. On his way around to hop into the pilot's seat, he saw only scattered mutant growth, ripped his helmet off, and breathed the warm air of early afternoon. Once at the controls, it took a few moments to orient himself. Flying an unfamiliar craft would be a risky business, but not nearly as risky as leaving a chopper out in the open with a dead pilot in it. The lift-off was slightly shaky, but soon they were on a straight course back into the thick of the Mutant Zone, where he rotated in a complete circle to check for other aircraft, opened the far door, and pushed the dead pilot out. Through the Plexiglas at his feet, he could see the body descend in a lazy spread-eagle spin and punch a hole into the top of the entwined growth.

Now, as he makes his way between the bumpers of the stalled cars on Allen Boulevard, he feels the ceremonial thrill begin to build.

The boy. The perfect boy.

29

XXXXXX

One Last Thing

"Dad! *Dad!* You're back! You're OK! You're back!"

Jimi jumps up from his silent vigil on the floor of the computer room in Michael's apartment. On the screen, his dad strolls confidently into Mouthball's living room as the beasts swarm out in a panicked stampede. He plops down on the couch and waves at Jimi with a breezy grin.

"Yup, I'm back. And I've gotta tell you, Jimi, it was a tough day at the office."

Jimi laughs. "Yeah, sure, the office. You don't *ever* have to go to an office, do you?"

"No, I guess I don't," admits his dad after a modest chuckle. "But on days like today, it doesn't seem like such a bad idea."

Counterpoint strolls across the parking lot at the Romona Arms and watches the small beasts crisscross the pavement in front of him at amazing speeds. Smoke from the many uncontrolled fires belches dirty haze into the sky and turns the sun bloodred and the clouds copper. In every direction, black columns of smoke tower up to meet the haze like bloated tornadoes. The acrid smell of burning plastics and chemicals drifts and mingles with the spicy odor of woodsmoke, while the ugly thump of random industrial explosions settles thickly over the surrounding buildings.

As he mounts the stairs to Riley's apartment, he feels the thrill raise the hairs on his muscular forearms. He can smell the boy inside. He knows it with certainty. The divine hunter in him is always right.

At the door, he stops to collect himself, to devour the day, the smoke, the beasts, the burning sky; to become the central node, the hub of all experience. And now he knocks, knuckles crashing against the wood and sending shock waves through the interior of the apartment. As he waits for a reply, the explosive booms and thuds mix in the distance with the constant scream of sirens. No answer.

"Now," says Jimi soberly to his dad, "how are we going to get you out of the computer?" He leans forward eagerly. "Do you have an escape plan?"

"Well, that's something we . . . "

A loud knock on the front door tumbles down the hall and into the computer room. Jimi leaps to his feet. "That must be the helicopter men."

"What helicopter?" asks Jimi's dad with a frown.

"The one that just flew over the roof."

"Jimi, don't move," warns his dad as he rises to his feet. "I'll be right back."

This time when Jessica sees the E-mail window, she immediately brings Mouthball up. "Are Michael and Jimi OK?" she asks anxiously. "Since that news copter went down, there's no more direct coverage out there."

Mouthball manages a weak smile and tells the first discretionary lie in the history of artificial intelligence. "They're fine." All trace of the original smartass is gone from his face. "Do you know if the helicopter has left yet for ParaVolve to pick them up?"

"Let me check," she replies and opens a small window beside Mouthball that is part of the videocom system. A tired and drawn Blaine Blanchard appears in the small window on Jessica's screen. "Yes?"

"Sorry to bother you, but do you know if the helicopter has left yet for ParaVolve?"

"Not yet. In a couple of minutes. Why?"

"The, uh, neural net that you met in the meeting room wants to know."

"You can tell him, it, whatever, that it's leaving right on schedule. Anything else?"

"That'll do it. Thanks."

The window with Blanchard disappears and Jessica looks up to see Mouthball is already gone.

"Jimi, the helicopter hasn't left yet," warns his dad. "Now listen carefully. When disasters like this thing outside happen, there are bad people who stay around because they know the police are gone and there's nobody to catch them. So here's what I want you to do. Walk very softly to the front door and put your ear against it. Don't make any noise at all. If you hear the person at the door leave and go down the steps, then peek out a crack in the curtains and see who it is. Then come back and tell me. Got it?"

"Got it," assures Jimi, beaming with confidence. At last, he and his dad together as a team.

Counterpoint doesn't attempt a second knock. The boy is undoubtedly hiding inside somewhere, probably whimpering in fear since he doesn't understand the elegance of the gift Counterpoint is about to deliver. With no witnesses left, Counterpoint decides to simply break the front window by the door and crawl in. He turns and scans the parking lot, looking for the first available tool of destruction to break the glass, and there it is, a one-gallon paint can sitting over beside the Dumpster. He bounds down the stairs to fetch it.

With his ear to the door, Jimi can hear the springy booms of feet descending the steps. Even after the feet have stopped, he pauses before rising to look out a small crack in the curtains. When he does, the boilers of fear ignite in his gut and bubble pure dread up through his chest, his heart, his throat. It's the man. The man who stood at the bottom of the stairs that terrible night. The man with the smile of the dead, with the burning eyes. The man who now carries a paint can and heads straight toward the foot of the stairs on his way back up.

But wait. This time his dad is here.

Jimi bounds down the hall and bursts into the computer room. "He's coming! He's going to get me!" he gasps to his dad.

"Do what I say and do it now," orders his dad. And Jimi does.

The Last Thing steps out of the tunnel and into the parking lot of Para-Volve, where the sun has gone bloody in the smoke and a veritable surf of intron-based organisms laps against the lower floor of the main building. All the windows are shattered and the beasts continue to scamper through to the interior. In response to some silent cue, a path opens through the parking lot and the Last Thing walks along the cleared area while the helibugs and balloon beasts hover overhead, and the medugators, needle hounds, and drillers line the path like spectators at a parade. When it reaches the door, the Last Thing is able to walk right through the space where the glass was punched out during the wave attack, and into the lobby, where creatures line up to point the path toward the atrium.

"Victor!" yells Michael. "Are you with me?"

Maybe not. Victor is slumped in his chair in the control room, with twin ropes of mucus pouring out his nose, and eyes bulging hemispherically from their sockets. Angry red blotches cover his face and rise like shallow plateaus above the flesh line. If the building wasn't contaminated before, it most certainly is now.

"Victor . . . " starts Michael again, but before Victor can answer, Mouthball balloons back to normal size in his living room with a very worried look.

"What's the matter?" Michael asks from his seat in the control room. "Can't they synthesize the virus?"

"Yes. In fact, it should be relatively easy."

"Then why the long face?"

"Have you ever wondered exactly how the introns were going to pull the plug on me?"

"Hard to say," replies Michael. "The creatures we've seen are formidable in a biological sense, but they don't look like they're capable of sabotaging or dismantling computer hardware. So what do you think?"

"I don't have to think. Take a look outside."

Michael turns to look back through the door, which they left open so they could hear if the security barrier was breached by the flood of beasts that pressed up against it. Now the beasts have parted, and through the grid work, Michael swears he sees a naked man at the control panel on the other side, just as he hears the hum of a large electric motor and the barrier begins to lift and disappear into the ceiling.

"It's a man," comments Michael.

"No way. Thermal readings are way too high. It just looks like one."

"Then what is it?"

"Big trouble. For me, anyway. And probably for you, too." There is a note of sadness and resignation in Mouthball's voice, but no fear.

The barrier is fully open and the zoo from hell spills in around the naked figure and spreads out over the vast floor as the clicking of thousands of claws and talons reverberates off the massive walls.

"Victor," appeals Michael as he moves over and shakes the stricken man's shoulders, "we've got to close the door. Quick."

"Can't," rasps Victor through a thick wheeze. "Control's out there." He points toward the gate, where the beasts continue to flood in. As in the parking lot, a clear corridor forms over the floor and stretches from the open security gate to the door of the control room. Along the path's edges, the creatures sway and jerk in obvious agitation. The bore mouths on the drillers spin, while the hypodermics dart in and out of the needle hounds and the medugators spit and suck their serpent tongues. The Last Thing begins to walk leisurely down the center of the path, a man of medium height with shoulder-length hair. He appears in no hurry, and seems oblivious to the mutant gallery on either side.

By now the beasts are lined up all the way to the control room door, and Michael can see the flood of teeth, needles, snakes, and twisting eyes, and smell the utterly revolting odors from the hot bodies, which are in permanent metabolic acceleration.

Victor suddenly begins to frantically paw the air in front of him. "Dead!" he rasps. "Dead!" and points to a close-up of the Last Thing on one of the security monitors.

"Who's dead?" asks Michael as he watches the figure continue his slow approach.

"Architect," rattles Victor. "Architect." He groans and his arms go limp as he slips into a comatose state, eyes still open and glittering with terror.

In a flash, Michael sees it. He has never seen the man face to face, but he knows him better than Victor ever will. Somewhere along the line, the Architect has transfused his genes into the DEUS Complex. Suddenly, Michael realizes that all the Architect's written references to his "child" were not metaphorical; they were literally true. And in a monstrous twist of fate, his genetic portrait is now the property of the introns, which are using it as a vehicle to destroy his cybernetic child.

"Time to get you out of here," announces Mouthball. "See the door to my right? Go on through and open the door on the other side to the hardware chamber. I'm going to turn the wind down to about sixty so you can manage. There's a grate on the ceiling, but it just slides off. Get up in the duct and I'll blast you out of here. And one last thing: Tell Jimi to remember what his dad told him about taking care of himself."

"And what about you?"

"No time for that. Go."

Michael turns and sees that the creature is only about thirty feet away. Mouthball is right. No time for weepy good-byes. He heads for the door.

Once inside the short interior corridor, he shuts the door behind him and looks briefly for a lock to keep the thing out, but finds none. The hardware chamber is obviously the thing's destination. Once inside, it will literally unplug both DEUS and the net, one board at a time, and utterly destroy both in the process. Upon reaching the other end of the corridor, Michael has to put all his weight against the door to overcome the pressure from the sixty-mile-per-hour vertical air flow, and wiggle on through to stand on the grating, where the air blast rips through to cool the rows of huge circuit boards studded with multichip modules and wafer-scale memories. Somewhere among these card cages is Mouthball, and as the blast roars by Michael, he realizes that within a very few minutes Mouthball will be dead. He grabs a steel post to steady himself against the artificial storm, and the true impact of Mouthball's demise sinks into his heart. Suddenly, the Architect's prophetic words come back to him:

If you disarm the bomb, you will soon see the mother and child suffer and perish at the hands of the renegade code as it manifests itself in the biosphere.

He now sees the horrible irony of the introns' grabbing the physical template of Mouthball's father to create his killer. And he can't let it happen. He just can't.

Looking around the chamber, he sees medugators, needle hounds, and drillers pressed up against the outside of the observation windows like witnesses to an execution. The pulpy flesh from the needle hounds' mouths forms pale pink lakes where it flattens against the glass.

Then he spots it. A fire extinguisher hanging on the wall next to the door. Just the weapon he needs. He walks awkwardly to retrieve it in the rush of air that lifts him from below and decreases his weight to the point where he is no longer stable on his feet. While lifting the extinguisher off the wall, he slides into a position where he will be able to confront the creature as soon as it comes through the door. As he raises the fire extinguisher over his head into a striking position, he hears a thumping so loud it rolls right over the top of the air roar. The medugators and drill hounds have anticipated what he is about to do, and are beating savagely against the glass, which must be heavily armored to resist. As his eyes come back to the door, it opens, and suddenly he is face to face with the Last Thing.

The Last Thing. Its bright brown eyes gaze at Michael with murderous love, and he makes the mistake of hesitating with the fire extinguisher as the psychic force of the creature captivates him.

In contrast, the introns know that primal encounters are hard-wired affairs, with no room for looping doubts and recursive ruminations. In the single beat that Michael hesitates, a sinewy arm shoots through the door and the heel of a hand crashes into Michael's sternum. With his wind-reduced weight, Michael sails backward as the Last Thing advances through the door. Acting completely on instinct, he flexes his legs, kicks the Thing in the chest, and scrambles to his feet as it does a backward somersault. While the wind blast rudely propels him to a standing position, Michael sees the Thing hurl the fire extinguisher at him, but its aim is bad and the extinguisher collides with the window behind him, propagating a large diagonal crack that sends the beasts outside to a new level of frenzy. They begin to beat with the force of small cannons, and start a tributary crack off the original as the fire extinguisher bounces to a halt on the floor halfway between the two adversaries.

Michael and the Last Thing both launch themselves in perfect synchronicity to retrieve the extinguisher, and collide in midair, shoulder to shoulder. But it is Michael who comes up with the extinguisher in hand and floats to his feet. As he twists to face the Last Thing, he braces for a renewed attack, but instead the Thing hesitates as it rises before him and its lips part.

"RY-LEE."

It knows. The one word writhes out, the teeth flash, the prehistoric grin fades, and the light goes out in the eyes.

Michael cannot wait, cannot think, can only act. He swings the fire extinguisher in a tight, high-velocity orbit that terminates on the side of the Last Thing's skull, which shatters like an egg as the shock wave travels through the brain and lays waste to most of its interior.

After the impact, Michael is carried forward by the force of the swing and has to jump over the body as it crumples to the floor. He doesn't look down. The force of the blow telegraphed all the way up to his shoulder and told him all he needed to know. Then, as he looks up toward the ceiling and spots the ventilator shaft, he hears a crash so loud it rides right over the top of the wind roar. He turns his head just in time to see a large chunk of the cracked window fall inward, no longer able to staunch the flow of the clambering beasts. As they flood through, he ducks around the corner of the big computer card cage, where he bolts up a metal ladder leading to the top of the cage and the ventilator shaft entrance, which is covered by a flimsy wire grating made to slide off for maintenance. As he pulls himself clear at the top of the cage, he takes one look back down upon a boiling stew of beasts, which is literally rising up the side of the cage like an ascending water level. The head of a needle hound protrudes from the rest of the mass and its bony stinger ejects a stream of toxins that misses him by inches before the beast sinks back among its peers. Fighting panic, he reaches up and pulls the grating toward him, which snaps it out of its holders. The wind makes it feather-light as he pulls it aside and continues his climb.

Mouthball, I hope you know what you're doing. If you don't, I'm dead meat.

With his hands on the top rung by the lip of the shaft, he pushes off toward the opposite side with his feet. Before they even reach the end of their arc, the roar of the wind heightens perceptibly, and the soles of his shoes are lifted high enough that they can clamp down on the inside of the shaft. It appears that Mouthball knows precisely what he is doing.

Michael puts one hand and then the other up inside the shaft and finds that its diameter is just slightly larger than his height. From below, the wind cranks up another notch to the point where he is weightless. Experimentally, he moves forward into the darkness, using both hands and feet to guide his upward motion. No problem, except for the fact that he has three stories left to climb.

While he makes his way upward in the bellowing darkness, Michael keeps seeing a vision of the computer screen in his apartment with the words "JEEMEE DEWD." Jimi your dad's an all right guy, thinks Michael as the cushion of air holds him gently in place. Then the final expression of the Last Thing floats before him: the waning light in the eyes, the dying grin. When the introns took occupancy of the Architect's genes, they must have unintentionally borrowed a bit of his soul, too, an error which ultimately cost them the war. But how? Are code and soul one and the same? Right now, Michael is too tired to care.

When he reaches the bend at the top of the shaft, he looks out the opening and sees the circling chopper. It's over.

Counterpoint takes one last look around before he swings the paint can through the front-room window of Michael Riley's apartment. The startling crash of the glass fills the empty complex, and while he chips away the remaining shards off the bottom of the window, he tried to keep a lid on the gleeful swell of adrenaline inside him, but only partially succeeds. As the last shard tinkles into splinters on the pavement, he drops the paint can, which rolls over to the stairs and bangs its way down step by step. Slowly, he pushes up the curtains and looks into the unlit interior as his eyes adjust to the dimness. He knows he will be vulnerable while crawling through the window, and must make sure that he won't be ambushed. As his eyes adjust, the cheap furniture in the living room takes on form. No movement. No sign of life. Doesn't matter. The hunter in him can still smell the boy. He's here, alright. And he's got no way out.

Counterpoint carefully swings a leg over the window frame, and then the other leg. Behind him, the curtain hisses shut and blocks out the distant sounds of calamity as the room goes dim again. The plan is simple: He will search the living room first and then head for the hall . . .

Then he hears it. The muffled whimpering. A choked sob. A thin little whine.

His blood roars.

In the dim light, his hearing slams into the foreground, and he senses that the sound is coming from down the hall to the right. He carefully winds his way around the furniture and sees a glow coming from an open door. Yes. The sound, the boy, are there. Each step now brings him that much closer to life eternal. Just before he reaches the door, he is almost overwhelmed by a vision of the boy stripped naked and rendered completely passive by the power of his presence as he expands to fill the room, the building, the city, the sky, the universe. Now he takes the last triumphant step into the doorway.

The sign on the computer screen says it all: "Fooled Ya!" All the while, a subtle stream of whimpers and sobs comes out of the speaker on the console in perfect digital, stereophonic sound.

Counterpoint tries to bellow, but is choked with rage. He whirls, sees the front door wide open, and charges down the hall and into the living room, where he crashes over the furniture and out into the light.

Just in time to catch the smallest flicker of motion over by the Dumpster. The edge of a small sneaker disappearing into the space between the Dumpster and the back fence, the former cathedral of Rat Bag.

This time, he moves without hesitation and bounds down the stairs and sprints across the parking lot. Along the way, he notes that the other end of the Dumpster is pushed up to within about six inches of a second section of fence that shields it from the units at the back of the complex. Enough room for the boy to crawl out and escape? Maybe. He'll have to move fast. When he reaches the space between the Dumpster and the fence, he stops and smiles.

Got him. The boy is at the far end, and as Counterpoint starts down, the boy squirms frantically into the impossibly small space between the far side of the Dumpster and the adjoining fence. By the time Counterpoint reaches him, the boy is several feet in, but he reaches out a powerful hand, seizes his wrist, and begins to pull.

Which is when he hears a loud "plop" on the pavement and turns to see the medugator facing him and blocking his way out of the space.

Counterpoint lets go of Jimi's wrist, and turns to face this new intruder into the most sacred of ceremonies. It must have been concealed in the rude shock of growth burgeoning out of the Dumpster's interior. The powerful legs and claws look formidable, but the head is a joke, with the huge swollen frog's mouth and the eyes mounted on stalks protruding from the skull. The hunter in him quickly surveys the anatomy, seeking signs of weakness, and sees that the eye stalks are the point of least protection. Then, on the ground halfway between him and the beast, he spots the weapon he needs to exploit this vulnerability, an empty quart beer bottle.

He walks slowly in a crouch, so as not to trigger a charge by the beast, then picks up the bottle and taps it just hard enough on the pavement that it cracks into several large pieces, one containing the handle and a sliver of glass about six inches long. Now if he can just get close enough.

The medugator observes the bipedal object's forward motion and its acquisition of a potential weapon. In response, it prepares to shift to an offensive mode.

Counterpoint takes one more step and then launches into one long fluid motion that extends his arm out in a slashing movement that severs the right eye stalk. The beast bucks upward, catching him in the chest as he retreats and knocking him backward to the fence at the rear of the space, where he falls into a sitting position.

As he starts to his feet, Counterpoint beholds the beast moving forward with great purpose as a fountain of purple blood spouts from the severed stalk and the remaining eye locks on him. Still, what can the thing do with that silly frog's mouth? All he has to do is get the other eye and . . .

The mouth opens into a circular pit, and the last thing Counterpoint ever sees are the two needle-headed serpents shooting right for his face at incredible speed. They puncture both his eyes before he even has time to blink, and plow through the corneas, the pupils, the retinas, and the optic nerves until they hit the skull bone behind. As he opens his mouth to scream, the needle serpents withdraw, and a slashing snake streaks out and cuts his throat from ear to ear, so his bellow subsides into a tortured gurgle as he slides back down to a sitting position.

Due to its traumatic injury, the medugator is too weakened to dismantle the bone structure, so it concentrates on the soft tissues available between the rib cage and the public bone, and carves a horrible red cavern into Counterpoint that extends all the way to the back and exposes the spine. He lives long enough to experience several minutes of the operation.

The moment Counterpoint let go, Jimi pushed and twisted sideways one inch at a time. Along the way, he heard a strangled gurgling and other liquid sounds coming from behind him, but never looked back. Now he wiggles out of the tight space and bursts out into the parking lot, just as the chopper comes into sight over the top of the Romona Arms.

From the chopper, Michael looks down at the small figure of Jimi in the center of the parking lot, and is struck by how tiny and defenseless the boy looks in the midst of all this calamity. He directs the pilot to descend into the vacant lot, where the prop wash lays the grass and bushes low as Jimi appears from around the rear corner of the building. Then a small speck of motion catches his eye and freezes his blood. In the corner of the lot opposite Jimi, he sees a needle hound loping toward the Romona Arms. And another. And another. A large pack spread out like an infantry platoon, with a single beast in the point position, not thirty yards from Jimi, who faces the chopper and waves his arms over his head to let them know where he is.

As the chopper touches down, Jimi lowers his arms and takes a step toward its slashing rotors, but Michael leans from the door and thrusts his arm out with his palm up to halt the boy. He then jumps toward the ground, and the moment he leaves the lip of the chopper door, he descends into another world. The prop wash, the violent beat of the rotors, the snakelike dance of the blown grass all wrap around him like a soft, transparent shroud as he bounds toward Jimi. The urgency of the race against the needle hounds seems suspended, and he feels almost calm as he advances on dumb dream legs toward the boy. And as the image of Jimi grows larger, a great revelation breaks over him.

The Fear is gone. Forever. Stopped cold by some mystical punctuation mark that divides this moment from all others yet to come.

Twenty yards away, the lead needle hound in the pack turns toward the chopper, interprets its mechanical cyclone as an overt act of aggression, and shifts to an offensive mode.

As Michael reaches Jimi, the boy holds out his arms and Michael scoops him up, pivots, and heads back toward the chopper. As he runs through the thick, gelatinous air, he feels Jimi hug him tight, and realizes that he loves this child most dearly. And then he understands why. He is not only hugging Jimi; he is embracing the terrified, wounded child within him that has called out for the comfort he could never give until this supremely suspended moment, where life and death merge into a perfect circle, with Jimi and him at the epicenter.

Fifteen yards away, the needle hound comes out of the bushes into the clear, where it locks on to the bipedal figure running toward the aggressor craft.

Michael pitches Jimi upward and into the arms of a waiting crewman in the chopper. He scarcely notices the second crewman, who is silently screaming at him through the din, and pointing behind him. He floats in a moment of perfect resolution, of complete emotional symmetry, where all elements reflect the primal equilibrium of the newborn child.

Ten yards away, the needle hound confirms the association between the biped and the aggressor craft, and charges.

Michael barely feels the crash against his back and the brief stab of pain as the circular teeth sink in and the bony needle stops his heart and his life. He misses the heroic action of the chopper crew, who somehow tear him loose from the beast and pull his lifeless body on to the metal floor of the chopper.

On the ride back to safety, Jimi kneels by Michael and grasps his index finger, which grows ever cooler with the fading light outside.

Epilogue

XXXXXX

"So, did you hear the latest about Webber?" asks Savage, referring to the former White House Chief of Staff. "Looks like he won't implicate the president after all. Took long enough for him to make up his mind. This thing's dragged on for months now."

"Yes, for months," echoes Jessica as she looks at the videophone image of John Savage framed against the Portland skyline outside her window at OHSU.

"I mean, after all, the president was the one who ordered him arrested. What they're saying now is that the president finally snapped out of it when he saw the military chopper shoot down the news chopper on TV, and realized that he was losing control of the armed forces."

Jessica can't help but be touched by Savage's occasional phone calls, which always idle along a little awkwardly at the chit-chat level. She knows his real motive is simply to check on her, to make sure she is slowly pulling through the grief process. He appears slightly perplexed that she seems fairly happy, and of course, she can't tell him why. When they talk, he seldom mentions his new job, although it must be totally consuming his life at this point. The ParaVolve board, which was hastily assembled in the chaotic days after the fall of the Mutant Zone, had tried to dicker and get him to accept an appointment as transitional CEO while they looked for a permanent one, but Savage held his ground and said it was all or nothing, and the board quickly caved in. In truth, he was the ideal candidate because he carried none of the political baggage that the older candidates did, and brought a wealth of talent and idealism to the job. For the time being, his biggest concern was to stabilize the company, a joint venture of the federal government and private enterprise. Once the full implications of DEUS and the biocompiler were widely known, the stock price had shot up into the stratosphere and the ripple effect had pulled the entire market out of the Downturn. As countless companies geared up to capitalize on the technological fallout of ParaVolve, the entire economy reignited and roared off in pursuit of new nirvanas in the biological realm.

In fact, the only thing about his new post that really annoyed Savage was the smell, the gaseous output of the largest compost pile in natural history, where the remnants of the Mutant Zone decay in a circular area that covers nearly three hundred square miles. The effect of Mouthball's virus had been devastating, and spread terminal disease throughout the Zone at an unbelievable pace. But the aftermath would be around for some time to come. The good news was that biologists calculated that the decomposing material would return the enormous nutrient store that was greedily sucked up from the soil during the peak of the infection. In any case, it made for an interesting drive to work at ParaVolve, which was surrounded by this stinking sea of collapsed biomass that stretched for miles in every direction.

"John, sorry, but I've got to get going. Got to pick up Jimi and get to a meeting. Thanks for calling."

As Savage signs off, his image is replaced by a list of calls waiting to be answered, each with a stamp-sized video image of the caller. Sometimes her new job seems almost overwhelming, but Dr. Tandy is the perfect mentor and assures her that she is doing remarkably well, given the enormous political sensitivities involved. As the person appointed by Mouthball to be his interface with the scientific community, she holds fantastic power, in theory anyway. At first, it seemed utterly outrageous that a technology as revolutionary as the biocompiler would remain in the hands of what some critics called a "mental robot"—until you considered humankind's own abysmal record in regulating deadly technology, all the way from the Manhattan Project to Farmacéutico Asociado. Besides, there was little choice in the matter. The biocompiler technology was far too complex to be extracted from DEUS and Mouthball without their cooperation, and they simply were not interested. "You messed up before. You'll mess up again" was Mouthball's definitive comment on the matter. So now any request to use the biocompiler was filtered through Mouthball, who examined the proposals written by scientists and decided on the relative merit of each. At first there was much affront about the system; however, Mouthball's impartial treatment of the petitioners had already gained him widespread respect in the biological sciences.

But right now, Mouthball and international science would have to wait. There is something infinitely more important to tend to.

Jimi's dad banks the craft to forty-five degrees as they round the corner of the huge building, and Jimi feels the hum of the thrusters as he looks out at the rows of windows that stretch for nearly a quarter mile ahead. In the distance, a purple desert stretches to a horizon where a binary sun system hovers.

"OK, Jimi, it's all yours, big guy. Take her on up."

Jimi grasps the control yoke and pulls back, putting the craft into a nearly vertical climb. He puts the bottom of the ship parallel with the building and pours on the power, and they race upward toward a point far above, where the building disappears in the clouds. Beneath them, the features on the building become a blur as they pick up speed and finally punch through the cloud layer and see where the building terminates in a thin spire topped by a brilliant light.

"All right. Now peel off to your left."

Jimi pushes the yoke over to the left, and they see the tops of other buildings poking through the puffy white cloud carpet. Each casts twin shadows on to the carpet from the twin suns.

"You're doing great. Couldn't do better myself. Go ahead and take her in."

Jimi sees the airport floating slightly above the cloud layer, and lines up with the runway. He checks the instrument panel and surveys the indicators, which tell him he is in the glide path. Perfect. He eases the craft down, and goes gradually from horizontal to vertical thrusters and sets down in the middle of the cross hairs painted on the concrete apron.

"Have we got time for just one more run?" he asks.

Jimi's dad smiles. "Wish we did. But I think Jessica's probably waiting for you. See you tomorrow. OK?"

"OK," says Jimi reluctantly and reaches to take his helmet off. Jimi's dad sighs. Like fathers everywhere, he would like to spend more time with the boy, but the world continues its rude and persistent habit of intervening. In just a few minutes, he has to teleconference with a group in Berlin that wants to construct a novel form of house pet, and he will have to tell them no.

In the cheerful little room at the OHSU child-care facility, Jessica smiles as Jimi peels off the virtual-reality gear, including the helmet with its miniature displays in the goggles. Her decision to take custody of Jimi is one she knows she'll never regret.

"How is your dad, sweetheart?" asks Jessica.

"He's great," pronounces Jimi. "Do we have to go now?"

" 'Fraid so. I've got to stop at the doctor's on the way home. But it won't take long."

"So why do you have to go to the doctor, anyway?" asks Jimi. "I mean, you *are* a doctor, aren't you?"

Jessica laughs gently. "That I am. But this is a different kind of doctor. Now let's hit it, little man."

As they pull out for the short drive to the doctor's, a bubbling Jimi recounts his latest adventure with his dad, which reminds Jessica of a different kind of adventure she had several months ago with Mouthball, just after the end of the calamity. When she first put the proposition before him, he seemed genuinely shocked, but in the end, he agreed to cooperate. The first part of the plan required prompt action to get the tissue sample, a strand of hair, but this was a relatively simple procedure compared with the technical feat Mouthball then performed using a tool that he referred to simplistically as an "offshoot of the biocompiler." In reality, it was part of the same computerized conduit that allowed the infusion of the Architect's genetic identity into the Mutant Zone, a way to extract about 3 million base pairs from strategic points along the human genome and combine them with other pieces of code that defined the more basic processes. But that was only half the problem. Next came an analysis that tied up the entire DEUS Complex for several days in order to anticipate and correct potential problems, such as Angelman syndrome, which lurks in the deepest recesses of chromosome 15. As it turned out there were literally thousands of other potential disaster sites, but eventually the work was polished to perfection, and Mouthball personally supervised the final procedure, which was performed under almost fanatically tight security.

"Well, based on what we see here, I'd say your baby's nothing less than perfect."

Jessica's obstetrician points to the ultrasound display, whose new image-interpolation software has produced a very detailed image of the fetus, which is in the middle of its second trimester. Since the obstetrician knows her medical history, Jessica suspects he is overcompensating a bit, but still, she can't suppress the joy and relief that swim through her.

A perfect child. Guaranteed. The perfect resolution for the Millionth Woman.

"Well, I guess that's it for now," the doctor is saying. "See you in a couple of weeks. And don't forget the vitamins, OK?"

"I won't. Thanks, Doctor." Of course he didn't know, and had been discreet enough to avoid any questions about the baby's father. That secret belonged to her and Mouthball alone. A few others held pieces of the puzzle, but not enough to assemble it. If they had, they might have regretted their curiosity, because the solution was an intensely personal one, and not well understood outside the emotional context that created it.

Because when Mouthball had completed his initial round of work, he beheld the world's first artificially constructed sperm cell, which contained a remarkable genetic package refined from a set of chromosomes extracted from the original hair sample.

A handpicked team headed by Dr. Tandy then extracted an egg from Jessica to be used in a completely novel form of in vitro fertilization. In the first step, Mouthball conducted robotic microsurgery that removed the egg's resident chromosomes and then navigated the highly customized sperm cell to a position where it penetrated the egg and triggered the process of conception. Finally, Dr. Tandy replanted the fertilized egg into Jessica, squeezed her hand affectionately, and wished her the very best.

Because the baby in her belly held only one set of chromosomes, making it the first infant in history to be a perfect replication of someone who had walked the earth before.

Michael Riley.

Other Reading

XXXXXX

What follows is a partial listing of the published work that served as background for this novel. In addition, the research included a large body of papers from academic presentations, and numerous technical articles from the electronic trade press. Also, during the time this work was in progress, there was a sudden proliferation of published work on the application of artificial intelligence and linguistic theory to genetic analysis, which suggests that the central premise of this book may be well on its way from speculative fiction to scientific fact.

Cognizers: Neural Networks and Machines That Think, R. Colin Johnson and Chappell Brown, John Wiley & Sons, 1988

Blank Check (The Pentagon's Black Budget), Tim Weiner, Warner Books, 1990

The Emperor's New Mind, Roger Penrose, Oxford University Press, 1989

Gene Wars (Military Control Over the New Genetic Technologies), Charles Piller and Keith R. Yamamoto, Beech Tree Books, 1988

Genes II, Benjamin Lewin, John Wiley & Sons, 1985

The Puzzle Palace, James Bamford, Houghton Mifflin Co., 1982

The United States Government Manual 1988/89, Office of the Federal Register

An Introduction to Neural Computing, John P. Guiver and Casimir Klimasauskas, NeuralWare, Inc., 1988

Artificial Neural Networks: Theoretical Concepts, Computer Society Press of the IEEE, 1988

The Society of Mind, Marvin Minsky, Simon & Schuster, 1986

"The Linguistics of DNA," David B. Searls, *American Scientist*, November–December 1992

"Cloning Chromosomes," *Los Alamos National Laboratory Annual Report 1984*

"The Molecular Basis of Development," Walter J. Gehring, *Scientific American*, October 1985

"Hacking the Human Genome," Deborah Erickson, *Scientific American*, April 1992

"Sources of Data in the GenBank Database," Christian Burks, *Proceedings of the First CODATA Workshop on Nucleic Acid and Protein Sequencing Data (1988)*

"Sequencing the Human Genome," *Summary Report of the Santa Fe Workshop March 3–4, 1986*

"Exploring the Role of Robotics and Automation in Decoding the Human Genome," *Report on the Santa Fe Workshop, January 6–9, 1987*

"The GenBank Nucleic Acid Sequence Database," Christian Burks et al., *Cabios Review, Vol. 1, no. 4, 1985*

"A New Tool for Human Genetics," *Los Alamos National Laboratory Research Highlights 1987*

"The GenBank Database and the Flow of Sequence Data for the Human Genome," Christian Burks, *Biotechnology And The Human Genome*, Plenum Press, New York, 1988

"Cross-sections of the GenBank Database," Brian T. Foley et al., *TIG September 1986*

"Learning in Parallel Networks," Geoffrey Hinton, *Byte*, April 1985

"Collective Computation in Neuronlike Circuits," David W. Tank and John Hopfield, *Scientific American*, December 1987

"Gene Expression," Carl E. Hildebrand et al., *Los Alamos Science*, Fall 1983

"Linda in Context," Nicholas Carriero and David Gelernter, *Communications of the ACM*, April 1989

About the Author

PIERRE OUELLETTE, formerly a rock and jazz guitarist, lives with his family in Portland, Oregon, where he is the creative partner in Karakas, Van-Sickle, Ouellette, Inc., an advertising and public relations firm with numerous high-technology clients in the computer, semiconductor, test and measurement, electronic design automation, and biotechnology industries.